BELLADONNA

ALSO BY DAŠA DRNDIĆ
IN ENGLISH TRANSLATION

Trieste (2012)

Leica Format (2015)

Daša Drndić

BELLADONNA

Translated from the Croatian
by Celia Hawkesworth

A NEW DIRECTIONS BOOK

Originally published in Croatian by Fraktura in 2012
Published in arrangement with MacLehose Press, London

Manufactured in the United States of America
New Directions Books are printed on acid-free paper
First published as a New Directions Paperbook Original (NDP1388) in 2017

Library of Congress Cataloging-in-Publication Data
Names: Drndić, Daša, 1946– author. | Hawkesworth, Celia, 1942– translator.
Title: Belladonna / Daša Drndić;
translated from the Croatian by Celia Hawkesworth.
Other titles: Belladonna. English
Description: New York : New Directions Publishing Corporation, 2017.
Identifiers: LCCN 2017013734 | ISBN 9780811227216 (alk. paper)
Subjects: LCSH: Memory—Fiction. | World War, 1939–1945—Fiction. |
Yugoslavia—History—20th century—Fiction. | GSAFD: Historical fiction.
Classification: LCC PG1619.14.R58 B4513 2017 | DDC 891.8/235—dc23
LC record available at https://lccn.loc.gov/2017013734

2 4 6 8 9 7 5 3 1

New Directions Books are published for James Laughlin
by New Directions Publishing Corporation
80 Eighth Avenue, New York 10011

Hodie mihi, cras tibi.

Quis evadet?

On Saturday, November 19, 2002, sixty people incarcerated in a camp for illegal immigrants *sew their lips together*. Sixty people with their lips sewn reel around the camp, gazing at the sky. Small muddy stray dogs scamper after them, yapping shrilly. The authorities keep postponing consideration of their applications for leave to remain.

Tereza Acosta is a woman who has decided not to remember. Tereza Acosta does not remember her childhood; it is as though she had not existed until her tenth year. Her amnesia is dense and immobile. Five different Tereza Acostas live in Tereza Acosta. Each has her own voice and facial expressions. None of them remembers conversing with the other Tereza Acostas. Each Tereza denies the existence of the other four. Each Tereza Acosta has her own opinions about marriage, love, work, life in general, quite different from those of the other Tereza Acostas. After many sessions, the doctor decides not to interfere in the lives of the five Terezas, he decides to leave them in their shared oblivion. In which they live harmoniously.

Fausta Fink did not remember her life before the age of fourteen. The doctors gave her antidepressants and she began to remember. She said, *Now I'm fine, I'm happy*, then she killed herself.

She threw herself from the fifteenth floor. In a red kimono. She fell, inflated like a balloon, fluttering. She soared. She crashed.

In an asylum in the south, or perhaps in the north too, thirty-nine *inmates* also sew their lips—with surgical thread. To carry out the sewing, the prisoners use a wide, curved needle, and each mouth is sewn with three, at most four, stitches. The patients were protesting against the staff who did not address them. Then, in the asylum, a still greater voicelessness reigned, a vast silence which now wafts like steam, like smoke, from the ceilings and walls of the ruined building in the back of beyond, and climbs in clouds toward the sky; in moonless nights that same voicelessness, that fateful human muteness, apparently insane, is borne back as a breeze; it falls like feathery rain on the opaque windows of our refuge in nowhere-land and, in order to survive, for that is their only air, the patients fill their by now slack, consumptive lungs with that sickly but odorless breeze, that invisible cobweb of silence. The landscape around the madhouse is sealed, petrified, motionless as a drawing. It lies beneath a lava of silence woven of inaudible footsteps that swish softly because they spill out of the asylum in which all slippers are made of felt.

He could do that too. Stop speaking. Stop remembering.

So.

Now he is alone.

In a dilapidated apartment in a small town.

He has talked, written, thought, about this apartment, and about this town, and he isn't going to do so again. He won't think. Not about the apartment, where it is cold and dark, neglected, as he himself has become, dark and neglected, and growing steadily colder, not about the town, which he has written off completely, as though it does not exist, as though it has collapsed, sunk into a cataclysmic sepulchre and now he is floating above that abyss (like Fausta Fink in her red kimono), becoming increasingly distant, growing smaller to the point of silence, to disappearance.

He could be anywhere, it does not matter now.

He no longer opens the shutters, maybe occasionally, when some kind of music comes into his head and startles him. When a tiny joy runs through his body, a small pale bolt of lightning that flashes and is swiftly extinguished. Then he opens the windows wide and looks out. From the fourth floor he watches the arrival and departure of trains. He peers into the hangars. Into the garbage bins where rats and cats are up early, he waits for them to dance through the trash and emits a brief *ah* which stops his breath. With an effort, he raises his eyelids and glances over the shred of sea, swaying there under the low mountain, then the clipboard claps, he withdraws into his cocoon again, and briskly, almost grotesquely, limps down the narrow eleven-meter-long corridor to snuggle like a mole into darkness, into his sepulchral wordlessness and feel once again the way the walls of that virtual tunnel shift, gather, approach one another and then he scampers crazily down that path, up-down hop up-down up-down hop, not to be crushed by its high walls, flattened into a thin line of death like the one on a hospital ECG monitor.

My pump, he says, my pump, one, a second, a third.

Then it's better. He can breathe.

He no longer thinks about anything. He has already thought out everything; his life. In little heaps, small piles, he has laid days, years, births and deaths, loves, the few there were, journeys, many, acquaintances, many, family dramas, his senseless chases and even more senseless small battles, on the whole lost, languages, foreign and local, landscapes, he has tidily classified it all, and tied up that baggage, that now unneeded burden, and arranged it in the corners of the spacious rooms as though yet another great removal awaited him.

A barracks, he says, *I'm living in a barracks*.

One of these days he'll ask someone to take it away, this debris, this garbage into which his life has shrunk, he'll get someone to move those accretions of his botched days out of his sight, so that he and those numerous piles should no longer look at one another as they begin to rot in the corners and give off a nauseating odor, not a frightening odor, but irritating, intrusive, steadily crumbling into dust and interfering with his breath. Take it all, he will say, take it. He has piled up the books, thrown some away, given some as gifts, sifted out the trash. He gives away his clothes as well, and his shoes, at times manically. Too much ballast has accumulated, all kinds of junk. He gives away coats, jackets, suits, sweaters, shirts, oh how many shirts he has, shoes, some never worn.

His mother did the same, some thirty years or so earlier, toward the end, as she traveled, leaving behind, handing out pieces of *her* life, he had not understood it then. When she returned from China from her acupuncture training, with a packet of needles, with enormous rubber ears, acupuncture points marked on them, with a three-foot plastic model of the human body, which could be taken apart and put back together and all the organs removed and examined, charming miniature *imitations* of organs, heart, lungs, liver, intestines, pancreas, everything, three-dimensional blood vessels, veins and arteries, bones, brain, everything could be dismembered, relocated, rearranged, turned over, put together like a jigsaw, the whole human insides, and the model always stands upright, stuck to a wooden base and impaled on a shiny metal rod, when his mother came back from China to them, to her family and her psychiatric patients, from China, from some Chinese province, he no longer remembers which, China is a vast country, varied, from that impoverished desert province where, she used to say, the Chinese food was nothing like the European Chinese food eaten in European Chinese restaurants, but meager and tasteless, watery, served (in field hospitals) in tin dishes, as once in the Yugoslav National Army, where she had her hair cut dry, his mother came almost without any luggage, holding a little note torn from a page of newspaper on which the diagnosis *ca corpus uteri* was written with a ballpoint pen (Chinese). She brought him a small antique Chinese tobacco box made of rosewood which had been gaping empty for a long time over there on his desk where he never went any more, she brought him a framed poem by Lu Hsun, and for his sisters Chinese robes, intensely azure and intensely crimson, with big golden dragons flying on them, and an old fan smelling of sandalwood, all that fitted into one suitcase, a small case in which his mother locked a glimmer of insight, which he later read as a decision and fear.

Now he squeezes that huge rubber ear with its reflex points for the whole body. An ear like a miniature fetus.

On that ear he sees a summary of his organs. All his organs. An overview of his pains. Sometimes he brings a needle, a toothpick or his nail to his ear and pricks his heart, his eye, his back, his brain, and he comes to life. For an instant. He pulsates. When he runs out of money, he finds the point for appetite control and becomes light, he sways as though about to faint.

Ears—a marvelous, ugly organ, repugnant, as is the whole human body, man in general, a grotesque being of discordant shape, with extremities that branch out from a central mass, with thin tentacles that flail around, with tips grafted on them where whitish pinkish formations grow ceaselessly, while at the top of that monstrosity, on a short, soft, mobile stalk rocks a ball-shaped organ with a larger opening at the bottom and two smaller holes in the middle with warm air coming out of them. Toward the top, two small watery balls set in hollows with movable covers roll about silently. In addition, this rounded mobile body is covered with hair that springs out of its top, and on the male also from the front.

There are a lot of ears in literature, there are ears for listening and ears for nonlistening, ears for dropping poison into and ears for cutting off. They say that ears keep growing. Old people have big ears, even those old people whose ears were small in their youth acquire large soft dangling ears with flabby lobes, deaf ears. That is why he was surprised by a recent event when, holding a pink folder against his chest, he got onto a bus, followed by an old gentleman wearing a hat, a man with a deeply lined, furrowed face, who asked him, *Are you also going to* that *building, for the meeting at four p.m.?* Then the old man who remained standing on the bottom step turned his back on him, the doors were open, and he observed the old man in a black coat from behind. The old man had small ears, unbelievably small, demonic ears.

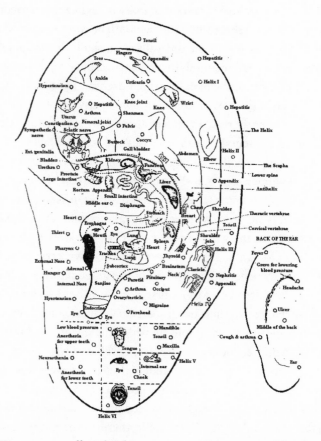

His ears are all right, his ears are quite respectable, decent ears without hairs. He can hear well, he can hear perfectly well, it would be better if that were not the case. Once, however, the sea had surged in his left ear, occasionally high waves had beaten, roaring, against his frontal bone and dissipated round his temple and nose, words were drawn out into slow unintelligibility with an unbearable echo. They put him in a soundproof room and tested his hearing. The doctor said, *Your hearing in your right ear is far above average. You don't need your left ear at all.* But this schizophrenic state of his ears, that noise in his head, that cacophony, only lasted a short time, after a month or two a becalmed sea swayed once again between the walls of his skull. Now he is again *surrounded* by terrible sounds that come from outside, which hammer on his brain and which he cannot exclude, by the appalling, rending din of this town, unlike any *normal* city noise.

He has recently read an article about Jewish ears. In it three women were discussing scanned irises and scanned faces in general, and the possibility of implanting chips into people. One of the three women said that she had been dismayed when she was having her photograph taken for a new passport in Vienna and was told, *Uncover your ears*, we have to *see your ears, both ears*, they said. That reminded the woman of her mother's war stories, she said. The other woman said that she was sent back twice by the police when they were getting passports for her grandchildren because her grandchildren's ears were, first, very small, and second, they were stuck close to their heads. After several attempts they succeeded in getting photographs on which the *tips* of the children's ears could be seen, but then there were problems with her grandchildren's eyes, because her grandchildren's eyes were not open enough to be scanned. When they got to the photographer's the children would immediately fall asleep. In passport photographs it is forbidden to laugh, even to smile, there was no problem with this second woman's grandchildren smiling, the second woman explained, because her grandchildren never smiled. In the end, her grandchildren did manage to leave with their parents. From Romania. To where they never returned. Then the first woman talked about her mother saying that in the Nazi era it was not permitted to touch up photographs on Jews' documents and that the *left* ear had to be visible, because the Jewish race was allegedly distinguished by the shape of the ear. The Nazis believed that Jews had *special* ears. In the article, the three women compared their ears but could not discern significant deviations even though one of the three pairs of ears was Jewish. In the end, the Jewish woman found the wartime identity cards of some of her relatives murdered in Treblinka and, indeed, in all the photographs the left ear was clearly visible.

For the time being the police have not analyzed noses although some scientists maintain that there is great biometric potential in scanning noses. The scientists complain that in biometric techniques noses have been unjustifiably neglected. Scanned noses could significantly speed up the recognition of people in the course of processing the entire photograph, which is not the case with standard biometric techniques. A nose does not alter with a change of facial expression, the experts state, while ears do, which is not quite accurate. When people smile, their noses broaden, while there are those whose ears do not stir when they laugh, although there are also those whose ears move up-down, forward-backward, while some people can move their ears even when they are not laughing, by an effort of will. Anyway, the scientific study of forty noses was first carried out in England, then this scientific testing spread through Europe, and now databases (of noses) for future testing are springing up all around.

He has a nice little nose. Regular.

He gathers up souvenirs from around the flat for the trash. He thrusts them into black plastic bags. Decisively, jerkily. Who needs his recollections, which not even he wants to remember, they *have fallen* into a pit of forgetfulness. And he lets them *sink*.

People collect idiocies to remember things by because that's easier for them, no strain—walks, landscapes, smells and touches, no time for that while life flows, or for most people trickles, he realizes that now. People half-wittedly arrange all their life's paragraphs on shelves and walls and from time to time cast an icy smile at them in passing and say, stay there, wait for me. When the lights begin to fade, people imagine that they will be together again, they and their derelict past squeezed into small dead objects, that they will touch each other again, tell each other mislaid, withered tales. Some hope. Memories die as soon as they are plucked from their surroundings, they burst, lose color, lose suppleness, stiffen like corpses. All that remains are shells with translucent edges. Half-erased brain platelets are a slippery terrain, deceptive. One's mental archive is locked, it languishes in the dark. The past is riddled with holes, souvenirs can't help here. Everything must be thrown away. Everything. And perhaps everyone as well.

He might keep the little china shoe his mother had given him, a little shoe that had not taken him anywhere. He would also keep the miniature antique grandfather clock, rusty, patinated, a clock with a crooked pendulum that looked as though it had escaped from Wonderland, whose hands moved only when a small coin was inserted into it—a gift from his son Leo. And Elvira, he'll keep Elvira—he takes her everywhere with him, close to him. There, that's what he'll keep.

His name is Andreas Ban.

He is a psychologist who does not psychologize any more.

A writer who no longer writes.

He is a tourist guide who no longer guides anyone anywhere.

A swimmer who has not swum for a long time.

He has other occupations that no one any longer needs. He, least of all.

He is sixty-five, he looks pretty good, like fifty. The upheaval for which he was prepared, for which he *had prepared* (he knew how to do that, he had trained himself for it), nevertheless happened in an instant, caught him unawares when a half-educated female colleague, a perfect bureaucrat, an obedient apparatchik, when that *frighteningly respectable* and reticent colleague flung in his face, in front of the whole staff, the fact that he was no longer needed by their institution, because, *you're about to retire*. Was that the trigger? *Your suggestions are irrelevant and won't get you anywhere*, she had said, *you're about to retire*. This happened when he and a few others were trying to tighten up the criteria for evaluating scholarly and artistic works, for evaluating one's presence in life, one's political, social and cultural visibility because, they maintained, the teaching staff had withdrawn into their cesspits, 1 percent of professors appeared in public, the others did not exist, like the majority of Croatian academicians who say nothing and have their photographs taken for various anniversaries and have no problems with their pension, so here Andreas Ban asked his colleague where and when she had ever spoken out, who had heard of her, who wrote about her, and she said, *That's not important, you're leaving, I'm staying.* And those tedious, deadly regular and empty Kafkaesque meetings of the faculty board chaired by four or five men dressed in blue suits and women in little waisted costumes with hairstyles à la Prince Valiant, directing their *cadre* to fill in senseless forms, to record *without fail* data of no use to anyone in *special little boxes*, persistently reading aloud documents distributed to them all, which were additionally reproduced in Powerpoint on the wall, as though 90 percent of the professors were attending a course on reading administrative nonsense, addressing them all anonymously, rolling titles through their false teeth, and then sending *all* that, this amateur sketch in the form of extended minutes, by e-mail, *by name*, to all the teachers, after which the "administration" informs the entire teaching staff, with the threatening notification that the message is "urgent," that the university mailboxes are full and they must *empty* them immediately.

There are university teachers who want to show they are engaged, so at meetings some women complain that there are no shelves in the toilets for women's handbags and then hold forth at great length on their toilet and physiological requirements, and ninety people say nothing and listen while the secretary takes notes. Then there is voting, which, as soon as some slightly delicate question appears on the agenda, results in either *mass abstention* or unanimous *for* or unanimous *against*, with no variation, a blessed harmony reigns, solid unity on the margin of life. Those who protest are quickly silenced, all according to regulations, according to the rule book, according to the statutes, a convenient hole is always found. When some, let's say more important, issue happens to come up, the assembly suddenly becomes tired, the more significant the issue, the more the teachers' fatigue increases in a geometric progression, the teachers are thirsty and hungry and meetings are interrupted, or *postponed*, so that in the end nothing is decided, or it is decided in an indeterminate, tepid and flabby way.

That's when it begins, when it condenses.

She, that malicious, uneducated woman with great scholarly ambitions in a small provincial university, will look repulsive in old age. She will have big ears. Her nose will become sharper still, and, weighed down, it will sink toward her top lip, upon which it will come to rest; because of a lack of teeth, her chin will turn upward, warts will break out all over her face, and her speech will come to resemble snarling.

Oh yes, he would have liked to abandon all those collectives that devour, those consumers of ideas, that cacophonous din, those blank masks that disguise a still greater nullity, and give himself up to cheerful occupations, nourish his brain cells so that they pulse and drum, but a pathetic pension in the small, ruined, pompous country in which he lives (how did this horror of destiny befall him, how?), in a country in which all rush headlong to leave if they can, in a country where a minister of education threatened to introduce *patriotism* as a subject into the school curriculum, in which publicly, in the open air and on television, in order for the message to reach the most remote village, people sing songs with the refrain *our Croatian mother bore me*, so that those whom the Croatian mother *did not* bear feel unwanted, while all those whom their Croatian mother *did* bear leap up, proud and superior, prepared one way or another *to eliminate* those whom the Croatian mother *did not* bear, by stoning if necessary, in this country, a country in which people want to believe that they are brought into the world by their homeland rather than by a woman, in a country of such false decorum and hypocrisy that people have executed names, and at work address one another as director, dean, professor, *boss*, a pension in this country earned after twenty-five years of education, studying, after forty years of work, guarantees a relatively swift and objectively awful—death; that pension, that *retirement benefit* that really makes one wind down, run down, insidiously and meanly drilling into one's ears on a dozen fronts at the same time *takes* one's life away. So he, Andreas Ban, cannot accept that his pension should dictate how he will wind down, that the undying *Croatian mother* should say when she has had enough of her son, and decides to take things into his own hands. He, Andreas Ban, cannot be *resigned* to living on chicken wings which he can't take, and if he could, and if he wanted to, that possibility eludes him because chicken wings are becoming increasingly expensive, in the end all that would be left to him would be the spleen and the lungs and other repulsive animal innards which some people feed to their dogs. He is already imprisoned, already chained, nailed to this little country because he can't travel, he can't run away (he has no money), even though he is mobile and still (though not for long) receiving a salary. He will not walk around in worn, outmoded shoes, he won't wear gray matted sweaters, he won't shove badly made dentures into his mouth, no. (He recently told somebody that his sweater was completely matted, and she laughed and said, *What a funny word, matted, what does it mean?*) He won't travel on buses to town in the morning (between ten and twelve) (even if the Croatian mother offers pensioners those rides for free), buses that are full of incapacitated, loud, deaf creatures carrying bags from the market, containing two apples, one bell pepper and instant polenta. He will not listen to:

> *They put her in a home, she hopes she'll get out, but she won't.*

Can she walk?
They put her in a home and sold her apartment.
Is she senile?
They haven't told her she doesn't have an apartment
anymore, if they told her she'd drop dead, she's not senile.

he won't look at those sagging, hungry, insatiable faces, those wizened people who cross themselves when the bus passes a church, mumble something into their chins and bow their heads humbly before "God," he won't look at those toothless faces rhythmically sucking the inside of their drooping cheeks with a revolting infantile smacking sound, those ravenous faces, which can best be seen on holidays and feast days when in town squares the Croatian mother bestows on them two sardines or a child's portion of beans, for which they wait for hours, patiently, lined up, while marshals watch them from the side, just in case, heaven forbid, they should have a rush of blood to the head and charge forward in a frenzy. Those benign feast days for the sick, the old, the abandoned fanatically in love with life, begin at nine a.m. and end at midday, when all that was on offer has been eaten and drunk, falling like a stone into those thinned, shrunken old people's stomachs, so that the squares can be cleaned with jets of water in time for the evening's musical entertainment for the young and well fed. Andreas Ban watches that horde of half-rotted living corpses, which multiply, proliferate, there are more and more of them everywhere, especially at clinics, waiting rooms are full of them, they go there for the company, in winter—for the warmth, they occupy *all* the chairs in waiting rooms, they go to doctors' offices and clinics because *they are anxious about their health*, they particularly like giving blood samples, although the lines at the laboratories are long and *there are no chairs*, there's no commotion, no relaxing, just wearisome waiting and shifting from foot to foot, in that line stretching over two floors, in which those old people touch, stick to one another, they wait, they stand and wait, where do they get such patience, such hunger and thirst for an already devastated, shriveled nothing of a life, a desire to live over the line, beyond beauty, in a desert, let them be downtrodden, it doesn't matter, they are those quiet, persistent, stubborn types accustomed to suffering and forbearance. One woman insisted she should have a cataract operation, although she was riddled with metastases, *You're riddled with metastases*, the doctors told her, *you don't have long to live*, they told her, that's medical practice today, throw it all in a patient's face, tell them the *outcome* but without explanation, just the bare outcome, because doctors don't have time for refinements, and that woman kept repeating, *I want to be able to see clearly*, she said, so the doctors relented, they did her a *favor*, they restored her sight, although it was questionable whether she had ever had it, so that she then had a clearer perception, without clouding, of her corroded, dying body.

Andreas Ban watches these bedraggled nags clutching their lives in their arms as they stagger and hobble their way across the road in a grotesque race, so what if someone knocks into them, so what if a car runs them down, that would at least be a worthy end, but no, their eyes are wide open, their mouths gaping, and, as though rescued from drowning, they leap onto the sidewalk, because they *love life*, because that life, that beautiful, rich life was gifted to them by their Croatian mother.

And Andreas Ban wants none of those calendars which the Croatian mother distributes to its pensioners before the end of each year, because, as if in some *régime* setting, in some *penitentiary*, in some *ghetto*, he would have to strike off his days.

In 2011, twenty-five members of the Macedonian organization UNIT, an association of dismissed workers, killed themselves. They could no longer bear life in poverty. They were all over fifty. Some hanged themselves, some jumped off bridges or buildings, and one set himself on fire. (Newspaper report)

He is a good-looking man, Andreas Ban, a refined decadent, former inhabitant of the big cities of the world, who, having battled for twenty years with this provincial town, was finally crushed by it. Now he is rapidly fraying, inside and out. Andreas Ban covers up the external fraying with clothes, for his own sake, so as not to have to look at it. He camouflages his flabby belly, his slack muscles, the puckered skin on his thighs and upper arms, his flaccid testes, he wears caps and hats, he is not entirely bald, he has his own teeth. As for his internal wasteland, he lets that spread. There had been an effort, yes, he had endeavored, he had tried with hoses and water cannon to shift, disperse that heavy desert sand around him, but got nowhere. Now he is tired.

What had been important to him he had registered and in his imagination touched at a distance, in the distance: old friendships, dead loves, abandoned towns, books, books, real and unreal characters, spending more and more time with writers, mostly deceased, but some living ones as well, because the small town had grown like dough steeped in yeast, enveloping him, sucking him into its porous entrails and finally swallowing him up. That is why he has difficulty breathing, wedged in that clammy mass. He is sinking.

He has found characters, male and female, who bear parts of his history, which he is now erasing. Those figures seem to him what is most alive in the shallow, dead town surrounding him. They crouch, squeezed between the covers, they thrash around, wriggle, sometimes they burrow through the paper like woodworms and he lets them sit at the table, lie down with him, accompany him on his infrequent walks, sometimes like crazed spirits, like swifts, they circle around his rooms, flying right up to the ceiling, then drop to the floor and drag themselves along, legless, and he is afraid he might step on them, trip on them, squash them, and what then? There would be unbearable loneliness, black silence.

> *In a crowd of tourists from many countries, on the shore of Lake Geneva, I found a man who was seeking solitude. The man had sat down on "my" bench, with his stick he drew a circle around himself in the sand and said, There, we're sitting on the same bench, I'm addressing you, you're listening to me, but this circle separates us and you are more remote from me than the remotest planet. That is solitude. But solitude is not only the force that sometimes raises us to the skies, sometimes casts us into an abyss, it is also a refuge for lost loves.*
>
> *My name is Edouard Estaunié, I am a writer of solitude. I know that our past, with all its secrets, winds around us, suffocates us, restricts our space, cramps our life, until it crushes it completely. Beneath our visible reality is hidden another that would astonish our acquaintances should they become aware of it. There is no sickness so terribly elusive as this one. The more it weighs us down, the deeper is our silence. Solitude need not be dramatic, but it is like a sack filled with stones, brimming with sorrow.*

Piling up experiences brings about changes in the brain, chemical changes. This can be seen clearly in animals;

there is no reason why it should be different with the
human brain. When two groups of adult rats,

Oh, Andreas Ban cannot bear rats. Stefan Biber had kept 1,300 rats in his apartment and heaven knows how many cats. The floors of the apartment were covered in rat and cat feces and urine. While the cats were loose, the rats were crammed into cages, many of them without eyes or legs. That is why the town authorities dislodge Stefan Biber from the apartment and he buys a ten-meter yacht to which he moves his rats and his cats. On Biber's yacht the situation with regard to the rats and the cats is no better than it had been in his apartment. Representatives of the Society for the Protection of Animals come onto his yacht and take away thirty-seven of Biber's rats and six cats, and report him for cruelty, for keeping animals in too confined a space. Veterinary examinations establish that all of Stefan Biber's animals are healthy. Biber gives a statement to the press saying that he is a victim of vengeance and persecution.

when two groups of adult rats, over the course of, say, eighty days, are exposed to conditions in which the rats from one group are isolated and put into poor environments, while the rats from another group are placed together (in good company, so they become lively), in environments "enriched" by various toys and activities, the mass of the cerebral cortex of the rats living "a rich life" increases, and the activity of the cortical acetylcholinesterase becomes more significant. With the other, from every point of view, the brain mass of impoverished rats shrinks, the brain empties, their experience evaporates, images disappear. Other areas of the brains of the rats living dynamic lives also show visible positive changes.

I'm turning retarded, my brain is shrinking,
says Andreas Ban.
Your voice is losing modulation, Andreas, your sentences
are slow and monotonous, you wash less frequently,
Andreas, and you twiddle your thumbs in silence.

An ambulance brings in a patient who had cut off his tongue two hours earlier. The patient had also cut off his testicles, but now that's not an issue. The patient is evaluated as normal. Before he had cut off a third of his tongue, the patient had injected an ampule of anesthetic (Lidocaine HCl 20 mg, Epinephrine 0.125 mg/mL) into its root and tip, so that he would feel no pain during the "operation." To prevent the doctors from restoring, sewing back on, the piece of his tongue, the patient had snipped it into little pieces with scissors. There was not much bleeding. The patient was given an antitetanus injection and sent home to recover. Two months later he killed himself playing Russian roulette. The patient was called Daniil Demidov and lived in the Russian enclave of Kaliningrad.

Estaunié's *Solitudes* remind Andreas of Loti's *An Iceland Fisherman*, a book that had moved him so deeply as a teenager that he wept. And now he hesitates—to abandon himself to "the insatiable sea" or continue to languish in solitude.

What a vast desert without shadow or water! Listen, Andreas, a man cannot open up even to his neighbor. That is the tragedy of all lonely souls who, parallel to their conventional, publicly visible lives, live terrible, painful, secret existences. They are silent sufferers. In your previous life, Andreas, you would have judged the state of men and women ashamed by their desolate, destructive silences as repression, quite professionally, according to the books, yet in that silence life does not stop, it does not end, but gradually expires, becomes paralyzed, languishes in secret, in darkness. Such a life in a glasshouse, a life of isolation, is a life of suffering. You know that now, Andreas. All that is needed is to be, to exist! Write, Andreas, write it down.

A quoi bon? A quoi bon? Andreas Ban asks Estaunié. Or perhaps he does not ask anyone, because there is no one, perhaps he just mumbles and catches his breath.

Then Conrad, that depressive who tries to kill himself but refrains, leaps up in front of Andreas Ban:

Who knows what true loneliness is—not the conventional word, but the naked terror? To the lonely it wears a mask. The most miserable outcast hugs some memory or some illusion. That's how I survived.

*Oh come now, Conrad, says Andreas Ban. What memory, which illusion. Memories are illusions, and illusions are elusive. Couéism is for idiots. Only the blind (and the insane) chant the mantra: Tous les jours à tous points de vue je vais de mieux en mieux.** *

Andreas Ban still reads, less and less now, but still. He seeks confirmation of his discoveries even though to him the situation is clear. He reads discourses on Dürer's *Melencolia*, that engraving from 1514, of which Benjamin affirms that it represents the deadening of emotions, a high degree of sadness. But he is not sad, Andreas Ban. *I'm not sad*, he says. Dürer's inconsolable angel evokes compassion

---

* Every day in every way I'm getting better and better.

in him, not identification. It is only that landscape, that landscape with the transcendent sea in the distance that disturbs Andreas Ban. *That is my vista*, he says, and glances toward his already rotten closed shutters. *That's it, end game*, he says. Benjamin believes that there is "enigmatic wisdom" in each object in Dürer's cataclysmic world; Andreas does not. *Foolishness*, says Andreas Ban, shuts the book and puts Dürer away.

Andreas Ban knows that the impasse he is struggling to cope with did not arrive overnight, it slunk into his days quietly and gradually, following his footsteps like a shadow, until he tripped over it. Ah, the disharmony, the collision of what had been and what is now, what a mess. That is why he is now standing, leafing, leafing through himself, through those close to him, through his surroundings, and before their final erasure all kinds of things leap out. Secrets that fall at his feet, uninvited, and outlines of the past, whose edges he endeavors to sharpen by squinting, shreds of memory that land, singed, on his shoulders, little sparks of joy under which he rests, imagining that they are small fireworks (or soft waterfalls). And then, like an immense deadly wave, he is flooded with unbearable irritation, fury and impotence.

Andreas Ban is lying on a doctor's table, bare to the waist. It is dark in the clinic. He is waiting for an ultrasound scan. Outside, it is raining. The drops drum on the tin gutter. He lies there, counting. He counts the drops that fall quickly, very quickly, he cannot catch them all. He leans his right arm, in a cast up to the elbow, against his side. *Raise both arms over your head,* says the doctor. His right arm is heavy, the plaster is heavy, they have put on too many layers of plaster, they have put the plaster over the splint, you should not do that, but it was easier for them. And quicker. This is the second time he has come to see Dr. Molina. He was here three days ago. He had woken up sweating, his face contorted with pain. *What have you done to your arm?* said Dr. Molina, *You're soaked through, tidy yourself up and come back the day after tomorrow.* It had been pouring then as well. In this town, it rains in spring, it rains in the autumn too, and in summer, the vegetation grows luxuriantly and sends out micro seeds that clog his bronchi, he drags little asthma pumps around in his pockets and as he walks he inhales like an addict sniffing glue and rolling his eyes. He does not roll his eyes.

In a transparent plastic bag he was carrying dry food, biscuits for his cat which disappeared soon afterward. She was the last to go.

He slipped. He has old shoes with frayed laces.

Laces?

We don't stock them.
Laces?
We don't stock them.
Laces?
What color?
Black.
No. Only red.
Laces?
What are they?
Ties?
What's that?
Cords?
Cords?
Shoelaces.
Oh, shoelaces. We don't have any.
Ties, cords, shoelaces, bootlaces?
What color?
Black.
Yes. How long?
Twenty-four inches.
No. Only forty-eight.
Go hang yourself on those.

He rushes out of the shop, the sidewalk glistens with rain, he loses his balance, the biscuits scatter, rolling over the smooth slabs, he lies face down, getting wet and watching his cat's biscuits swell, the little brown dots in the shape of a trefoil on the smooth stone slabs cheerfully raising their heads like little mushrooms, sounds vanish, *Who turned off the sounds?* nice shoes, men's and women's, pass his head, he could stay like this, he could fall asleep in this rain, then someone lifts him. *My foot fell,* he says, *my spine's no use.* He looks at his right arm, his wrist is bent at an angle of forty-five degrees, as though someone had broken a twig.

Now that arm, lying in a gymnastic pose above his head, is being held by his other arm, while Andreas Ban waits for Dr. Molina to switch on the machine, to rub him with jelly, that heavy arm drags him down, it will turn him over.

In the trauma clinic they tell him, *The doctor is at lunch.*

The pain is off the scale.

After sixty-seven minutes (his laces break, his shoes keep falling off) an oldish paunchy doctor arrives in a half-clean white coat from which a gray sweater with a rice pattern protrudes. He waits for the doctor to examine a dozen patients before he is called in. In the surgery there are two enormous posters, one on each wall. The Pope (the previous one) and President Tudjman.

What are these posters doing in a fracture clinic? he asks.

The doctor says, *Who are you?*

I need both my arms for writing, fix it somehow, he begs.

Then the doctor asks, *Are you going to Leipzig, there's a lot in the papers about the book fair in Leipzig, is Aralica going to Leipzig?**

He takes an X-ray of his hand and wrist, and says,

All the small bones are broken, go and get it set.

That's where they graft this horror onto him.

Dr. Molina feels Andreas Ban's thorax. *When did you notice this lump?*

Are you going to give me good news or bad news? asks Andreas Ban while Molina circles over his chest.

Molina is silent, silent for a long time, then he says, *I'm afraid it will be the latter.*

His heart detaches itself. Andreas Ban feels his heart falling

* Ivan Aralica (b. 1930). A pro-regime novelist and essayist during Franjo Tudjman's government.

through his back and slowly sinking onto the floor beneath the exam table he is lying on. He turns onto his side and watches his big swimming heart pumping in the air as though it were panting, very slowly. With his left hand rounded into a ladle, he scoops up his heart and returns it to its rightful place.

Dr. Molina says, *Sit up and we'll have a chat.*

Andreas Ban says, *Fuck off*, and walks out into the rain.

He doesn't know what to do with that diagnosis, *carcinoma mammae*, a tumor of one centimeter. Should he tell someone? He stands on the narrow sidewalk and watches the traffic. A boy passes carrying a small pink umbrella. A little girl in a wet yellow dress runs after him. They are laughing. At the corner, under eaves, a woman is frantically tapping out text messages, not looking at the screen as she taps, her eyes dart about as though something important was happening, but it is not. Another girl appears with a mobile, yelling into it ciao ciao ciao ciao ciao bye bye ciao bye ciao. Andreas feels like shaking her. The raindrops hurt the crown of his head like a Chinese torture, as if he were waiting in Venice in the prison on the Bridge of Sighs for that last drop to fall onto his brain, to finish him off. That drop does not come. He turns his head from left to right and counts the cars. He ought to have his hair cut.

He has been invited to dinner, he has bought wine.

Venice?

The shop windows near the Rialto glow, Murano necklaces sparkle, both cheap and costly, very young and very old Americans yell, Yugoslav dinars are exchanged for peanuts. One should go to the island opposite, to Giudecca, where the gondoliers live, and glass blowers and fat Italian mamas, where people are poor, the streets firm, the trees green, and the fish come from the open sea. Where the children are grubby and loud.

He kissed Zoja in a cheap hotel room coated with bedbugs, under dusty covers and damp sheets and it was good. In that rottenness, he imagined dead Elvira, decayed, her maggoty thighs gripping him, her one charred breast, which he sucked, which he bit until thick, dark blood ran from it. In a spasm, he pulled Elvira's hair, elusive (nonexistent, fallen out from cytostatic drugs), and sticky as a cobweb. He kissed Elvira's empty eye sockets until Zoja said, *Andreas, that hurts.* Soon afterward Zoja abandoned him. Or he abandoned her. They abandoned each other.

It is twenty-five years that Elvira has been gone. For Leo, Elvira is a fairy tale that cannot be made real, an invented recollection, an imagined love. For Andreas, a ball of string that rolls around his chest, a closed ball whose melody is fading.

Thirty-five years since the death of his mother Marisa.

In men cancer of the breast is a very malignant cancer. The prognosis for breast cancer in men is significantly worse than in women. Of the total number of patients at any stage of the illness, 36 percent live for five years and 7 percent for ten.

Marisa departs at fifty.

Elvira at thirty.

Father is ninety-two, he wants to die but he is not dying.

Andreas Ban calls into the antiquarian bookshop around the corner. He often calls in there, has a coffee with Oskar and leafs through books. He brings old postcards, historical documents, black-and-white photographs, family "mementos" with famous figures from the world of politics, for the most part copies (he keeps the originals), clearing out his drawers. At the door, Oskar smiles. *Should I get a haircut?* Andreas Ban asks. Without waiting for an answer he says, *I've got breast cancer.* Oskar stops smiling. Cruising around the bookshop is a seventy-year-old, who then addresses Oskar in Italian, *Avete delle vecchie fotografie famigliari?*

Among the photographs that Oskar lays out in front of the old man, Andreas Ban notices some that he had discarded, some of his own family, photographs from the beginning of the twentieth century, copies of sepia photographs of his great-grandmother about whom he knows nothing, not how she lived nor how she smelled, who is a complete stranger to him, and therefore unnecessary; he catches sight of some distant uncle in hunting boots, with a curled mustache, he does not know what he was called, he looks at those relatives, those tiny flat figures and at the old foreigner dipping into the little pile of ghosts, then hears him saying, *Ecco la mia nonna, ho trovato la mia nonna*, he says, *Comprerò tutto*. Andreas Ban says nothing, he is thinking of his breast. The old man leaves the bookshop with a heap of paper-people crumpled in a plastic bag, and Oskar says, *He's from Trieste, he comes regularly, looking for his relatives*.

He's bought my kin, says Andreas Ban, *strangers' lives*.

Three years have passed since then. The situation was new then. For Andreas Ban it had been the third new situation in the space of a year. After that more and more new situations kept coming, as far as the eye could see. The first situation had to do with his spine, a year earlier, when his instep had collapsed. He had begun to fall apart. His body was falling apart, and with it his days began to dwindle.

In recent times, people have begun to write more and more about the body, the body as a geographical map, the body that remembers, the body that punishes, the fat body, the thin body, the muscular body, the flabby body, the body that loves, the cult of the body, the cleanliness of the body, the body and its signals, the body that dictates, determines, organizes, the body that rebels. The body that surrenders? It is mostly women who write about the body, about the fact that not only do they have bodies but that they *are* their bodies. He is beginning to find this irritating. Andreas Ban is convinced that between him and his body a constant war is being waged, over which is the stronger. Andreas Ban can go hungry, he can go without sleep, he can stay still, he can do as he pleases with his body. He has only to find the control buttons.

The woman sitting next to him in the clinic slurps and clicks at regular intervals. Her dentures are loose. He would like to say, *Madam, fix those castanets in. Or take them out.* Everything irritates him. The voices surrounding him pierce his brain like needles, set off a storm in his chest, create echoes in his ears. Otherwise, now, when he is alone, it is quiet in his head. No one speaks, nothing can be heard. Now and then a thought sneaks into his skull, whirls around slowly then evaporates. Danger comes from outside.

Walking becomes increasingly painful, so he makes the rounds of clinics on his crutches. He goes through everything, through all the examinations, all the analyses, it all drags on interminably. After the X-ray of his spine, the radiologist erupts from his office shouting, *This is the spine of a ninety-year-old, shame on you!* Andreas Ban says, *My bones hurt, could it be a kind of cancer? I don't know*, says the radiologist, *go and get a CAT scan immediately.* After ten days of uncertainty, Andreas Ban discovers that he does not have bone cancer, but that he will have to have an MRI for which you have to wait at least six months.

When he had undergone that too, that magnetic resonance, they told him, *Go to a neurosurgeon to see what your next step should be.* All in all, for ten months he had been totally preoccupied with his spine, his deformed vertebrae, his pain and how to overcome it when he lay down, when he sat up and, the most terrible of all, with every step he took.

He has begun to limp. So, now, as he walks, he sways. Like a mast, as Kiš would say.

The neurosurgeon looks at his MRI, while a dreadful, pulsating silence gets into his ears where it beats to the rhythm of his heart. His jugular vein throbs crazily like a mechanical hen pecking at grain.

How much shorter are you? asks the neurosurgeon.

He knows he has lost two inches. Fortunately, he had been tall so he could permit himself that reduction. He is now a decent height, six foot one, which still annoys small men. It would have been terrible if he had gone from five foot seven to, say, five foot five, he would have become a midget and thrown his weight around in company; as it was, he could still stand.

You have severe degenerative changes, the neurosurgeon continues, *how do you manage to walk at all, this is your spine, the spine of a ninety-year-old, these are the vertebrae of a ninety-year-old, how old are you, how old are you, how do you manage to walk at all?*

Then he asks the neurosurgeon, *What do we do now?*

The neurosurgeon says, *We could remove two or three or four vertebrae, as many as necessary, and replace them with steel, or rather Teflon vertebrae. On either side of your spine, we would insert a steel mesh around which we would have to wrap your muscles, mind you*, says the neurosurgeon, *that's very painful, that's three months of unbearable pain, it's a difficult operation and the outcome is uncertain.*

Don't sweat so much, you're very pale, says the neurosurgeon. *There's a more conservative variant, rehabilitation, electric currents, waters, exercises, magnets, you need to devote time to your body.*

And then? asks Andreas Ban.

Then you'll be able to mess around in the garden, says the neurosurgeon.

I don't have a garden, Andreas Ban observes, *and I don't like messing around in gardens, what would you do?*

I'd mess around in the garden, says the neurosurgeon, *I enjoy that, I adore messing around in the garden, it relaxes me.* Then he adds, *Without an operation, I give you four years.*

Till what? asks Andreas Ban.

Till a wheelchair.

Then, in 2007, Andreas Ban takes out a loan and goes for treatment. Social Security refuses to pay for the treatment because he is not yet incontinent and can still limp around unaided.

The receptionist at the hospital says, *You must be glad that you haven't got a brain tumor.*

He says, *Should be,*

and the receptionist says, *Yes, you must be glad,*

he replies, *You should be glad,*

and the receptionist raises her voice, *Don't get upset, you must be glad.*

So, he is supposed to be glad that he doesn't know when he's going to die.

When Yugoslavia fell apart, Andreas Ban was still working in Paris. He is sent to Paris because he is trusted, because he was born in Paris after the war, when his father, a national hero and bearer of a 1941 Partisan medal, was sent there to establish connections. Cultural, political and economic. His parents did not register him as a citizen of the French Republic, that would presumably have been unpatriotic, so his arrival in the world was recorded in the Yugoslav Register of Births. When he was old enough to change this state of affairs, he had more urgent business, so becoming a Frenchman didn't cross his mind.

When Yugoslavia was falling apart, Andreas Ban returned to Belgrade from Paris, where else would he go? And is dismissed. Now you are an enemy of the state, a Croat. He has his name, he does not consider the fact that he is a Croat significant. But someone does. Andreas Ban gnaws at his savings, which are minimal. Close friendships crumble. His colleagues become supporters of the Serbian nationalist leader Šešelj. Andreas Ban roams the streets, visits graves. Acquaintances who meet him are surprised he is still there, in Belgrade. *Aren't you with the Croatian national guard?* they ask. Now, from Belgrade, he could be mobilized, they could tell him, *Go to Croatia and liberate Yugoslavia.* They could tell him, *Feel free to go and kill.*

He grew up in Belgrade, Andreas Ban had lived in Belgrade

from his seventh year, he got his degree in Belgrade, from Belgrade he went to do national service in Skopje, Third Military Sector, Marshal Tito Barracks, VP 4466, from Skopje he returned to Belgrade, he got married in Belgrade, and it was in Belgrade that he buried his Elvira, Elvira the pianist who on her deathbed said, *I love you as if I were Madigan.* What was he supposed to do? Kill himself like Sixten Sparre? He buried his mother in Belgrade, she had said, *When I die, take me back to my Split, to the sea.* They didn't take her back. They did cremate her, but they didn't take her back, it would have been a nuisance. Now that cheap urn has probably disintegrated, peppered with little holes through which the ashes seep, through which tiny grains of Marisa have long since spilled into the earth. But the pine they bought in a pot for New Year 1979, a little pine, a pinelet, which they planted by his mother's head, is now a big, powerful and imposing pine into whose roots Marisa has grown, light, like fine dust.

In Skopje they live like lords, and in Skopje Andreas Ban acquires the nickname "Lord." In the morning, Andreas Ban distributes bread around the barracks, in the afternoon he works in the office where they hand out passes for going into town, in the evening he organizes the duty roster, guards and fire officers, but mostly he reads. He spends his free evenings in bars or at the theater. In winter, a heavy, suffocating cold rolls through the barracks' rooms until the soldiers chop enough wood to warm the stoves and make their fingers flexible again. Otherwise, there were days, especially the snowy ones, when that Skopje Marshal Tito barracks, with its ghostly silence, darkness and desolation moved into the world of Edgar Allan Poe. When the soldiers were absent en masse, and most often at weekends, the sound of dripping water from the collective but empty bathrooms drove Andreas Ban crazy in the little office where he was preparing lectures for the "sprogs" and materials about mechanics which he later turned into handbooks that "his" No. 2 platoon used for studying. The dripping echoed in the low washbasins resembling water troughs for cattle like the ticking of a nonexistent clock, marking time that did not pass, that was stifled by its own resonance.

Andreas Ban could now recollect his military days in detail. The way the younger ones, the "sprogs," called the "old" soldiers "old ruts," "old hooks," "nails" or "old bones." "The old hook lies under his Deutz, while a sprog scratches his balls," they used to sing to one another. They used to call him "grandpa" too, he was twenty-four. He could remember the way they protected the homeland from the enemy who was just about to attack, but never did, or the registration office in front of which he planted roses with Albert from Osijek, Andreas Ban could remember "Tarzan," the barracks commander, who swayed like a dry twig, "Fall in!" or "Mouse," a diminutive blue-eyed Captain 1st Class who stank of sour cabbage. He could remember the clap contracted on a one-night stand when Ruta the Strumpet shrieked *Yes, oh yes, let me have it* ... But he refuses to remember. He had inhaled anxiety and vomited anxiety. He had sunk into the morgue of time, he had become a cadaver wrapped in senselessness, in idiocies, in the grotesquely devised absurdity of soldiering with an aura of the dramatic. He refuses to remember. He is repelled by those forced reminiscences with which, for years after they finish their military service, men in bars feed their masculinity, their eternal friendships, while those eternal friendships have rapidly dispersed into nothingness, into shabby memories. Then into war.

While they are in Skopje, waiting for their imaginary enemy who is supposed to come from Albania via Prizren, in ancient T-59 tanks (Chinese copies of the famous T-55s), Enver Hoxha hysterically sows bunkers all over his country and south of Tirana develops the airbase Berat-Kuçovë with hunter-bomber squadrons,

MiG-15/19 and 21, F-13 version, all Chinese products, with the mark F-5/6/7.

Those 750,000 bunkers in which Albanians crouched for decades in the mud, "at the ready," lying in wait for *their* enemy, are today being refurbished as narrow, dark living spaces, little cafés or discotheques, tourists visit them with a smile and tepid surprise and buy miniature models of the half-century of horror with which a whole nation was riddled. The tourists place those souvenirs, those little bunkers, which remind people from somewhat more fortunate countries of nothing at all, on shelves or, in the case of those in the shape of an ashtray, use them to extinguish their smokes.

He will go to Albania, he has not managed to go yet, but he will. When a group of his acquaintances went to Albania in 2008, Andreas Ban had to have an operation on his nodule, just then, it coincided the way some real, urgent business that cannot be put off coincides with dreams that afterward leave a hole in the heart. His surname, Ban, is of Illyrian origin, Albanian, Arnaut, his roots are shriveled up somewhere there under the mountain massifs among the long since disintegrated bones of weary warriors, before his distant ancestors fled to Istria in the face of the Turkish invasion in the fifteenth century. Nevertheless, coincidence or not, through the reality of Andreas Ban, Albania draws miraculous threads like rusty fasteners, apparently forgotten threads, which like the tributaries of every history at times come to life to rearrange the tidily placed blocks in the lives of those close by. But then, as he looked toward the Albanian border imagining a world walled up, petrified, and the sad small impoverished lives from which smiles, even tears, have been stolen, of that, Andreas Ban had no inkling.

Many years later, in a book entitled *Trieste*, Andreas Ban finds a chapter about the life of an Italian family in Albania during the Second World War. In that chapter he comes across the name Ruben Ketz, and Andreas Ban raises his eyebrows and says, *Impossible. There are many different people with the same name and surname*, Andreas Ban assures himself as he reads the book entitled *Trieste* in which the Italian-Jewish-Fascist Tedeschi family moves to Valona in 1939, where some six hundred Jews still live, and that the then sixteen-year-old Haya in her old age remembers only Fanny Malli because she used to walk her rabbit on a lead, and Ruben Ketz because he had pockets full of black pebbles and spoke Albanian better than she did. After that insignificant, allegedly fictitious fact a faint unease settles in the thoughts of Andreas Ban, quite incidental for his life. But, as time goes on, new cracks in the history of the Ban family open up, benign cracks, admittedly, painless, yet nonetheless gaps which once again confirm that our existence is more invented and imagined than real, and so now Andreas Ban does not know what to do with his present state, confused, chaotic and exhausted, now that he is beset by all kinds of major health issues that deposit the alluvium of a suppressed, unspoken and rigged reality.

At the end of the 1960s, Andreas Ban's sister, the one who dies of a stroke in Ljubljana in 1997, marries a certain Carlo Ketz, a civil engineer from Trieste, whom she divorces a short time later, because of "temperamental incompatibility." They have no children. Almost immediately after the divorce, Carlo Ketz is placed in the psychiatric department of the San Giovanni hospital in Trieste, which was modeled in the 1960s after the psychiatric hospital in Gorizia by the renowned Franco Basaglia and on the facade of which stood in once-bright red letters the graffito *Therapy is freedom*, while the building itself was for a short time renamed Casa Rosa Luxemburg. Andreas's former brother-in-law Carlo Ketz is subjected to treatment for loss of identity, that is for his low sense of himself and his times, after which, given that he is having increasing difficulty understanding who he is, he decides to become several people whose destinies he lives in parallel, like those Tereza Acostas, which only confirms that this illness connected with the awareness of the self, with a distorted reflection of our lives, is not a specific kind of illness, but a phenomenon more or less common in the fragmented, perforated times we live in.

The San Giovanni hospital is integrated into its surroundings in a humane way, young people stroll around, there is a discotheque nearby, little cafés, restaurants and confectioners, even a small theater, the landscape is lovely, as it was around some Nazi concentration camps, the architecture is Secessionist, the neighborhood multiethnic with an interaction of cultures, oh, wonderful, the patients go out when they feel like it, some, admittedly, accompanied, in other words, it could be said that Carlo Ketz, the former husband of Andreas's sister, is, in his middle age, currently living in the psychiatric wing of the San Giovanni hospital peacefully and integrated, as if he were not where he is, but among us.

Franco Basaglia, aware of how destructive psychiatric institutions are for the human identity branded "from the cradle to the grave," advocates democratic psychiatry and the deconstruction of psychiatric hospitals which mercilessly catapult a person even deeper into a mental and spiritual abyss. When the patient finds himself clamped between the walls of a psychiatric hospital, says Dr. Basaglia, he steps over into a new dimension of emotional emptiness, into institutional neurosis. Andreas Ban thinks that to fall into institutional neurosis it is not necessary to be hospitalized, it suffices to sit in any office, to be an employee, even in a university, perhaps especially in a university, because university staff are packed behind an impenetrable rampart of false autonomy and academic corruption, about which Kafka has already had something to say. When he enters a psychiatric hospital, says Dr. Basaglia, a person enters a space originally conceived to make him harmless, tame, calm, gentle and submissive, everything in the spirit of a Christian, especially a Catholic worldview, one of the most destructive worldviews, which, loaded with lies, kills the spirit, which is in fact a tedious propaganda play lasting centuries, a badly costumed production full of hollow texts and kitsch staging, at the head of which, under a heavy cloak threaded with gold, and in small red Prada shoes, the grotesque figure of the Pope parades.

When a person is placed in a psychiatric hospital, affirms Dr. Basaglia, those "responsible" have in fact thrust him into a space in which, treated with medication, they metamorphose him into someone acceptable to the outside world. Paradoxically, says Dr. Basaglia, the patient instead undergoes a complete annihilation of his individuality. If mental illness is essentially characterized by a loss of individuality and freedom, in a mental institution the patient loses himself entirely, becoming the object of his illness from which he recovers with difficulty. In such institutions patients are deprived of a future, in such institutions people stumble around without a present, deprived of decision-making and resistance, constantly dependent on the will, directives and dictates of others, says Dr. Basaglia.

Where am I, asks Andreas Ban, *inside or out?*

The fact that Carlo Ketz, the former husband of Andreas Ban's older sister, was "interned," Andreas Ban discovers while he is living in Skopje in the 1970s, in the Marshal Tito barracks, VP 4466, examining his roots, as he faces the Albanian frontier, prepared to defend his homeland from the attack of an enemy force that is invisible and never seen.

But it is only when he comes across the surname Ketz in *Trieste* that a chapter opens up before Andreas Ban, which he knows nothing about and whose heroes dash into the footnotes of his life. Whence the Italian family Ketz, how does it end up in Albania? Does the Ketz family have any connection with his sister's husband, whom he had seen only once, thirty or forty years earlier, at their wedding? Why did Carlo Ketz fall apart, and now, if he is still alive, is he assembling the debris of his days? So, seeking and annihilating his past, in the corners of which he is losing himself, peeling away the layers of time that clasps him in the embrace of forgetfulness, Andreas Ban feeds himself with other people's lives on his journey toward death, that most powerful goddess of ultimate oblivion.

In 2010, two years after the operation for carcinoma of the breast, at the invitation of his Belgrade friends from the 1990s settled in Nova Gorica, Andreas Ban crosses the nonexistent border and visits the retrospective exhibition of Zoran Mušič (1909–2005) in Gorizia. By chance, if there is such a thing as chance, at the exhibition he meets Haya Tedeschi, the one from the book *Trieste*, because someone whispers, *There's crazy Haya; it seems she's found her son and repented of her sins.* Andreas Ban invites aging Haya Tedeschi to Café Joy to tell him about Albania and that Ruben Ketz who had pockets full of black pebbles and spoke Albanian better than she did.

That's how Andreas Ban discovers that, as early as the 1930s,

Italy casts its eye on Albania and offers the country credits that it cannot repay. King Zog gives in to Italian blackmail and in 1936 signs twelve economic-financial agreements, which will undermine Albania's independence. Rome demands that Tirana place an Italian administration at the head of the Albanian police, that it affiliate with the Italian customs union, that it guarantee Italy control of Albanian sugar production, a monopoly on the organization of the mail and telegraph systems and the distribution of electricity, that the Italian language be introduced into all Albanian schools and that Albania accepts Italian colonizers. Albania is already run by a number of Italian companies, particularly construction firms. Ferrobeton, Simoncini, Marinucci, Tudini and Talenti and many others are already there. As well as Italian banks.

After the Italian invasion of Albania, in April 1939, there are twenty thousand Italians living in Tirana alone, Haya Tedeschi tells Andreas Ban. *That's when we arrive in Valona,* she says. *My father was a banker. The engineer Massimo Ketz lived nearby, he could have been around forty years old, an employee of the Immobiliare company that built the Durrës–Elbasan railroad. Sensing the impending war, Massimo Ketz sends his family, his wife Marcella and two sons, Carlo and Ruben, from Valona back to his Fascist homeland of Italy, to his father's luxurious villa in a suburb of Monfalcone, where the family continues to live its separate, peacetime life, multiplying and dispersing, procreating and dying, according to the laws of life and human nature, until the present day,* says Haya Tedeschi. *As early as 1940, my little ten-year-old friend Ruben Ketz,* says Haya Tedeschi, *the one who had pockets full of black pebbles and spoke Albanian better than I did, disappears from the picture and enters a different story. I discovered the rest recently,* says Haya Tedeschi, *when I was at the Trieste Red Cross, where I had gone to look for new information about the disappearance of my son and met Ruben Ketz, whom I would of course not have recognized, nearly seventy years had passed since we parted. In the office of the Trieste Red*

Cross, someone suddenly shouted signore Ruben Ketz! and I was, natu-rally, startled. Ruben was looking for information about his family; then he told me what had happened since they left Albania.

So, when he has settled his wife and sons in Monfalcone, before his flight to Albania, in Trieste the engineer Massimo Ketz tries on some field boots (for his return to Valona), which are tenderly drawn onto his foot by the shop assistant, the Slovene Dora Dag, a tall red-haired beauty with white hands and no rings. That same evening, in the Trieste restaurant run by the married couple Perica on Piazza Cavani, between the engineer Massimo Ketz and the shop assistant Dora Dag (b. 1900) a passion erupts that neither can un-derstand, after which Massimo Ketz says, *Come with me to Valona.*

I remember them arriving, says Haya Tedeschi, *because we only left Albania in 1943.*

Then, in 2010, in Café Joy in Gorizia, Andreas Ban also learns from Haya Tedeschi that Dora Dag leaves her husband and two children in Trieste and flies with Massimo on the airline Ala Lit-toria to Tirana. Massimo and Dora, along with several thousand Italian and Italian-Albanian families, survive the war, survive the German occupation of Albania and live to see the regime of Enver Hoxha after which a heavy iron curtain of immobility and fear falls over their lives, forty years of poverty, hunger, surveillance, arrests, release, renewed incarcerations, pursuits and executions, general misery during which, until 1992, there was no prospect of returning to Italy. Even though after the war Enver Hoxha needed the Italian colonists and their offspring to rebuild the country, they were later, as "agents of imperialism," "saboteurs" and "en-emies of the revolution," deprived of their language, nationality, memory and existence, and forgotten, living out their bunkered lives in a trap.

Dora and Massimo from the Mediterranean Vlorë, sunk in gar-dens and olive groves,

Ah, what a beauty, our Valona, says Haya Tedeschi,

in 1947, by order of the Central Committee of the Communist Party of Albania, Dora and Massimo are moved to Burrel, a little town of some fifteen hundred inhabitants in the north of the country, where they die—Massimo in 1982, Dora three years later. For their children, Giuseppa (1942), renamed Zefi,

I remember when she was born, said Haya Tedeschi,

and Rosa, Roza (1945), reality immersed in suffering rolling by heavily and slowly.

Albanians still call Burrel the birthplace of Skënderbeu and Ahmet Zogu, the Land of Kings. In communist times, it was a mining town covered in invisible particles of poisonous chrome, which constrict the lungs, so that breathing becomes doubly difficult. In Burrel, the engineer Massimo Ketz supervises the mine by digging in it. In Enver Hoxha's time, Burrel is best known for its cruel prison for criminals and political traitors. Massimo Ketz spends time in that prison on several occasions, for spreading "anticommunist propaganda and agitation" among miners. The Sigurimi controls his life.* The metastases of Sigurimi creep everywhere, into every nook of life. At Easter, secret agents rummage through trash cans looking for colored eggshells, at Christmas for broken decorative balls and wrapping paper, even though decorative balls and paper are not available, they look for dried pine branches and then they arrest people. In prison, Massimo Ketz gets to know Fatos Lubonja, sentenced to twenty-five years of which he spends seventeen in Burrel and Spaç and whose novel, written on cigarette paper, he does not manage to read; he meets Pjetër Arbnori, sentenced to twenty-eight years, hears appalling stories, sees beaten bodies, toothless skulls. The hideous times of a rampaging mind, the interminable rule of an ouroboros.

* Albanian secret state police; Stasi, KGB, Securitate equivalent.

In 1992, the new Albanian government allows Roza Bufi, née Ketz, to travel to Italy to look for her half brothers, Carlo and Ruben Ketz, said Haya Tedeschi. *Whether there was a meeting also with the children of Dora Dag, married name Ketz, I don't know. At that time, fifty-eight-year-old Carlo Ketz lives in a bachelor flat right beside Trieste's San Giovanni hospital, occasionally visiting psychiatrists. I'm well now, states Ruben's brother Carlo Ketz. For fifty years Carlo Ketz had lived with the conviction that his father, Massimo Ketz, had perished on the Albanian front, defending it for the Fascist Kingdom of Italy, and had no clue that any Roza Bufi, née Ketz, existed. So he told her, Dear Roza Bufi, this is my family, pointing to the old framed sepia photographs hanging on the wall. They were people dressed in velvet and silk. The men wore shirts with frills and jabots down the front, the women wore lace gloves and smiled wistfully. Ruben says,* said Haya Tedeschi, *that Carlo Ketz used to visit antique shops from Trieste to Koper and Rijeka, buying framed strangers' lives and his imagined past.*

And so, for the nth time Andreas Ban confirmed that we are all traveling along parallel tracks, tracks that touch for only an instant through the crazed sparks that scatter from under the wheels of an eternally rushing train.

Avete delle vecchie fotografie, famigliari? Delle fotografie famigliari, echoes in Andreas Ban's head.

That's a man from Trieste who comes regularly, looking for his relatives, says Oskar the secondhand bookseller.

Ecco la mia nonna, ho trovato la mia nonna, says the Italian. *Comprerò tutto.*

He bought my relatives, Andreas Ban tells Oskar, *strangers' lives.*

Maybe not so much strangers' lives as it seems, Oskar concludes.

Now, two or three years later, as he listens to Haya Tedeschi, all that remains for Andreas Ban is to smile at the realization that the old man in Oskar's antiquarian bookshop, his former brother-in-law Carlo Ketz, had once again wandered, even if briefly and only for a moment, into his life, the scattered rags of which he had dragged to distant hiding places.

Yes, Andreas Ban has a good time in Skopje, apart from the fact that even then he is plagued by scrambled thoughts. In the Skopje Drama Theater, he sees a play by Arthur Kopit, he doesn't remember the title, something about the way a lie becomes the truth and the truth a lie. He reads the recently published poems of Bogomil Gjuzel, *A Well in Time*, poems about weeping without weeping, about robbed Hamlet who has no one to dine with, and so, terribly alone, with a plate of hunger before him, he sits in the castle of Elsinore surrounded by guards—ghosts; he listens to Gjuzel asking how one can now bear witness to the legibility of this world of memories, how one takes hold of the threads of stories so tangled that they are barely recognizable, woven into knots and rags, he hears Gjuzel fear that the proscribed and forbidden, locked in a trunk, might appear alive at the door and shout, *I am a kid cooked in its mother's milk!* In verse, Gjuzel transforms *temple stairways into pigs with an unavoidably familiar stench*, until *darkness like dust covers the losers and the victors mixed together in heroic blood and cowardly excrement*. Andreas only now understands that, like a cursed visionary in the particles of existence scattered about like randomly tossed peas, Gjuzel reads our perpetuated today:

> *And the wind brought people*
> *who had let their plows rust;*

solitary people tilling the sky,
reaping the harvests of summer nights,
the fat grain of early stars,
leaving it all unwinnowed.
Instead they used swords;
their plowing was of bodies, their furrow cut to the heart;
they plucked out hearts like tree stumps,
they burst gall bladders,
with livers they fed the vultures on their shoulders.
At the last they rolled away the skulls
like stones for building,
but for building there was never time.

So, when the soldier Andreas Ban is granted leave, he does not go home to Belgrade, but to the Struga Poetry Evenings, into the center of the world. He plunges into yet another history, into hundreds of personal histories, which drive some people mad and others to write poems. He looks at Lake Ohrid, resembling a small enclosed sea over which one cannot sail away. The Golden Wreath is won that year by Pablo Neruda (in absentia), the symposium is led by Viktor Shklovsky and the Miladinov Brothers' Prize is awarded to Gjuzel, at whose table, in a little prefabricated house erected after the Skopje earthquake, Andreas Ban will many years later drink and listen to Bogomil's latest poems, stories of his friendship with Czesław Miłosz and Isaac Bashevis Singer, stories of his political past which evoke anger, impotence and nausea, to whose wife he will flee from his current provincial languor into an embrace as secure as a mother's.

That year, 1972, from West Germany to Struga comes Nikolas Born (1937), seven years later he dies of cancer, while from East Germany arrives Sarah Kirsch (1935), for the first time permitted to leave the country and accompanied by the trusted mediocre poet Eva Strittmatter (1930–2011), whose books at that time have print runs in the millions and whose husband Erwin Strittmatter, a novelist of rural themes, it is discovered in the 1990s, served during the Second World War in the 18th Regiment of the SS police, deporting Jews from Athens, then lived briefly in Poland as a guard of the Kraków ghetto, then, after taking some courses in anti-Partisan warfare, went to Slovenia. When the Berlin Wall is erected, Erwin Strittmatter becomes an informer for the Stasi, while his writing becomes increasingly permeable and popular. That year, 1972, in the little Struga backwater, cut in half by the Black Drim River, Nicholas Born and Sarah Kirsch try to patch up their country with illicit embraces. And do not succeed. In that year, 1972, Andreas Ban also meets the attractive W. S. Merwin (1927), now the renowned Carolyn Kizer (1925) and Peter Henisch, who makes every effort to arouse the empty-headed sinners of this planet, who keep on reproducing, crawling all over the place and depriving others of air. As early as the 1970s, it was with Peter Henisch that the publication of so-called Vater Literatur in Austria and Germany began, about the secret sins of fathers, which, in Eastern Europe, including Croatia in 2010, is decanted into sentimental, artistically irrelevant, historically insignificant campaign against an uneducated readership, not confronting history, fumbling around with trivial family traumas of writers. That quasi-literary settling of scores with dead fathers, the ironing of one's crumpled conscience, those furies of impotent sons cowering in the shadows of their progenitors, those variations on self-pity, guilt, hatred and fear written in a cascade of semiconsciousness, provoke in Andreas Ban nausea, disgust and sorrow. Even Kafka was afraid to confront his living father, so he wrote a letter to him, in cautious steps (*petits pas*) at odds with his inner turmoil, and asked his mother to hand it to his father which she did not, so that his problematic letter only saw the light of day once all the protagonists were long since dead.

Henisch's *Negatives of My Father* (*Die kleine Figur meines Vaters*, 1975) disturbs the Austrian-German public, which, long after the war, scrupulously consigns to oblivion its desecrated soil. The little figures of Henisch's father are thematically selected photographs by Walter Henisch, one of the most prominent photographers of the Third Reich. Walter Henisch tells his son Peter Henisch, *Listen, little one, I had no connection with the politics of the Third Reich, I was completely apolitical, just as I am apolitical today; I did my duty, and my duty was to take photographs for the homeland, for our Germany.*

And Peter tells him, *Listen, old man, I shall write a book about you and all the horrors that you witnessed with a smile on your face and a Leica at your eye. And I shall write that you participated in the crimes and that after the war you made no mention of them, and that you are lying now.*

Oh, I am proud of the professional way in which I conducted my wartime duties, says Walter.

Yes, in the service of Nazi propaganda, says Peter.

The half Jew Walter Henisch (1913–1975) began his career in his native Vienna in the 1930s, and continued it from 1939 in the Wehrmacht, of which he was a member until the end of the war. As early as 1940, Henisch was part of Goebbels's machine, taking photographs on the front lines in Russia, Poland, France and the Balkans, he also clicked away in 1944 in the course of Operation Rössel-sprung, i.e. the Seventh Enemy Offensive, or the Raid on Drvar, when he raised the soldiers' morale. Then, after 1945, Henisch first worked freelance (no newspaper would employ him, in light of

his wartime past) and much later placed himself at the service of the social-democratic press. He had received awards for his work during the war, including several of Hitler's Iron Crosses. But then came the Austrian new age, followed by a wave of oblivion.

The early 1970s. In Vienna's Rathaus the political and cultural elite are gathered, the atmosphere is festive, it is touristy, the city is clean, *Judenrein*, and onto the stage climb a throng of *citoyens* to whom their country is indebted. Among them is Henisch whose exceptionally reduced biography, with the war years omitted, is recited in a chirpy voice by the young hostess. A member of the Austrian government then cordially praises the photographic achievements of Walter Henisch, particularly those that display his exceptional sensitivity to the social and communal issues of his postwar homeland, and also his unforgettable portraits of children (in peacetime), while the whole ceremonial is recorded in silence by new young photographers. In the background, classical music plays, as befits the Viennese hall. And so, after transience had swallowed up the years between 1936 and 1948, historical and collective memory has folded. The *fotographischer Standpunkt* that reflects the gaze, and *distorts* it, remains a powerful tool to this day. That's why Andreas Ban no longer believes photographs.

Andreas Ban's obsessive thoughts

After Peter Henisch come increasingly acute public show-downs in literature and film by the traumatized postwar generation with their SS fathers and grandfathers. That painful process still continues to jolt the German and Austrian literary-historical scene. In the book *Trieste*, Andreas Ban reads about the well-known graphic artist Christopher Meckel and his book *Such-bild. Über meinen Vater* and *Suchbild. Meine Mutter*, about Monika Göth (daughter of the infamous commander of the concentration camp in Plaszów, condemned to death by hanging), who today seeks out camp survivors, victims of her father Amon Göth, asking for their forgiveness, she wanders through the world, repeating, *I am not like him*; about Peter Sichrovski and his book *Born Guilty: The Children of Nazi Families*; the book *Trieste* mentions Beate Nie-mann in the documentary by Yoash Tatari *My Father, the Murderer*, and Peter Schneider and his novel *Vati* ("Dad"), and Dan Bar-On, Andreas's colleague, born in Haifa in 1938 to parents of German origin, who writes the essay "Legacy of Silence: Encounters With the Children of the Third Reich," and then there's Niklas Frank. Unlike those for whom it took fifty or more years to discover the truth about their Nazi fathers and who now portray themselves as the traumatized victims of history, in *Trieste* Andreas Ban reads about how Niklas Frank protests from the end of the war until to-day, emerging from that painful struggle devastated but victorious.

Until 1945, Andreas Ban reads, life in Wawel Royal Castle, which dominates Kraków and from which there is a spectacular view of the Tatra mountains, seems like a dream to Niklas Frank. While his father Hans Frank, "the King of Poland," is working on the liquidation of the Polish elite, maintaining that "Poland has to become a land of workers and peasants," with no educated class, throughout the Generalgouvernement he shuts down theaters, schools and universities, forbids the population to listen to radio broadcasts, destroys libraries, proscribes the printing of books and eliminates the Polish language, while he limits the distribution of provisions to a level below that required for survival, the Frank family lacks nothing, from food to servants and stolen artworks, Hans Frank entertains high SS functionaries, including Himmler, and, with caviar and champagne, strums piano keys, playing—oh, what splendid times—Chopin. From that book *Trieste*, Andreas Ban discovers that, writing and talking about those days, Niklas went on an excursion with his nanny Hilde Albert to a place where some jolly prankster was forcing very thin people to mount a donkey that would kick, throwing them to the ground, and those very thin people found it hard to get up. *I watched the performance and laughed as though I was at the circus*, Niklas Frank says, *and I went to a camp for forced labor, in the so-called subcamp of a nearby concentration camp*. Niklas Frank becomes an angry teenager and a fanatical hitchhiker, he travels through the western part of his divided country of Germany and takes its pulse. *As soon as I said I was the son of a famous Nazi executed at Nuremberg, the drivers would buy me lunch. In all my years of hitchhiking only one driver stopped, opened the door and told me to get out*, says Niklas Frank. In the Berlin Documentation Center Niklas Frank studies his father's dossier (which Beate Niemann could have done as well). Niklas Frank visits the archives, reads Hans Frank's diaries, visits aging Nazis who had once been connected with his father and close associates, visits servants who worked for the Frank family in Berlin and Kraków, goes to America and talks to the priest Sixtus O'Connor from whom Hans Frank sought God's forgiveness before he was put to death. *Was the noose over his black hood tied tightly enough?* Niklas Frank may have asked himself. *Was there a crack when the chair was removed? Could it be heard loudly enough?* he may have wondered. *I imagine myself biting into Hans Frank's heart while he bellows like a wild beast, and I sink my teeth ever more deeply and he howls ever louder and the blood spurts and then his heart stops, empty and dead,* he says. *For a long time after the war, Germany bathed in collective denial of individual responsibility for the war,* says Niklas Frank. *My father was a coward and depraved and he was guilty of the deaths of two million people.*

What Niklas Frank discovers in the course of long years of searching is converted in 1987 into a lifelong obsession, into a mission imbued with fury because of the deafness that oppresses the country, transforming it increasingly into a Beckettian landscape in which the players are left at the end of the game with just a few pawns and a limited number of moves. In his book *Der Vater*, not *Mein Vater*, but *Der Vater*, Niklas Frank enters a dangerous duel the outcome of which not even Freud could decipher, for which no Greek tragedy has an answer.

Then, in 2005, Niklas's new book *Meine deutsche Mutter* is published. Niklas Frank does not let go, Niklas Frank does not give up. "The Queen of Poland," Maria Brigitte Frank, unscrupulous, greedy, calculating and promiscuous, and already long since dead, fares no better than her "King." Niklas Frank continues to howl in a cosmos of deaf and lifeless silence.

So, in Germany and Austria, almost seventy years after the end of the war, ever new serials of undigested Nazi trauma keep appearing, while in Croatia, in a patriotic trance, Ustasha crimes and their perpetrators dress up in carnival robes of rotten nostalgia, their descendants keep quiet or lie about their fathers' and grandfathers' pasts, at Christmastime masses dedicated to the leader Pavelić are still held, it is a deaf age of defiled silence through which pigs grunt as they stampede over the paving stones of memory. And Andreas Ban languishes in his exile in a mouse hole on the edge of the world.

Besides, what's so terrible about being a photographer in Goebbels's propaganda hell, or a journalist, musician, writer, painter, a poet loyal to Pavelić's State Information and Propaganda Office (DIPU), or the Main Directorate for Propaganda (GRP); what is so terrible about making films, conducting symphony orchestras, composing, acting in national theaters, writing wishy-washy poetry, "fireside" fiction that is thrust forth as the standard of supreme art, nauseating, singing to the people, encouraging the people not to falter in their love for their beautiful, enlarged, future homeland (their Croatian mother) of pure blood, for "culture" strengthens the people's spirit, makes them better and they, the people, swallow all that, this great Mass of dedication, while somewhere out there, "in forests and mountains,"* people die singing quite different songs, far away from the everyday, enclosed by walls and wire or under gas showers, or with an Ustasha curved knife at the throats of Jews, Serbs, Roma and antifascists, millions of the "unsuitable," the vast heap of "human trash," transformed into an army of skeletons, "freed from work," they listen to the heavenly music of obliteration.

In October 2010, at the age of eighty-one, in a clinic in Schönau—oh, the irony and "happenstance"—near Berchtesgaden, with a lovely view of Obersalzberg, the location of Hitler's favorite mountain spot Berghof, the producer and writer Thomas Harlan

* "Po šumama i gorama," a partisan war song.

dies of emphysema. Thomas Harlan was the son of the famous Veit Harlan, extremely popular during the Third Reich, a bon vivant and ladies' man, the blue-eyed and fair-haired creator of the infamous anti-Semitic film *Jud Süss*. This "artistic" propaganda product, melodramatic and heartrending, which ends with the bloodthirsty execution by hanging of the greedy, ugly and smelly Süss, while the masses scream "Kill, kill the Jew," inflames people throughout the Reich, including many Croats in the NDH (Independent State of Croatia).

Because many Croats in the NDH are already organized, prepared, blinded, conditioned and loyal. As early as 1941, anti-Jewish propaganda and the struggle to protect the Aryan blood and honor of the Croatian nation are prospering and pecking at their brains, as advertisements do today. The newspapers are obedient and loyal, they keep warning of the danger of "the Jewish spirit that emerges from Jewish blood," but they also remind Croats of the good fortune that the Croatian countryside has preserved "its pure racial foundations," because "Croatian blood in the countryside has not been infiltrated by a foreign, Jewish influx." The Zagreb newspaper *Novi list* calls for "a biological regeneration of our milieu," which would completely cure the Croatian national organism. It is necessary, therefore, to eliminate Jewish blood from the cells of that Croatian organism, because at present, due to the Jewish blood that still circulates here and there, its threat is enormous. That is why the introduction of race laws is the best defense of the purity of Croatian blood, the newspapers, that is the journalists, say. Their names no longer matter, do they, they are dead, and the fact that their children and grandchildren don't wish to talk about it, that's their right, isn't it, their right to silence, the thick, suffocating silence, pumped full of the poisons of patriotism. The registration of Jews begins, yellow stars are sewn on and other yellow scrap-like tin badges resembling grotesque brooches are pinned to the "defiled" chests, and in May 1941 journalists remind their readers that every Jew is a parasite on the body of every Croat, a worm that corrupts him, and with its great destructive strength destroys the Croatian family, Croatian villages, Croatian municipalities, towns and the whole Independent State of Croatia. Those Jews, those foreigners, aliens, make use only of lies, deceit, cunning, dishonesty, and if necessary murder, the loyal Croatian journalists report.

The State Information and Propaganda Office (DIPU), later renamed the Main Directorate for Propaganda (GRP), run by the journalist and chief censor Ivo Bogdan,* the devoted Ustasha, powerful ideologue of the Independent State of Croatia, the rabid radical clerical fascist in love with Franco, this GRP, then, has eyes and ears for the entire public and private life of its beloved homeland of Croatia. That DIPU and GRP, that is, the Leader's sycophants, determine what will be published, which gramophone records will be sold and which will be destroyed, which films will be shown, what the radio will broadcast, so that the life of the Croats should flow smoothly and securely, so that the cafés should be full, evening outings relaxed and entertaining, the women well turned out, fluttering and smiling, the music in Sunday matinees melodious among horticultural greenery, and the church tranquil. (Quite incomprehensibly, while Andreas Ban imagines Zarah Leander

---

* Ivo Bogdan (Šipan, 1907–killed in Buenos Aires, 1971). In 1944 appointed director-in-chief of the Main Directorate of Propaganda of the NDH On May 6, 1945, with the other members of the Educational Battalion, flees to Austria from where, like many NDH functionaries and even hangmen, via Italy, that is via the Catholic rat-run of the Holy Roman Church, and with the help of the priest Krunoslav Draganović, he reaches Argentina. There, together with a whole team of Ustasha émigrés, he edits the journal *Studia Croatica*.

soothing tense Nazis, stoking passions suppressed by their fanatical patriotism, with the aura of Zyklon B, he finds in his storeroom, in a cardboard box amidst a heap of Bakelite 78 records, one with the label "Elektroton, Zagreb," most probably from the NDH era, on which Zarah Leander sings compositions by the well-known Theo Mackeben, who spent the entire war actively conducting, composing and making films, cheerfully scampering around the cinematic and musical scene of the Third Reich.)

Journalists, filmmakers, international congresses, exhibitions, cultural cooperation with the Third Reich, oh bliss, everything is under control, as it should be. New criminal laws are instituted, the disobedient brought to order, above all order, effort and re-education.

Poglavnik!* exclaim the NDH journalists and all the editors of the Zagreb newspapers at a reception hosted by Pavelić in 1941, as they sip Herzegovinian wines and nibble authentic Livanj cheese, *dear Poglavnik*, they exclaim, *Croatian journalists are now and for ever more, for the Homeland—ready!*

So, in addition to politicians, and journalists and scientists and students and artists—painters, writers, musicians, singers, actors, producers, and priests and young people and *children* too, so many are *ready* (not all, to be fair) to contribute by law to the "protection of the Aryan blood and honor of the Croatian nation" and its "national and Aryan Croatian culture." The scene is set, the terrain sounded out, and so, with great pomp, on July 1, 1942 in Zagreb, in the Art Pavilion on Strossmayer Square, the exhibition is opened "about the development of the Jewish population and their destructive activity in Croatia before 14.10.1941," which also illustrates "the solution of the Jewish question within the NDH."

* Führer!

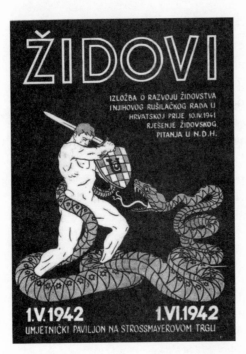

In the introductory text to the catalogue of that famous exhibition about Jews, "someone" explains that *freedom must be realized through numerous seemingly insignificant acts, independence must be realized in all areas of national activity, what must be achieved is inner liberation, national purification, the strengthening of national consciousness, the permeation through all spiritual life of pure Croatdom, a new national state must be built, and to retain in one's milieu the enemies of all nations, Jews, is the same as planting a young fruit tree with worms nesting in its roots.* Visitors are benevolently instructed that *The State Information and Propaganda Office undertakes to inform the Croatian nation of all the reasons that guided the Leader in the introduction of anti-Jewish laws and decrees and the carrying out of an anti-Jewish policy. Everyone must realize,* it says in the catalogue, *that despite their individual harmless appearance, Jews have never been, whether consciously or unconsciously, anything other than units of international Judaism, they have always been the enemies of everything that is expressly Croatian, that may assist Croats in attaining a better future. This exhibition, sponsored by the State Information and Propaganda Bureau in the city of Zagreb on May 1, 1942, is a contribution to the process of understanding Judaism and serves the anti-Jewish consciousness of the Croatian nation.*

One important fact must not be overlooked, the anonymous agitator gloats throughout the catalogue: *This exhibition was not created by employees of the State Information and Propaganda Office, it has been created by the entire Croatian people through their donations. Day after day, the Reporter on the Jewish Question received packages of books on the subject from citizens in the provinces. The people of Zagreb personally brought armfuls of books, data and documents about the evils the Jews have inflicted upon the Croatian people, experts from the universities have voluntarily placed at our disposal their knowledge and their time to organize this vast accumulated material ... The exhibition contains just a few examples of Jewish bloodthirstiness from their earliest history on.*

Finally, as a reward, all visitors to the exhibition "The Jews" are offered, free of charge, enjoyment of "the excellent films of German production, *The Eternal Jew, Rothschild* and *Jud Süss*," which will be shown at the Danica picture house (now the ZKM theater) each day at three thirty p.m. and on Sundays at a matinee at eleven a.m.

The infamous film *The Eternal Jew*, made under the strict control of Joseph Goebbels (like the even more terrible *Jud Süss*), depicts Polish Jews who, living like rats, rule the world economy and commerce and threaten the racial "purity" of mankind.

To prepare the audience for a "quality emotional experience" during and after watching these appalling films, the Croatian

Voucher for free entry to Danica picture house for the screening of "Jud Süss"

Voucher for free entry to Danica picture house for the screening of "Rothschild"

Voucher for free entry to Danica picture house for the screening of "The Eternal Jew"

newspapers teemed with "facts" and "authenticated statements," such as those of the well-known socially active Ustasha, the carpenter and terrorist Vjekoslav Blaškov,* who observes that at last an end has come to the Jewish abuse of thousands upon thousands of girls of Aryan blood who had been obliged to sacrifice their honor to obtain employment with Jews or in their companies. *In Zagreb*, Vjekoslav Blaškov bellows, *in Zagreb there are innumerable Jewish companies in which Jews exploited not only the labor force, but also the honor and morality of their female workers, where Jews kept special female personnel for the whims of their sons. Most prostitution in Zagreb*, bellows Vjekoslav Blaškov, *has its origin in Jewish firms.*

Not since the screening of *Jud Süss*, in the history of film, has there been a work that has succeeded to the same extent in inflam-

* Vjekoslav Blaškov (Donje Selo on the island of Šolta, 1911–Zagreb, 1948). Accompanied Ante Pavelić on the occasion of his visit to Hitler in September 1944. In May 1945, he escaped to Austria, then to Italy, and in 1948 entered Croatia illegally. He was captured in the same year and sentenced to death by the Supreme Court of the National Republic of Croatia.

ing the masses as that core cultural product of Goebbels's anti-Jewish campaign. As soon as it was released, *Jud Süss* became a sensational hit throughout Germany and elsewhere in Europe. Showing and watching the film became the main propaganda entertainment at "friendly evenings" for Hitler Youth, SS informers, concentration camp guards and other *kulturträger*, including the "ordinary, innocent" urban and rural masses. The audience went home from the screenings in a trance, overwhelmed by an emotional cocktail of patriotism and hatred, ready for official as well as small individual *actions*. At the 1941 Venice Film Festival, to the general enthusiasm of both audience and critics, *Jud Süss* (in which, by order of the SS, the extras were Jews collected from the Łódźghetto) won the Lion d'Or.

Veit Harlan, star of Third Reich propaganda films, is the only director to be charged twice for crimes against humanity, and ultimately released. Veit Harlan died in 1964, with divine forgiveness, a cleansed conscience and a smile on his lips.

Jud Süss is still banned in Germany. In Sweden, even at the beginning of 1941, the Nordisk Tonefilm company sought permission from the government to show it, but the request was turned down. So, in the course of the war, the film *Jud Süss* was not shown publicly, although the German Embassy in Stockholm organized a screening for selected guests.

The rights to the film *Jud Süss* are held by the Friedrich-Wilhelm-Murnau Foundation, owned by the German state. The Foundation permits the film to be screened exclusively with advance explanation of the context and the times in which the film was made, as well as the influence that it was intended to have (and succeeded in having) on its audience. Nevertheless, in July 2008, the anti-Semitically charged brothers Sándor and Tibor Gede, devotees of Szalasi's anti-Semitic Fascist Arrow Cross party, publishers of Hitler's speeches, active associates of neo-Nazi web portals, organize, illegally, in the middle of Budapest's Jewish Quarter, a public screening of the film *Jud Süss*. Five hundred delighted souls arrive outside a hall with one hundred seats, but the zealous Gede brothers reassure their loyal public that before September 13 there will be three additional screenings of the banned film *Jud Süss* in the same hall, there, in the middle of Budapest's Jewish Quarter. *You won't regret it*, exclaim the neo-Nazis Sándor and Tibor Gede. *This magnificent film by the renowned director Veit Harlan*, exclaim the Gede brothers, *is a true work of art, and tickets are only 4 euros 50.*

Two years later, on June 16, for the sake of continuity, for the sake of snatching it from oblivion, for the sake of the struggle with the greedy Jews who, in the twenty-first century, continue to shape the destiny of the careworn Hungarian people, the Gede brothers organize the screening of yet another propagandist artistic creation of the Third Reich—the film *The Eternal Jew*. There is delight in the hall. People applaud, laugh and shout, the atmosphere reaches fever pitch. Then the police arrive, arrests are made and the show is (temporarily) suspended.

After the war, Thomas Harlan, son of the Nazi "artist" Veit Harlan, is overwhelmed by his father's past and goes to study philosophy in Paris. In Paris, Thomas Harlan works with Gilles Deleuze and Klaus Kinski, he participates in left-wing debates and in 1959 begins to rummage in the Third Reich archives, and thus becomes an obsessive searcher for the truth, a Nazi hunter, a revolutionary and lifelong critic of Veit Harlan, taking upon himself the unrepented and unrepentable sins of his father. What a burden.

And so, Thomas Harlan's research lead to the prosecution of more than two thousand German war criminals.

*Yes, one has to carry a burden like this to the end of
one's days. Responsibility for what my father did must
pass to my children and my children's children, and to
their children, and so on. That past, which is also my
past, circulates like shrapnel through my body, causes in-
eradicable, unbearable pain, and ravages it. That murky
brown and black German past follows me through life.*

*As a child I was spoiled and cared for. On my birth-
days the Gestapo would, on Goebbels's orders, open
Wertheim department store just for me in the middle of
the night, the store was seized, of course, from the Jewish Wertheim family, so that I, "their dear Thomas,"
could stroll undisturbed from floor to floor and choose
my presents.*

The NDH also enters the race. As early as April 23, 1941, in Zagreb, the Directorate for Film is founded at the State Secretariat
for National Enlightenment, which on May 3 publishes a circular
intended for all film companies and cinemas in the country:

*From now on, the Independent State of Croatia permits
only serious and exemplary advertising which will, in
a realistic way, emphasize the content and meaning of
a film and even its message, insofar as it is favorable
and beneficial and in the spirit of the new age ...*

*When advertising their films, cinemas and film com-
panies must take into account that in the Independent
State of Croatia cinema is now placed at the service
of the Croatian people and State and is no longer an
ordinary business. Cinema must also give expression to
the new spirit and new age, which will be increasingly*

felt each day in the world of cinema in the Independent State of Croatia.

The following year, 1942, the NDH opens the state company Croatia Film in Zagreb, under the auspices of which it makes and distributes *cultural* propaganda journals and short *educational but significant* documentary war films and occasional *naive* feature films with prominent Ustashas in leading and supporting roles, little films about the carefree Croatian Aryan Youth dancing and singing, then marching, and in the end killing; about splendid Croatian landscapes: about Croatian villages in which people live clean, authentic lives without electricity, drainage or water, but where sheep are raised and wool is spun and the sun shines over the renewed, enlarged and cleansed "independent" Croatian countryside and the state whose fighters selflessly lay down their lives on the altar of the homeland, or open and oversee concentration camps where people work cheerfully for the well-being of a bright future, which, five years later, deformed and defiled, ends up on a garbage heap, in sewage pipes which flow to this day and continue to emit their stagnant, putrid stench.

So, from 1942 to 1945, part of the Croatian cultural elite makes uplifting films about the voluntary spring cleaning of river banks and sea shores, and the winter clearing of piles of snow from the streets of Zagreb, newsreels about weavers, about the founding of the Croatian-German Society in Berlin—on a stage beneath unfurled red-and-black flags with swastikas and with Croatian-German friends, their arms raised, *Heil!*, ditties are recorded, little works about life in Bosnia, which is in fact part of the NDH, is it not?, audiences enjoy watching the Domobrans, the Croatian Home Guardsmen, taking the oath, also with one arm raised, *Heil!*, and documentaries about how clothes are made from *rabbit fur*, clothes later worn by lovely blonde "pure-blooded Croatian women," short films about idyllic lives on the Adriatic coast (what was left of it), and about the Leader Pavelić's visit to Adolf Hitler, *Sieg Heil!*, and about Vjekoslav "Maks" Luburić,* that half-literate

---

* Vjekoslav "Maks" Luburić (Ljubuški, 1914–Cargagente, Spain, 1969). Commander of the III Division of the UNS (intelligence, counterintelligence and political police). After completing the first year of secondary school, he takes a job in the Croatian Employment Agency. Sentenced in 1931 to five months in prison for embezzlement of funds. Having served his sentence, emigrates to Hungary, where he becomes the camp treasurer in the Ustasha military camp in Janka Puszta. At the beginning of April 1941, he enters the Kingdom of Yugoslavia illegally, and in mid-April joins the newly established government of the Independent State of Croatia (NDH). He works in the management office of the military command of the Ustasha headquarters, and after Mija Babić is killed, is appointed Commander of the III Division of Ustasha defense, that is, commander of all the Ustasha camps in the NDH He founds Jasenovac concentration camp, which he visits often to oversee its work and to personally execute prisoners. At the beginning of 1942, on Pavelić's orders, he goes to Herzegovina. The Germans complain that he is interfering in their units' activities in Herzegovina, and ask Pavelić to recall him. At his own request, in the summer of 1943, Luburić places himself in internment in Šumci near Lepoglava, where he lives under the false name of Matija Ban. He reappears in public toward the end of August 1944, when he participates in putting an end to the Vokić-Lorković putsch and works on the "defense" of Sarajevo.

During the reorganization of the NDH's armed forces in the autumn of 1944, Luburić acquires the rank of General of the Croatian Armed Forces. Just one day before the entry of Partisan units into Zagreb, May 7, 1945, he is appointed Commander of the Armed Forces of the NDH and so oversees their withdrawal toward the Austrian border. He does not surrender to the Allies, but returns to Croatia and with groups of "crusaders" (Ustasha terrorists) is active in the districts of Bilogora and Slavonia until November 1945, when he retreats to Hungary, from where, under the pseudonym Maximilian Soldo, he goes to Spain. In the struggle for supremacy, Luburić falls out with Pavelić in 1955 and is expelled from the Ustasha movement. With a group of like-minded people, he founds a printing company where he publishes propaganda pamphlets and his speeches. In 1967, Ivan Stanić takes a job at the printer's and two years later kills Luburić.

overseer of all the camps in the Independent State of Croatia, including Jasenovac, where he stops by to kill a few prisoners (the films do not show that) and to have his photograph taken with a dove on his chest, about that butcher with the rank of general (oh, how history repeats itself), that fugitive about whom, even today, bigoted émigrés and their descendants write sentimental, warmongering pamphlets; then there are films about the Croatian Parliament, renamed the Croatian State Parliament, then reverted again in 1991, just as in 1993 the NDH currency, the famous filthy Croatian *kuna* is resurrected. Then, there are films of the Leader's speeches given here and there, exterior and interior shots, and so on, the people, rural and urban, are stubbornly fattened, strengthened, invigorated in their hatred of the Partisan bandits and those dreadful Allies who would like to deprive a magnificent people (the Croats) of their autonomy, of their hearth and tradition.

As early as 1942, at the Venice Film Festival, the NDH medium-length propaganda documentary *Guard on the River Drina* wins a little bronze medal, a great triumph for this puppet statelet dedicated to glorifying itself and Nazi Fascism, and in that year of 1942, when the main prizes, Copa Mussolini and Copa Volti, are awarded to the only director to be accused of crimes against humanity, Veit Harlan, and his wife, the actress Kristina Söderbaum, for the films *Der Grosse König* and *Die Goldene Stadt*.

Guard on the River Drina, that creation of sick minds, pregnant with dramatically packaged lies, talks about "non-Slav and un-Croatian nomadic tribes" which, straight after the declaration of the Independent State of Croatia, rise against the Ustasha authorities, and these bandits plunder and kill and carry out acts of bestial terror against the powerless population, but then the legendary Black Legion is formed, whose commander, after the death of Franetić,* is the semiliterate boor and butcher Rafael Boban,† who used to tour village fairs before the war, selling spangles and tobacco, and who disappeared from sight after the war, and so, like many SS members never taken to court and like his own fanatical émigré Ustasha brethren, remains for some a tender memory. And the Black Legion, under the command of Rafael Boban (the 9th Battalion of the Croatian Defense Forces was named after "Rafael the knight Boban," as were the 1st battalion of the Croatian Defense Forces from Livno and a unit of the Croatian Defense Council in 1942), this Black Legion "demonstrates the greatest heroism, and the Croatian Liberation Forces (HOS) hurry to the aid of their

---

* Jure Francetić (Prozor, near Otočac, 1912–Slunj, 1942). In *Feral Tribune* of May 20, 2004, Boris Rašeta writes: "There are numerous eyewitness reports of the crimes of Jure Francetić and his Black Legion. Among the most moving is that of Milovan Đilas, which was quoted in the second volume of his 'Diary' by Vladimir Dedijer, describing in detail the massacre of civilians, for the most part women and children, in Serbian villages near Kupres. Nevertheless, the myth of Jure Francetić lives on to this day, and to criticism of his person and acts or to the idea that his statue should be removed from the center of Slunj, his apologists reply that he has not been condemned of anything and never committed any crimes." (The monuments to Francetić in Slunj and in Sveti Rok to Mile Budak, writer and Minister of Culture in the NDH, a convicted war criminal, are removed in August 2004.)

"The lean commander of the Black Legion, Jure Francetić, the Ustasha colonel, posthumously promoted to the rank of flank commander, honored as the Leader's 'knight' and Commander of the Ustasha army," writes Boris Rašeta, "has in recent years become the greatest star of right-wing websites in Croatia. The website of the Black Legion alone has had over half a million hits!"

† Rafael Boban (Sovići near Grude, 1907–?). Ustasha colonel and general of the Croatian Armed Forces.

brothers under attack in Bosnia"—as in 1992—"and capture hordes of bandits who call themselves Partisans, rampaging without restraint … The Black Legion continues to cleanse the eastern border of Croatia" (Bosnia), the narrator continues in *Guard on the River Drina*, then "the captured bandits are taken to camps where they are set to useful work," and, as the narrator puts it, displayed as "characters"—Partisans—"whom the Bolshevik infection has made more pathetic than animals … men who leave their own children to the mercy of hunger and death," says the narrator, "while the Croatian State authorities take care of their placement into special reception centers, so after days of misery, hunger and suffering from all possible diseases, they are offered medical aid and assured a dignified human life," in the care of gentle, smiling nuns.

> *What dignified human life, what special reception centers! I rescued children from the so-called children's hospital in Stara Gradiška, from a camp under the command of Maks Luburić. With superhuman effort and the help of some nuns and friends, we saved thousands of children from certain death in other Ustasha camps and reception centers. There were terrible dilemmas, to take or not to take the children who could not even stand up and who would die in just a few hours, how to bear the pain of separating children from their mothers, and how to transport to Zagreb so many sick and starving nameless youngsters with their large intestines hanging from them and covered in flies, whose mothers had long since been sent to German camps.*
>
> *Once, as we drove, I could not move in the wagon for fear of stepping on someone. The older children sat the whole time on potties, while the little ones soiled*

*themselves. The floor was covered in mud and chil-
dren's worms. I endeavored as best I could to move the
children to get them out of the filth. Toward morning,
people at the stations came and saw this misery, and
brought us water. During long stops, the healthy children got out of the wagon. For the weak ones in the last
two wagons, there was no question of taking them out.
I managed to get hold of a rake, so I could at least dis-
pose of the worms. It seemed that before a child died the
worms left its body, because, toward morning, when
some of the children in my care became weaker, whole
tangles of worms left their bodies. My name is Diana
Budisavljević. I died in Innsbruck in 1978 at the age
of eighty-eight. I kept a diary from 1941 to 1945. Today
I am forgotten.*

Then the camera in that pugnacious "documentary" film *Guard on
the River Drina* shows children "whose parents had been killed by
the Partisans," all in faultlessly tailored and ironed little Ustasha
uniforms, stepping out cheerfully, "their hearts full of content-
ment, on their faces a smile of happiness" as they dance the kolo
in the burgeoning countryside. In the background, the beautiful,
clear River Drina roars, in reality the bloody Drina in which the
mutilated corpses of "the undesirable" float, the river that for centuries, to the present day, reverberates and rushes in an effort to
cleanse itself of the blood of the innocent, and "order and peace
reigns once again over Bosnian villages, for they are protected
by the Ustasha guard." The narrator tells how "the Croats of the
Muslim faith, in whose veins runs pure Croatian blood, made huge
sacrifices in the battle for liberation from the bandits," and that
now "their blood flows like a river, but life is returning, people are

returning to their homes," people are building, plowing, the masses are cheerful, they compete with one another, throwing rocks from their shoulders, in the background intoxicating popular music plays, the atmosphere is ebullient, Croatian Ustasha Youth come and help to establish Croatian life, the Leader comes, "cordially received, with the love of his grateful nation," small children offer him bouquets of freshly picked wild flowers, little boys with neat haircuts and faultless partings, little girls with their hair drawn back into braids, in little white dresses and white crocheted knee socks, while he, the Leader, tenderly pats them on their little heads, "joyous tears flow," one mother carrying a baby lifts its arm in a Nazi salute, throughout Bosnia the NDH flag flutters, this is the small film of big lies and monstrous ideology, awarded the bronze medal at the Fascist Festival in Venice in 1942, a little film which makes some people today, overwhelmed with nationalist resurgence, wonder why "in former Yugoslavia there was a ban on films from the NDH era." This film was directed by Branko Marjanović, a key employee of the State Cinematic Company of Croatian Film during the Independent State of Croatia, head of newsreel and documentary production, and so on.

Andreas Ban no longer knows what to think. Who is that excellent director, Branko Marjanović, trained in Prague who, immediately after the war, as early as 1949, without any criticism from the Communist authorities, with no reference to his NDH patriotic film activity, with screenwriter Joža Horvat makes the socialist-realist propaganda film *The Flag*? A film in which a ballerina assures her colleagues that "a real artist takes inspiration for his art from life and this is the only way to create enduring and valuable works," and then that ballerina, whose name is Marija, but everyone calls her *Meri*, saves the Partisan flag and sets out, enlightened, into the battle against fascism. What must Branko Marjanović do or not do, what must he agree or not agree to, for the new censors to approve of him making what somehow turned out to be Partisan films? Films about those same "bandits," who are now heroes, brave, honest and just, but who in Marjanović's film *Guard on the River Drina* plunder and murder and instigate unheard-of bestial terror against the powerless population, whom the "Bolshevik infection had transformed into animals who even abandon their own children to the mercy of hunger and death." How can it be? One minute this, the next that? Andreas Ban searches, he searches for information about this Marjanović and finds many facts about his postwar career as a director, while Marjanović's NDH artistic work is somehow bypassed, forgotten, like Walter Henisch's SS photographic career. All right, the film *Ciguli miguli* that Marjanović makes in 1952, also with screenwriter Joža Horvat, is embargoed, but a mere four years later comes Marjanović's fine, human, Partisan omnibus *The Siege* (script by Slavko Kolar, Zvonimir Berković and Nikola Tanhofer), in which wounded Partisans in a house that is surrounded talk about Zagreb's illegal antifascist movement and their flight from the cruel NDH police, about love, about goodness and humanity. Then Branko Marjanović turns to directing documentaries, films about nature, about pure, authentic, *liberating nature,* untouched by human hand and the sick human mind, films about Istria, about the Karst, about the coast, about vultures and trout, weasels and foxes, about young bears and little fish, about the European dormouse, about glowworms, even about the coast of Africa, all small miracles of great nature, all excellent documentaries, praised and winning prizes everywhere, which reminds Andreas Ban somehow of Leni Riefenstahl's biographical journey and her career.

Or perhaps this Branko Marjanović was connected with the Partisan Movement and worked during the war undercover? If that is the case, why is there no information about this, why does no one talk about it today? Andreas Ban knows that there were such situations, his mother was rescued from prison by a guard who was an Ustasha member of the Communist Youth Alliance. Do the collaborationists, true or false, who survive after the war somehow redeem themselves? Andreas Ban would like to know how, by what means? Do they perhaps live under the burden of a secret past life that runs through their veins, the ballast of which lies on their chests, so their breathing becomes shallow and their words soft, until it suffocates them to death?

In Zagreb in Matica Hrvatska Hall on March 18, 2010, and on April 8 and 9 (avoiding the 10th),* in the city libraries in Split and Imotski, two books were launched by a certain Carmen Vrljičak, according to the newspapers, "an Argentinian university lecturer, writer and journalist originally from the Imotski region." The books are called *Croacia, cuardernos de un país* ("Croatia, Notebooks about a Country") and *This Is How It Was*. Andreas Ban leafs through the newspapers, seeking any kind of statement by Professor Carmen Vrljičak connected with her family's past, at

* The NDH was founded on April 10, 1941.

least a parenthesis about her parents' worldview and activities; in interviews published at this time, in March and April, Andreas Ban searches for some allusion to the time of the NDH from which, after the collapse of that monstrous, satellite, sponging and bloodthirsty creation, the family of Carmen Vrljičak (with many other families) flees, and finds nothing. Does this mean that Carmen Vrljičak condones what happened in Croatia between 1941 and 1945 under the government of the Leader Ante Pavelić, in which her parents participated zealously, or does the writer and university lecturer Carmen Vrljičak believe that those are *i tempi passati*, and pointless to rake over? From the newspapers Andreas Ban discovers that in her books, the journalist, writer and university lecturer Professor Carmen Vrljičak describes the natural beauties of her former homeland of Croatia, its folkloric tradition and also the enchanting and complex landscapes of her second homeland of Argentina.

Anyone can search online and find the following: The mother of Carmen Vrljičak, Mira Vrljičak, née Dugački (1917–2004) was a functionary in the NDH, Independent State of Croatia. While still at secondary school, she writes for the magazine *For Faith and the Homeland* and is a member of the Croatian Eagles' Union, that is, a crusader. With the establishment of the NDH in 1941, Mira Vrljičak takes up the position of Chairwoman of the Women's Ustasha Youth organization. In 1942, at a functionaries' meeting in Zagreb, Mira Vrljičak gets acquainted with the district leader of the Dubrovnik branch of the Women's Ustasha Youth organization, Dolores Bracanović, and suggests that she take over her function in that jovial organization for the corporeal and social strengthening of Croatian girls and young women, the future *multiparae*, who go to rallies and scamper joyfully *in the Croatian countryside*. Ah, how this obsession with nature so integrated in the psychophysical complex of crazed rightists, fascists, Nazis, Ustashas and other defenders of the hearth becomes a nauseating, porous front for hypnotizing the Lord's flock, so that Andreas Ban, under attack by that natural dominion, increasingly shuns nature, *I can no longer stand nature and its beauties*, he says, shutting himself in his miniature Hades.

So, the honored and nationally conscious "pure-blooded" Croatian woman, Dolores Bracanović accepts her new office with enthusiasm and a full heart, which beats for the Independent State of Croatia, while Mira Vrljičak, as the wife of Kazimir Vrljičak, Consul of the NDH in Madrid, goes off with her husband to give birth to new and great little Croats. The end of the war finds the family in Spain, so it does not occur to the family, loyal to the NDH, to return to Croatia, which is no longer an independent Fascist state, instead the family, with their three children, one of whom is future *journalist and university professor* Carmen of this story, move to Argentina, where, entirely in the spirit of their Catholic worldview and nationalist ideology, the *grand multipara* Mira Vrljičak brings a further five little Vrljičaks into the world. In Argentina, the now fairly numerous Catholic Vrljičak family immediately join the activities of the Ustasha émigrés and live their undreamed dream.

It does not appear to occur to the journalist and university professor Carmen Vrljičak, as she walks freely through her former (lost) homeland of Croatia, to visit, say, an archive or two and take a look at the press which her parents followed with ardor and zealously supported. So now Andreas Ban, quite senselessly, and agitated, is doing that for her, determined to post whatever he finds on Professor Carmen Vrljičak's Facebook page, in the faint hope that it will perhaps bring her to her senses. But it won't.

And in 1991, Dolores Bracanović, former chairwoman of the Women's Ustasha Youth, bigoted Catholic and teacher of German and Italian, hurries to Croatia and to a certain Tomislav Jonjić, and just before she passes, in 1997, well over eighty years old, into the other world, she wails about the beginnings of her "tortured" émigré life when, after the collapse of the NDH, she flees her beloved homeland and sails under a false name from Genoa to Argentina where, poor thing, she is first obliged to do physical work, what a tragedy, to sew jute sacks and, with a dose of revolting pathos, nostalgically recalls the announcement of the establishment of the NDH as "a moment of general enthusiasm for all Croats," beginning almost every sentence with that "well" so beloved of Pavelić. And she, this Dolores Bracanović, also remarks, well, *Let us not forget*, she says, *that a good number of the crimes committed "in the name of the NDH" were not carried out on the orders or intentions of the government, but represent actions of individuals and groups which in those chaotic circumstances exploited opportunities to act of their own accord*, says Dolores Bracanović authoritatively, and Andreas Ban seems to hear the yelling of contemporary Croatian right-wingers in relation to the crimes committed by the soldiers of various contemporary Croatian Armed Forces against the non-Croatian population in the 1991–1995 Homeland War.

This Dolores Bracanović talks about the time Mira Vrljičak introduced her to the Leader, who made an excellent impression on her, because the Leader was, she says, *a straightforward and witty man, exceptionally close to the people. The Leader had a rare ability*, says eighty-year-old Dolores Bracanović in 1991, *a rare ability to speak warmly with both laborers and intellectuals.* She had met numerous other high dignitaries, says Dolores Bracanović, well, she says, she did not have frequent contact with them, but was in contact with the wonderful Professor Oršanić,* and with lieutenant

* Ivan Oršanić (Županja, 1904–Buenos Aires, 1968). One of the leading Ustasha functionaries in the Independent State of Croatia. Administrative commander of the Ustasha Youth organization, member of the Croatian State Parliament. One of Pavelić's most trusted colleagues.

Dr. Lovro Sušić,* and she had particular contact, she says, with the supreme and ideal fighter for the Croatian cause, Božo Kavran.†

Oh, and here comes Joža Vrljičak, the brother of "our" Carmen, editor of the Argentine journal *Studia Croatica*, whom the Croatian Government in 1995 decorates with the Order of the Croatian Triple-Strand,‡ while in June 2010 the journal *Studia Croatica* itself, which is "generally held to have played an important role in the life of Croats on the South American continent and beyond, publishing thousands of pages about Croatian literature, history, culture and politics," is presented by President Dr. Ivo Josipović (in absentia) at the Croatian Center in Buenos Aires with a Charter of the Republic of Croatia designed in the worst possible kitsch style of modern folkloric traditional "art." Everything would (perhaps) have been all right, the tenderness and compassion for those disconnected Ustasha clerical-Fascist émigrés, who had, on the face of it, sobered, and had the apparently civilized concern for their fine, educated offspring, if only those émigrés somewhere, somehow, publicly apologized to their victims, if their children and grandchildren at least glanced back at their forebears' ideology of

* Lovro Sušić (Mrkopalj, 1891–Caracas, 1972). Attorney. In the NDH, Commissioner in Ogulin, Economics Minister (signed the first kuna banknotes).

† Božidar Kavran (Zagreb, 1913–Zagreb, ?). Senior Ustasha functionary; from 1943 managing commander of all Ustashas and deputy director of all Ustasha organizations. He goes abroad on May 7, 1945, but returns to Croatia in 1948 as the key organizer of the Ustasha-terrorist-spy group of 96 in the "April 10" action. Arrested by the Secret Service (UDBA) in the autumn of 1948 and sentenced to the loss of all citizen's rights, confiscation of his property and death by hanging. The exact date of his execution is unknown. Apparently, in May 1995, at the Pharmaceutics and Biochemistry Faculty of Zagreb University, he is rehabilitated as a Croatian intellectual and Master of Pharmacy.

‡ Troplet, Early Croatian three-strand design. Translator's note.

blood and soil. But no. Muddy little islands of poison continue to float through the Republic of Croatia. When founded, the journal *Studia Croatica* appoints as editor-in-chief the businessman Ivo Rojnica (1915–2007), the most prominent figure in the Ustasha NDH government for the Dubrovnik region and the main instigator of all the mass crimes and murders, torture and deportation to camps, torching, plunder and destruction of property, in other words, all the crimes carried out against Jews, Serbs and Croats from the beginning of the Italian occupation until September 1941 in the territory of the Greater Parish of Dubrava. And while various international organizations call (unsuccessfully) for the extradition of Ivo Rojnica, the established owner of Argentinian textile factories, proclaimed a war criminal in 1946 in the Federal National Republic of Yugoslavia, while, in other words, the progressive world calls for this Ivo Rojnica, also known as Ivan Rajčinović, the first chief editor of *Studia Croatica*, to be brought to trial, in 1993 President Franjo Tudjman appoints that same Ivo Rojnica Plenipotentiary of the Republic of Croatia in Argentina. Even though, under pressure from international public opinion, Franjo Tudjman soon relieves Ivo Rojnica of that duty, "the first Croatian President" makes amends by decorating the Ustasha Rojnica with the Order of Duke Trpimir, for "promoting Croatia in Argentina, and in particular for his work in bringing together the political, cultural and civic values of the Croatian people since the Second World War," and now somewhere in Buenos Aires that medal shines to the delight of the eternally Great Croats.

After Mr. Rojnica, another senior functionary of the Independent State of Croatia becomes editor-in-chief of the leading archaic Croatian journal *Studia Croatica*, as today's Croatia has the ever-growing prospect of becoming: archaic, hidebound, poor, and the servant of revised tradition abandoned by the world, but with splendid natural beauty and drinking water soon to be marketed. Dr. Radovan Latković, as glorified by Croatian neo-Ustasha, neo-Fascist and neo-Nazi websites, was director of Croatian State Radio and played "an important educational role, culturally enlightening the Croatian people via radio stations in Zagreb, Sarajevo, Banja Luka and Dubrovnik, and transmitting stations in Varaždin, Petrinja, Ogulin, Požega, Osijek and Hrvatska Mitrovica." In 2001, in Zagreb, Jurčić Press publishes a book by this same, allegedly former Ustasha Radovan Latković, with the sentimental title *We Lived and Worked for Croatia*, and the still more abhorrent subtitle *My Recollections of the Struggle for Croatian State Independence and the Freedom of the Croatian People: Memories and Documents 1930–1990*.

Then yet another editor of that benign culturological journal, *Studia Croatica*, is appointed: Danijel Crljen, the NDH ideologue and Ustasha colonel in charge of education and propaganda in the Ustasha headquarters (GUS), secretary to the Ministry for Foreign Affairs and director of the State Directorate for Propaganda.

The function of editor-in-chief of the journal *Studia Croatica* is also carried out by Franjo Nevistić (1913–1984), district leader in the NDH of the University Command and editor-in-chief of the weekly newspaper *Spremnost* ("Readiness").

Soon after the proclamation of state independence, after 1992, members of Pavelić's family return to Croatia, finding nothing better to do with their time than to disturb the public with their fascist statements about the NDH as a lost paradise on earth. Pavelić's bigoted daughter Mirjana, brought up on Ustasha ideology, and her husband Srećko Pšeničnik, also a functionary in the NDH and after the war, in exile, president of the terrorist organization the Croatian Liberation Movement, once Croatia had long since been saved from an absolute catastrophe by the Partisans and Allied forces, addresses, in one of the Tudjman years, inflamed masses in Bleiburg with the ominous prophecy: "You, Croatian soldiers,

Ustashas and home guards, you had to be slaughtered because that is what the Communist occupiers wanted, but your spirit will lead to the resurrection of Croatia. The cursed enemy from beyond the Drina wished to crush forever the spirit of the Croatian people, but I say that, without Bosnia and Herzegovina, Srijem and the Bay of Kotor, there can be no free, sovereign and democratic state of Croatia. Our struggle was not in vain, and we find ourselves now on the eve of a final Croatian victory ..."

Andreas Ban torments himself with all the scraps of information he digs up, rummages through, which seem unimportant, like desiccated data rotted in time, but they enter his rooms, sit at his table, knock into him in the street, and this is why he goes out less and less, why he refuses to listen and to hear.

Pavelić's granddaughters come, they want their property back, one of them, with a bit of sadness and a great deal of determination, Ivana Sheridan-Pšeničnik, like her father, exclaims, "Today we have lost Bosnia and Herzegovina, the heart of the Croatian State. If Pavelić were alive, I believe he would be a member of parliament!"

In Melbourne there is a little restaurant, Katarina Zrinski, in which for many years April 10, 1941 has been celebrated and homage has been paid to Ante Pavelić. The *Jerusalem Post* of April 17, 2008, records that Croatian émigrés celebrate the genocidal policies of that leader of theirs, policies that led to the death of four hundred thousand Serbs, Jews, Roma and Croats. This event celebrating the leader of the Croatian Fascist Ustasha Movement is a shameless offense for its victims, but also for all those whose morals and conscience oppose racism and genocide, states Efraim Zuroff, the famous Nazi hunter. A local newspaper reports that there was a large photograph of Ante Pavelić hanging in the restaurant and that guests were able to buy T-shirts with his portrait on them.

This does not surprise Andreas Ban. In the little Istrian town of Rovinj there used to be a café in which a picture of Pavelić also hung, and under his gaze people chatted and greeted one another, he did not dare go there or say anything and risk getting beaten.

Then in 2010 Radoslav appears, son of that Andrija Artuković,* saying that he would like to bury his father in his native Herzegovina. That would be perfectly all right, even President Josipović states in a conciliatory tone that everyone has a right to his own grave, but on January 14, 1988, when (after a lengthy public trial and passing of the death sentence) the war criminal, the butcher Artuković dies in a Zagreb prison hospital, Radoslav organizes a memorial mass for his father in Los Angeles, attended by four hundred nostalgic Ustasha souls and at which, to the horror of the American public, he announces in a military manner that his dear father Andrija Artuković was the victim of huge injustice and energetically denies all claims of mass murder committed on his father's orders during the Second World War. A scandalized *Los Angeles Times* journalist explains to his readers that Andrija Artuković was a fascist, Minister for Internal Affairs and keeper of the state seal in the puppet government of the Independent State of Croatia, and that his son Radoslav is lying for all to see, lying and stating that his dear papa was an ordinary civilian minister and knew nothing about any concentration camps. The journalist explains that the American Supreme Court had ordered the extradition of Artuković so that he could be tried in Yugoslavia

---

* Andrija Artuković (Klobuk near Ljubuški, 1899–Zagreb, 1988). Minister for Internal Affairs in the NDH government and one of those most responsible for carrying out the policy of genocide. Twelve days after the NDH is founded, he announces that the government will soon solve the Jewish question in the same way that the German government had done. With all severity, Artuković announces, "the government will oversee the strict application of the racial law in the immediate future."

for war crimes and for mass murder, specifically for the shooting of 450 men, women and children in 1941, and for the elimination from the face of the earth of the entire population of Vrgin Most and neighboring villages in 1942.

But Radoslav Artuković, like Gudrun Himmler, daughter of Heinrich Himmler, Himmler's favorite, her daddy's "Puppi," who dreams Himmler's dreams and till her death mourns her father, as fanatical a Catholic as he was a racist, Radoslav Artuković, in that church in the center of Los Angeles, over his father's empty coffin says, "He believed in God, in his state and in his people and I am proud to be his son." Oh, horrors.

So, from 1991 on, elderly, retrograde, clerical-fascist right-wingers, more or less prominent figures of the Ustasha Movement, crawl through Croatia like rats, some in secret, some with pomp-ous announcements in the state-controlled media, many of them having lived secretly as émigrés, changing their names and sur-names, but not their love for the NDH, a nondescript, backward, black little hanger-on of a country, leaving behind them their foul rats' droppings, and now, with their children and grandchildren, howl the same threadbare, patriotic song:

> *See, they return; ah, see the tentative*
> *Movements, and the slow feet,*
> *The trouble in the pace and the uncertain*
> *Wavering!*
>
> *See, they return, one, and by one,*
> *With fear, as half-awakened;*
> *As if the snow should hesitate*
> *And murmur in the wind,*

and half turn back;
These were the "Wing'd-with-Awe,"
Inviolable.

Gods of the wingèd shoe!
With them the silver hounds,
sniffing the trace of air!

Haie! Haie!
These were the swift to harry;
These the keen-scented;
These were the souls of blood.

Slow on the leash,
pallid the leash-men!

So, Andreas Ban returns to Belgrade from Paris, his military service report lies in the Ministry of Defense, in the Belgrade military department, and he realizes that he is in their sights, that they will summon him, if for no other reason than for a little conversation, so that the Belgrade Ministry of Defense can mobilize him, so that they can tell him, *Go to Croatia and liberate Yugoslavia*. They could tell him, *Feel free to kill*. At that time, one of his two best friends, oh, how many shared games of *preferans*, how many swimming contests, how many confessions, love affairs, chats in cafés, how many journeys, exchanged intimacies and secrets, that friend for whom he had been best man, from a well-known Belgrade family of medics, himself a successful psychiatrist, told him, *There's nothing to be done, one may as well die for the homeland, if necessary.*

That is when he starts corresponding with Clara.

Until then, Clara had existed largely as an abstraction. There had been some distant summers when he was sent from Belgrade to his uncle's to go with Clara to the town beach, when he used to listen at night to Clara's parents quarreling in the dark apartment of a building that once belonged to Italy. The apartment is near his present one, he has not set foot in that apartment for fifty years, and when he did, it was for Clara's mother's wake. Clara's father, his uncle, died long ago, in another town, in another family with which Andreas Ban also has lukewarm, rare contact. Clara's mother remarried and Clara was brought up by her maternal grandmother whom he never met. Clara was very pretty and very devout (her granny's doing). Clara was a devout doctor who played the piano brilliantly, who smoked as much as Andreas Ban did, who could even drink when required, living by straddling the chasms of the sacred and the everyday secular.

When he reaches Croatia at the beginning of the 1990s, when he deserts, in fact, numerous problems arise. Existential, political, linguistic, he would prefer not to go into it. Before that, Andreas Ban sends his nine-year-old son Leo through Ljubljana (by bus) to friends in Rovinj, and he pays for a two-day tourist excursion to Budapest, from which excursion he never returns to Belgrade.

In Budapest, Andreas meets his cousin Printz, known as "Pupi," who is staying in the same hotel. *I'd like to get into Croatia*, says Printz, *but Rikard won't hear of it, mother Ernestina is dying. I got out secretly*, he says, *I know someone who can help me*. Andreas says nothing. They go to the island of Margitsziget, where on the eastern side, near the ruins of the Dominican monastery, they wait for Pupi's contact, for seven hours, until it gets dark, they pee, kill mosquitoes and wander up and down. For four hours it rains in sheets, forming transparent curtains that fall from the sky like woven wet cobwebs and through which the greenery of Margitsziget is reflected. *I'd like to enter that greenery*, says Printz, *enter it and lose myself, that green is like the green of Safet Zec's paintings.*

Printz's contact does not come.

In the hotel, a man, not very tall, in cracked black patent-leather shimmy shoes, is waiting for Printz .

The short man says, *It's pouring and Budapest is deep green.*

Printz asks, *Are you a poet?*

The secret agent smiles mysteriously.

Your contact is dead. Your contact has been killed, or he may have killed himself. That is what the short man in the dark-brown leather jacket says.

What do I do now? asks Printz.

Nothing. You'll do nothing. You won't cross over. You'll go back. Tourist style, the way you came. That's how it is. There's a war on. We're being attacked and we're defending ourselves. People are being killed, buildings destroyed. That is what the man from the neighboring country says. Then he leaves.

What do I do now? Printz asks Andreas.

You'll go back. I'm going solo, I don't have a contact, I'm a deserter, says Andreas Ban.

Printz asks the porter, the hotel porter in a blue-and-gold uniform, he asks him, *Where is the grave of Ignác Semmelweis?* Printz wants to visit the grave of Ignác Semmelweis at once, that's why he asks the porter *Where is the grave of Ignác Semmelweis.* The porter is polite, porters do not ask superfluous questions, guests usually ask questions, porters answer. This yellow-blue porter is not in the least interested in why someone would want to visit the grave of Ignác Semmelweis, that is quite clear to Printz. It is also clear to Printz that porters do not need to know anything about Ignác Semmelweis, even if they are Hungarian porters, Budapest porters.

What would porters want with Ignác Semmelweis?

Take a taxi, says the porter. *The cemetery is called Kerepesi.*

Printz wants to see the monument to Ignác Semmelweis, because with the departure of the short secret agent, Printz is suddenly plunged into sadness because of Ignác Semmelweis.

A terrible injustice has been done to Ignác Semmelweis, Printz tells Andreas Ban. *Come with me to Kerepesi cemetery. When one comes to Budapest as a tourist, it makes sense to visit Kerepesi cemetery, doesn't it? There are many famous people at Kerepesi,* says Printz, *and you aren't leaving till tomorrow. Besides,* says Printz known as Pupi, *when you're a tourist you have to see as much as possible because you never know whether you'll be able to repeat that trip, whether that trip can be repeated. You don't know.*

There is no Ignác Semmelweis at Kerepesi cemetery. Just a monument, and beneath it—nothing. The monument to Ignác Semmelweis rests on the ground like an ornament, a large ornament of yellowed stone, with soft sods of moss, because Ignác Semmelweis died long ago, and Kerepesi cemetery is damp, that is why there is moss. Ignác Semmelweis was burned and poured into an urn, and the urn is kept in a glass case at the Museum of Medical History.

Well, after all it's stupid to go to foreign cemeteries, says Printz to Andreas Ban, *there's no one close in foreign cemeteries. We don't need that. We'd do better to eat cake. Come, Andreas, let's go for some cake.*

In the cemetery brochure, Andreas Ban reads the story of Ignác Semmelweis, evidently important to Printz, although Andreas does not know why. And he does not ask. He learns that Semmelweis dies aged forty-seven on August 13, 1865 in Vienna, in fact at the National Institute for the Mentally Ill in Döbling, he was a doctor and—mad, they say. Mad! Vienna would not have him. Vienna tells him, *Go away, go back to where you came from, go to your Budapest.* Ignác Semmelweis goes back to his Budapest and in his Budapest he helps women give birth, they don't die of pyemia but stay alive, they don't die of puerperal fever like all those women giving birth in Vienna, because Ignác Semmelweis washes his hands in chlorinated water and in Budapest it is no longer permitted to dissect bodies and then attend births with unwashed hands. Why the sick Ignác Semmelweis returns to Vienna, or rather to Döbling, is not known, perhaps he is taken by force to the National Institute for the Mentally Ill. Is there no hospital for the mind in Budapest at that time? Or perhaps they no longer want him in Budapest either. Printz cannot go back to the country where he was born, the people in whose country he lives are killing people in the country where Printz was born, and who knows what is in store for Andreas, will he too be moved back and forth, will he too be told, *Go back to where you came from, that Belgrade of yours.* He will be. Only Andreas Ban does not know that then, in Budapest.

Walking to the exit from Kerepesi cemetery, Printz stops at plot 28, where there is an enormous statue, completely white, frightening.

The four horsemen of the apocalypse, all four of them in stone, petrified, says Printz to Andreas, *look.*

In plot 28, beneath the white horsemen of the apocalypse, lies József Attila.

Sad life, says Printz and embarks on the story of József Attila, son of a washerwoman and secret member of the secret Communist Party, telling him József Attila was an impoverished child, an impoverished student, an impoverished poet, terribly impoverished, his father left, abandoning him and his mother, while József Attila was moved from one family to another, and none were kind to him, and while he was still small, only nine, he tried to kill himself. Then his mother died although he, József Attila, was not quite grown, he was only fourteen, indeed he was completely unprotected, his mother, the washerwoman, died, exhausted, worn out, withered and done for, and József Attila was left alone. He spent some twenty years figuring out how to kill himself and in the end, of course, he killed himself. This time successfully, forever. He threw himself under a freight train, József Attila, a brilliant student, József Attila, a poet whose poems no one read at the time. Later, much later, some people decide to remember József Attila and make him famous, only that is of no use to him because he has already been dead for a long time, as indeed has Ignác Semmelweis. Ignác Semmelweis is often mentioned today, people write novels and plays about him. *Unhappy people, unlucky, both of them,* says Printz to Andreas and bends toward the gravestone: József Attila, 1905–37. *You see, Here inside is suffering/outside is the explanation, he wrote that,* says Printz.

Listen, Pupi, says Andreas Ban, *when Dezső Kosztolányi's town of Subotica ended up in Yugoslavia, he wailed, Where is my face? Where is my past? Where is my resting place? Where is my grave? You see, situations recur. It is possible to live without a face and without a past, without a resting place and without a grave, fuck the pathos, Pupi, go back to Belgrade.*

Printz is having a hard time, Printz is not well, Andreas is afraid that Printz will come to grief. So he says,

I read in Oto Tolnai that every evening he passes a butcher's shop in which people stuff hot sausages in their mouths, wolf down smoked ham and crackling and where soft bacon from pork belly hangs on hooks, whole wreaths of frankfurters, garlands of liver sausages and black puddings in luxurious variety. In that illuminated shop window, Oto Tolnai caught sight of a statue representing Sándor Petőfi reciting poems with his arms outstretched, while his defiant, shaggy hair rose to the heavenly heights of freedom and ecstasy. He was as white as snow, writes Tolnai, and at the beginning he thought that he had been sculpted from Carrara marble. But he soon realized that Sándor Petőfi was carved out of fat, of top-quality pig fat. There, Pupi, maybe our realities are unreal, but with time we learn to sidestep them. Pascal often felt an abyss was gaping on his left side, and he put a chair there to calm himself.

The patisserie is elegant, it's called Gerbeaud. Oh, that Gerbeaud, what a gourmet! No one knows why he left his native Switzerland, but he did, people leave their home countries, it happens all the time. There are people who never leave the country in which they were born, they refuse to. They think it is not OK, it's like leaving your mother.

I don't agree, Andreas, says Printz. *You have to leave your mother,* especially if your mother is called Ernestina. When he left Switzerland, Gerbeaud invented a magical sweet filled with cognac, with a firm, dark-red morello cherry floating in it, drunk with pleasure. That was how Gerbeaud compensated for the loss of his homeland and his mother. And the loss of his large Swiss chocolate factory. Sweets compensate for various losses, that's a well-known fact. After Germany, France and England, Gerbeaud settles in Hungary, and in Budapest creates his Gerbeaud dessert. As yet another compensation. That compensation brings him fame. And fortune. That contact did not need to fail me right now, says Printz, he could have failed later, when he had gotten me across. Now it's finished, and Ernestina refuses to die.

Printz leaves Budapest. The tourists sing. The tourists also leave Budapest, they return to the town on the confluence of two polluted rivers, they return from their excursion, from their shopping trip. The tourists are happy, you can see, because they sing. Budapest is a beautiful city. Printz hears shells falling on the other side (Vukovar?), he sees bombers flying over there, the woman beside him in the bus says, The Hungarians have excellent cheeses and cheap salami, no worse than our Gavrilović, not at all. Is Gavrilović a Serbian name?

Meanwhile Andreas's friend Bruno from Budapest drives him to Maribor, where he takes the train to Croatia. Andreas Ban arrives in Croatia with one pair of pajamas, three pairs of underpants, two shirts, toiletries and fifteen hundred German marks to begin his circumscribed, trimmed-back life. Earlier, Andreas Ban exchanges his elegant Belgrade apartment for this neglected barracks with single-glazed, peeling windows in which the panes rattle because the putty falls out in lumps, partly it's age, partly the din of traffic and the yelling of idlers walking the streets, he had exchanged his apartment for this one with the yellowing six-foot double door, impossible to clean, the ceiling that leaks, soaking the electric wires whenever the pipe upstairs detaches itself from the washing machine or dishwasher, dug-up parquet with burn marks from wood fires like black bugs of various sizes. And he can never again buy a car. So he is immobile, he could only escape by submitting to the poor and infrequent bus timetables, he could not even consider trains because where he now lives there exists a railroad station at which almost nothing and no one ever arrives, from which almost nothing and no one ever leaves, where even the clock has stopped ticking.

Clara wanted to help. His cousin Clara brings warm pie and beer while Andreas strips wallpaper with gigantic mountain landscapes where falling water murmurs, with landscapes of nature that fill the spacious rooms with darkness and cold, as he paints and arranges his furniture, none of which goes together, the space becomes small, then small and displaced, lost in the space, as he and his son are lost in that space. At the same time, Andreas Ban runs from one school to another in order to register his nine-year-old Leo in fourth grade, he appeals to the Ministry responsible and its local branches, trying to convince the blinded officials of the idiocy of their demands that Leo first pass the exams in Croatian language, Croatian history and Croatian geography from the first, second and third grades, and only then will he be permitted to attend classes, to which he responds that in the first, second and third grades of primary school these Croatian subjects (apart from language) are not studied at all, what is studied is something that is senselessly called understanding society and nature, senseless because children in school do not learn anything intelligent about society or nature, rather what they learn is fairly grotesque, and sometimes monstrous, but they do learn how to kneel in prayer and how to be silent, because what leaps out of Leo's reader is the idiotic, imbecilic and loathsome ditty by Pajo Kanižaj:

I first cried in Croatian
I speak Croatian
I whisper in Croatian
I'm silent in Croatian
I dream in Croatian
even awake I dream in Croatian
I love in Croatian
I love Croatian
I write in Croatian
when I don't write I don't write in Croatian
everything I do is in Croatian
Croatian is everything to me.

Later, Pajo Kanižaj publishes ever more appalling creations:

When Serbs stop lying,
dry sticks will turn to herbs!
Not all Serbs are Gypsies,
but Gypsies are all Serbs!

and then Kanižaj somehow disappears, maybe he falls into a sewer where, with other crazed *Croatian* rats, he flows into the backwaters of *Croatian* history, listening and biding his time.

After Pajo Kanižaj's poetic slap, nine-year-old Leo practices making Croatian versions of familiar words. He turns the spines of all ten volumes of his Cyrillic children's encyclopedia to the wall and when he listens to music by Balašević, he tries to lock the loose-fitting windows that look out onto the underpass-overpass street. Only the bathroom window overlooks a stunted concrete playground with no children in it, a playground which must be reached through tunnels from the neighboring buildings, which Leo and Andreas do not even attempt to do. In the neighborhood there are no parks, no greenery, no children, no ball games, not so much as a swing.

All told, this is a town with a restricted outlook, a town on the sea without a view of the open sea, a town which surveys its decrepit interior, its physical and social decay the way an inquisitive child picks at its belly button. This is a town with no silence, a town with a unique quantity of senseless, hollow noise into whose core pedestrians fly and are immediately deafened. This is a town that has transformed its pedestrian zone into a rural living room into which musicians drag their shabby armchairs from which yellowing foam rubber pokes, in which tents blast music which is not music, in which Croatian kitsch is sold, as though this town were set in the middle of an Arabian desert where at any moment sheikhs will ride up on camels or black steeds, visiting the wretched oases of the common people.

Now it does not matter. Leo has gone. Now on the outside wall of this refurbished bathroom window that shuts admirably well, a strange (wild) plant grows, the seed of which was probably brought by the wind or a small quiet bird, and that little plant branches out and has pink flowers and Andreas Ban monitors its life wondering whether (when) it will wither. Like that film he saw when he was six years old, discovering many years later that it was a film based on O. Henry's story "The Last Leaf," in which a young painter is dying of pneumonia and as she's passing away she sees through the window a wall overgrown with ivy and gazes at the wall and counts the leaves that fall from the ivy, while the wind blows and the rain pours and it becomes increasingly cold and the young painter tells her friend, *When the last leaf falls, I shall die*, and her friend brings an old painter who then, at night, on that bare stone wall, *draws* just one leaf, realistic, already a little wilted, motionless admittedly, but still, and after that the young painter gradually recovers, though soon afterward the old painter himself, soaked and frozen, dies of pneumonia. Perhaps that little plant growing out of the loosened bricks beneath the window of Andreas's bathroom will decide not to wither, perhaps it will go wild, go mad and stick to the pane and spread its stems until it covers the window, until the bathroom becomes completely dark, until the whole apartment grows dark and he, Andreas Ban, is left even more constricted in his prison.

All right, Leo does go to school. Andreas Ban comes across a head teacher who is a Czech by birth who says, *Bring your son, we'll register him.* Fortunately, Leo does not learn either how to whisper or how to keep quiet or how to dream or how to love in Croatian, he completes his schooling, attends courses in computer design and film workshops from which his spirited documentaries emerge, he swims, travels, grows and becomes strong, gets a degree in medicine and—leaves. He said, *I'm off.* Andreas Ban said, *Quite right, off you go.* For Andreas Ban an enormous emptiness descended then, the apartment trembled with its resonance. Like dominoes, little tiles with fading images of the past fall onto his chest. For a long time he wears a washed-out T-shirt designed ages ago for an American theater for the deaf and dumb by his friend Oskar. He dreams of a screeching woman's voice threateningly telling him, *Praise be to God!* and freezes. He looks at their two bicycles, Leo's and his, leaning against each other, as if Leo were here. Then, somehow unexpectedly, in that tomb that had walled itself in of its own accord, little lights begin to glimmer in the corners. Those lights flicker from Leo's shelves, sending out rays of warmth, as though waving. Then peace settles in Andreas Ban, a small happiness that whispers, *It's all good, we made it.*

Where did he get to? Clara.

Clara tries to drag Andreas Ban out of his unshakable atheism into her unshakably religious world through stories about regular town meetings and philosophical-religious debates with educated

Church figures, *patres nostri* and *patres vestri*. Today Andreas Ban thinks, *I could at least have listened to her*, wondering whether Clara could have been a distant echo of Simone Weil, but presumably he would have guessed that. Clara had two sons and a husband, she did all the housework herself, she had her medicine and her music and black hair that was rapidly turning gray. Some ten years later, he met her walking alone in town, slowly, almost aimlessly, *I'm looking for a Turkish coffee pot*, she said, which sounded senseless.

Then they find that Clara has a brain tumor and she dies six months later, frightened. He knows several others with brain tumors, he had watched them go, Angelo, Esteban, Julia. He had also known people with metastases on the brain, he had watched them lose their sight, lose their sense of balance, lose their words and leave little notes around to remind them of life. He had watched them become paralyzed, stagger then fall—Ivan, his femur breaks, eroded, loose, so it tears the muscles, pierces the skin and protrudes, and Erik, completely paralyzed, who opened his eyes wide and let out animal cries because he could no longer speak.

Clara remained an enigma to Andreas. His relations on his mother's side possess a warehouse of undiscovered secrets, because his mother had no space for telling stories. His father had confiscated the space. But from time to time some of his distant relatives step into that storeroom, that place where little family boxes are kept, and start rummaging around. They search for silent mementos which disintegrate when touched, all the singed remnants of a former life. So, in the flea market of a used-up age Andreas Ban sifts through the junk bequeathed him by these unknown people, quite unexpectedly. At funerals, at weddings, at pointless, mercifully rare festive lunches, they throw into his pocket or onto his plate small packaged riddles, whose thin veins, brittle and filled with now diluted (family) blood, stretch toward him. They destroy his concept, his philosophy of life, they loosen

the screws that hold the framework of his life together, they penetrate the picture and bring commotion into his molehill. The
greater the distance, in time and space, the better, the simpler.

When she was taken ill, Clara called him, *Come so we can talk*,
she said, *everyone on my father's side has disappeared, just a hole left.*
He went. Once. Her arm was paralyzed (because of the tumor,
which radiation had not diminished), her head was bald, with a
scar from the operation that had not succeeded, *Let's light up*, she
said, and asked him, *How old are we?* He called a few months later,
at the moment of her death. *She has just passed away*, said her son.
For years Andreas Ban has been trying to interpret that moment.

Twelve months later Andreas Ban has merged with his serious degenerative changes, he has become one great degenerative change that can no longer run and climbs stairs with difficulty, he has become a limping degenerative change waiting for that degenerative change to ossify, to pitch camp, to stiffen in his body which will grow ever more crooked and bent, completely degenerated. So he'll wish to get rid of it. As they wanted to get rid of that art. When he moved to the small provincial town he considered to be somehow degenerate, to have, no one knows how or when, degenerated, some people said he had infiltrated it, which could mean that he was quite wrong, that the town had not degenerated at all, but that he had degenerated because his assessment of life in this town was erroneous, because if he had infiltrated it, then he was an infiltrator (like a tuberculosis bacillus) who had nested in the healthy fabric of the province and was destroying its vigor, its life. Such relativity offered Andreas Ban little solace.

In fact, many people limp. In streets all over the world people limp, some even energetically. The people who stagger most are little old ladies in brown coats with tight perms, for the most part obese. Under their coats one can see their diamond-patterned home-knit sweaters, dark-colored sweaters, sometimes also dark red. Red-brown combinations are the ugliest and the most common. Those are old people's combinations. Until he began to limp,

Andreas Ban thought that lame people did not walk, he thought that lame people just tottered around their rooms and along their dark corridors (as he does now), because that was where they were safe. But no, lame people like to go out and hobble around publicly. In public, lame people have priority, the public takes pity on them and with time lame people may become arrogant and inconsiderate lame people. He tells himself, *Andreas, mind that does not happen to you.* Then, as he staggers, he imagines that he doesn't limp at all, he alters the expression on his face into a healthy, smiling expression and puts his scowl into his pocket, to take out when things get difficult. So, he began to go out. He accepted his limping as a normal state. That was four years ago. Some young people limp. Men limp too.

The therapy in Opatija wasn't successful.

He spent the whole day counting: lengths of the pool times twenty-five meters up to a thousand, exercises, one-two, one-two, up to ten, in the course of which he could listen only to orchestral music because the vocals of the music that played in the reha-bilitation rooms would have distracted him, confused him as he counted and he would not have known where he had got to. At that pointless Opatija spa, he spent half the day at the entrances of different clinics, waiting. This sort of current, that sort of cur-rent, ultrasound, magnets, underwater massage, walking between room 33 and room 45 and back, trying to read Hrabal, but the pa-tients were loud and confessional, cacophonous, and their voices fell onto Bohumil as though he were a springboard, then flew into Andreas's head where they multiplied into vomit.

The dinners are unimaginative, alternately turkey and frozen hake and there are Slovenians who behave as though they are on a skiing holiday. In the pool, few people actually swim; both men and women, especially women, just float and chat, then they stand un-der the jets, close their eyes, stretch their lips into an obtuse smile and sink into the bliss of chlorinated water at thirty-three degrees.

Oh, how he wished he could swim long long distances as he had when he was training in fifty-meter pools, when his arms and legs did their work, calmly and rhythmically, harmoniously, when his breathing embraced his body, protected it, drew him toward infinity, not like today when he wrestles with it, when it rages within him, ravages him, constricts him, hisses as he tries to fall asleep and, shallow as his breathing is, insidiously crushes his lungs which are unable to open and take into themselves the elusive, colorless but miraculous food for the mind, ordinary air. When he used to swim long distances, in pools and outside them, toward the open sea, for hours, he leafed through books, read poems, sang, wrote, sculpted, but now, with no air, he is completely drying up from the inside, contracting, diminishing into a quiet, uninhabited, almost cataclysmic microworld.

In the course of those three weeks spent in Opatija, he watched all the TV shows he had not known existed, he did not read a single book, he strengthened his stomach and back muscles, while his spirit fell ill. But when he got home, he wrote. He still wrote.

He skips the first phase, the phase of rejecting the illness, he's no fool. So he confronts it. The second phase, the phase of anger (fuck off!), settles down, he no longer shouts at the doctors, he's tame. He rushes into the third phase, bargaining, with one sentence— *Give me ten years*—to which Dr. Toffetti replies, *Perhaps. But then you'll come back for another ten*, and Andreas Ban falls silent. He had hoped, if the tests didn't show disturbing changes, deterioration, that he would be able to accept his condition and live with it, and thus avoid that enigmatic phase, depression, which is hard to tame. Andreas Ban knows all this, he has studied books and observed cases in the course of his professional life. So, with the ultrasound diagnosis, with the little photograph that Dr. Molina handed him, the following day Andreas Ban goes for a needle-core biopsy, they give him an appointment at once, breast cancer in men is after all a rare (aggressive and fairly malignant) phenomenon. *Ah, great,* one of the oncologists lets slip, *at last I'll be able to show this to my students. Breast cancer in a man never comes our way.*

The surgeon, Toffetti, inserts a wide needle with an extraction mechanism into Andreas Ban's breast. Andreas Ban turns his head away, he doesn't want to look, but he hears the needle click and feels it grab a small piece of the tumor. Then again, and again, and again, the soles of his feet are cold, his nose itches, his arm under the cast itches, he doesn't breathe. In ominous silence, Dr. Toffetti collects the samples of that not yet entirely aroused substance that has settled inside him, conceived who knows when, who knows in what hustle, bustle, house-move and impecunity, perhaps in the course of some great solitude that threatened, like a flood, to drag him down to depths so deep he would not be able to surface, but it did not, it left him, as in a film, beached, in semiconsciousness from which he did nevertheless extract himself. Then Dr. Toffetti exclaims, almost cheerfully, *Oh, what a beautiful sample, big and compact,* as though he were looking at a slice of Black Forest gateau.

A week later, in Dr. Toffetti's clinic, Andreas Ban reads the result of his needle-core biopsy as if he were reading a bad review of some melodrama. From the small piece of paper the word *invasive* flies up and, like a bullet, hits Andreas between the eyes. *How invasive is it now?* asks Andreas Ban. *What has it attacked, where, how much has it attacked,* he asks. *If they are malignant, they are all invasive,* says Dr. Toffetti with discreet irritation, as if to say *Don't try to be clever.* Andreas is silenced, he is diminished, but diminished in a way that makes him want to lie down, curl up and pull the covers over his head, because his nose is getting cold and that annoys him.

The surgeon Toffetti looks for a free date on which to perform the operation, operations are done on Thursdays, because *Thurs-*

days are our sentinel day, says Dr. Toffetti. What kind of sentinel, sentinel—guard, French *sentinelle*, Italian *sentinella*, probably from the Old Italian *sentina*, vigilance, from *sentire*, to feel, Indo-European root, what is that sentinel, how big is it, whom is it guarding, what is it guarding, is it guarding him, Andreas Ban? During that operation what will they do to his sentinel, will they remove it? Because, soldiers, sentinel-guards threaten arrivals (malignant tumors?), they prevent their potential attacks on, on what? On a town? On fortifications? On a body.

When he arrives in this town from hostile Belgrade, look, he feels, he touches the walls of the fortification he is entering quietly, almost submissively, with the permission of the town's authorities, but sentinels nevertheless follow his footsteps, for a long time, suspicious. Because he spoke differently, he laughed differently (loudly), he dressed differently (sloppily), he had forty-five years of a past which those inside the walls knew nothing about (and still don't), in other words, for those inside the walls he had a mysterious past, a potentially dangerous past, which would need first to be investigated, then eradicated, space made for a new past resembling this one here, a small, cramped, shared past, virtually a family past.

He was supposed to become Otto the rabbit, then it would be all right. Otto the white rabbit lived in a henhouse and sat on the eggs with the hens. Otto the rabbit jumped onto the perch, clumsily to start with, falling a lot, but then he became adept and was able to stay up there for a long time. Today, Otto the rabbit does not sit on his owner's lap nibbling carrots. Otto the rabbit eats everything the hens eat and scampers around the run with the hens. For the hens, Otto the rabbit is a hen. When he sits on the perch with the hens, Otto the rabbit sometimes tucks himself under their wings and huddled up breathes quietly, protected and invisible.

But Andreas Ban—a superfluous man in his new homeland, neither a local nor a nomad, an *exception*—hovers in emptiness, catapulted into Never Never Land, into *Narrenschiffen*, into *non-lieu*, and becomes human debris. In order to be included, in order for them to include him, he first passes through a fine, quiet, several-year-long purgatory of radical exclusion, through a ritual of cleansing, a ritual of undressing, so as to "buy" his rite of passage. sto eliminating potential chaos in the threesome dance, in that amorous spasm, in that ménage à trois of territory, state and nation. Therefore, in order to subsist, to survive, he tries not to remember. Lacan. He is not a patient with symptoms that have to be illuminated, with puzzling symptoms whose cause is unknown, so he asks, *Who am I?* And Lacan tells him, *You are your past.* Joke. He, Andreas Ban, is nailed to his own being, to his body; his organs, his blood, his pain languish in a mildly aseptic society, anesthetized and mechanized, an ironed society with no creases.

Andreas Ban thus ekes out his existence in the prisons of that town with the homeless and the indigent (on benefits), with his son and his increasingly porous memories, until the sentence of isolation that was never recorded is finally revoked, after enough years have left him with damaged organs, lungs whose bronchi contract wildly, whose bronchi clench crazily, suffocating in their own mucus, suffocating him too, at times leaving him with a pipette for inhaling air.

It's then he decides not to remember. *It's over, the sentence has been served,* he says, though so far he has not been able to understand what that sentence was and why it had been imposed. Life had somehow gone on, had dripped rather than flowed, but he had been able to work, he had been able to write, to publish, after many trials and tribulations and overruling he had been taken on, at a pitiful salary, in some kind of state institution, an employee had retired and he leaped in, he did bits and pieces at the university, did honorary teaching, he even got a doctorate, because that was required of him, he was fifty-five when, between writing "his own" articles he succeeded in scraping together a dissertation on "Aspects of Aggression in Different Social Strata and Self-control as a Potential Intermediary," which did not interest him in the slightest, that dissertation, that quasi-research, but they tell him, *If you are thinking of teaching, if you want to fit in, if you want us to accept you, you cannot do only what you like, writing is not a job,* they tell him, *writing is relaxation, a little entertainment carried out on weekends,* because on various faculties individuals do that, they have little creative hobbies—they do amateur sketching, they write literary balderdash, *writing is not an art,* they say, *because in Croatia there is no school that teaches writing, therefore here, in this country, at this school, the School of Social Sciences, you cannot have a position as a writer-artist, but exclusively as a psychologist-scholar, because you are not a painter, nor a sculptor, nor an architect, not even a landscape architect, you are not a dramaturge, or a musician, or a pantomime artist,* they tell him, *nor a designer of lights or visual communication, you are nothing, your interests are disparate, undefined, you are not focused on one field, you don't research one area in depth,* they say, *that's not good, take it or leave it,* they say, because they write humanistic "original scholarly" works, presentations, all so decent, washed, harmless and soothing.

As in Zagreb, when he participates in a conference on the intellectual and war, a conference entitled "Intellectuals and War, 1939–1947," and a woman participant gives a paper on intellectual women in the Independent State of Croatia, mentioning two with a university education, the others were all knitters and childbearers who exclaim "Our duties to the nation are great," which is the title of the paper by the participant glued to the academic charade, "Our duties to the nation are great," but she said nothing, condemned no one, concluded nothing, so when Andreas Ban asked whether after the war, in Argentina, some of those rural "intellectuals," or perhaps some of their descendants, had opened their eyes, when he asked whether any of their descendants, sons, daughters, grandchildren had apologized to the victims of their Ustasha fathers and grandfathers, because this woman scholar had talked with those bigoted ninety-year-old women, she, the scholar, shook her head in denial and everyone in the audience immediately shrieked at him, Andreas Ban, *That's not the subject now*, and he asked, *What is the subject then and what's all this about?* At that "scholarly" conference about intellectuals in the war, at which there was no audience, at which the audience consisted of those who had come with their little papers and little stories to convince one another that everything was now clear, that the past had no connection with the present, instead of Social Sciences students attending the conference about intellectuals in the war, another participant rambled on for twenty minutes about the tragic destiny of Milivoj Magdić who, as editor of the Ustasha journal *Spremnost* ("Readiness"), smuggled in subversive articles about the writing of Thomas Mann, Edgar Allan Poe and the surrealists, so shattering the poetics of the native soil and the hearth, and in fact opening "free space," that is what he said, *free space* (in the monstrous NDH), cracks through which to glimpse different kinds of "landscape," because in that Ustasha *Spremnost* they published also humorous writings, novellas and articles by Mayakovsky, Zoshchenko and Babel, Russian avant-garde writers in other words, this historical researcher maintained under the aegis of dispassionate analysis of the Ustasha Movement, which in Andreas Ban's eyes does not bear relativizing, just as Nazism does not, there are no minor Ustashas, there are no minor Nazis, and that new *kulturträger* of the new Croatia, in defense of Ustasha *kulturträgers*, did not remotely relativize the prison sentences and executions of the new Communist authorities which, he said, *had mercilessly and unjustifiably* condemned the *elite* of Croatian Ustasha journalism for cultural cooperation with the enemy. The researcher of the Croatian wartime journalistic past did after all admit that those, to him subversive, editors and journalists, for the most part supporters of the NDH, to keep their positions, did not dare touch the Leader, it never occurred to them to criticize the Ustasha struggle and the Ustasha order of things, *nor was it important*, he said, because *those who were concerned with the essential aspects of literature, aesthetics, narrative technique and so on, did not stick their heads in the sand*, he maintained, *they were preoccupied with their profession, because literary criticism was not a free space for the expression of opinions of all kinds; it was for opinions about literature.*

Sickened by this tepid and amoral paper, this evasive theater planted on the worn-out columns of clichés, Andreas Ban leaves the conference. Hearing about that little rotten "free space," propagated by that right-winger, reminds him of the confession of the protagonist of Littell's book, Dr. Max Aue, who, just like these little Ustasha journalists, had before him a great space for freedom (of choice). Because, while Milivoj Magdić and company had published what had been for the Ustasha regime allegedly subversive pieces by Surrealists, Jasenovac was filling up and Auschwitz was smoking.

They could hardly wait to get rid of him. On that little faculty, at that little university, there are some fine people, and clever ones, it's just that they are few. There are many meek, frightened souls who use every opportunity to practice a porous severity and comic stiffness. There are many self-effacing people, many cowards, and many who are silent. Meek souls talk about Andreas Ban having communication problems because he does not communicate the way they think one should, indirectly, but that is no communication, just half-heartedness, nodding and formal correspondence full of clichés which travel with incredible frequency from the first floor to all the other floors and back to base (the Dean's office). They do not want direct communication because communication on an equal basis means responsibility. They do not want responsibility. So, they sprinkle and iron, starch, sprinkle and iron, starch and embroider to the point of exhaustion.

There is a woman, a psychologist unfortunately, who, when she gets upset, and she gets upset whenever anyone opposes her, opens her mouth wide and roars. They say that this psychologist, presumably for educational, if not for sadistic purposes, used to tie up her daughter's hands so she could not scratch. Why the daughter of the psychologist scratched herself compulsively the psychologist had presumably not researched, because had she done so she would not have tied up her daughter's hands but disentangled the issues that made her daughter scratch. That tying up of people, tying up the weak, is becoming popular in academic circles, if not everywhere then at least at some universities. There is a woman who is supposed to teach literature, who fancies herself a writer, and when she produced her tiny "original" works, in which she was to analyze texts already analyzed and assessed in the literary canon, she fails in her interpretation. People say that she used to tie her son to the radiator, and that he wriggled while she observed him with the eye of a jailer. At the university there are also insufferable boasters squeezed into dark-blue suits who look horrific, especially in summer when there is color and life everywhere. Departments, like the School of Social Sciences, are meant to produce an intellectual elite, instead they create meek people who hide in mouseholes. Who talk but say little. Who are not heard outside their classrooms, and speak softly, muttering to themselves.

> *All shuffle there; all cough in ink;*
> *All wear the carpet with their shoes;*
> *All think what other people think;*
> *All know the man their neighbor knows.*
> *Lord, what would they say*
> *Did their Catullus walk that way?*
>
> *Yours, Yeats*

The apex of Kafkaesque academic correspondence, which is the last straw for Andreas Ban, is a half-literate letter addressed to him, Andreas Ban (CLASS: 602-04/11-01/182, Our Ref: 2170-24-01-11-01), a letter of absurd content and demands, in other words a senseless letter in the first person plural (we) signed by one Dean:

> *Dear Hon. Prof. Dr. Ban*
>
> *We write to inform you that, in keeping with art.*
> *102 of Statute 6 of the Law on academic activity and*

tertiary education your contract comes to an end on
30.09.2011.

A contract of work for an employee in the scholarly
teaching profession comes to an end with the end of the
year in which he has reached the age of sixty-five in
order for him to retire.

We request that you resign and propose a suitable
replacement in your field to ensure continuity in the
teaching profession.
Respectfully,
Dean

Given that some kind of law does exist and in it an art. 102, Statute 6, what is Andreas Ban supposed to say in his resignation, what is he supposed to report and to whom? What kind of replacement should he propose, now he's on the way out? So Andreas Ban does not respond, although the Dean's office impatiently awaits his resignation, they send reminders, notes that begin "you are obliged" (are they threatening him?), so they can zealously, in time, according to the law, (de)classify and file away (where?) his reply, that is him, Andreas Ban.

Andreas Ban wrote about the death of the intellectual, but since the majority of his then colleagues hardly read anything outside their own fields, they selectively read articles in their field, they had no clue, or rather they didn't give a damn about what was happening in the world, nor did it cross their minds to go beyond their own turf. For that reason, when he leaves, he sends everyone on the faculty in which he spent thirteen barren years an abridged version, a compilation of his articles on the theme of academics whose claws cling to the walls of their dark, moldy cocoons. He sends his resignation, his statement, his adieu.

To the majority who imagine they are intellectual, Andreas Ban writes that Edward Said too states that there are virtually no genuine intellectuals any more. He sends extracts from his favorite Julien Benda who, as early as 1927, and again in 1946, writes that intellectuals committed treason by joining movements such as Nationalism and Fascism, movements founded on false premises, on practical activism and violence, which is the case with a number of university lecturers in Croatia during Tudjman's 1990s of extermination, liquidation and purges. Benda maintains that the intellectual is a person who nurtures, preserves and propagates independent judgment, a person loyal exclusively to truth, a courageous and wrathful individual for whom no force of this world is too great or too frightening not to be subjected to scrutiny and called to account, which those lecturers, the so-called former colleagues of Andreas Ban, are not and never will be. Andreas Ban lays Said and Benda and Chomsky out in front of them because otherwise they would never read what he is writing (this way they might at least glance at his article), because they are so blind and stupefied that they need prominent, mighty names to believe in something, the matter at hand is not enough, especially if the writer is, to them, unknown. So Andreas Ban announces to the faculty that Said considers today's intellectuals to have had *their teeth pulled out*, reduced to *producers of assent*. (Generally speaking Croats do not do well with their teeth; gap-toothed as they are, they roll their easily digested porridge around their mouths, or bite cautiously with their dentures, and with denture glue in their pockets, repeat the mantra, *The hard walnut is a peculiar fruit. You'll not break it, but it will break your teeth.* Stone deaf to that saying, *Strong teeth can crack even the hardest nut.*) A true intellectual, a genuine one, is always an outsider, Andreas Ban attempts to explain, he is a person who lives in self-imposed exile on the margins of society. He speaks to the public, in the name of the public; he is on the side of the powerless, of those whom no one represents, of those who are forgotten.

Then, Andreas Ban reminds them of Umberto Eco, in the hope that the mention of the late maestro of sharp tongue and mind will enlighten their spirit, not because of Eco's books and essays, but rather because of the film *The Name of the Rose*, for them, who splash around blissfully in the Kafkaesque waters of pointless bureaucracy, in not-at-all-benign threats and obtuse conventions, and he tells them that Eco sees the intellectual as an extremely hazy category. If such a hazy, befogged intellectual chooses the space of tactical silence, writes Eco, then reflection about war demands that this silence be *expressed aloud*, which few university professors did then or do now. It's true that at the end of his *Tractatus Logico-Philosophicus* Wittgenstein states that with things one cannot talk about one should remain silent, but that implies that we remain silent about something when we know exactly why we do not speak, why we remain silent. That is why Andreas now, while he has the opportunity, a rare occurrence, says no, it is precisely about things which it is impossible to speak of that one must speak, although this revolt of his is ever quieter, a shot in the dark. Andreas Ban had wanted to serve up to these people, these cowed conformists of mediocre ability who shun directness, because they are so pathetically and emptily refined, to serve them a portion of Karl Jaspers about individual responsibility, but he changed his mind. He gave them crumbs of Debray, Gramsci, Wright Mills, Fanon, Adorno, Hamilton, Chomsky, y Gasset, Sontag and some others, just enough to season his accusation. In truth, Andreas Ban could not resist quoting Kołakowski who says *the priest is the guardian of the absolute; he sustains the cult of truths accepted by tradition as ultimate and unquestionable. The jester is the impertinent upstart who questions everything we accept as self-evident ... In order to point out the unobviousness of its obviousnesses and the nonultimacy of its ultimacies, he must be outside it, observing from a distance; but if he is to be impertinent, and find out what it holds sacred, he must also frequent it.*

Then, supporting himself on Hofstadter, Posner and Jacoby (because otherwise they would have skipped this part), Andreas Ban writes to them, to those who thank goodness Ban will no longer encounter even in this small town, because they don't move around, are not interested in anything outside, he writes about the *castrating influence* of the university, the university *codex* and *constitution*, on the independence of the intellectual, because that *structure*, so reminiscent of the *ecclesiastical structure* of the fanatically rigid General Ignatius Loyola, anesthetizes (and punishes) the public activity of free intellectuals who as a species are dying out, shut up within the walls of the university, writing monographs and articles for a select minority (who may or may not read them), who look neither back nor to the side, whose gaze is locked onto professional journals and conferences, which drives them deeper into conformism and mediocrity, and kills the independent spirit which owes obedience to no one. The intellectuals got lost in the universities, from independent critics they have turned into academic careerists, Andreas Ban then quotes Chomsky.

A military-religious structure, a military-religious ideology wrapped in military-religious terminology, writes Andreas Ban to the amorphous mass, in universities, including their own, often serves as a cover for the legal practice of unfounded, outdated or worn-out authoritarian power, preserving power through fear from a position acquired long before, paired with an offensive, slimily paternalistic attitude toward those who occupy positions lower in the hierarchy. Why are dissertations not presented or expounded before some kind of commission, but defended, as though someone was attacking them? asks Andreas Ban. How is it that for the most part there are no first-rate artists at universities, nor first-rate writers, nor first-rate architects, nor first-rate musicians, nor first-rate philosophers? asks Andreas Ban. There are none, he writes, because such people need varied and unbounded spaces of freedom, and since with time a military-religious structure leads to serious psychic frustrations, it happens that this lethargic university cadre reach for cathartic activities such as amateur, by and large worthless, artistic creation, to mask its creative impotence. There is no freedom within an institution, concludes Andreas Ban. An institution offers security, freedom destroys it.

Andreas Ban is not revealing anything new to his colleagues. As early as 1907, as a delegate to the Second Anarchist Congress in Amsterdam, Emma Goldman says, *The school, more than any other institution, is a veritable barracks, where the human mind is drilled and manipulated into submission to various social and moral spooks, and thus fitted to continue our system of exploitation and oppression.*

You behave like private intellectuals, Andreas Ban writes to them, *and a private intellectual does not exist. You are not responsible intellectuals either, for responsible intellectuals cannot be passive observers, which is what you are. This is a message from Edward Said,* Andreas Ban tells them, *not from me.*

Your morality is questionable, because you passively observe injustices and social and political anomalies, you incur moral omissions, Andreas Ban writes, and then, unable to resist, seasons his text with Jaspers, *and moral omissions create the basis for political wrongs and crimes. Innumerable tiny omissions, conformist accommodation, cheap justification and imperceptible acceleration of injustice, contributions to a public atmosphere that renders clear vision impossible and makes evil possible, all this has consequences.*

In the meantime Radomir Konstantinović dies. Andreas Ban is not sure how many people at the School of Social Sciences, let's say in Rijeka, let's say in the English, German, and Croatian Departments, in the Departments of Psychology, History and Art History, how many people have heard of that writer, poet and philosopher, let alone read him. Maybe a few, not many, but in the Pedagogy and Polytechnic Departments—Andreas Ban is certain—none.

Andreas Ban now plays his ace. He uses *Filozofija palanke, The Philosophy of the Province* written by that courageous and wise visionary, cruelly isolated and eliminated from public life even in Serbia in these gloomy times. And he ends his pitiful and irrelevant tirade with a nod at the idea of the provincial, endeavoring in the most straightforward possible way to explain to the ignoramuses he is addressing what makes them as parochial as they are. The provincial does not imply settlements pushed out of the center—small towns, villages—but a state of mind, writes Andreas Ban, quoting Konstantinović. The size of an inhabited locality is not proportionally commensurate with its openness and cosmopolitanism, he writes. Consequently, a whole country, that is to say its inhabitants, may be imbued with that provincial spirit, the spirit of the "kingdom of darkness." The provincial world is neither a village nor a town. Its spirit, however, is a spirit between the tribal, as ideally unique, and the international, as ideally open. The spirit of the province preaches the religion of closure. Opposes action with passivity, because action, activity, is capable of transforming the provincial spirit, of betraying it. A provincial person is not an individual on a personal journey, he is the *summum* of experience, he is an attitude, a style. The provincial person has an exceptionally strong sense of style, for he has a strong sense of the collective, frozen or embodied in that style.

The provincial spirit is the spirit of homogeneity, of the ready-made solution. In the provincial world, it is more important to maintain established customs than to be a personality. Anything predominantly individual is undesirable, because it is the embodiment of versatility, the pure personification of sound, which for the provincial spirit is the music of sheer hell. Having renounced his own will, stylized according to the model of collective will, the provincial takes refuge in the security of the general. The provincial spirit as the spirit of super-I, the spirit of collective will, takes us under its wing, protects us from everything (especially ourselves), from the provocation and temptation called "I," personal responsibility and personal action. The provincial spirit does not like the unfamiliar. That is one of its fundamental attributes, defining its history, its culture, its mental world. Provincial life is a life of routine. The provincial spirit is a tribal spirit with no awareness of the individual.

The impulse to exclude, by mocking, by negating what is outside the norm, is strong in the provincial spirit. The provincial spirit registers everything, every difference, linguistic, ethical, physical, cultural, it remembers everything and does not acknowledge any variation. The provincial world is transformed into a great theater of life. The provincial spirit makes tragedy impossible, sentimentalism becomes a substitute for sensibility. The provincial possesses the consciousness of the collective, becomes the collective hero which in tragedies explains the destiny of the protagonists while remaining outside the tragedy.

The philosophy of the province is a philosophy of a closed circle that does not allow an apostasy, without which there is no creativity. The philosophy of the province is a normative and normalizing, suprapersonal and impersonal philosophy, it shuts out all aspects of life, education, sport, nutrition, nature, love, work, language, religion and death (which is far from being the death of an individual) replacing life with rigid forms of the normative which apply to all.

The province is fanatically afraid of the world because it is afraid of chaos. The province is incapable of absolute rebellion. Its world is ruled by the spirit of order and self-discipline. The province takes its banality for granted, an archaic condition in permanent retreat from the Other, whom it sees as the enemy and whom, because of its own restrictive spirit, it frequently promotes to renegade, intruder, and often also "jester." The spirit of the province is the creator of the vision of the "small man" and his small life, a semilife of semiwill.

So Andreas Ban leaves that invalid horde of former colleagues comfortably settled in the Abgrund hotel, in Hotel Abyss, to quasi-philosophize from time to time in a melancholy fashion. Poor Andreas Ban. His letter addressed to his former colleagues will be read only by few, by that aggrieved critical minority, already weary and sickened. Most will wonder, *What is this drivel? What does he want? Maybe he's deranged?*

Twenty years have passed since he came here. It might seem that he has fitted in.

> He has not
> At least he has someone to write to.
> He does not.

When it gets tough, when it gets bad internally, when his insides clot, when they contract, Andreas Ban sings "*Ich hab' noch einen Koffer in—Belgrad,*" although that's a lie. If it turns out that twenty years later an abandoned suitcase, a small piece of cardboard baggage still languishes there, not much will be left inside: two cracked urns, Elvira's and Marisa's, a few reliable addresses with altered names, some physical contacts which are pulling away, aromas mingling, and misty glances. Marlene Dietrich did not return, she just flew over Berlin. When he sings that song "*Ich hab' noch einen Koffer in—Belgrad,*" Andreas Ban calms down for a while, he doesn't need his asthma pump.

I, like a river,
Have been turned aside by this harsh age.
I am a substitute. My life has flowed
Into another channel
And I do not recognize its shores.
O, how many fine sights I have missed,
How many curtains have risen without me
And fallen too. How many of my friends
I have not met even once in my life,
How many city skylines
Could have drawn tears from my eyes,
I who know only the one city
And, by touch, in my sleep I could find it …
Yours, Akhmatova

In Andreas Ban and around him, nothing flows any longer, it is a time of *stasis*. Like Joyce's Dubliners, he is stretched out under a snowy coverlet on the verge of sleep. They, the Dubliners, paralyzed as they are, constantly remember, they don't live, they remember the living monks who lie in their coffins, who rest in life, they remember the dead who shiver under snow. With those memories they pump up their brittle blood vessels. Andreas Ban does not even want that anymore. He has packed his past as one dumps old clothes into plastic bags. Sometimes, though, feeble flashes appear before his eyes, sparks, but as his sight is steadily weakening, with time they too fade, one by one, silently. What was it Pessoa said? "Now nothing inside me can cut off—the nothing."

Ich hab' noch einen Koffer in –

The last time Andreas Ban goes to Belgrade is on October 27, 2011. After twenty years he has been invited, officially and in a friendly way.

I'm going to get my life back, he writes to Leo. *I'm coming to get my life*, he writes to his friends.

May 14, 1992, eight a.m.. In the apartment there's nothing left. Just nailed-up wooden crates and taped-up cardboard boxes in which, squeezed and crumpled, airless, lie once vigorous years. On the walls only dark gray outlines where pictures once hung. Two plastic coat hangers on the floor. Built-in bookshelves, empty. Lowered blinds. Darkness.

The ginger cat, Ivo (*Is your cat Croatian?* the six-year-old twin girls ask Leo), has been given as a gift to the Lebovićes, Zlata and Djordje, who move to Israel shortly thereafter. Without Ivo.

 Andreas Ban runs across the highway to the police station, registers his departure. *Why are you going to Reka?* asks the woman at the desk. *Rijeka*, he says.

The neighbors come and cry. *Why are you crying?* says Andreas Ban, as Leo picks up the neighbors' garbage left outside their door the night before. *Here, take our flowers*, Andreas Ban tells the neighbors. They did not buy potted plants again, Andreas and Leo. For twenty years there were no potted plants in the apartment.

Leo in the third year of primary school. *Your father writes for the newspapers, stand in front of the class and read this article of his*, the teacher, Nada Milošević, says to Leo. Leo reads, Leo is little, he is eight. *You see, children, Leo's daddy is an enemy of the state*, says Nada Milošević, *Leo's daddy is a state enemy.*

He brings a chocolate cake to the clinic as a "farewell." The director of the clinic says, *It's good that you're leaving, you like the sea.* A female colleague says, *It's good you're going, one can see in your face you're not a Serb.* A male colleague sheds a tear, *Have I contributed to your leaving?* Prior to that, some people said, *that Ustasha Ban.* He takes the cake to his patients.

He said, *I'll come to Belgrade when Milošević falls.* He stays in a hotel then. It's all quite sick. He meets people who want to hug, but there's no chance of that. He meets friends, they fall into each other's arms. *As though I'd never been away*, says Andreas Ban. He goes to the cemetery. He takes mimosas to Elvira and his mother. Then the aperture closes.

It gets dark again. He returns to nervous Croatia.

Some people from Belgrade come to Croatia, so his relationships seem unaffected. As if nothing much has changed. He sees actors, writers, directors, doctors, painters, colleagues, among them some close to him, he shops with them for sandals and clothes for their wives. Some people he misses. There were many in his former life. He used to correspond with a few, no longer. He still sees some of them, in the summer, they grill mackerel. They swim. Healing little visits, though pointless—they nourish the illusion of time standing still. Here there are not many he is close to, not many at all.

Two or three times Andreas Ban goes to Belgrade—always for a short time, in haste. That doesn't count. One October, irrationally summery, he goes to the Čubura restaurant in Pejton with some good, weary people and there in the garden sits Brana Crnčević.* Relaxed and carefree. Andreas Ban wants to leave immediately, *This is too much*, he says. *Pretend you haven't seen him*, his friends try to distract him. Miša brings him some new books about Rovinj, the following summer Miša dies.

He cannot remember which is ulica Kolarčeva. That disturbs him, but at the same time it is liberating.

---

* Branislav "Brana" Crnčević (1933–2011) was a well-known Serbian writer and politician, and during Milošević's rule a hard-core nationalist.

Leo "returns" to Belgrade after sixteen years. He calls Andreas and says, *All the time I feel like crying.* Then he shoots a documentary entitled "My Belgrade." A sad but acerbic film. A tough little film, not at all sentimental.

When they first arrive in Croatia, Leo's schoolmates say, *Ban is a Serbian surname.* Of course it's not. Leo asks him, *Is Ban a Serbian surname?* but Andreas is silent, he does not say anything.

Recently, they brought Leo's children's books down from the attic. Leo opens his *Greek Myths* and says, *Look, Nebojša gave me this in Belgrade, for my birthday. Look, I covered up the dedication with big stickers,* says Leo. *The dedication was written in Cyrillic,* he says, laughing. Andreas Ban does not find it amusing. His stomach contracts. It's the first time he sees Leo's fear of twenty years past.

 Andreas Ban goes to Belgrade in May 2010 as well. For less than two days. He has no time for anything. On the way to a meeting, he walks from Kalemegdan Park to Marx and Engels Square (which is no longer called Marx and Engels Square, he knows) and is surprised to see trees growing there. He runs into Goran Marković and they say *ciao*, as though they often meet. At the beginning of December 2008 Andreas Ban sees Goran's film "The Tour" in Pula. Then Goran gives him his book *Small Secrets*, he hasn't seen him since, Andreas wants to say something about that touching chronicle, with its dedication: *For Andreas, after so long, for the years ahead.* That mess with time turned out to be a serious complication. That ebbing away of punctured, hole-ridden time.

 He walks along some streets and remembers the numbers of buildings in which his friends lived, 51, ulica 7. Juli, only, that street no longer exists. 16, ulica Tadeuš Košćuški. Zagorka no longer lives there, she died.

In the former Toplice Hotel, he has a meeting with Ognjen. Ognjen orders lamb soup, Andreas pours Coke into himself because he's had a stomachache the whole time he's been in Belgrade. Both of them are graying. They don't talk much.

There are some terribly dilapidated facades. On the ground floor of the crumbling, pockmarked buildings are elegant shops selling imported goods. The statue of "The Boy from the Čukur Fountain" is no longer in ulica Dobračina, it disappeared. There is only a vacant plinth. The statue is the work of the uncle of Andreas's grandmother, Paško Paskoje Vučetić, from Split (1871–1925), who goes from Split to Trieste, to the art and craft school Nordio, from there to Venice to the Accademia, then to Munich Akademie der Bildenden Künste, then back to Trieste, where he works with Rendić and finally ends up in Belgrade in the arms of a certain Marija with whom he now lies embraced in the New Cemetery, where they also placed Andreas's mother. Elvira is somewhere else. For Croats, Paško Vučetić is an important Croatian painter; for Serbs, Paško Vučetić is an invaluable Serbian artist. So, four years after he won first prize at a competition, Paško Vučetić's monument to Karadjordje is erected in Kalemegdan Park in 1913. But the monument is destroyed as early as 1916, during the Austrian occupation of Belgrade, with the excuse that it had been damaged in the course of the fighting. Today that spot is occupied by Meštrović's "Monument of Gratitude" to France.

On the grave in which Andreas's mother Marisa also lies there is another of Paško's pieces, "The Boy with a Jug." Cvijeta writes that it is damaged, that someone had tried to take this one down too and sell it for a "fee" of fifty euros. Paintings by Paško Vučetić hang in the National Museum of Belgrade, some are in galleries, some sold at auction. They ought to be on display in Split.

Those facades have completely shattered him, Andreas Ban. Belgrade is like an old man. A treacherous old man. As he taps his way along its streets, Andreas Ban feels like Arsenije Njegovan, like "a man who eats death," who is eaten by death. In Croatia, Andreas Ban has almost no one to talk with about Belgrade, five or six people maybe. Not enough for healing. With others, a lot of misunderstandings, their Belgrades differ in image, in time, in completeness. Even now, when he is not in Rijeka and wants to say that he has left something there, in Rijeka, Andreas Ban says, *I forgot it—in Belgrade*. Presumably in that suitcase in which what is there is not there at all. The deceit played by his tongue and mind irritates him, but pleases him as well. The fact that this tattoo is hard to erase.

He does not buy *kaymak* in Belgrade then, in 2010, others from the group—who do not live in Serbia—do, they take it home, to Croatia. Unfounded adoration with no ties.

Within himself Andreas Ban carries layers and layers of Belgrade. From the nursery school in ulica Užička, the primary school with the mustachioed teacher Branka who won't let him write with his left hand (though he does) and the First Belgrade Grammar School and university, publishers and editorial boards, dentists and doctors, psychologists, painters and sculptors, architects and plumbers. To Ksenija Anastijević with whom he recently had a painful conversation after Bogdan Bogdanović died. Four years earlier, in Vienna, Bogdan asks Leo, *How do you, young man, feel about Romanticism?*

No one has ever talked with me so wisely, says Leo.

Thirty-eight years. And yet.

The ruins of the Headquarters continue to embellish ulica Kneza Miloša. But the statue of Boris Kidrič is no longer there. It was an enormous statue, on the plateau below ulica Narodnog fronta (National Front Street), near the building in which Marijetka Kidrič lived, she looked extraordinarily like her father. Marijetka Kidrič is no longer in Belgrade either. When Belgrade was shelled, Erik called and asked how the Croats were reacting.

No how, he had said. *They're not dancing.*

Erik said, *It's terrible in Belgrade.*

Is there electricity, is there water, is there food? Andreas asks Erik. He asks him whether he knows how long the siege of Sarajevo lasted. Does he know that during the winter the people of Sarajevo did their business in plastic bags, that the contents would first freeze and then, with the coming of spring, thaw. When Vukovar fell, Erik had said, *So what, fuck 'em all.* Who? In Rambouillet, before what a small bombardment, Milošević & Co. had tapped at the keys of a piano and ordered bottles of expensive wine while the world waited. One ought to forget.

He rarely used the wrong word for lightbulb. At a Belgrade market, in 1991, he had asked for a light bulb in Croatian. The stall-holder told him, *Piss off!*

Andreas Ban is not Marlene Dietrich. He doesn't have beautiful legs and he is still alive. He has nowhere to return to. He has nowhere to put down roots. What remains is his language. A mishmash of languages which exclude him, with which he excludes himself. Which "betray" him, with which he "betrays" himself.

New people are coming, with shorter memories. Perhaps the air will blow with fewer gap-toothed emotions. But for Andreas Ban that is small consolation. Too late. The train left the station. And under it, under that train, he now lies motionless. Crushed.

Even so, Belgrade was done with somehow. After that last visit, Andreas Ban said to his sister, *Belgrade's no longer in my dreams. For twenty years I've been dreaming of Belgrade, now I've stopped. It seems I'm finally done with Belgrade.* And now, what will Andreas Ban dream about? What?

Andreas Ban does not have a column in any newspaper, no one has offered nor does he ask. He can no longer ask, he will not plead, no. While he had no work (five years), he asked the local paper if he could write reviews, scholarly or literary, anything, the editors kept changing, but the reply was always the same: *The section's full.* Eventually, one of the cultural editors suggested, as a magnanimous gesture to Andreas Ban, that he write digests of new books, in fact copy the blurbs from the jackets, which seemed pointless. So Andreas Ban said, *No, thank you.*

It's tedious to think about it all, about the impenetrable silences that grip the ribcage and stop the breath, even his characters speak about that, how many times must he go over those facts, and for whom? Literature and life are full of human trash and debris. At first Andreas Ban feeds on those slaps in the face, he contemplates his sullen expression in the solitude of his bathroom, and he says, I give up. He no longer examines himself, he's forgotten what he looks like. To start with, when he first got here, he sold paint and varnish for a chemical company, but the company soon went bust. Then he wrote speeches for the mayor (insultingly meager payment), he translated the itineraries of foreign delegations: reception, luncheon at three p.m., evening visit to the bay, formal dinner; he worked occasionally in a school as a psychologist, then they told him, *We don't need a psychologist, our children are healthy;*

over the summer he took little groups of tourists around Istria, he looked for any kind of full-time job, typing in an office, at least that, he asked in the 1990s, but was told, *No way, you're overqualified.* Back then, Andreas Ban was still angry, as they say—defending his integrity of which all that was left was a thick splotch like melted chocolate or smeared shit. In the beginning he would not give in, he would not be crucified on his own cross, nailed to his own body, as a piercing penetrates the tongue, nose, navel, penis or clitoris. He would not permit their story to be etched onto his skin, to let himself be branded with some identity from over there, constricted, local, provincial. Just one. He wanted, like a schizophrenic, to roam through his own lives, free.

And now, again.

It's not that Andreas is completely inert, it's not that he does not take steps, tiny steps admittedly, quiet steps, let's say he asks in a dignified way, but nevertheless he asks, then he stops. As twenty years earlier, he goes again to the mayor and says, I have nothing to live on, the same old story, only the mayor is different. He has meetings with advisers to the president of the state, with ministers, with country councilors, with newspaper proprietors, he presents them with his books, award-winning and translated, while they shake their heads and lower their gaze. In Istria they tell him, *You're not from Istria*, in Zagreb they tell him, *There are problems here*, in this little town they don't say anything, they scribble in their notebooks and can hardly wait for him to leave. Andreas Ban visits all these people but never again, and so his little tale ends "not with a bang but a whimper" and he now watches his present slipping away from him, crawling, sliding to the office counter where they give him his free annual bus pass to all four zones, which he does not want to use, which he will never use. *No one is going to help you*, Angela had told him bluntly, *Give it a rest*, she said. The only person to stand upright was the colorful publisher from a small Croatian town who said, *I'm sending you a book to translate*. And, for a moment, as if gathering up scattered seeds with both hands, Andreas put his dispersed life back together.

Some cockatoos with behavioral problems get depressed if their surroundings are forcibly changed and start plucking out their feathers, usually from their breasts—because that is presumably where the weight oppresses them the most. Some cockatoos also peck at their legs until they bleed, piercing holes in them. One bird chewed off its claw and died of blood loss. To prevent further self-harm in their pets, psychiatrists recommend that their owners treat them with sedatives and tie a stiff collar around their necks to immobilize their heads.

And now this sentinel, this nodule, this invasive tumor like a long line cast into his innards, has shaken everything up. It sends his brain little bubbles of memory that then burst. The images blur, double, move out of focus, tremble as if in flames.

A body like a town.

A body like a citadel, a tower, a fortress. Under siege.

There are sentinel tablets for dogs (and cats), given to dogs (and cats) once a month to protect them from heartworms (*Dirofilarije immitis*), from parasites carried by mosquitoes, which settle in the right-hand side of a dog or cat's heart and in their lung arteries, and the animals quickly tire, they breathe heavily, they cough, lose weight, stagger, get fluid swellings in their rear extremities. Enough! Andreas Ban is like a dog, like a sick dog. Perhaps that's why he has a growing tenderness toward dogs, toward small creatures in general, especially birds.

A sentinel is a lymph nodule. A guard before the web of lymph nodes, the keeper of the door of the armpit, the first site where metastases settle, protecting the other lymph nodes from attack, until it runs out of energy. A biopsy of the sentinel (under anesthetic) reveals whether the tumor has emerged from its case and begun to branch out. Thus, if the sentinel has been seized, the whole web of lymph nodes is removed, if the sentinel is found to be clean, only the tumor is removed, but then the sentinel is no longer there, it has been sacrificed, slain, cut up, chopped, sliced into thin sections, examined and discarded. This makes Andreas Ban think of the people who set fire to themselves in the name of some imaginary better tomorrow, as Jan Palach did, and people first stopped to look, then went on their way.

So, the surgeon Toffetti looks for a free slot for the operation, operations are carried out on Thursdays, and Thursdays are booked up as far as the eye can see, two months ahead. Andreas Ban will not be able to carry his tumor around for that long, he will break, he will listen to it waking up, stretching, spreading out its tentacles, he will go mad but it's the wrong moment, he has some jobs to attend to, to complete. For the first time in his life, Andreas Ban asks for help, which makes his shoulders sag under the weight of shame. To the director of the university (otherwise a medical doctor, so thank God he doesn't have to lay out the details, nor modulate his voice into helplessness), he says, *Find me a Thursday not too far off*. Two weeks later the surgeon Toffetti says, *We've fitted you in.*

In the meantime, I'd like to go to Leipzig, says Andreas Ban.

Go, says surgeon Toffetti. *And when you come back, get that cast off your right arm*, he says, *I need that arm for the anesthetic.*

In Leipzig, the pain in his plastered arm does not stop. Andreas Ban swallows three boxes of painkillers, in vain. The cast is increasingly heavy, it has come loose, it moves around, sliding to the tips of his fingers, and Andreas acquires the tic of pushing it back up to his elbow. When he returns from Leipzig, Andreas Ban goes to Lovran. There Dr. Salomon exclaims, *What have they done to you? Your hand is ruined. We'll have to break every bone that's grown together. Reposition your wrist.* Dr. Salomon vividly prophesies the future of Andreas's hand. He says, *Your hand will be completely out of commission unless we break the large and small bones that have grown back together crooked.* He says, *Otherwise you won't be able to lift anything with that hand, not even an empty ashtray.* And he also says, *If we don't break it, your hand will be left as crooked as when you twisted it in your fall, at an angle of forty-five degrees,* which would have looked especially frightening, completely crippled.

Andreas Ban is placed on a table and his arm is pulled into a sort of inquisitorial torture machine. A groove for each finger. They first stretch it with a winch, separating the hand and each of the fingers from their joints. Then they begin winding, or rather unwinding it. Andreas Ban lies on Kafka's torture machine dreamed up for his tender letters to Milena Jesenska, and in that terrifying sketch sees himself:

There are four posts, with poles running through the two middle posts to which the "delinquent's" hands are fastened; poles for the feet are run through the two posts on the outside. Once the man is thus secured, the poles are slowly pushed outwards until the man is torn apart in the middle. The inventor is leaning against the column with his arms and legs crossed, putting on airs as if the whole thing were his original invention, whereas all he really did was watch the butcher in front of his shop, drawing out a disemboweled pig.

Andreas Ban was rent apart. He had disintegrated, his integrity was shattered.

Dr. Salomon is pleased. *I've reduced the angle from minus forty-five degrees to minus fifteen,* he said. And added, *I thought you were going to pass out. Go home and waggle your fingers,* says Dr. Salomon. (That evening Andreas Ban's fingers turned completely black and swelled up like fresh blood sausages, it was impossible to move them.) *Your arm will remain somewhat crooked,* Dr. Salomon said, *but in a couple of years we'll be able to break it again, under full anesthetic.*

Then Eliot sprang up. He stood in front of Andreas Ban and said, *Do not disturb the universe.* He said, *In a minute there is time for decisions and revisions which a minute will reverse, and then what? I have known them all already, known them all,* he repeated, *have known the evenings, mornings, afternoons, I have measured out my life with coffee spoons, I know the voices dying with a dying fall beneath the music from a farther room …*

Enough, Eliot, says Andreas Ban. *Get lost.*

But Eliot scampers after Andreas Ban, he talks, and talks, and talks, increasingly loudly, increasingly loudly, he shouts, *Listen, I no longer dare disturb the universe, I am sprawling, pinned and wriggling on the wall, how then can I begin publicly to spit out all the butt ends of my days and ways, how?*

Andreas Ban leaves the orthopedic hospital. *I won't write any more,* he says.

Andreas Ban will have to go for the operation on the small tumor on his left breast, in a week's time now, with a cast on his arm.

He goes for all the preoperative tests: blood count, pulmonologist, internist, ECG, anesthetist. There are lines everywhere, he waits everywhere, wastes time, everywhere the nurses tell the patients, *Sit here, sit there, sit, don't talk,* as though the patients were dogs, and the patients, as though they were dogs, are obedient, they sit and for a moment are silent. Otherwise, in the waiting rooms, they converse, they chatter, babble, grow close, the moment they leave the clinic they are strangers. Most patients stand, there aren't enough plastic chairs in the waiting rooms, and besides, the clinic chairs are uncomfortable, they are joined together with steel rods so the patients don't pull them out and make a mess, so they don't make themselves too comfortable, so they don't keep coming back, which otherwise patients do, they come, regularly, ever more frequently, they love going to doctors. The patients are tense, anxious, they twist around, they wriggle and frequently sigh. They babble. They have nothing to focus on but their fear. Of course, in waiting rooms no one ever reads, because in waiting rooms it's dark and because the people waiting are frozen with uncertainty, they are in suspense, and besides, people don't read, even on intercity bus journeys which can last from two to twenty hours, few people read, especially at night, though in buses there are those little lights above the head, designed specifically for reading. As soon as it gets dark, even in winter when it gets dark by six, maybe even by five, the passengers sprawl like hens and fall asleep. Or they peck at their mobiles, or converse through those little devices, mostly spewing nonsense, sometimes unimaginably loudly. So, in clinics, the waiting people abandon themselves to time which devours them. They leave the hospitals or polyclinics worm-eaten, amorphous. Andreas Ban follows the conversation of two women.

Do we know each other? asks one. *Your face looks familiar, it rings a bell*, she says.

This business with bells ringing comes from various TV quiz shows in which the contestants always hear ringing when they don't know the answer and mostly they don't.

Didn't you work at the market, asks the woman with many eight-carat gold rings on her fingers. *I used to work at the market.*

Andreas Ban feels his stomach suddenly clench.

Andreas thinks about working at the market when he retires, he'll see what can be done.

Yes, I used to work at the market, says the second woman, *I sold fruit and vegetables.*

In Crikvenica?

Yes.

I sold clothing. Now I don't sell any more, it's not worth it. I work in Italy.

You look after old people?

Old people have too much skin. Like mastiffs. Their eyelids are thick and their eyes sunken. Their upper lip thin, their ear lobes long, and their skeleton fragile. Their vertebrae degenerate, their spine bends. The diameter of men's chests can be reduced by as much as four inches, women's by six. The shoulders narrow, the pelvis broadens. The thorax takes on a sagittal aspect, especially with women. The muscles atrophy, the joints lose mobility, osteoporosis takes hold, there are frequent breakages.

Excuse me?

What do you do in Italy?

I look after old people.

I don't sell fruit and vegetables either.

On his other side, Andreas hears one woman say to another, *She keeps dying and dying, but never does, fuck her.*

Then his name is called and he goes in. The anesthetist asks him, *Do you by any chance have asthma?* Andreas says, *Yes.*

Go at once to the pulmonologist, says the anesthetist. *Then come back so I can determine whether you can have the operation.*

The pulmonologist is in another hospital, on the other side of town. There they take X-rays of Andreas Ban's lungs, then Andreas Ban waits for three hours for the image of his lungs to fly by computer from the first floor to the fourth where the pulmonologist's office is. They take another blood sample, he blows into little tubes so they can assess the capacity of his lungs, they are surprised, *You have great capacity*, they say. Swimmers usually have great capacity and a big heart, Andreas knows that, but says nothing. No sign of the pulmonologist, five people are waiting for him, it is late afternoon, this is the morning residue, leftovers, dreg-patients. Andreas Ban knocks on the door of the doctor's office and asks, *Shall we get on with it?* The pulmonologist is eating a dry roll, crumbs fall onto his chest, onto his white doctor's coat. The pulmonologist is astounded by Andreas's intrusion into his privacy but says nothing. The pulmonologist thinks he is God. A plump woman comes up to Andreas, she is also waiting for someone, for something. *You seem familiar,* says the plump woman. *I'm from Rovinj,* she says. *I used to sell bread and milk at the top of ulica Švalbina.*

Yes, Andreas remembers. The woman has swelled up now.

I've retired, says the woman, *I don't work in the shop any more. I'm having an operation on my thyroid, but I have to get back to make* sarma *for the children.*

Then she says, *My parrot died.*

Maybe it got bored with life, your parrot, says Andreas to the former shop assistant.

It didn't get bored. It was alone. It had always been alone. It never had a companion, but it had a mirror and used to kiss it. So it wasn't alone.

What were they thinking, that because of his asthma Andreas Ban would expire on the operating table?

The pulmonologist tells him, *You've got COPD, Chronic Obstructive Pulmonary Disease, stop smoking.*

COPD has nothing to do with smoking. Parrots don't smoke, but the blue-and-gold macaw can suffer from COPD too, it has the same difficulties breathing as he, Andreas Ban, does. In one veterinary clinic, in the course of five years they hospitalized twelve blue-and-gold macaws suffering from COPD. This beautiful long-tailed parrot is very sociable and exceptionally intelligent, it can learn to speak and, when it learns to speak and does not feel well, it says, *It's stuffy here, cramped and I can't breathe.* The blue-and-gold macaw is an endangered species. When it develops the unpleasant chronic obstructive pulmonary disease, the blue-and-gold macaw can hardly inhale and exhale, it is tormented by hunger for air, its breathing becomes shallow, the skin on its face turns blue and it keeps coughing dryly, squeakily, straining its lungs horribly. Over time, the illness gets worse. It is only when this powerful, tame bird returns to its spacious forests that the blue-and-gold macaw can recover a bit. Even though there, in "the wild," there is no one to teach it to speak, even though it will never utter a single word.

The day before the operation, Dr. Toffetti asks Andreas Ban into his office and explains what is going to happen. From the top pocket of his white coat, Dr. Toffetti takes a wad of paper torn out of a notebook, scrawled with blue ballpoint. Andreas Ban has already heard it all. Dr. Toffetti had drawn his armpit and his tumor when he had prodded at his breast earlier, and later, when they were setting the date. He made a large dark-blue smudge. While he was speaking, Dr. Toffetti bored his pen into the paper, creating a circle which grew, outgrowing the size of Andreas's tumor by one centimeter. Now the surgeon looked for a clean piece of paper to continue sketching the course of the operation on Andreas's tumor. Among the sheets of paper, Andreas notices "his own."

There it is, he says, *that's my tumor.*

Dr. Toffetti raises his eyebrows. Dr. Toffetti explains to Andreas the procedure with the sentinel.

Sentinel, Andreas repeats, *the guard.*

Dr. Toffetti raises his eyebrows again, a bit higher this time. *What shall we do about the cast?* he asks.

Andreas says, *It hasn't knitted, another three weeks.*

All right, we'll think of something. The body has a lot of veins.

Andreas likes Dr. Toffetti. He came to him because Dr. Toffetti happened to be in the clinic when he ran into the hospital with the ultrasound picture in his hand, when his doctor friend had telephoned and said, *See this man today.* He'd heard that some women, who got stuck in a line as he had, went to another well-known surgeon, not Dr. Toffetti, they had not heard of him. But

Dr. Toffetti is a big man, calm and relatively young. He does not talk much and he does not smile politely. When he smiles, he lifts the corners of his lips barely perceptibly and blinks slowly, soothingly. Dr. Toffetti has big hands with soft fingertips, which are able, like probes, to feel small tumors, the very smallest. So Andreas Ban abandons himself completely to Dr. Toffetti.

Before he is admitted to hospital, Andreas Ban goes to the theater, he quickly forgets what he sees. He finds theater productions tedious, they are turning into kitsch spectacles with bad acting and acrobatics. No longer able to distinguish good from bad, the audience is whipped up, it loses its capacity to judge, and shallow emotion trumps reason. And so the audience applauds. *Bravo! Bravo!* The previous winter, for the New Year holiday, Viktor had come and they had gone to a concert, in spite of themselves, Viktor was a theater man. Otherwise, for a week, they cooked and ate, sat and drank, watched films by Peter Greenaway, Quentin Tarantino and Lars von Trier and raked over *les temps passés*. At that New Year concert the musicians sat on maroon plastic chairs, but as the theater presumably did not have enough maroon plastic chairs, a few wooden chairs were put on the stage, while the women (musicians) were dressed dramatically, each one differently, in long dresses with frills, mostly in combinations of violet and red, which all in all looked alarming. The auditorium, full to bursting with excited people, dolled up, smiling as they clapped in total rapture, gave the event an additional provincial dimension. During intermission, Viktor and Andreas learn that a former male dancer at the theater spends his nights in casinos and his days begging.

Instead of watching the play, the evening before going into hospital Andreas Ban observes with great concentration a plump little old woman with a pretty face and thin hair pulled into a ponytail with a rubber band, the kind used for sealing jars of jam and chutney. The old woman had hooked a large plastic hairclip over the rubber band, a white one, which slipped, because her little ponytail was thin and greasy. Andreas Ban does not dress up for the performance, to someone in the foyer he says, *Soon I won't be able to afford tickets and I won't have anyone to push me in my wheelchair to the theater.* At the end of the performance it is pouring, so from the open cloakroom Andreas Ban borrows someone's umbrella and calmly leaves the building. It's windy. The south wind blows the rain wildly in all directions, slapping the sky. Andreas Ban stops and watches a seagull battling with the wind, unable to take off.

Had it not been pouring, he would have sat in the unsightly fenced park right beside the theater, a little park with low-growing shrubs, dwarf trees and gravel paths, a park where by day there is no shade nor quiet nor real greenery, but which passersby visit and sit pointlessly on benches fixed in a circle.

Over the last few years his friends and acquaintances have been dying. Poof—just like that, they vanish. Bunched, they go, one after the other. It is a time for dying and suicide.

BEKIM

Thank you, Andreas, says his Branka every time she meets him.

BOGDAN

His Ksenija, there in Belgrade, was always elegant, she had black hair, very tidily brushed, a distinguished bearing, restrained, although she wasn't at all restrained, when required Ksenija is very direct, and before they, Ksenija and Bogdan, left Belgrade, Ksenija said to Andreas, *Come and see us, we are so isolated,* she said at some meeting of Reformists at the Duško Radović theater or perhaps at a meeting of the Yugoslav Democratic Initiative, who knows now, they were excluded because they had understood, too soon according to some, they had understood what was happening, Bogdan had written about it, Andreas remembers everything, everything, what people said, how they behaved, there in Belgrade, from Žika the carpenter and Mića the painter, and the writers, Antonije, Dragoslav, Dušan and Moma, some blinkered writers, foaming at the mouth, but also psychologists, then directors and actors, and so, Ksenija said, *Do come*, because someone had written a "U" in huge letters on the corridor walls, right up to the door of their apartment, Bogdan comments on it in his book *The Cursed Builder*, but Andreas Ban knows, he was there, he saw the "U," in *The Cursed Builder* is also one of the loveliest love stories Andreas has ever read, it's called "*Les nuits d'octobre*," when an old man writes about love, he does so with a lot of terrible, powerful, liberated passion. He still has to look for the grave of Bogdan's grandfather in Delnice, that is what Bogdan told him the last time he was in Vienna, *Try to find that grave*, he said, *it won't be hard, it's a grave with the headstone in Cyrillic*, he said, *if it hasn't been removed*. By chance (really?), at that time Andreas Ban is living in Vienna at 11 Davidgasse and Bogdan and Ksenija, now only Ksenija, at number 9 Davidgasse, in the 10th district, a working-class, peripheral district, as more or less all of them are now, among peripheral people who talk with an ease that evokes the bliss of a dream followed by a dangerous uneven beating of the heart, if that is medically possible.

ZAGA

Buy me the latest crosswords. And a roll.

TOM

JASENKA

BOŽIDAR

BRANIMIR

JOŠKO

NELA

it's terribly aggressive, it metastasizes quickly, I can hear its hoof-beats scraping over the dry earth: da-dum, da-dum!

RUBEN

he has radiation treatment at the same time as Andreas, in 2008, when Andreas Ban is thinking mostly about his breast and has no idea that Ruben is ill, because there is no chance of meeting him anywhere, around the hospital, in the street at least, because their streets diverge along distant meridians, there is no possibility of asking anyone, *What's up with Ruben, where's Ruben?* There are no friends to tell Andreas, *Ruben's ill*, out of that group of school-mates, no one visits this country, and it is only three years later, in 2011, that Andreas discovers that Ruben is no more. Ruben Han, a world expert in nuclear medicine, he dealt mainly with the pre-vention of disorders caused by iodine deficiency, so when Cher-nobyl happened, Andreas brought four-year-old Leo to him with the question, *How can we protect him?* Chernobyl is still emitting and Leo is little, really close to the earth, in Pazin they pick dan-delions in the park and Ban smiles, *Shall I make you a wreath like a king?* he gathers dandelions and breathes in particles that tremble invisibly on the tiny flower suns, and he says, *Look, little broken suns have fallen onto the park.*

KLAJA

from Rovinj he returns to Amsterdam and leaves his glasses on Andreas's table.

MARKO

and his aunt are killed in Srebrenica. Marko sells hot dogs from a cart on the streets of Toronto because he has no one to whom he can offer his skills in applied linguistics, in psycholinguistics, so he brings hot dogs, together with small bags of fine oriental teas, to him, Andreas Ban, who is displaced in Toronto too. The Bos-nian refugee Marko leaves Canada because selling hot dogs pre-vents him from completing his doctorate. He goes to Budapest, where he works as an editor, then returns to Belgrade and dies aged thirty-five. Not from drugs, which he had given up, but from kidney failure. In his computer, Andreas Ban keeps his, Marko's, published and unpublished works.

He is still alive, Andreas Ban.

The night before the operation, Andreas Ban calls Leo in Zürich. Leo lets out a bloodcurdling cry and arrives early the following morning.

That night Andreas Ban is visited by miniature people resembling statues, small people in various poses, sitting, lying, running, with legs outspread, with open arms, kneeling, jumping, crawling, each person wrapped in a tiny cellophane packet tied at the top with a red ribbon. Like children's gifts, lead figurines fall from above interminably, burying Andreas Ban.

God, where can I go, he asks, *I'll suffocate*, he says.

All the patients for the next day's operations have been admitted and registered, then distributed around the wards. That takes five to six hours. It's a sunny April day. Early afternoon. The doctors leave, the nurses walk around, some are medical nuns, they skate and float. The majority of the patients jump into their pajamas, put on clean socks, all the women wear white socks, they drag their slippered feet around, some cruise the corridors mindlessly, some lie down, stiffen and gaze straight ahead, exhausted. The women wear new housecoats in pastel shades, long, made of velour or terry cloth, they roam around. It looks frightening. Andreas Ban puts on a tracksuit and goes into the hospital garden. There he walks and smokes.

One of the women is about to have both breasts removed. *They're cutting both of mine off*, she says, looking out of the hall window. She is calm. There are ten men in Andreas's ward. All cancer. Testes, prostate, throat, lung—that man can hardly breathe, he keeps coughing, hacking. *You can get medication to stop smoking,*

Bruno writes to Andreas from Budapest, *it's not based on nicotine*, he writes, *I tried it and for me it worked, only I started smoking again. The medication is very expensive, but it's worth trying*, writes Bruno from Budapest. *It's called Champix*. Should he tell the man who's coughing? The one who will have half his lung cut out tomorrow? Four years later, still smoking, Andreas Ban reads that Champix has been withdrawn from sale because it has serious side effects: anxiety, depression, suicide.

Viktor comes, he brings cakes. Andreas and Viktor eat cakes with their fingers in the hospital garden, chocolate cakes, with cream. They break out of the hospital complex and go to a nearby café. There they sit and talk about nothing in particular, as though nothing was happening. Viktor has seven and a half acres of lavender, at thirty-six hundred feet above sea level. *I've been harvesting*, he says, *we made bouquets and sold them*. Viktor had also planted rosemary and thyme, ginger and chives and Italian basil. Viktor likes gardening, he had tired himself singing, his voice had given out. Viktor and Andreas know each other from their past life. They left Belgrade at roughly the same time, twenty years earlier. Viktor is now the closest friend Andreas has in the little town. Viktor did not get by. The opera theater is small, they did not need his singing, his singing stood out, Viktor's singing was first class, world class, so Viktor performed as a guest artist in Vienna, a bit in Venice and Trieste, a bit in Berlin. Then he gave up, age and weariness got into his vocal chords, dripped into his lungs, constricted his windpipe. So Viktor starts breeding pedigree dogs, but that fails. Now he lives in a village in Istria, checks on his olive trees and plants potatoes. He looks well. He has pink cheeks and cracked hands.

When Andreas Ban returns to his ward, everyone is already asleep. Some have taken out their teeth and their mouths are puckered like an asshole, while others gape like corpses. One man is sleeping with a thick black wig on that has slipped to one side and covers half his face. He had been given a course of chemotherapy to reduce the size of his tumor, then they decided to operate. Another has been waiting for his operation for two weeks now, guarding his bed. His badly washed socks and a small yellow towel are steaming on the radiator. On all the bedside cabinets stand bottles of beet and carrot juice. Oncological patients believe that beet and carrot juice can save them. And soy. As well as green and red vegetables. So they pour those juices down their throats and stuff themselves with broccoli and tomatoes. They also believe, and the sicker they are, the more fanatically, that white foods are poisonous, very harmful, so they don't consume them, they don't consume sugar, flour, sweets, milk or soft cheese and then they calm down, they believe they are, sort of, saved.

What keeps my mother going most is praying to the Holy Virgin in our little village chapel, the man in the drugstore says after blowing four hundred euros on all kinds of shiitake, maitake and reishi in various aggregate states, on powders, tablets, Beta-Glucan, Bio Bran and spirulina and an extract of goat's milk. He, Andreas Ban, only takes vitamin tablets, vitamins are antioxidants, C, A, E and selenium, to counteract the impurities that attack him.

So Andreas Ban goes into his hospital ward. The sleepers, to a man, look old and worn, shabby. In the weak fluorescent light coming from the hallway, they look like huge dummies, *des poupées gargantuesques*, giant puppets, marionettes, limp rag dolls—bluish rigid corpses in a storeroom of lifeless, rejected figures—mannequins.

Andreas Ban cannot lie down, he does not want to become an exhibit in that grotesque display of rejected human flesh. So, like a visitor to some long-ago exhibition of degenerate art, he sets off to peer into the wards. Everywhere he finds immobile figures in clean striped pajamas, figures on which a procedure had already been carried out or was about to be. Processed bodies, deadened. Manipulated bodies, some visibly, others invisibly deformed, completely surreal, or perhaps that's only how it seems to him, Andreas Ban. Perhaps those flickering images are little fata morganas, *You have a vivid imagination*, the doctors tell him when he describes his vision of his damaged internal organs. Ward after ward, it is as though he is looking at the injured on a battlefield, mutilated, crippled, as though he is in a concentration camp where every incarcerated being that by faith, ideas or blood does not conform to the mystical German (or Croatian) spirit, rural, moral and ennobled by ancient wisdom, is sadistically mutilated. Are these people of weakened, damaged egos, who seek salvation in the reconstruction of their bodies, like those who expose themselves to plastic surgery, to implants, or are they simply the victims of an aggressive notion of the purity of the race? No matter. That hospital routine of sleep at nine, lights out, of forced waking at six, the patients' acceptance of obedience, collective bathrooms with a rotten, damp wooden grid under the shower and chipped ceramic tiles, the lack of toilet paper, the severity of the hospital staff, the commanding tone, especially from the nurses, the order, all this oppresses Andreas Ban before the next day's operation and he is vaguely aware of the sanctions of the powerful over even the slightest creative, rebellious chaos, and says, *I'm trapped.*

Andreas Ban walks through the hospital hallways, surrounded by captive, dysfunctional, mutilated humanoids. The healthy are outside, although their bodies are merely a shield, a prosthesis for supporting distorted images of their own organism, of the damaged, rickety construction of their ego. And so, after the operation, Andreas Ban obsessively observes pedestrians, the audience at meetings, performances, matches, parades, and endeavors to grasp how many of them are carrying lethal cells, small or large tumors with numerous visible or invisible branches, without any inkling; who are the marked people walking around, eating, sleeping, crying, kissing and fighting in the company of living cells clustered in little balls that glide through their bloodstreams or sway in their brains, in their lungs, in their livers, in their testes, ovaries, bones, in their pancreases, while they know it, while they do not know it.

However, the people outside, the ones with healthy young bodies, unmarked, have no time, have no cause to long for bodily contact, because they are integrated, because their lives flow, they do not pause, they do not stop. While a sick body is condemned to suffer to its corporeal limits, violence upon violence. A clean body as opposed to a rejected body. What are the limits of a person's control over his own sick corpus? The oncologists decide on chemotherapy for Andreas Ban, in the best case just radiation, they will prescribe antihormone medication, recommend regular ultrasound monitoring of the organs which could be reached by metastases, at first three-monthly then six-monthly blood tests and analysis of blood markers, an army of strangers will crowd around him, fiddling with his organs, his erythrocytes and leukocytes, peering at his liver, listening to his breathing, touching him, palpating him here and there, in his groin, and mostly near his collarbone to see whether any kind of tumor has appeared on his lungs, which he, Andreas Ban, would find particularly annoying, because there, near her collarbone, his mother had felt a growth and said, *You see, these are metastases on the lungs*, so now whenever doctors' fingers approach his neck, Andreas Ban says, *Don't, I check myself.*

What is left for him? He will after all form an alliance with the doctors, cooperate with machines, with that Oncor and Mevatron, he will hand his body over to others, share its functions with others, entirely rationally, entirely in the spirit of Western civilization which treasures control. He will pack away his emotions, because emotions blur the vision, fog the perception, he is fed up with emotions in everyday life, he is fed up with sentiment in literature, in film, in empty logorrheic speech, he is sick of the diluted weepiness that threatens to drown the brain in formaldehyde, he has had enough of life as advertised.

Andreas looks at the pile of sleeping bodies and sees undressed, lifeless dolls. And in the morning, when he wakes up, when they are shaken awake to start moving around, they will go on being just that, dysfunctional machines constructed of mechanical, poorly wired moving parts.

So he says, disgusted,

Ça me fait pisser.

Since she was eight years old, Andreas Ban's mother had borne a huge scar on the calf of her left leg, brownish skin with no pigmentation. Andreas's mother Marisa acquired that large burn trying to save a favorite doll that had caught fire, the rag doll had human hair which her father, Andreas Ban's grandfather, arranged on its head, the grandfather Andreas Ban had never met because this grandfather of his, otherwise a wigmaker with a leather-bound collection of Goethe and Schiller in the original, was from 1923 until his death a member of the Austrian Communist Party and because he died in Zagreb in 1943. Afterward, Andreas's mother was put into a plaster trough because of the burn and broken bones and lay there, rigid and misshapen, with twisted, turned-out extremities like a Bellmer *Puppe*, immobilized for six months.

In ward 42 one man's arm has slipped off the bed and is hanging to the floor, one of his legs is in a cast, hooked up to a small swing installed at the foot of the bed. In the corridor, on a white bench, propped up with pillows, the woman who will have both breasts cut off has nestled down and does not stir. She looks like an art installation. Andreas Ban touches her shoulder to see whether she's alive. *I can't sleep*, the lady says, *all the women in the ward are snoring*. In the ward where the women are snoring, one is sleeping naked but she is not naked, she is swathed in bandages, mostly around her belly, they must have dug, chopped, rummaged, removed something down there, her breasts flattened so she appears to have none. Another is breathing deeply and clicking her dentures which she has forgotten to put into a glass, tkk—pause, tkk, pause, tkk, tkk. In ward 39, a man has a tube attached to his penis that connects to a plastic bottle at the edge of the bed, the bottle is half-full of brown liquid. In the same ward another man has tubes sticking out of his nose, and tubes attached to his veins into which some solution is dripping from a bottle on a stand. In the women's ward at the other end of the corridor, one woman has her head in bandages, stained with congealed blood, maybe they have been rooting around in her brain and when she wakes up she will no longer be herself; another has her chest bandaged to her waist, on her left side a swelling can be made out, her right side is flat, they've probably chopped off her right breast, *people don't die that quickly*, Dr. Toffetti had said, *There are women who won't go under the knife and drag their breast tumor around for ten years until the breast rots and falls off on its own*. No one is awake. Or they are pretending to be asleep. But in ward 47, Andreas Ban finds one man who is not asleep. *I've shat myself*, he says. *Call a nurse*. The corridors are filled with wheelchairs. Andreas Ban imagines how crowded it will be in the morning when invalids, cripples, set off for walks, milling cheerfully around.

Dolls, Andreas's obsession, Andreas's weakness and longing. He buys a rag doll for two-year-old Leo and draws a fat red heart on its chest. Now, twenty-eight years later, Leo's doll is torn at the seams, but the heart is still there. All the dolls he comes across, in life and beyond, mirror old stories, Andreas Ban knows that, stories of sexuality and birth, of patriarchy, tales of men and women, hidden tales, buried and uncovered, sometimes dangerous, fascist, cruel and incomprehensible tales. But he cannot think about that now, before the operation, although all kinds of images dart before his eyes, in the sterile, clinical semidarkness. Was it Adorno or Horkheimer who wrote that Nazis see the body as a moving articulated mechanism, a skeleton covered in flesh. Like armor. That Nazis extol the body above all else, the splendid superhuman male muscular body in movement, oiled for the photograph, and the supple female body leaping, also naked. And he says, Adorno or Horkheimer, or both, that these godlike gymnasts are inclined to kill, just as lovers of nature are often hunters. That fascist sculpted body (fitness clubs, gyms) makes the other body, the body of the *other*, weak, ugly, decadent, undesirable. The "potent" body is a defense against everything fragmentary, noncompact, fluid and elusive, so, because it is powerful, the protected body annihilates, alienates and destroys everything that is broken.

Oh, from the beginning of the twentieth century right up to the present day, deviant artists have been carrying out all kinds of experiments on mannequins, to the irritation of ideologues and the propagandists of the Aryan body and spirit. There are bald dolls, dolls wearing thick nylon wigs; headless dolls, whose skulls roll at their feet; dolls covered with lettuce leaves over which crawl three hundred edible Burgundy snails, those *bisexual gastropods* which are capable of crossing a razor blade unharmed; mannequins with dislocated limbs, with glass eyes or with no eyes at all, with a penis instead of a nose, a vagina instead of a mouth, with protective goggles on the snout of a shark; hermaphrodite mannequins with the torso of a woman and the head of a man with a bearded face, like Dali's "sexy lady" Christopher Columbus on which is written *I'll be back*. That "I'll be back" will echo through the twentieth and twenty-first centuries ominously, not reaching deaf ears, reverberating unheard. There are hybrid mannequins, Siamese twins joined with horror; monstrously dressed or half-naked little girls in provocative poses with innocent white socks and patent leather shoes on their feet; there are soldiers, war cripples (*Kriegskrüppel*); female mannequins with a blindfold over their eyes, lacking one or both arms, with several limbs or without any, some with two torsos, with two pelvises and four breasts, dressed in men's jackets, wearing men's shoes; women with little green lobsters scattered over their naked bodies; women with mustaches, *les mannequins moustachés*, wrapped in wire (behind the wire); and ones that shed crystal tears; there are *hidden dolls*, covered in transparent, ethereal veils, and Masson's beautiful doll, one of Andreas's favorites, its head stuck in a wooden birdcage, with a band over its mouth from which a pansy hangs, silent, silenced, in a cage, with a narrow red ribbon concealing its sex and with little stuffed birds in its armpit.

All these dolls, all these mannequins can be dismembered, parts of their bodies moved around, swapped over, discarded or multiplied, so that it is no longer clear whether they are male or female dolls or at the same time both male and female dolls, like some people. Ah, all those "real" dolls under the noses of the blind, so different from today's living (Nazi) dolls which propagate the Aryan norm, that magnificent, dangerous kitsch. A whole disturbing, warning world of phantoms, object-beings that come to life, that caution, and to which, Andreas Ban senses, he himself belongs, deformed, dislocated, with his arm in plaster, his hand twisted, his spine crooked, with damaged lungs and myopic eyes, lame, and soon with a torn-up breast. A well-known mannequin, a phantom with no voice, no eyes and no face sometimes visits Andreas Ban, both in his sleep and when he's awake, and it is with him now, gliding behind him along the hospital corridors, and Andreas Ban says, *Maybe that's me, a total mess, ever closer to death.*

Yes, Andreas Ban, in fragments, in rags with which he is trying to cobble together a whole.

Then, those books of his, Andreas's, in which he endeavors somehow, perhaps feebly, with firm, black ribbons, to tie the idea of blood and soil to the present day, as if to tighten a terrifying corset in which it is hard to breathe, those books of his have begun to annoy their readers. But this too is one of Andreas Ban's diseases which he does not know how to cure, because the attacks, although they come in waves, do not wane, after a brief remission, the symptoms return and Andreas's immunity weakens. People write to him, people, uninvited, with no provocation, tell him their old yellowed stories, in case he (oh, the irony), the psychologist Andreas Ban, might show them a little passageway to tranquility.

Andreas Ban looks at what he has packed and is surprised: people usually buy new things for a hospital stay, new socks, new pajamas, new dressing gowns, new toothbrushes, new underwear, new soap, new slippers, as though intending to display their tidiness, their orderliness, the order that reigns in their disordered, disintegrating bodies, as though they will emerge from the hospital reborn, remade, repaired, new. Andreas brings everything old, flawed; a washed-out tracksuit with its right pocket coming off and legs covered in cigarette burns, Leo's alarm clock with no hands, a clock with its numbers rubbed off on which time stands still, on which there is no time. He brings thin slabs of black chocolate with 80 percent cocoa, he brings Marina Tsvetaeva (in English) and a few pieces of music which make him feel stylish. He then arranges all those elusive scraps of desiccated dreams, illusions of polish and the sublime on the cabinet beside his bed.

Not long ago Andreas Ban read a manifesto by the master of street graffiti, the subversive *enfant terrible* of the contemporary art world, the puzzling Banksy enamored of rats of which he says,

They are everywhere, they attack from all sides, the lowest levels have them, the highest levels have them, Banksy whom the obedient and correct, the categorized and sterilized Aryanized robots call a dangerous antisocial vandal. In that manifesto Banksy quotes a section from the diary of Lieutenant Colonel Mervin Willett Gonin who was, in 1945, among the first British soldiers to liberate Bergen-Belsen:

Corpses lay everywhere, some in huge piles, sometimes they lay singly or in pairs where they had fallen.

It took a little time to get used to seeing men women and children collapse as you walked by them and to restrain oneself from going to their assistance. Early on, one had to get used to the idea that the individual did not count. One knew that five hundred a day were dying and that five hundred a day went on dying for weeks before anything we did would have the slightest effect. It was, however, not easy to watch a child choking to death from diphtheria when you knew a tracheotomy and nursing would save it, one saw women drowning in their own vomit because they were too weak to turn over, and men eating worms as they clutched a half loaf of bread purely because they had to eat worms to live and now could scarcely tell the difference.

Piles of corpses, naked and obscene, with a woman too weak to stand propping herself against them as she cooked the food we had given her over an open fire; men and women crouching down just anywhere in the open relieving themselves of the dysentery which was scouring their bowels, a woman standing stark naked washing herself with some issue soap in water from a tank in which the remains of a child floated.

It was shortly after the British Red Cross arrived, though there may be no connection, that a very large quantity of lipstick arrived. This was not at all what we men wanted, we were screaming for hundreds and thousands of other things and I don't know who asked for lipstick. I wish I could discover who did it, it was an act of genius, sheer un-

adulterated brilliance. I believe nothing did more for these internees than the lipstick. Women lay in bed with no sheets and no nightie but with scarlet red lips, you saw them wandering about with nothing but a blanket over their shoulders, but with scarlet red lips. I saw a woman dead on the postmortem table and clutched in her hand was a piece of lipstick. At last someone had done something to make them individuals again, they were someone, no longer merely the number tattooed on their arm. At last they could take an interest in their appearance. That lipstick started to give them back their humanity.

It is late. A nurse appears and says to Andreas Ban, *Go at once and take a shower, put on your pajamas and get into bed.* Andreas Ban says, *No. Tomorrow. I'll do all that tomorrow.* Standing in the corridor, Andreas Ban eats a cold chicken leg that was brought that morning, for lunch. The nurse gives him a suppository, *Put this in to clean out your bowels,* she says. It is not clear to him why he should clean out his bowels, his digestion is in order, and the bowels are a long way from his armpit and breast, the surgeons will not go anywhere near his bowels. He puts in the little suppository and it rips his guts. Till they bleed.

A BEDTIME STORY—*Bambole senza guerre*

Once upon a time, in the kingdom of Italy, there lived a man by the name of Peppino Russo. When war broke out, Peppino Russo joined the Resistance Movement and set out, gun in hand, to fight the Fascists and Nazis who were oppressing his people and his homeland. One night, with a group of his co-fighters, Partisans, Peppino Russo arrived in a small mountain village after a terrible massacre carried out by enemy troops that slaughtered all its inhabitants and burned down their houses. But in a hollow full of corpses, Peppino Russo caught sight of a little girl whose wide-open eyes

151

showed signs of life. He took the little girl in his arms, carried her to his home and looked after her. When the child grew up, she and Peppino Russo became man and wife. The years passed. One New Year's night, as was the custom, on a square in Rome people burned old, worn-out, no longer usable objects. Among the rubbish Peppino Russo caught sight of a doll with wide-open eyes. It reminded him of the little girl he found in the hollow, among the corpses in the burned-out mountain village. Peppino Russo pulled the doll from the flames, returned to his little town and hung the doll on the fence in front of his house. Then something in him clicked. Peppino Russo set off in search of broken dolls, first in Rome, then throughout the whole of Italy. Many years later, in the foothills of Monte Maria, the highest hill in the environs of Rome, a field of two and a half acres stretched out, covered with more than a hundred thousand damaged dolls. In 1983, traveling through Italy, the Russian photographer and director Valeriy Sirovsky, coming across Pep-

pino's graveyard of discarded dolls, spent two days photographing it, taking more than seven hundred photos which he later exhibited in Moscow. It was a very moving exhibition. At the exhibition, one visitor declared, *The hecatombs of deformed dolls—with no eyes, with no arms or legs—are horribly reminiscent of photographs from the Second World War and the concentration camps.* And Rilke said, *Inside, a doll is empty, it emits a chilling silence.*

Peppino Russo died at the beginning of the 1990s. His wife sold the land and a bulldozer obliterated the collection. And Valeriy Sirovsky's assemblage of photographs also ceased to exist long ago.

*

When Andreas Ban was living for a short time in Zagreb in the mid-1950s, at his grandmother's house, 24 Medvedgradska, the street was dilapidated and impoverished. Small one-story houses without plumbing, with taps in muddy courtyards and little craftsmen's workshops, strung in a gray, *sfumato*, on the edge of the town center. At number 24 there also lived disheveled, crazy Klementina, her feet wrapped in dirty rags, who shouted from the balcony to passersby, *Fuck me, fuck me, now!* In her arms, crazy Klementina rocked a large rag doll, flecked with spit from Klementina's drooling kisses and the food she fed it in little spoons, while the rag doll's arms and legs swung limply to and fro as if doubly dead.

With Hans, who lived opposite the building at 24 Medvedgradska, right beside the cramped, dark shed used by the cobbler Lojzek, it was said he was the illegitimate son of some SS officer who roamed Zagreb in the NDH days, Andreas Ban made catapults and shot at people and birds. At number 24, on the floor below Andreas's grandmother, there were Mrs. Koch with her fair-haired blue-eyed daughter Anneke, also named Koch. Before the end of the war, the low-ranking SS officer Otto Koch abandoned Mrs. Marija Koch, leaving her his surname and his child, for ever. In 1943, this same Otto Koch informed on Andreas Ban's mother, then a medical student, to the Ustasha Intelligence Office, so, instead of joining the Partisans, Andreas Ban's mother ended up in prison. After the war, Andreas's mother avoided Mrs. Koch, while Anneke was involved in casual prostitution, which everyone in the street knew about. When Andreas Ban (with his sisters) was living briefly with his grandmother, no cars passed along Medvedgradska, but carts with tall milk churns clinking on them. One day Hans hit the horse with his catapult, the horse reared and its hoof hit ten-year-old Petar, who was kicking a ball in the empty street, right on the forehead. Petar fell, never to get up again. The whole street was beside itself, because Medvedgradska was a family street, fairly compact. In the attic of number 24 lived Ante, a train dispatcher who mended clocks. In the courtyard of the building numbered 24, Andreas Ban's sisters put on puppet shows. The puppets would fall and lose parts of their bodies. The doll maker Albert also lived in the street, also in a shack, and Andreas's sisters would take their maimed puppets to him to be mended. The doll maker Albert's street window was full of deformed, not yet mended or unmendable dolls. That window was spooky.

Inside the doll maker's workshop it was even more terrible. *I am a doll doctor, my clinic has to look like this*, said Albert to the horrified Andreas Ban. Glass eyes of various colors, green, blue, brown, with eyelashes and without, rolled around everywhere. Scattered, over shelves, tables, even on the floor, were plump little porcelain or stuffed arms and legs, and also rubber ones. There were all sorts of heads everywhere, broken, with holes in their napes, some with both eyes, others with only one, some with none. *These are my surgical instruments, I use them to cure my little patients*, said Albert, a little bent, in his white coat. At one time, Andreas Ban used to visit "Dr. Albert" nearly every day, overcoming his fear. *I've seen all kinds of things*, said Albert. *I've brought more than ten thousand dolls back to life*, he said. Albert the doll maker also made little shoes for his patients, little leather shoes, with proper buckles. And he planted real hair in his dolls' heads, blond, brown or black, curly or straight. Even then, in the 1950s, Albert was quite old. Today, where his shack used to be, there is a modern five-story building with a pink facade.

Many years later, in Vienna, Andreas Ban meets the doll maker Arnold Meyer, a former guard at Mauthausen concentration camp. Arnold Meyer had an impressive collection of miniature curly wigs made from real hair the color of honey, and in the glass-fronted cupboards with hundreds of little drawers that lined the walls of his workshop, were various colored plastic and glass eyes, paired and separated. Mengele had a collection of glass eyes too.

Arnold Meyer recalled a secret order from August 1942, requiring that all the hair cut off the camp inmates be sent to Alex Zink in Nuremberg or to the Paul Reimann company in Friedland. Both firms paid half a mark for a kilo of human hair.

If he's prescribed chemotherapy, he'll go bald. He won't buy a wig. A tiny fear wrapped in feathers rolls along the hospital corridor. Old Bette Davis gropes her way toward Andreas Ban. *Fasten your seat belts*, she says, *it's going to be a bumpy night.*

It is the 1970s. In New Belgrade, on the sixth floor of one of the "Six Corporals" as you see them from the bridge, a retired Yugoslav Army officer sells processed aloe vera in green Fruška Gora Riesling bottles, with the labels still on; there is great demand, but also great mortality. The thick gray liquid is meant to be rubbed onto radiation burns, nowadays one does not hear about such terrible burns, oncology has become more decent. Andreas's mother's skin is falling off in tatters. They rub her. The officer calls his liquid "balm." They rub his mother with balm. Andreas also makes a tincture of aloe vera for drinking. He goes with his sister to Kisvárda, a village on the Hungarian–Russian border where in winter tears freeze. Their mother is young. In the train the conductresses are Russian, in blue homespun uniforms, all of them with swollen knees in short skirts. The uniforms have gold buttons, like the uniforms of captains on long-haul ships. The conductresses are Russian because the train continues on to Moscow, it only passes through Kisvárda. The conductresses sell weak Russian tea in glasses, hot, and do not sleep at all. Kisvárda is a village like those in the Banat region. It has an inn and good goulash. It has frozen mud. In Kisvárda Dr. Baross sells anticancer drops in a little room with a low ceiling. The little room is suffocating in carpets and rugs, they line the floor and the walls and are thrown over the armchairs, because the armchairs are threadbare. There is also a microscope, out of date. One enters the room through the kitchen in which the doctor's wife sits in a blue fustian housecoat; the doctor's wife sits at a wooden table, in a vase on the table there are stiff plastic snowdrops. In the kitchen there is a cabinet, reseda-green, glass-fronted, with upside-down coffee cups on which pale women in crinolines float. People come in droves, people arrive from all of Yugoslavia, because this is Yugoslavia's day, other countries have *their* days. Tito is still alive, their mother dies before Tito. The doctor's drops do not help.

They try everything.

Including Paris.

In Paris Andreas sleeps with the tramps, the sky is clear, Parisian-blue and it is winter again. Their mother bleeds. The blood soaks through the mattress and drips onto the polished floor of the Institut d'Oncologie, in the complex of the Paris Faculté de Médecine, or perhaps it does not happen in the complex of the Paris Faculté de Médecine at all, although there are indications that this is precisely where Andreas Ban's mother lies as they try out various new medicines on her, they carry out trials. His mother—a submissive, half-dead guinea pig, still beautiful—*We are experimenting,* they say, *we have nothing to lose.* Maybe Andreas's mother is falling apart and bleeding in the military hospital Val de Grâce, although he does not know why his mother would be lying in the military hospital Val de Grâce since their family has never had anything to do with the army, and particularly the French army, for a long time, for generations, their family has been an ordinary civilian, urban family. Perhaps Andreas's mother is lying, and draining away, in the Hôpital Cochin. There is also the

Hôpital Laennec, they tell him, near the Panthéon, and Maternité Port Royal, he does not remember, he only remembers the Panthéon because that is where Voltaire and Hugo and Zola lie, and the spry Jean Jaurès and the tame Rousseau who all mean nothing to him, unlike his mother, absolutely nothing, and without them his life is entirely possible. In Paris Andreas Ban sees Bergman's "The Serpent's Egg" and in the stuffy apartment belonging to the gallery owner and antiquarian Bojon, he eats steak tartare with Ema's brother out of a soup plate, with a spoon. Ema's brother is called Jean, he was once called Jovan, his wife also dies of cancer, many years later. In Paris, at the open market he buys *crêpes*, a circus troupe dances, the sky is frighteningly blue. It is the 1970s.

When she bleeds, Andreas's mother's mucous membranes fall off, from inside she is peeling in layers, disappearing. Andreas buys her shoes, but she can no longer walk. The shoes are burgundy. Later, he gives the shoes to Katja Romany who also dies, but of a heart attack. The stockings are burgundy as well. Those he does not give away. There were a lot of moves, international and transatlantic. The stockings wait a long time, then Andreas's sister takes them. Thirty-five years have passed. That sister died as well. With Elvira there was no time for surprises or anger, for journeys, for examinations and small lies. Elvira was a shock. Elvira melted within three months. She just vanished.

Andreas fell asleep in his tracksuit.

he is in a long black limousine. he's at the wheel, his mother is sitting beside him. they drive along narrow dark streets and he realizes that he can't go any further. he wants to go back, he turns his head to look, the street has closed into a cleft so narrow a person couldn't pass, let alone a car. his mother says, the road has disappeared, there's no way back, let's keep going, a broad street opens up in front of them, quiet and filled with sunlight.

The next day, he takes a shower and shaves both armpits. In the misted mirror he looks at his torso. He raises his shoulders, he inhales. He touches both breasts. His gaze falls to his belly and he shudders. *My belly button's gone*, he says. Then he puts on his pajamas. They do not take him to the operating theater until the afternoon. They keep saying, you're next, you're next, he is the last on the list, he is thirsty and hungry, he wets his lips, *nothing to eat, nothing to drink, be patient, keep still, wait*, they instruct him. He roams around the corridor and secretly smokes out a window. Three men are brought back to his ward, operated on, unconscious. Cut to ribbons.

The room outside the operating theater is sterile and full of mobile stretchers. This is where Andreas Ban is prepped, they look for veins in his legs, prick him to take blood, prick and try again, it does not work, they break the cast on his forearm and finally succeed. He says nothing and watches the preparations for a brief death. Beside him lies a sturdy young man with piercings on his face and tattoos on his upper arms and chest, blue crosses pressed into his skin gleam with sweat that runs down his fingers, making little puddles on the stone floor. The young man is beside himself, his eyes wide open, he is trembling, big as he is. The nurse says to the young man, *Relax, your veins are tight, we can't inject you.* Andreas feels like singing, but he does not sing well. The nurse orders him, *Take out your dentures.* This annoys him, he is ready to quarrel. They are his teeth, white and healthy, with no crowns, despite his smoking. These teeth are an important trump card for Andreas in the poverty that besets him. He watches, he listens to people forever commenting on his teeth, attacking his teeth, irritating him. When Andreas Ban begins to lose his teeth, people around him will calm down, the last trace of his stylishness, his otherness, his not-belonging will disappear, he will become one of them, and they will think, now you are nondescript, we love you. And so, when he finds himself out there, Andreas Ban looks attentively at other people's mouths, he sees hundreds of dentures clicking, growling, gleaming, some dentures are expensive, some are not, all produce stiff smiles, frightening and cold, which make Andreas nervous.

After the operation they take him back to the ward, he wakes at once, with a clear head. Dr. Toffetti says, *It's good, the sentinel is clean, the lymph nodes have not been affected.* They put lovely long white stockings on Andreas Ban's legs that make his thighs look younger; the stockings reach from his feet to his groin. Andreas admires his legs, now firm and strong as they once were. He feels like strolling through the town in these white elastic mesh stockings for ever. The next day they take them off, his skin and flaccid muscles droop, falling flat on the bed. After the operation, Leo sits next to him watching the intravenous fluid drip. *I'll speed up the drip*, says Andreas Ban, *so that I can eat, I'm hungry.* From a nearby restaurant Leo brings *pasta verde con frutti di mare*. Andreas likes that. They eat together. In the hallway. And drink red wine. The nurse says, *What are you doing, you can't do that!* Andreas asks, *Why?* She says, *Because.* Andreas goes onto the balcony with Leo, he takes two drags on a cigarette. *It's no good*, he says, *I'll keel over.* The next day Andreas's sister comes. She brings him *pasta verde con frutti di mare*.

There is euphoria in the ward. All the patients have had their operations and are shameless. They compare their bellies and penises, they fart. Priests come to offer solace. Andreas Ban turns his back on them. Some women come from the "Hope" society and offer psychological support. Andreas Ban does not need psychological support, he needs his breast. Physiotherapists demonstrate exercises to stop their arms from swelling. Andreas Ban wants to go home.

It turned out more or less OK. According to the histopathology results, there is no calcification, the edges are clean. There is no need for chemotherapy, just radiation.

A week later Andreas Ban is back at work. It is summer. The appointments for radiation therapy are all booked up. He'll have to wait a month. The temperature rises to forty degrees Celsius. Gershwin's "Summertime," "I Got Plenty o' Nuttin'" and "It Ain't Necessarily So" alternate in Andreas Ban's head, like a broken record. Andreas sings to himself, silently. As he walks. Gershwin drives him crazy. Gershwin, in fact Jacob Gershowitz, born into a Russian-Jewish family, dies of a brain tumor. He complains of unbearable headaches and is pursued by the smell of burnt rubber. He dies suddenly because the tumor spreads quickly and he keeps blacking out, he becomes lost. Until he disappears. In the thirty-ninth year of his life.

When he is not working, Andreas Ban goes for walks. He still goes out and walks. He still has moments of liveliness although other walkers often irritate him. They walk slowly, they take up the whole sidewalk, so he cannot pass, and he shouts, *pardon*, and the walkers snort. When they come toward him they block his way, they want stubbornly to pass him on the right, but one should pass on the left, so he does not let them, so they aim at each another on the sidewalk, or he stops, stiffens, and lets them attack.

He is still drawing his salary.

He waits.

And waits.

One night from his window he sees an old man picking his way with small steps along the sidewalk. The street is deserted and the old man is talking to himself. Maybe he, Andreas Ban, is that old man.

On him, on his chest, they have to radiate, they draw with a dark-red felt-tip, from his neck to his waist, he is marked. He must not wash that part of his torso because the lines would come off. The heat is terrible, the color melts with his sweat, around his (nonexistent) breast there are smudges. The nurses and doctors frown, they raise their voices, press their lips together, grind their teeth, their jaws dance, they have to do the measurements again, they have to draw the lines again, he has to go back to the simulator, which is fully booked, there are more and more patients, there is an epidemic of carcinomas, they say. In other countries, they make shallow tattoos so the lines do not rub off, so the patients can wash. Andreas Ban buys liquid henna in a small tube and draws the lines himself. No one notices anything. At last he can have a shower.

There is no radiation on weekends. They prescribe him thirty-three sessions. Thirty-three sessions last seventy-five days because the equipment breaks down. He is on his summer holiday and he is still undergoing radiation. He spends the weekends in Viktor's little Rovinj apartment, near their former house. When this new war broke out, Andreas and his father sold the stone family house for peanuts to some nice Italians from Bologna who now sit in the summer on "his" terrace, with a view of the bay. Andreas's sister was left with the basement of the house, a room dug in under the earth level through which underground waters roar and moisten the walls, a room with a door into a little garden, overgrown with bushes and enclosed by a crumbling wall. Andreas's sister is a biologist. Her name is Ada, in the family she was called Bubi. Bubi is close to Andreas. She hopped into his life from time to time, she was like a little mother to Leo. That is not important now. Ada is drawing her pension as well, she is on her own as well, her daughter has gone. As soon as she enters retirement, Ada exits her life. In Belgrade, Ada works for the pharmaceutical company Galenika, she studies the effects of estrogen on spatial learning and neuron morphology of the hippocampus in rats. That is her doctoral thesis. When she comes to Croatia, a bit before Andreas and Leo, there is no space for her in Croatian laboratories because she is too old, forty-seven. She teaches biology in a secondary school in a small coastal town. Now Ada lives in the Rovinj basement through which underground waters roar and moisten the walls. She wears old clothes. She is poor. She is fat, she used not to be. She eats cheaply. She has a gray streak. She has no husband, her partner died long ago. Her teeth are falling out. Recently, she had a small vacuum prosthesis fitted, which is prone to come loose when Ada laughs, she mocks her vacuum prosthesis. That is not the laughter Andreas knows. In their family kitchen, Ada and Andreas used to talk late into the night over fine cheeses and noble wines. They were looking for a way out of the trap.

He travels to and fro on buses, on Friday evenings toward Viktor, on Monday mornings to the hospital. He gets to know the drivers. He observes the passengers. Many rustle their plastic bags frantically, chew, smack their lips, click, clean their teeth, ruminate and talk loudly, drowning out the turbo folk music from the National Radio. When darkness falls, the passengers sit in the dark, the drivers do not switch on the lights above the seats. Once an old lady sits down next to him with a white beard five centimeters long. Another time, a young man with beautiful hands. His, Andreas's hands, are sort of shriveled, their backs covered in freckles. In the bus he also sees a man with very long eyelashes. Andreas's eyelashes are short and point down. Like a pig's. Andreas has pigs' eyelashes, bristles. Later, that will change. That summer, in the course of his regular comings and goings, he observes all manner of bus people. Bus people one can observe because they sit, they do not pass by: a man who twitches his head for two hours, raises and lowers his shoulders and sniffles. Andreas offers him a handkerchief and sees two shallow, dead eyes, those of a heroin or cocaine addict; a woman who during the journey lasting one and a half hours runs her hand through her hair fifty-nine times; another, fat and shabby, does not stop rocking, forward-backward-forward-backward, as though in psychosis, in some kind of serious regression that she wakes from only when the bus stops. Beside her dozes an old woman who has stepped out of a Beckett play, the one with the garbage cans. She is well turned out and eats bananas. Bananas are sticky, so the old woman smacks her lips. As she eats, she gazes steadily in front of her. As soon as she finishes a banana, her head bows and she falls into a half sleep, into a stupor. That happens five times. Until she reaches her destination, onto which, it seems to Andreas, she has no desire to step, because her legs are paralyzed, or because she no longer has any.

In Poreč, where the evening bus takes a ten-minute break before continuing its journey, an old toothless man in gray worker's trousers waits regularly, but not to meet anyone. He looks at the passengers, shakes his head and hops. Later, when Andreas Ban no longer goes to radiotherapy, when he no longer travels on weekends but spends the whole summer there, at Viktor's, the old man is not there. For years afterward, at the bus stop in Poreč, Andreas looks for the old man, in vain. Once he sees on the platform a pygmy woman, a dwarf with a large head, yellow strawlike hair, huge thick lips and short limbs scampering around the legs of her lover of normal height and build. Her head reaches his groin into which she pants shamelessly. Andreas imagines them in the spasm of love, which seems oddly pedophiliac. Then, from some lagoon in his brain onto the bus station platform surface the seven dwarfs of the Ovitz family, the seven "pets," Joseph Mengele's seven Jewish test guinea pigs and (for Andreas) their grim circus performance begins.

Andreas Ban watches the smiling, but old by now, Rozika, Francika, Avram, Frida, Miki, Elizabeta and Piroška, known as Perla, members of the Lilliput Jazz Troupe, dancing a Hungarian *csárdás*, greeting passengers and seeing them off, passengers who circumvent them, bypass them, because they neither hear nor see them, they pass *through them* while, during their ten-minute breaks (before they set off again), they run to the toilets, for a bottle of beer or a hot dog.

For a year and a half, the Angel of Death (Mengele) keeps his seven dwarfs in a human zoo and examines their insides.

*The worst were the gynecological experiments. They
would tie us to a table and the systematic torture could
begin. We got shots into our womb, they took blood from
us, samples of our flesh and fluid from our spinal cords,
they pierced and cut us, pulled out our hair, examined
our brain, our nose, our mouth, our legs and arms, they
dug around and drilled through us in the name of "future generations," in the name of living dwarfs and in
the name of those who will come. I am Elizabeta.*

*While he talked to his colleagues about our genetic de-
formities, in front of the older Nazis Mengele would
line us up as naked objects on display, then he would
gaily clap his hands and say, Come on, Lilliputians,
play and sing, and we played and sang German songs,
standing there like that, small and naked. I am Piroška,
I was the last to die.*

*I died first. The Angel of Death even made a short film
in which we acted, and sent it to Hitler as a gift. Hitler
liked watching films, entertaining himself. Miki.*

*Yes, we survived Auschwitz. Thanks to Mengele. Af-
terward we performed all over Eastern and Central
Europe and did our Totentanz for him, for our Angel
of Death. Rozika.*

*It was the worst for twins, for twin children. I don't
know whether any survived. Mengele explored their
eyes, he researched twins with different colored eyes,
particularly those with one blue and one green eye.
Mengele would first kill the little twins, then dig out
their eyes and send them to Berlin.*

*He sent them to Otmar von Vershuer and to Karin
Magnussen in the Kaiser Wilhelm Institute of Anthro-
pology, Heredity and Eugenics. Not one was taken to*

court. Mengele died on some Brazilian beach, with waves lapping at his feet. Magnussen died at eighty-nine in 1997, when of all my sisters and brothers I was the only one left. Piroška-Perla.

> *Oh, fuck off you circus performers, you dwarfs no one needs, a threat to the pure Aryan race, get lost, you dirty Gypsies, the only thing of any value were your eyes, and I was able to collect enough of them in time, I have a fine, rich collection for my research. I was the one who decided which races and people were worthy of life in the Europe of tomorrow. I was the one who worked on eliminating the Black Danger that threatened the West, I was the one who worked on stopping the Bolshevik advance in the East, I was the one who was concerned with the fundamental question of all the European states, that of the Jews. Because the Jews, who still enjoy the hospitality of Europe, are our greatest and eternal enemies. Karin Magnussen.*

The driver calls *All aboard* and the Lilliput Jazz Troupe flies to the skies, gliding over their native Transylvania back to Haifa.

That summer Andreas Ban sits under a sunshade at the swimming pool and watches water polo training and swimming training and gazes out to the open sea. With the water polo players he drinks beer, plays chess and *briscola*, in his swimming trunks. At first people stare at his scar, the breast that is not there, then they relax. Distant swimming days, his youth, hover inside him. Andreas Ban spends all his summer weekends in the shadow of his former good health. Drawn on, violet and yellow-red. The henna and felt-tip merge on his breastbone like additional scars. Andreas Ban lives in two worlds, perhaps even in three. He begins to miss waiting outside the clinic for his radiation therapy. He misses his companions in sickness, in treatment. In summer, plastic chairs are placed outside the clinic, someone brings terracotta ashtrays in the shape of a smiling sun, the patients wait, drained, bald and drawn on, smoking and exchanging life stories. Togetherness bonds them in an invisible circle of air. Sometimes one's turn comes quickly, in half an hour, in an hour, sometimes one waits from morning till noon. When the radiation is finally done, the patients do not disperse, as though they have nowhere to go, no one to go to. Most people who come from far away for radiation stay in the hospital during the week. Those who have transport or can afford to rent an apartment do not stay in the hospital, they do not walk around on the hardened, dusty earth, over dry lawns in their pajamas and old tracksuits, they do not roam around, dragging their frantic thoughts as if they were aging pets, blinking their desultory gaze into the void. By the entrance to the radiation room, there is a small dilapidated house, with beds for those who, from Monday to Friday, wait for hours for their two-minute therapy. On Friday afternoons they all disperse, there is a lot of running around after which a two-day silence thuds.

The Mevatron and Oncor machines, my companions, says Andreas Ban as he lies on the table watching the globe above him send lifesaving rays into his body, he feels like hugging them, but he isn't allowed to stir, *Don't move! Don't breathe!* so he directs tender and grateful glances first to Mevatron, then to Oncor. With their invisible tentacles, Mevatron and Oncor grasp the potential (or existing) micrometastases which are waiting for their moment, gathering strength for a leap, for an attack, and now there is no sentinel to protect Andreas Ban. Andreas Ban feels like a slug. The radiation room is empty and cold. Just the two of them, twenty-five intimate encounters with Mevatron, eight with Oncor, both working soundlessly apart from the starting and finishing clicks. Heavy, two-minute-long immobility reigns, interminable. On a shelf to his left there are four rows of white latticed masks like those used by fencers. Andreas feels as if he is being watched through each of those masks by Hannibal Lecter. They are masks for cancer of the throat, nose, forehead, mouth, Andreas concludes, the masks have their owners, on each hangs a little label, Andreas cannot see the names.

Madame Ema is always well turned out. She comes to her radiation in a pink silk suit, or a light-green casual outfit. She changes her brooch regularly. She has a neat hairstyle. She sits on a bench, leafing through women's magazines. She is very calm, sometimes excessively cheerful, then loud. Andreas does not remember what Madame Ema talked about. Andreas knows nothing about Madame Ema. He concludes that Madame Ema lives nearby, otherwise she could not change her suits and outfits, she could not be well turned out. Then one day Madame Ema comes with a turban on her head, in a dirty white terry cloth robe under which can be seen the crumpled legs of hospital pajamas, striped, prison-style. The turban is crooked, beneath it can be seen Madame Ema's bald skull. No brooch on her chest. She does not have summer sandals with straps, there is nothing delicate, feminine about Madame Ema, no rouge (from a little box) on her cheeks, the corners of her mouth, cracked and bloodless, hang, slack. Madame Ema sits on her bench, in her place (the others move out of the way), and looks at her little socks. Then she says, *I'm sick of this comedy, I'm an inpatient, I don't even go home on Fridays, I've got no one to go home to.*

This illness is deceptive. People with cancer are excessively euphoric or excessively secretive. The secretive ones monitor their bodies without showing it. Those who do not want to hear, pretend to be deaf. The most euphoric soon die. Such exalted optimism irritates Andreas.

Ivetta is in her seventies. She does not wear little suits or outfits, she is not starched like Madame Ema, who is in her sixties. Ivetta carries a refined decadence in her gait and voice, it is summer, Ivetta wears a wide checked taffeta skirt in blue-green tones, a skirt that rustles with each of Ivetta's steps, just as his, Andreas's, mother's step had sounded, just as Elvira's hair had rustled. Ivetta comes back with her PET scan, the patients in the courtyard wait expectantly in the July sun, they smoke in silence, they look at Ivetta. From the cool interior of the clinic, in her green ballet pumps, Ivetta enters a shimmering ring of heat, of invisible extinguished fire. She lowers herself onto a wobbly plastic chair against the wall and says, *Metastases all over.* The silence following her words, full of leaden weight, drags everyone down. Then Ivetta stands up, breaks off a twig of wilted rosemary covered in the dust that has invisibly fallen over everything surrounding the hospital that summer, because the street is close, and she says, *I'll make a marinade for my family.* And goes away. Each to his own ploys.

As he waits for his turn, Robert reads Virginia Woolf, *Mrs. Dalloway.* He does not converse with anyone. Andreas likes that, at least someone is reading, the others talk. *Mrs. Dalloway*, a little book about a disturbed woman from the upper middle class who experiences a moment of epiphany when she feels like killing herself, and reconsiders, because finally she finds herself. Instead, someone called Septimus kills himself, he does not find himself, on the contrary, he is completely lost, destroyed and rejected. *Mrs. Dalloway* is not exactly popular reading matter, and for oncology patients there are more cheerful books. *What do you think?* Andreas Ban asks Robert who immediately writes him a note: *I can't speak, I've got throat cancer.* After that Andreas just smiles at Robert, he imagines him lying under the Mevatron with that hanniballecterish helmet-muzzle on his head, are his days numbered?

That summer Andreas receives by mail an invitation to some

kind of healthy food promotion in a café in the railroad station. Leo says (telephonically), *Go, it might do you good.* Nothing will do him any good, he already knows all he needs to know about healthy food, about nutrition, Leo would not be so handsome and big and healthy, without a single filling ever, but all right, it's not the weekend. It is five o'clock in the afternoon, the sun is scorching, a crowd of dolled-up pensioners is pouring into the café, fresh from their afternoon siesta, pensioners begin their day early, they get their tasks, their insignificant duties done early, as though they were in a hurry, as though they were going to be late, as though they had important things to do. The women are revoltingly neatly combed and fat, in synthetic floral blouses, the men freshly shaven, sometimes with a little cut on their chin, a spot of dried blood (shaky hand), they all wear checked summer shirts, perfectly ironed, by four o'clock, perhaps three, these re-tired couples sip their thin afternoon coffee and now they set off in a cheerful mood, in expectation of a lovely outing. An occasional train goes by and toots, but rarely, for this place, like the pensioners gathered in the café, is on the edge, outside. Andreas waits for the healthy food, but the bright young demonstrator is using a transparent saucepan to prepare a small chicken for the twenty old people assembled there, a chick so small that it fits into the palm of her hand, and she reels off a memorized speech that Andreas does not understand. Then the young demonstrator adds one potato to the pot, while in a food processor she prepares an "aperitif" for the guests, one carrot, one small apple and one other thing which together barely cover the bottom of the plastic cup. This is the festive meal that the toothless pensioners knead with their gums. Andreas feels a cocktail of nausea and disgust rising within him. Then the demonstrator announces the prices of those transparent healthy saucepans, which are astronomical, especially suitable for pensioners, and then onto the stage steps the main demonstrator, a man who, in 40°C heat, advertises special bed-clothes made of pure fleece wool at a price of five thousand kunas (666 euros) for a small single-bed set. Andreas gets up, he wants to go home to down a glass of Rémy Martin, but the demonstrators protest, they shout after him, *Aren't you going to have dinner, here's a pair of complimentary slippers made of pure fleece wool, come again.*

The radiation comes to an end as well. Andreas Ban grabs a summery September fortnight for himself; he swims when there is no sun, in the early morning and late afternoon. He reads, off and on, in fact he leafs through books, browses through other people's thoughts, buries his own. On Viktor's terrace he makes light suppers for acquaintances and an occasional friend, suppers which, to Andreas's surprise, blend into tedium, because his old friends are no more, they've remained over there and are already scaled down, whether because of old age and dying, or because of never thrashed out, never clearly articulated attitudes in connec-tion with the last war, particularly in connection with Bosnia and Kosovo. At these suppers of Andreas's someone occasionally ut-ters a witticism or two, there are those who ask stupid questions, but also those who do not talk at all, who just eat, because these si-lent people at his table have their own truncated past, their youth, their memories, their experiences, impossible to share with him. So, at a dinner which lasts from nine until two in the morning, M. says, *The meat is excellent,* and an hour later adds, *This dessert is tasty.* The dessert is *crème caramel,* Andreas's specialty, which on this occasion, for the first time, collapses, falls apart when he turns it out. But then, and for a couple of years thereafter, in his little coastal town, in his Rovinj where he still feels like the old Andreas Ban, even though his home has fallen apart, even though he is fall-ing apart, in that little town he is at home, and in that little Istrian town in the summer, an occasional old, elderly metropolitan pal, a swimming chum, a cardplaying mate does nevertheless call on

Andreas, then there's a celebration, fireworks of adventures summoned up, an encyclopedia of names from their lives at nursery, primary, secondary school, university, their sporting, love, military and professional life, oh, how many shared circles in whose whirlpools they spin like terns. Then it all stops. Little doses of decency are filled to the brim, Andreas Ban relegates them to the trash basket of his diminutive Croatian life, and in the place of that past life, in his head, in his chest, a hole opens up through which a mirage, weightless as a ghost, moans. And Andreas Ban decides to pine away in silent solitude.

In the small town where he lives, during the day, and particularly at night, there are times when all the traffic lights could go out. No one passes, nothing passes. The streets roll along of their own accord. The traffic lights flicker tirelessly in a void, to themselves. For themselves. In a town for itself.

In the small town where he lives the days are sometimes composed entirely of not-having, so Andreas Ban lives a life of nonliving.

All right, sometimes he does go to a restaurant. His acquaintances persistently and thoroughly leaf through their youth. He cannot join in. Andreas Ban knows no one from their youth. He has no one from his youth, from his life in this small town. So he listens, he watches these people nevertheless remote to him clearing a path to their past, so their past swells and fills the gaps of not-having, and they laugh.

Oh, Eliot.

> Yes, milord,
> Footfalls echo in the memory
> Down the passage which we did not take
> Towards the door we never opened
> Into the rose-garden.

As in some thriller, for twenty years Andreas Ban has been living undercover. Not anymore. He has no reason to. The town inside him has collapsed, his town, his towns. The avenues have been dug up, skyscrapers flattened into hovels, there is darkness all around. The cheerful bustle, stylish as music, swells into an insupportable cacophony of noise, crude and hysterical, like a woman who pulls out her hair and beats her breast. His poetry is stifled in the din, in the blaring that drums inside him, devastating his being, organ by organ, breaking him from within. He lies in the ruins, shakes his head and snatches increasingly shallow breaths. Andreas is like a ravaged city. Like a leveled city. His landscapes are imprinted in every cell of his body, that scenery with which he has been branded from birth, the little genetic archetypes like the remains of minute insects buried in nuggets of amber, those hallmarks, now all smashed, crushed under a monotone, monochrome, limited space that paralyzes him.

Andreas Ban tried, it's not that he didn't. Over these twenty years he has tried to hold onto at least aspects of this alien, discordant imprint, but it has proved unstable, shallow, in the long run impossible. That outer landscape, for Andreas false, has sucked up, demolished, devoured his internal world, he was too alone, too weak to plant it into new scenery. His hourglass is now an empty glass jar through which nothing flows.

> *Andreas, only a person who has departed for good will understand this. All my images are etched inside me. That which is absent is present like a wound, like a wound that does not heal, present like the presence of pain. Look after your fragments. A fragment can be a remnant, something from which and with which the always risky reconstruction of the lost begins. Such is the fragment that is a remnant of the destroyed, the res-*

> idue of the vanished, that mutilated whole that bears
> witness to destruction, the obliterated whole, an un-
> earthed ruin or preserved document, every trace that
> confirms existence and disappearance, as well as the
> often barbaric, violent destruction of a spiritual and
> existential complex.

Finci, there are no more fragments inside me. They are
beneath the ruins.

> Then record your nothingness by writing down the
> fragment, because the description of annihilation is the
> right fragment, because it is itself an expression of the
> destroyed whole. The event of destruction exists even
> when it is no longer happening, because it returns and
> is ever repeated in memory, for through memory it is
> annihilated anew.

But I am destroying my memories, I pluck them from
their bed, because their bed is under water.

> And I can't help you.

It is the end of September 2008. The nights are colder, Rovinj is
emptying. For several days Andreas does not make his bed, the
room is crumpled and narrowed. A gloomy day is coming, with
rain on the verge of falling, Andreas goes to the main street, recently paved with white stone, beautifully meandering and cheerful, and now, at the end of summer, blessedly deserted and quiet.
He catches sight of an old man dragging out "*O sole mio*" on an
accordion, but nobody passes, there is no one, only plump pigeons
walking and staggering (as does he, Andreas Ban), so he sits opposite the player, on the ground and, leaning against the wall of the
old palace, listens. The old man has gnarled fingers and a shaky
voice and he smiles at Andreas. The clouds linger. The sky is ominously dark. Andreas heads back up the hill at a limping run. *The*

swifts are coming, he says. That summer, that autumn, Andreas is maddened by swifts, as once when he had almost touched them, sitting under the sky in the house where strangers now live. Long ago. After Elvira's death.

Something breaks, that late summer of 2008.

A crack opens and grows.

In Andreas a longing for small creatures continues.

In the Rovinj evenings, before rain, a low-flying flock of swifts circles frantically in the sky. They emit ominous, rhythmic cries.

The little cosmopolitan birds, perhaps the most powerful and surely the fastest fliers (sixty meters a second, up to two hundred kilometers an hour), with their strong pectoral muscles, long, narrow wings, hardly know how to walk. Swifts have short legs covered in down, barely visible, they seem not to have any at all. Apodidae, creatures that only fly, for whom walking is a threat to their life, for when they land, they are slow, lame, vulnerable creatures, they waddle awkwardly, turning their heads this way and that.

What freedom! Swifts spend their whole life in the air, they feed in the air, they mate in the air, they sleep in the heights.

They slide, circle, squeal. And they move from sky to sky.

On the earth, swifts land on vertical surfaces, on chimneys and trees, on rough walls, as far from people as possible, and there they build nests. On their miniature feet with sharp four-toed claws, trembling, terrified, they approach for them dangerous humans.

Little birds, swifts. From nine to twenty-five centimeters long, with a wide wingspan. Light as a breath, they weigh from two to five hundred grams. Andreas Ban would like to put several swifts on his chest to rest, to breathe with him like sleeping children.

Little black birds like cheerful death. Painless.

Little birds with big eyes and a small beak, which peck noiselessly at his insides, see what is there and are silent.

Andreas Ban stretches his arms toward the sky, imagining that he is flying, imagining himself in a flock of swifts and lets out a stifled cry.

Small birds, they die when they are alone.

He, Andreas Ban, is alone.

Apus apus, the European swift, a bird without legs, manages well in dark places, in caves for example, where it rests, where no one intrudes. So he, Andreas Ban, will step into unconsciousness, into unworldness, when the time comes.

Now Andreas Ban watches that black playful flock drawing near, performing astonishing acrobatics while the sun goes down and the swifts with their short beaks draw a dark curtain across the sky, and Andreas Ban sees himself melting into the darkness, disappearing.

Not long ago on a high wall in the hospital complex Andreas Ban had seen a blackbird facing the closed windows of the psychiatric ward. There are bars on the windows of the psychiatric ward. The blackbird was standing motionless as though waiting for someone to appear at the window. No one came. Mesmerized, Andreas watched the stillness of the small black bird, while people passed, shaking their heads suspiciously, why is that man standing there when there is nothing to see, when nothing is happening. After half an hour, Andreas whistles a short tune and the blackbird looks at him. Between the bird and Andreas Ban flits a small black shooting star, a comet.

Had he not at first every three months, then every six months, gone for tedious checkups (markers, blood tests, ultrasound scans of his chest and abdomen, appointments, referral slips, waiting), had his diary not been scribbled with reminders of painful hospital meetings, had his mobile not regularly reminded him when, what and with whom, Andreas Ban might have forgotten that whole cancerous episode, or at least ignored it, he would have given himself up to life as seen in advertisements, with a smile, but also energetically, even hysterically, with the euphoria of a consumer, and thus repressed the sense of a beauty acquired genetically, but also through life, a feeling for an exalted, complicated and decadent aesthetic he is composed of and which keeps him uprooted. And which requires a lot of money. But poverty is swelling all around him, threatening. Soon he will find himself in an overcoat of pennilessness, in a cage with no way out, locked in, and he will toss and turn, with heavy limbs and labored breathing, to extinction. He is stalked by a tedious unease, particularly when he passes the hospital or walks through the hospital garden, which is collapsing. As time passes, as his medical problems pile up, the garden becomes ever darker, dampness sways from its bare, sickly trees, the stone paths are now dug up, the lawns covered in dead leaves and undergrowth. In spring, violets suffocate under the piles of debris and rotting matter and Andreas Ban sometimes liberates their petals with his foot, bequeathing them uprightness.

So, Andreas Ban continues to live more or less normally, mostly observing, participating less and less. But small pointless tensions, episodes of groundless anger, more frequent swearing, are the first indicators of his disintegration, his decomposition. *I'm changing*, says Andreas Ban.

On the bus, the woman in the seat in front of him is turning her head with lightning speed left-right, left-right as though she is watching the landscape pass by, there is virtually no landscape, nothing is happening either to the left or right, while she keeps turning her head like a frenzied sparrow pecking at a breadcrumb. Andreas taps the woman in front of him on the shoulder and asks,

Why do you keep spinning your head like that? The woman turns around and shoots Andreas the gaze of a madwoman hidden in the tightened pupils of her swimming pigs' eyes. *Who's spinning?* asks the woman.

He got hooked on Skype, but then gave it up, along with idiotic Facebook. But he did find Oskar and, as if playing a game of patience, they combed through their student days. Forty years had passed. Andreas and Oskar celebrate their masters' degrees in a dark tavern in Chicago's Little Italy, breaking lobster tails offered at bargain prices that evening. Afterward they cruise through London, Brussels, Amsterdam and Paris and end up in Rovinj. After they have thoroughly gone through all those past years, there is nothing left for Andreas and Oskar and they lose each other again.

Andreas also finds Violeta with whom he had gone to secondary school, Violeta from a little room in the attic of the inn "At the Sign of ?" opposite the cathedral. Violeta studies technological engineering, marries an Italian from Trieste, has two daughters, takes another degree in Italy, this time in chemical engineering because the Italians do not recognize her Belgrade diploma, her husband died twenty years earlier, she teaches math in a school in Udine and is fearful of approaching retirement. While she waits, Violeta plays golf and travels, a bit to Morocco and a bit to Portorož because of the warm sea water pool and low prices in winter, and spends time with her grandchildren and says, *Let's meet up.* Andreas says, *OK,* but when they eventually settle on a date, he sends Violeta a message, *I'm ill, another time.*

He finds loads of people, even some former friends, once close. That lasts for about a year, maybe two, that foray into long ago, that swimming through the thick waters of twenty, thirty, forty years before, then Andreas Ban says, *I'm sinking,* and signs out of Skype, signs out of Facebook, out of his email, signs out altogether. In the meantime, that slow burning up, that gradual disappearance, that scrambling toward the waters of Lethe opens up paths of forced continuity, tracks along which Andreas Ban (nevertheless) seeks landings of salvation.

On the terrace of a tall building (what is Andreas Ban doing on the terrace of a tall building?) he sees a couple. The young man has thick curly black hair, dirty from physical work, the girl is zipping up his fly, *We won't make a little girl,* she says.

Then the hemorrhoids appear.

Pain, bleeding, humiliating examinations, tedious therapy, ointments, cold compresses, potassium permanganate, showers, diapers. Waddling grotesquely, Andreas Ban hurries into the doctor's clinic, waves that crooked hand of his and says, *If this is some kind of cancer again, a shit bag is out of the question. It's not cancer,* they say, *the treatment is lengthy and tedious, if it doesn't work, we'll operate.* Andreas Ban spends a year occupied with his bottom, he (almost) forgets his breast. *Go for walks,* they say. So he goes for walks. Fanatically and aimlessly. Then he gives up. Because while he walks his thoughts walk too and currents of tension pour through Andreas Ban's body. When he tries to block out his thoughts, his walks feel hollow.

They open a jetty in the center of town for pedestrians, 1,730 meters to and 1,730 meters fro. The pedestrians are delighted, the view is wonderful, they say. And Andreas Ban sets out on that walk, but he hurries back home, sweating. The view is nothing, ugly. He can see the view of the small town every day (if he wishes, but he does not), so why would he also want to look at it from a distance which makes the town seem ever smaller. From the left, down the length of the jetty, there is a high protective wall with enamel tiles that warn *No climbing!* so from the jetty the sea cannot be seen, nor infinity, nothing sparkles, nothing twinkles, only, as one walks, on the right, the small, narrow, elongated town gazes at the crazed, idle walkers. Nonetheless, on that jetty, where on the left the wall comes to an end and on the right the town, there is a dizzying point. For fifty centimeters at its end, at the edge is a point of breakthrough, a point *for* breakthrough, for departure. That point of stupefying spaciousness before death is where suppressed aromas blend, childhood shines, youth beats against the temples, a fifty-year past like a slimy snail squashed into its fragile little shell.

Couples walk along the promenade. They walk slowly. Older women walk, slowly. But Andreas Ban marches with his limp as though hurrying somewhere, to a place he does not reach, as though treading briskly on a crazed fitness track.

By the edge of the quay, in the sea with its patches of oil, on whose surface float the remains of food, apple and pear cores, cigarette stubs, plastic bags swollen like cadavers, a diver is swimming in full gear.

A north wind lashes and Andreas breathes with difficulty.

The Case of Rudolf Sass

Rudolf Sass, *pruritus ani*, of the itching anus, Rudolf Sass scratches himself constantly. For seven years Rudolf Sass scratches himself to the point of frenzy. To the point of drawing blood. Rudolf Sass is a doctor. He is about sixty when Andreas Ban is almost forty. Rudolf Sass lives an orderly life. He has an orderly marriage. A grown-up daughter. He has a granddaughter and savings. He has a handsome face, a bit pockmarked, but handsome. He is a good height, he has no belly, he is not flabby. He is not bald. He has made a fine job of his life.

Like Andreas Ban many years later, Rudolf Sass goes for examinations, rectal and ultrasound, has laboratory tests, tries out a multitude of therapies, reappraises the possible causes and comes up with ... nothing. Seven years of scratching one's anus is a lot. Rudolf Sass loses concentration, he is superficial in his work with his patients, he eats little, sleeps badly, he is beset by fears that prowl around him like tiny beasts lying in wait, *They'll get into my head*, Rudolf Sass says, *they'll addle my brain, drive me mad*. Like poisonous gases those fears spread through Rudolf Sass's space, internal and external. Rudolf Sass feels a sickening swaying that forewarns of danger. *I could become aggressive, I could harm my wife, my granddaughter, pedestrians. It's not good*, he says.

Rudolf Sass sinks into depression. A deep, acute depression. Rudolf Sass comes from Switzerland (where he lives and works) for consultations with the then clinical psychologist Andreas Ban, employed at the university hospital of the city of Belgrade. Realizing the complexity of Rudolf Sass's case, Andreas Ban sends him to a psychiatrist, a friend from his school days, Dr. Adam Kaplan.

The neuropsychiatrist Adam Kaplan then embarks on a lengthy process of probing into Rudolf Sass's life. Adam Kaplan slips under Rudolf Sass's eyelids, rummages, delves and turns his life, his childhood, his past, distant and recent, upside down. Miraculous landscapes open up, surfacing out of dense fog, swamps of quagmire, amputated memories. In the repository of his soul Rudolf Sass has been storing a horde of dormant ghosts that now, risen, stir into a mysterious, macabre dance that he finds petrifying.

In 1941, Rudolf Sass is fourteen. Almost overnight, Rudolf Sass's face becomes sensitive to cold. Large swellings, lumps, appear on his cheeks, his forehead, his chin, around his eyes, particularly on his lips, distorting Rudolf Sass's face, making it unrecognizable. This unpleasantness is repeated every winter until he meets with the psychiatrist Adam Kaplan. Admittedly, over the years the unpleasantness becomes more bearable (milder), because Rudolf Sass develops small tricks to protect himself from the cold and the resulting frostbite. Nevertheless, Rudolf Sass continues to find this inconvenience irritating and somewhat perplexing. *I'm simply allergic*, he repeats, *that's all there is to it.*

It is not.

So, Rudolf Sass is fourteen, it is Sunday, February 2, 1941, it's snowing, the wind makes walking difficult, and in St. Anne's Church, in the small Serbian town of Šabac, Candlemas is being celebrated, candles are lit as a representation of the Lord who brings "light to lighten the Gentiles," people who only become enlightened, if ever, when it is too late. That evening, February 2,

1941, young Rudolf Sass does not feel well, he is shaken by a mild fever, he would prefer not to go to the service, to that church which always gives him an upset stomach. Rudolf Sass's father says, *There's no question, we're going!* because Rudolf Sass's father is a devout father with a hard face and calloused hands. In church, Rudolf Sass can hardly stand, he sways as he watches through half-closed eyelids the flickering of the candles which believers bring to be blessed by the Blessed Virgin Mary and St. Anthony of Padua, as though they were both alive. Through their sticky lips the believers whisper something to St. Anthony of Padua and the Blessed Virgin Mary, with their submissive eyes they watch them humbly, they raise their heads, they stare at them obtusely, fall at their feet, which in itself resembles a dumb slapstick comedy, because both the Blessed Virgin Mary and St. Anthony of Padua remain silent, stiff and immobile, expressionless, so this worshippers' performance, entirely meaningless, provokes in Rudolf Sass a new horror, because the Blessed Virgin Mary and that St. Anthony of Padua are ordinary statues, pieces of carved and painted linden wood, he in his Franciscan habit, balding, she with a veil on her head. Then his father says, *Go up to them and kneel*, but Rudolf Sass says, *No*, wild laughter could have burst from him, he could have kicked the Blessed Virgin Mary and St. Anthony of Padua, which would have made them collapse in a frenzied amorous embrace onto the little flames of those hundreds of candles at their feet and vanish in a magnificent blaze.

That same evening, Rudolf Sass has arranged to see his friends Kari and Enzi, a few years older, to whom he is supposed to take some partly collected and partly stolen money, altogether a negligible sum, a contribution to their renewed attempt to flee to Palestine. So Rudolf Sass leaves the service surreptitiously and hides beneath the internal stairway determined to escape. Crouching there, he falls asleep, overwhelmed by a terrible weakness. His father wakes him. *Is the service over?* asks Rudolf Sass while his father stands over him like a giant, casting a black shadow. His father does not say anything. His father lifts Rudolf Sass by his hair onto his feet, where he sways. His father pulls his ears, twists them as though he were opening a tin can, as though he were unlocking a door, then lands him two hefty slaps, which make Rudolf Sass's head swing first to the left, then to the right like a poppy in the wind. The marks of his father's fingers are imprinted on Rudolf Sass's cheeks. Rudolf Sass says nothing. His father takes Rudolf Sass back into the church, but at prayers Rudolf Sass faints. Then someone lifts him (not his father) and carries him home. The next day Dr. Bata Koen, who will soon cease to be, comes and says, *Rudi is seriously ill.* The diagnosis: *variola minor*—chicken pox. The treatment is lengthy. Rudolf Sass spends the days in his room, in bed. His father rarely visits him, there is no question of any, of even a mild effusion of tenderness toward his son.

My father seems to have surfaced out of a Haneke film, Rudolf Sass will tell Adam Kaplan many years later. *The same feeling, the same hatred, the same fear. His white ribbon around my neck, redemption of sins where there were none, loads of accumulated fury into which violence and guilt poured alternately.*

That is when Rudolf Sass becomes sensitive to cold, in 1941. Every winter his face tells him, *See how your father's hand has disfigured me*, but Rudolf Sass does not hear. At the same time repulsion, intolerance grows in Rudolf Sass toward believers and all religions, so it does not cross his mind to satisfy his father's wish that he enroll at the Higher Theological School in Djakovo, for Rudolf Sass wants to be a doctor.

On the evening Rudolf Sass faints, there are worshippers gathered round the Šabac synagogue as well, among them many newcomers, non-Šabac dwellers, all kinds of mysterious people telling terrible tales, but also youngsters having fun, some lads are excellent soccer players, there are girls dancing ballet, playing the guitar or piano, and these people speak various languages, German, French, Czech and Polish, there are older people, and there are children, there are people in love. Rudolf Sass makes new friends. In those years life in Šabac is as exciting as it is terrible, it's filled with foreboding that creeps into spaces that until now have been hidden in the quiet little town. Šabac touches Europe, Europe comes to Šabac bringing with it wondrous landscapes. Šabac grows from outside and within.

Andreas Ban knows this story, this little wartime story which is not included in encyclopedias or in world history, perhaps it just glimmers from time to time at its edges, in some preserved letter or diary chronicle like that of Father Grigorije Babović, or a few people post it online for the sake of remembering, for searching, for not-forgetting, in broken images, and so also in the past of Rudolf Sass, in names, which at the end of the 1980s Andreas Ban hears from his friend Adam Kaplan, and acquires a visa for an extended but crippled life. And now, in 2011, this story draws Andreas Ban off into a quite different world, into a different time, far from the sickness of Rudolf Sass, far from the pains in his, Andreas's, degenerated spine and his lame knee, far from his hemorrhoids, his glaucoma, his asthma and the blackened scar on his left breast which is no longer breast, and so he, Andreas Ban, forgets how often he has, by means of some knot, some decades-long strap, unbreakable, endeavored to connect, bring close, clasp and tie periods of human existence to find meaning in their madness.

With relief, with a strange, short-lived gaiety, Andreas Ban plunges into that remembrance beyond his life, he embarks on a mental excursion of flashes of borrowed images. Because Andreas Ban is not a Jew, nor does he have any connection with Šabac. That is why he observes the Šabac wartime story as he might watch a film, he tries to decipher whether the story has any connection with Rudolf Sass's diagnosed depression. And perhaps with him, Andreas Ban.

As early as April 1, 1938, as though it were a hideous April Fool's Day joke, a train transporting prisoners, including around sixty Jews, sets off from Vienna to the concentration camp of Dachau. Whoever grasps what is going on—and there are not many who do—flees. It is mostly the young who flee. Less than two months later, on May 23, among the prisoners destined for Dachau are an additional fifty Jews. The following day all the police stations in Austria receive the order to arrest immediately every Jew who had ever come into conflict with the law. This marks the beginning of raids, of a frenzied manhunt. Those arrested are taken straight to the police prison of Rossauer Lände in Vienna, and from there to Dachau. On May 30, 1938, a new transport train sets off from Vienna carrying five hundred Jews, on June 2 a further six hundred, on June 16 another six hundred Jews disappear, and on July 15, the last transport for Dachau, another six hundred souls depart. Vienna empties. Vienna is cleansed and purged, 2,310 citizens of Vienna have been dispatched, last stop—Buchenwald. By order of the Gestapo, the remaining women and men, teachers, doctors, shopkeepers, bakers, butchers, and jewelers, perform gymnastics in pajamas in the squares and scrub the streets of Vienna with toothbrushes, their shops are marked with the handwritten word "Jude," Jews are thrown out of their apartments while some other people waltz, enjoy cabarets and eat Sachertorte. The way it usually goes in wars.

> On Saturday, February 6, 2010, the Croatian daily newspaper Jutarnji list publishes a small photomontage of 104 pages, with some 120 photographs from 1941–45

entitled "Life in the NDH"* *In these pictures, Zagreb is*
nothing but banquets, celebrations, parades, and full of
idyllic scenes. The head of state Pavelić, as "the father of
the homeland," spends time with sweet, smiling children,
with peasant women in ornate national costume, with
devoted soldiers, while his wife Marija humbly takes care
of war orphans. Culture and sport flourish, the ladies are
au courant with European fashion, around the pavilion
in the central park of Zrinjevac, crowds of citizens de-
light in a military band. At the same time, in the deserted
town under curfew, night raids are carried out, families
which no longer exist are carried off and their property
plundered; trains for the Jasenovac camp and Auschwitz
are full; large groups of hostages are shot, publicly hanged
victims dangle from lampposts in the suburb of Dubrava.
In other words, not everyone is singing and dancing.
There are citizens of Zagreb who resist Evil and there-
fore lose their lives. I am Slavko Goldstein.

Austria is annexed to Germany, fused in submission and evil. Then
comes the night on which the Neptune monster, accompanied by
heavenly crystalline chords, dances his macabre *Tanz*, the night of
November 9 to 10, 1938. Ninety-six Jews are killed, hundreds are
injured, more than one thousand synagogues are burned, almost
7,500 shops are destroyed, graves desecrated, schools demolished,
thirty thousand Jews are arrested and sent to camps.

In November 1939, groups of young people begin to organize
the illegal emigration of Jews to Palestine, illegal because from as
early as May of that year, Great Britain, on the basis of the Mac-
donald Letter, that is his White Paper, bans all Jews from the Third

* Independent State of Croatia.

Reich from direct immigration into Palestine, they are considered "enemy aliens."

So, according to existing regulations, during that winter of 1939, a total of 822 people set out illegally from Vienna, 130 from Berlin, fifty from Gdansk, and in Bratislava they are joined by another hundred Czechs and Poles. The winter of 1939 is harsh, the harshest of the wartime winters. The Danube is frozen over, river traffic is erratic and the refugees wait for ten days before finding a boat prepared to take them. The refugees finally embark on the excursion boat *Uranus* and look with unease at the Nazi flag adorned with a swastika fluttering on its prow, but at the Hungarian border the *Uranus* is turned back to the port from which it departed. In the middle of December, the refugees set sail again from Bratislava and get halfway, before they are sent back once more. Thanks to the Union of Zionists of Yugoslavia, that is through the connections of its chief secretary Šime Spitzer* with Mossad, the institution in Europe concerned with the illegal settlement of Jews in Palestine, 1,102 passengers are transferred to the excursion boats *Tsar Nicholas II*, *Tsar Dušan* and *Queen Marija*. This journey too is interrupted at the three-country border of Yugoslavia, Romania and Bulgaria. There is no letup in the unprecedented Arctic winter. Ice floes float on the Danube. Temperatures sink to twenty below zero. Winds whip. At the turn of the year 1939, the boats sail toward the small, remote town of Kladovo, fifty kilometers from the nearest railroad station, cut off from the world and frozen in time. For nine months, in deplorable conditions, in filth, cold, without adequate food, more than a thousand people first waste their days on boats, then in huts thrown up on the marshy ground around Kladovo. Epidemics of malaria and various infectious diseases spread, there

* In September 1941 he is arrested and taken to the camp at Banjica, where he is interrogated and tortured. In the camp he is executed by the SS Major and doctor Friedrich Jung.

are cases of typhus and polio. There is no news of the arrival of any kind of ship to transport the refugees to Palestine. Anti-Semitic Romania expressly forbids the passage of Jews over its territory. And so, on September 22, 1940, this motley crowd of all ages, all professions, varied education, confronting the essence of evil and united, as it seems to Andreas Ban today, in a senseless effort to survive, this rabble of people thrown together haphazardly, needed by no one, discarded souls, is offered protection and hospitality by the mayor of Šabac, the doctor of law Miodrag Petrović, former Yugoslav consul in Bern, Trieste and Zadar. Into that small town of barely sixteen thousand inhabitants come 1,300 new people. Šabac, in which in addition to Serbs live some Slovaks, Roma, Russians and an occasional Croat, has its own integrated Jewish community, some hundred old settlers, and possesses that miraculous quiet and benevolent openness that propels small towns into the world of good and protects them from the world of evil. Unlike those other small towns, loathsome, through which flow the black waters of submission with deposits of decay; whose inhabitants are transformed into hounds, which at the command of their masters tear apart anything foreign, or like puppies put their tails between their legs and crawl on their bellies.

The majority of the new citizens of Šabac move into the mill belonging to the wine merchant Jakov Vukosavljević, others go to the warehouse of the Prague Bank, adapted to their needs, yet others are dispersed through the homes of local people, some of whom are well off, others not at all. A hospital is set up in a building in which a dozen newly arrived doctors and two locals work, everything in that hospital with some twenty beds is clean and safe.

After numerous conversations during which the psychiatrist Adam Kaplan, like a patient and experienced angler, draws out of Rudolf Sass's deep pit of oblivion blurred, bleary images from his past, many of which are so brittle they are on the verge of falling to pieces, Rudolf Sass begins to construct the fragmented puzzle of his life. And recollections roll.

In 1941 the tailor Simeon undertakes small repairs for the Sass family, for Rudolf he shortens his father's old trousers, turns his mother's coat inside out. An improvised Jewish school is opened, someone composes choral songs for performances there, mostly they sing "*Wir Packen, Wir Auspacken*." The Šabac football club Mačva is reinforced, "first-class" players are brought onto the field, the short but speedy spectators' favorite Kurt Hilković, then the goalkeeper Otto Ferri, two halfbacks, Mandl and Goldschmidt, then Hermann Steiner and the fullback Emil Silbermann, who runs barefoot.

The cobbler Josif makes wooden sandals with leather straps, everyone wants them, Rudolf Sass wears them in the summer to Šabac's wild beaches where he goes with Ernst Wiesinger, little Lili Mendelsohn and Suzanne Zwicker. And, of course, there is his beloved Karl—Kari Kriss who just cannot scrape together the money for his escape. The "Zorka" factory runs at full tilt, there are increasing numbers of workers who make themselves understood in various languages, Russian, Polish, German and Hungarian, which is unheard of in Šabac. The streets are full of people. Even in winter. Children are born. In Šabac, the war is still only a whisper.

Then, April 1941, the bombing of Belgrade—darkness falls on Šabac.

Germans in uniforms move through the town.

In May comes dense rain and difficulty breathing. The SS officers arrest twenty prominent citizens of Šabac and take them away as hostages. Civilians are ordered to hand over their vehicles to the German Command. The Paris cinema is closed. Food is increasingly expensive and there is less of it. No singing, no celebrating, silence grips the town.

The SS officers hand out yellow ribbons to the refugees. Enzy Deutsch, in Šabac known as Zoran, throws his ribbon in protest at the feet of the SS officer and goes to the mill, not emerging for days.

Jewish shops are marked.

Near the Paris Restaurant someone breaks the window of "Mignon," where shoes are sold.

The railroad station is deserted, trains do not run, the bridges are destroyed.

No sugar. No oil, no coffee or lemons, no tobacco. The shops are emptied, the German soldiers take, steal, whatever they find. Food coupons are distributed. The mill chimney emits no smoke, the Jews go hungry.

No silk stockings for love or money. Silk stockings are worn by … Rudolf Sass's mother.

In June the Gypsies no longer play in Šabac's restaurants, Jewish doctors are prohibited from working. Various notices with prohibitions hang all over town. The people of Šabac are denied access to the Green Garland Hotel, where German officers eat, binging at night, while unknown heavily made-up women sing. One night Rudolf Sass's father comes home tipsy and says to Rudolf Sass's mother, *I've brought you silk stockings.*

All radios are confiscated. People hug their radios, rock them like babies as they carry them to the German Command—at the Green Garland Hotel. The Sass family does not take anything to the Command. In the Sass family home the stations of the Independent State of Croatia, Croatian wavelengths, are received (and secretly listened to).

Rudolf Sass no longer goes to the wild beaches by the Sava River. Anyway, in June it rains a lot. No one goes swimming. Corpses float down the Sava. Someone says they are Serbs from the NDH The corpses are unrecognizable.

No flour. No salt. Peasants knock on doors offering eggs, chickens, maize, even flour—for a little salt. For a small cup of salt Rudolf Sass's mother gets a large fattened turkey.

All the Jewish refugees, 1,107 of them, along with sixty-three indigenous Šabac Jews, are taken to the old Šabac castle on the Sava, now a concentration camp.

It is July 1941. Rudolf's friends are gone, Kari, Enzi, the little "ballerina" Lilli who flits on the tips of her toes.

In August Rudolf Sass's father entertains the commander, Captain of the Ustasha Army Josip Hübl, the noncommissioned officer, Sergeant Gjuro Majdak, and the corporal Franjo Kasa, all from the 37th Rifle Company, all in Ustasha uniforms. They go to evening Mass in civilian suits. Rudolf Sass does not go.

In August 1941, the killings begin. The doctors are killed, Dr. Bata Koen is killed, some shopkeepers and farmers are killed, Rudolf Sass does not know their names. From telegraph poles in the town hang the citizens of Šabac, shot by firing squad. Rudolf Sass's father says, *Don't look, pretend you don't see.* But Rudolf Sass looks, Rudolf Sass wants to and has to look as he passes through on his way home. The ropes around the necks of the hanged soak up their blood, the lifeless bodies slip out of the noose and fall to the ground. Why they hang up murdered people Rudolf Sass cannot understand. Several days later the Germans take prisoners, the Jewish refugees, to a nearby camp; those ordered to hang up the bodies of the shot now load the Jewish corpses onto carts that take them out of town. Rudolf Sass looks again. The carts are crammed with corpses, their arms and legs tangled, bloody and filthy, they sway. A collective funeral procession with no escort, with no tears. The people in the street are frozen.

September 26, 1941. Some five thousand citizens of Šabac and 1,057 Jews from the camp on the Sava are transferred to Klenak and, from there, under blows from rifles, are forced to run twenty-three kilometers to the camp in the Srijem village of Jarak.

At the beginning of October General Franz Böhme* announces that members of the Wehrmacht have to shoot 2,100 Jews and Gypsies as a reprisal for the killing of twenty-one German soldiers, according to the principle of a hundred for one.

On August 12 and August 13, 1941, all those interned in the camp near Šabac are taken to Zasavica and shot.

There was a storm brewing, Rudolf Sass tells the psychiatrist Kaplan. *The sky turned dark, the wind swirled down the empty streets of Šabac, stirring up dust. The night was ominously quiet. The next day, I hear from school friends about the massacre in Zasavica. In our house no one talks. Forty-five years later I listen to the recollections of Milorad Jelešić, then a farmer and witness to the shooting. On Michaelmas, Jelešić said, I was taken with forty other men to Mačvanska Mitrovica and from there to Zasavica. We thought they were going to shoot us. They dropped us on the marshy ground and told us, We aren't* going to shoot you, you're here to bury people. *Then a German company of about fifty soldiers arrived bringing fifty men in civilian*

---

* Franz Friedrich Böhme (Austria, April 15, 1885–Germany, May 29, 1947). After graduating from the Military Academy in Graz, he serves in the Austro–Hungarian army as an officer in the Headquarters. In 1938 he is appointed Chief of Staff of the Austrian army. He was also military observer in the war in Abyssinia. He takes part in the military campaign in Poland and France. He comes to Serbia in September 1941, with exceptional powers granted him personally by Hitler. Remembered for the infamous punitive expedition of September to December 1941, which left devastation and death in its wake. He introduces the "death key": a hundred Serbs for one dead German and fifty for each German wounded. Up to December 5, 1941, (in just two and a half months) 11,164 hostages and 3,562 insurgents are shot. After this "mission," Franz Böhme leaves Serbia and is reassigned as army general to Norway, where he is arrested. At his trial in Nuremberg he states that everything he did was in order for the population of Serbia "to achieve tranquility and peace as soon as possible." On May 29, 1947, he commits suicide by jumping from the fourth-floor window of the prison where he is interned. He is buried in Friedhof St Leonhard in Graz.

clothes. Right away I realized that they were Jews. The soldiers said, Go to those stakes, *and the stakes were driven into the ground at intervals of a meter or two, Jelešić said,* Go to the stakes and straddle them. *All the civilians were facing a pit, Jelešić said. Then four German soldiers came, went up to each of the Jews with a blanket and spread it out among them, each Jew threw something into the blanket, probably money or valuables. After that, said Jelešić, an officer gave the command and German soldiers with rifles aimed at the back of the Jews' heads—two at each one. We had to go up to the dead at a run and throw them into the pit, but before that we shook out their pockets and took anything of value, watches, money, and we had to take off their rings, this didn't go smoothly, Jelešić said, it was sometimes impossible, so the Germans gave us pliers to cut the rings off, while the Germans pulled out their gold teeth, except that this didn't always go smoothly either, and when it didn't, they kicked the teeth out with their boots. Then we threw the dead into the pit. When they finished with the first group, we had to run some distance away, while the Germans brought another group out of the stubble field to the firing squad, and so it went on, all over again. In the evening they took us back to Sremska Mitrovica, some forty of us, and shut us in a wagon. In the morning they took us back to Zasavica and the shooting went on as on the previous day. On the first day they killed only Jews, the next day there were some of our Gypsies, there were more Gypsies than Jews, they had probably already killed all the Jews. The whole time some German soldiers were taking photographs, they like doing that, clicking away, as though they were at some kind of performance, Jelešić said, they photographed different moments, they photographed the victims before they were shot, straddling those stakes, they photographed us throwing the bodies into the pit, they photographed the firing squad, from close up, different moments. On the first evening we left the pit open and the next day when we came we found a lot of dogs gnawing at the bodies. Then a German started killing the dogs, he pointed to the pit and shouted, Curs to curs, Ješelić said. Not all the Jews were obedient, Ješelić said. They did not all hand over their valuables, they did not all stand beside their stakes, some smoked, some embraced each other, one young man refused to leave his accordion so they shot him with his accordion on his chest. There, that is what I learned some forty or so years later,* Rudolf Sass tells Adam Kaplan, handing him a photograph streaked with the white veins of age. *This is my friend Kari Kriss, the one for whom I collected money to help him escape, money my father had but didn't want to give me. Kari Kriss taught me to swim, Kari Kriss was killed in Zasavica. He was nineteen.*

Rudolf Sass could not tell Adam Kaplan how, during his visit to Vienna in 2007, he had been stopped in his tracks when he wandered into the little neighboring town of Mödling and came across Günter Demnig's *Stolperstein* dedicated to Hermann Dasche. On that polished brass cube 10 x 10 x 10 cm embedded in the sidewalk, on that stumbling block in front of the house in which Hermann Dasche had once lived, that is 8 Eisentorgasse, the following is engraved:

> *Hermann Dasche*
> *Born February 23, 1910 in Hohenau.*
> *Killed on October 12, 1941 in Zasavica.**

---

* Hermann Dasche, son of the shopkeeper Bernhard Dasche and Gisela, née Schnabel, was married to Felicija Winter and worked as a debt collector. He had to move from Mödling to Vienna, to 1 Sperlgasse, into a Sammelwohnung (the Nazi name for a shared apartment) on March 20, 1939. While his wife managed to escape to the United States, Hermann had tried to reach Palestine with the so-called Kladovo transport.

In that year, 2007, Rudolf Sass, already an old man of nearly eighty, could only sigh: *The past is haunting me again.*

But then, in Mödling, the somewhat calmer Rudolf Sass (because of help from Adam Kaplan?) had already learned to cope with his ghosts. So he bent down to make out all the letters of the inscription, repeating in disbelief and out loud *Zasavica, Zasavica buried in Austria*, which might have looked as though Rudolf Sass was bowing, as though he was praying, paying his respects to the vanished Hermann Dasche.

 In November 1942, the women and children from the Kladovo transport are sent, on foot, in bitter cold, through snow, to the Sajmište camp near Zemun. Old women, the sick and children die on the way. Four-year-old Luci, the daughter of Dr. Bata Koen, dies in the arms of her mother who then goes mad. Two of the children of Irma Hilković, wife of the popular soccer player Kurt, by then shot, die on the way, while the third, born in Šabac, freezes to death on her chest. Those of the Kladovo transport to survive, along with other prisoners, are killed by exhaust fumes in so-called soulstranglers, Saurer brand trucks which could carry between fifty and one hundred victims per "session."

The commander of the camp was SS-Untersturmführer Herbert Andorfer, accused of participating in the murder of 7,500 Jews, mostly women, up to May 1942. As the direct organizer of liquidations, every day except Sunday, Andorfer accompanied the mobile gas chamber from Sajmište to the killing field of Jajinci, after first telling the mothers that they would be traveling to Romania or

Poland, where better days awaited them. He printed leaflets about considerably easier conditions in those fictitious destinations for Jews, and then oversaw the burial of children and their mothers in the Jajinci pits.

The Nazi criminal Andorfer, commander of the Sajmište camp, comes before Austrian court in 1967 charged with participating in the murder of Jews in the Sajmište camp. He defends himself by affirming that he sympathized with the victims, that the murderers gave orders sitting at their desks, that he did not construct the mobile gas chamber, nor did he himself turn on the gas that killed 7,500 people. He was sentenced to two and a half years in prison; he died in 2008 in Austria. His deputy, Edgard Enge, was brought to court in Stuttgart in June 1968, twenty-three years after the end of the Second World War. In spite of all the evidence presented, including the statements of witnesses to his crimes, Edgard Enge was declared innocent.

In June 1945 the mass grave at Zasavica is opened. The mortal remains of the Šabac Jewish refugees, murdered on October 12 and 13, 1941, are taken from Zasavica to the Šabac Jewish Cemetery, and in 1959 to the Sephardic Cemetery in Belgrade.

Requiescant in pace

1. Albinum Alfred, 17, schoolboy from Šabac
2. Albinum Josef, 35, from Šabac
3. Albinum Samuilo, 19, student from Šabac
4. Abrahamović Berta, 47
5. Abrahamović Salomon, 48, Germany
6. Adižes Rabiner, 56, from Šabac
7. Adižes Sofija, 40, housewife from Šabac
8. Adižes Amada, 20, schoolgirl from Šabac
9. Adižes Margareta, 18, schoolgirl from Šabac
10. Adižes Rachela, 25, seamstress from Šabac
11. Adižes Reina, 13, from Šabac
12. Adižes Sarah, 23, housewife from Šabac
13. Albahari Salomon, 73, merchant from Šabac
14. Albahari Bukas, 63, housewife from Šabac
15. Aleksander Herbert, 37
16. Aleksander Ruth, 30
17. Altman Leo, 22
18. Altman Maksimilian, 34
19. Amzanowsky Aron, 48
20. Amzanowsky Sima, 49
21. Antserl Rosa, 33
22. Antserl Oskar, 44
23. Aschenbrenner Margarete, 26
24. Aufrichtig Egon, 34

25. Austerer Moses, 45
26. Avramović Ascher, 20, dental technician from Šabac
27. Avramović Jakob, 27, tradesman from Šabac
28. Batscha Dr. Albert, 56
29. Baile-Malke Mader, 50
30. Bader Lydia, 20
31. Bader Pavel, 21
32. Back Arpad, 32
33. Bana Moses, 44
34. Baner Haim, 56
35. Bararon Jakob, 49, tinsmith from Šabac
36. Bararon Roas, 50, housewife from Šabac
37. Bararon Eugenia, 10, from Šabac
38. Bauchbar Dr. Israel-Hans, 51
39. Barsai Ester, 49
40. Bartz Margot, 28
41. Baron Elias, 44
42. Barbe Alfred, 34
43. Bär Walter, 30
44. Baran Mehnla, 42
45. Baran Heinrich, 50
46. Bassist Otto, 30
47. Bassist Berta, 27
48. Batsa Blanka, 47
49. Bazman Otto, teacher
50. Bauer G., teacher
51. Bauer Alice, 22
52. Bauer Rolf, 21
53. Bauer Walter, 32
54. Bauer Walter, 21
55. Baumann Paul, 19
56. Baumgarten Irma, 54
57. Baumgarten Josef, 41
58. Baumwoll Simon, 41
59. Baumfeld Friedrich-Egon, 26
60. Beer Anna, 57
61. Beer Bethold, 18
62. Beer Frieda, 30
63. Benner Haja, 53
64. Becksmann Alfred, 29
65. Bendit David-Karl, 50
66. Berényi Ilona, 41, from France
67. Berger Edith, 20

68. Berger Helene, 57
69. Bergeld Adam
70. Bergmann Dr. Herbert, 23
71. Bergmann Emilie, 51
72. Bergmann Otto, 56, from Germany
73. Bernbach Adolf, 48, from Poland
74. Bernstein Rachel, 52, from Germany
75. Bernstein Thea, 19
76. Berkmann Julius, born 15 April 1886, from Germany
77. Bergwerk Felicia, 43
78. Bergwerk Dr. Salo, 45
79. Blatt Kaja, 44, from Poland
80. Blaustein Edmund, 26
81. Blitz Rosalie, born 26 December 1860
82. Bloch Eugen, 48
83. Bloch Margot, 22
84. Bloch Herman, 27
85. Blumenthal Judith, 32, from Germany
86. Blumenthal Lili, 23, from Germany
87. Böhm Dr. Oskar, 50
88. Bohrer Max, 19
89. Bolezk Minna, 41
90. Bolezk Noah, 36
91. Boschković Karl
92. Braslawsky Margarete, 48
93. Bialogowsky Hersh, 22
94. Bialogowsky Max, 48
95. Binderfeld Robert, 20
96. Bichler Wilhelm, 26
97. Breier Sigmund, 57, from Vienna
98. Breier Gustav, 48
99. Breier Hilda, 37
100. Breier Abraham, 38
101. Brenner Lili, 20
102. Brenner Anna-Edith, 20, from Hungary
103. Brestiker Jakob, 23
104. Brettholz Norbert, 21
105. Brings Liese, 20, from Germany
106. Brod Aleksandar, engineer
107. Brodski Flora, 40
108. Brocky Aleksandar, 41
109. Broner Rachele, née Speiser, from Poland
110. Broner Rosa, 20

111. Broner Jakob, 9
112. Brunner Leonora, 20
113. Brunner Eva, 37
114. Brunner Hugo, 48
115. Brunner Rosa, 43
116. Brunner Emil, 48
117. Burnstein Rifka, 41
118. Burnstein Wolf, 40
119. Buchelović Robert, from Vienna
120. Bucković Norbert, 29
121. Battel Rena, 21
122. Damit Joachim, 38
123. Danziger Eugen, 20
124. Banker Fredo, 41
125. Danemark Abraham, 54
126. Dasche Hermann, 31
127. Daskalović Elizabeth, 40
128. Daskalović Samuel, 39
129. Datz Sarah, 39
130. Datz Hermann, 45
131. David Marcel, 21
132. David Otto, 37
133. David Werner, 37
134. David Martha, 20
135. David Grete, 43
136. David Wilhelm, 32
137. David Luise, 20
138. Dermer Abraham, 44
139. Dresner Bernhard, 36
140. Deutsch Bernhard, 30
141. Deutsch Johann, 29
142. Deutsch Edith, 20
143. Deutsch Beno, 57, from Vienna
144. Deutsch Fritz, born 2 December, 1923
145. Deutsch Ernst, 21
146. Deutsch Heinrich, 19
147. Deutsch Ignatz, 30
148. Diamant Adolf, 28
149. Dodal Rifka, 23
150. Donskoj Max, 41
151. Dorfmann Jakob, 57
152. Dorfmann Rebeka, 50
153. Dorfmann Adolf, 22
154. Dornreich Hans, 49
155. Dornreich Marianne, 43

156. Dortort Haim-Fischel, 44
157. Drucker Gertrude, 23
158. Drucker Ernst, 28
159. Dvoriansky Vera, 44
160. Dvoriansky Daisy, 22
161. Dvoriansky Walter, 22
162. Eckstein Heinrich, 21
163. Edel Dr. Jakob, 54
164. Edel Gisa, 49
165. Eger Fritz, 37
166. Eger Moses, 36
167. Eger Gertrud, 36
168. Egert Lilli, 21
169. Ehrenkranz Heinrich, 36
170. Ehrlich Ester, 49
171. Ehrlich Erwin, 28
172. Ehrlich Kurt, 29
173. Ehrlich Bruno, 31
174. Ehrmann Max, 35
175. Eisenhammer Robert, 46
176. Eisland Etel, 44
177. Ellbogen Lothar, 41
178. Elefant Rifka, 28, from Hungary
179. Elefant Ladislaus, 25
180. Eisner Dušan, d.o.b. unknown
181. Ellenberg Gerson, 62
182. Elias Edmund, 57
183. Elias Irma, 51
184. Engel Edith, 37, from Germany
185. Engel Blanka, 26
186. Engel Oskar, 45
187. Engel Grete, 57
188. Engelmann Moses, 52
189. Engelmann Lea, 50
190. Engelmann Cilli, 29
191. Engelmann Mirianna, 29
192. Engler Edith, 37
193. Engler Alfred, 41
194. Eppler Felix, 19
195. Epstein Perl, 46
196. Epstein Viktor, 48
197. Epstein Erich, 22
198. Ereitner Robert, 54
199. Erlbaum Hans Moritz, 52
200. Eugen Juda, 42

201. Fabian Max, 25
202. Feder Tommy, 31
203. Feder Hermann, 35
204. Feigl Erich, 33
205. Feintuch Paul, 30
206. Feldmann Hilda, 51
207. Fenichtel Otto, 21
208. Feral Bruno, 21
209. Ferri Otto, 21
210. Ferschko Rosa, 20
211. Ferschko Edith, 26
212. Ferschko Erwin, 26
213. Feuerstein Wolf, 48
214. Feuerstein Jetty, 48
215. Fieselson Isak, 48
216. Figdor Elsa, 33
217. Figdor Regina, 51
218. Figdor Ernst, 25
219. Finder Lisa, 20
220. Fingerhut Salomon, Rabbi from Ruma
221. Fink Josef Moses, 35
222. Fink Walter, 32
223. Fink Faite, 41
224. Fischer Paul, 19
225. Fischer Gideon, 23
226. Fischer Serena, 38
227. Fischer Saul, 45
228. Fischer Gisela, 24
229. Fischer Eduard, 24
230. Fiscks Lucy, 20
231. Fiscks Stella, 41
232. Fiscks Ignatz, 48
233. Flaschner Egon, 51
234. Flesch Leopold, 21
235. Fluss Erich, 19
236. Fotel Hanni, 28
237. Forstenzer Margarete, 48
238. Forstenzer Paul, 50
239. Frankfelder Josef, 21
240. Frankfurter Sophie, 22
241. Frankfurter Heinrich, 22
242. Frankfurt Sigmund, 52
243. Freud Dr. Erich, 45
244. Freud Frederike, 45
245. Freud Hans, 34

246. Freund Margarete, 33
247. Fried Dr. Kurt, 30
248. Fried Arnold, 25
249. Fried Gotthold, 60
250. Fried Hans, 39
251. Friedel Ernst, 38, from Germany
252. Friedland Louise, 21
253. Friedfertig Abraham, 41
254. Friedmann Aron, 53
255. Friedmann Vera, 20
256. Friedmann Isak, 28
257. Friedman Emil, 46
258. Friemet Simon, 28
259. Fromm Leib, 34
260. Fromm Anna, 30
261. Fuchs Heinrich, 36
262. Fuchs Aurelia, 32
263. Fuchs Erwin, 22
264. Fuchs Leo, 59
265. Fuchs Gertrude, 20
266. Fuhrmann Alfred, 20
267. Fürst Edith, 47
268. Fürstenberg Marian, 24
269. Fürstenberg Martha, 17
270. Gans Oskar, 45
271. Gans Fradella, 45
272. Gänser Dr. Moses, 52
273. Gänser Rachela, 39
274. Gelbard Batja, 45
275. Gelbard Arie-Leib, 52
276. Gelbberger Theodor, 20
277. Geller Alfred, 21, from Vienna
278. Geri Heinrich, 29
279. Gerschen Gerhard, 21
280. Gerson Minna, 21
281. Gerecht Eiseg, 54
282. Gerecht Rosa, 55
283. Gidić Gedalja, 20, housewife from Šabac
284. Gidić Naum, 49, trader from Šabac
285. Gidić Delisia, 20, housewife from Šabac
286. Gidić Samuilo, 7, from Šabac
287. Gidić Fatima, 43, housewife from Šabac
288. Gigulsky Wolf, 43, from Russia
289. Glase Max, from Vienna
290. Glaser Walter, 29

291. Glaubauer Josef, 20
292. Glück Erich, 23
293. Glück Lotte, 16
294. Glückmann Hanna, 48
295. Glückmann Adolf, 53
296. Glückselig Hugo, 27
297. Goldberg Richard, 27
298. Goldenberg Gustav, 28
299. Goldberg Berta, 46
300. Goldberg David, 46
301. Goldschmidt Eduard, 27
302. Goldschmidt Wilhelm, 42
303. Goldschmidt Anna, 33
304. Goldschmidt Rosa, 44
305. Goldschmidt David, 52
306. Gottesmann Haim (Hermann), 56, from Vienna
307. Gottesmann Sima, 45
308. Gottesmann Pinkas, 44
309. Gottlieber Chaim Kurt, 20, from Vienna
310. Gottlieb Greta, 33
311. Gottlieb Alexander, 37
312. Goldring Eduard, 27
313. Gorlitzer Alter, 39
314. Graf Grete, 44
315. Grenek Simon, 30
316. Grebler Sabse Sigmund, 42
317. Griffel Alfred, 33
318. Groiner Kurt, 20
319. Gröniger Ida, 54
320. Grossfeld Sarul, 41
321. Gruber Gusta, 46
322. Gruber Moses, 53
323. Grünberger Herbert, 21
324. Grünsfeld Wilhelmina, 20
325. Grünfeld Regina, 20
326. Grünstein Tibor, 26
327. Günsberger Julius, 73, merchant from Šabac
328. Gutstein Leo, 19
329. Guttmann Freidle, 36, from Poland
330. Guttmann Bär, 34
331. Haas Hans, 29
332. Haber Josefine, 20
333. Haber Max, 22

334. Hacker Alfred, 27
335. Hacker Helene, 49
336. Hacker Josef, 51
337. Hacker Hilde, 28
338. Hacker Samuel, 33
339. Hacker Malvine, 45
340. Hacker Siegfried, 29, from Germany
341. Hacker Arnold, 59
342. Hacker Johanna, 52
343. Hoffmann Leopold, 35
344. Hahn Fanny, 52
345. Hahn Berthold, 50
346. Hahn Robert, 31
347. Halbkran Franz, 28
348. Helpern Rosa, 32
349. Hambach Fedor
350. Hamm Josefine, 39
351. Hamber Antonia, 43
352. Hamber Hugo, 52
353. Hammerstein Gerda, 27
354. Hammerstein Fritz, 35
355. Hana Rachela, 45
356. Handler Heinrich, 21
357. Hand Margarete, 39
358. Hand Dr. Richard, 50
359. Hartmann Hans, 28
360. Harmann Maria, 50
361. Harmann Juda, 53
362. Hass Greta, 19
363. Hasserl Rosa, 51
364. Haas Moritz, 62
365. Hauser Georg, 28, Vienna
366. Hauser Grete, 29
367. Hauser Oscar, 40
368. Hauser Cilly, 40
369. Hauser Oswald, 22
370. Hauser Berta, 49
371. Hauser Gottfried, 59
372. Hecht Siegfried, 36
373. Heimbacher Eli
374. Heilbrunn Kurt, 28
375. Helmrich Herbert, 19
376. Heller Heinrich, 22
377. Held Heinz, 19
378. Held Alice, 20

379. Held Siegfried, 41
380. Hönig Hans, 27
381. Hönig Livia, 53
382. Hönig Matje, 53
383. Herschenbaum Natali, 20
384. Hermann Kurt, 21
385. Hermann Paul
386. Hertz Manfred, 18
387. Hess Otto-Sami, 18
388. Hess Selma, 22
389. Hess Benö, 27
390. Hertze Nelly, 24
391. Hertze Hans, 34
392. Herschmann Leonora, 21
393. Herschmann Georg, 23
394. Herschel Siegfried, 23
395. Herschel Josef, 36
396. Hofmeister Klara (?)
397. Hochhaus Alfred, 32
398. Hofmann Cipolea, 53
399. Hofmann Wolf, 56
400. Hollenberg Mordko, 32
401. Holz Gertrude, 21
402. Holz Johanna, 29
403. Horowitz Israel, 46
404. Husserl Marsel, 52
405. Hilković Wilhelm, 29
406. Hilkovic Irma, 27, and three children,
    one of whom was was born in Šabac
407. Hilkovic Kurt, 30
408. Hirschenhauser Eugenie, 19
409. Hirschhorn Bernhard, 21
410. Hirsch Fritz, 21
411. Hirschl Margarete, 25
412. Hirschl Samuel, 32
413. Hirsch Hildegard, 22
414. Hirsch Martin, 26
415. Hirsch Svibnjaer, 52
416. Hvat (Chwat) Mardo, 47
417. Immergut Herta, 20
418. Jäger Ignatz, 25
419. Jakob Ilsa, 19
420. Jakobi Rachel, 40
421. Jakob Jack, 60, businessman from
    Šabac

422. Jakob Sarina, 53, housewife from Šabac
423. Jakubitz Nathan, 26
424. Jedlinsky Walter, 23
425. Jakobowitsch Miklaus, 21, from
    Germany
426. Joffe Manfred, 20
427. Jecić (Jetzitsch) Tauba, 52
428. Joachimson Agnes, 33
429. Joachimson Franz, 29
430. Julius dr. Leopold
431. Jungleib Elka, 24
432. Kachane Wolf, 46
433. Kachan Mosche, 22, from Hungary
434. Kahn Eva, 21
435. Kahn Helmut, 28, from Germany
436. Kahn Wolfgang
437. Kagan Leon, 38
438. Kaiser Barthold, 20
439. Kalisky Hans, 22
440. Kamlot Fanny, 55
441. Kanditor Haim Isak, 32
442. Kanditor Mali, 51
443. Kandel Pinkas, 34
444. Karpeles Maria, 45
445. Karpeles Otto, 55
446. Karpeles Fritz, 60
447. Kari Otto, 20
448. Käser Herman, 27
449. Kassierer Heinz, 23
450. Kastner Karl, 30
451. Kaster Otto, 24
452. Kastner Salika, 29
453. Katz Blanka, 28
454. Katz Amalia, 28
455. Kaufmann Josef, 53
456. Kerner Israel, 63
457. Kerner Ester, 57
458. Kessler Ernst, 28
459. Kessler Walter, 27
460. Kiefer Ernest, 21
461. Kinberg Isidor, Berlin
462. Klapp Melanie, 20
463. Klapp Rudolf, 20
464. Klawon Erna, 48
465. Kleinberg Sofia, 38

466. Kleinberger Ignatz, 33
467. Klein Isidor, 63
468. Klein Isak
469. Klein Karl, 50
470. Klein Otto, 21
471. Klein Walter, 28
472. Kleiner Heinz, 21
473. Klimka Mikulas, 22, from Slovakia
474. Klug Markus, 63, from Vienna
475. Klug Therese, 63
476. Knesbach Osijas, 53
477. Knesbach Jetti, 49
478. Knobel Bernhard, 56, from Poland
479. Koen Luci, 4, from Šabac
480. Koen Elsa, 29, widow from Šabac
481. Kohn Siegfried, 42
482. Kohn Sidonie, 46
483. Kohn Josef, 30
484. Kohn Ella, 25
485. Kohn Wolfgang, 21
486. Kohn Hilde-Ruth, 27
487. Kohn Anna, 22
488. Kohn Friedrich, 40, engineer
489. Kohn Hermine, 21
490. Kohn Isidor, pharmacist
491. Kohn Lea, 21
492. Kohn Oskar, 25, from Germany
493. Kohn Kurt, 31
494. Kohn Franz, 42
495. Kohn Friedrich, 24
496. Kohn Friedrich, 23
497. Kohn Kurt, 19
498. Kohn Maximilian, 22
499. Kohn Rudolf, 20
500. Kohn Sigmund, 25
501. Kohn Wilhelm, 31
502. Koffler Ester, 46
503. Koffler Jakob, 49
504. Kolnik Benzion, 48
505. Kolnik Edith, 40
506. Kolb Gertrude, 22
507. Koppstein Alexander, 20
508. Kopper Alfred, 20
509. Koppel Malvine, 23
510. Koppel Klara, 20

511. Komornik Silvia, 20
512. Kornfein Walter, 21
513. Körner Max, 29
514. Korn Hanna, 50
515. Körner Elka, 32
516. Kornblut Gertrude, 20
517. Kormann-Gabel Rosa, 44
518. Kormann-Gabel Josef, 52
519. Kozminsky Martin, 20
520. Kozminsky Friedrich, 53
521. Krahl Kurt, 19
522. Krainer Artur, 57
523. Krainer Zlata, 50
524. Kraft Josef, 43
525. Kraft Aurelia, 36
526. Kramer Haim, 45
527. Kramer Nikolaus, 45
528. Kramer Rosa, 42
529. Kramer Robert, 52
530. Kreutner Wilhelm, 23
531. Krebs Heinz, 19
532. Kriss Karl, 19
533. Kriss Regina, 38
534. Kriss Alfred, 42
535. Kriegsmann Karl, 27
536. Kriegsmann Frieda, 29
537. Krishaber Dr. Lazo, 29, dentist from Šabac
538. Krishaber Riki, 22, housewife from Šabac
539. Kuh Viktor, 24
540. Kulka Lilli,17
541. Kulka Olga, 45
542. Kümmelheim Leon, 39
543. Kupfermann Karpel, 49
544. Kupfermann Sara, 46
545. Kuttner Cveta, 29
546. Kuttner Isak, 21
547. Kutscher Simon, 34
548. Lackenbacher Anna, 78
549. Lagstein Paul, 21
550. Lagstein Moses, 21
551. Lamp Georg, 20
552. Lampl Rudolf, 32
553. Lampl Margarete, 29

554. Landau Laibis, 55
555. Landsberg Jakob, 19
556. Landskroner Hersch, 44
557. Lang Theodor
558. Langsam Aron, 39, Vienna
559. Langenbach Werner, 22
560. Lassmann Leo, 19
561. Lauringer Moritz, 27
562. Lautner Dora, 48
563. Lautner Klara, 21
564. Ledenheim Alexander, 29
565. Leihkram Gisele, 17
566. Leinwender Benno, 56
567. Leinwender Emilija, 56
568. Leinkram Paula, 42
569. Lemb Karl, 24
570. Lemberg Sita, 44
571. Lemberger Erich, 27
572. Lamberger Antonia, 52
573. Lampel Dr. Oscar, 32
574. Leozisky Brandla, 49
575. Lerch Dr. Markus, 43
576. Lerch Anna-Eugenie, 38
577. Lewinson Karl-Filip
578. Lewniowsky Malvine, 31
579. Lewnowsky Minna, 29
580. Liebling Friedrich, 26
581. Liebert Heinz, 21
582. Liebreich Ignatz, 38
583. Liesback Majlec h, 20
584. Linder Kurt, 19
585. Linsen Paul, 32
586. Linker Leon, 34
587. Linker Hedwig, 24
588. Lion Margarete, 32
589. Litwitz Liese, 48
590. Löb Max, 19
591. Löbl Lucie, 61
592. Löbl Agnes Rachel, 25
593. Löffler Emil, 45
594. Laserstein Gertrude, 17, from Germany
595. Löwl Šandor, 27
596. Löwy Sigmund Moritz, 56
597. Löwy Lilli, 21
598. Löwy Hermann, 23

599. Löwy Irma, 27
600. Löwy Gustav, 20
601. Lustig Grete, 24
602. Lustig Max, 33
603. Mader Beile Malke, known as Berta
     Mader, born in Nazissenfeld, 50
604. Mayer Kata, 22
605. Mayer Siegbert, 22
606. Mayer Benno, 56
607. Mayer Aron, 49
608. Mayer Anna, 46
609. Makowsky Heil, 34
610. Mamber Ottilie, 31
611. Mandl Emmerich, 61
612. Mandl Elsa, 50
613. Mandl Rosa, 25
614. Mandl Maria, 53
615. Mandl Ernst, 19
616. Mandl Leib-Ignatz, 25
617. Mandel Leib, 52
618. Mandel Theodor, 29
619. Manswirth Friedrich, 23
620. Mantler Kurt, 24
621. Mantler Grete, 30
622. Marchfeld Walter, 24
623. Marbahn Karl, 44
624. Margulis Felicia, 51
625. Margulis Moses, 51
626. Markbreiter Ignatz, 30
627. Markstein Ernst, 46
628. Markus Ida, 52
629. Markus Kurt, 20
630. Markus Frieda, 43
631. Medina Buchora, 71, housewife from
     Šabac
632. Medina Binja, 73, merchant from Šabac
633. Medina Salomon, 50, householder
     from Šabac
634. Medina Rebka, 42, housewife from
     Šabac
635. Medina Benno, 20
636. Medina Ignatz, 17
637. Melamed Samuilo
638. Melamed Jakob, 54, merchant from
     Šabac

639. Melamed Lika, 35, housewife from Šabac
640. Melamed Nissim, 25
641. Melamed Isak, 22
642. Melamed Sultana, 17, from Šabac
643. Melamed Samuel
644. Melamed Silva, 12, from Šabac
645. Melamed Jeanina, 10, from Šabac
646. Melamed Nissim, 5, from Šabac
647. Melser Susanne, 21
648. Mendelsohn Genter, 28
649. Mendelsohn Lilli, 11
650. Mezies Klara, 31
651. Milcinsky Harli, 36
652. Milcinsky Pailine, 23
653. Mittelmann Samuel, 49
654. Mittelmann Regina, 66
655. Moorberger Rudolf, 53
656. Möller Josef Hirsch, 47
657. Moreno Moritz, 39, merchant from Šabac
658. Morgenstern Ester, 49
659. Morgenstern Fritz, 31
660. Morgenstern Netti Sara, 20
661. Mondschein Renée, 29
662. Müler Berthold, 31
663. Müler Henry, 19
664. Müler Sulamith, 22
665. Münzer Felga, 45
666. Münzer Moses, 50
667. Münz Anny, 34
668. Münz Adolf, 30
669. Nachmann Samuel
670. Nasimov Felix, 19
671. Neiger Karl, 24
672. Német Jakob, 47
673. Német Berta, 41
674. Neuberger Ignatz, 34
675. Neufeld Lilli, 36
676. Neuhauser Leopold, 32
677. Neumann Bernhard, 35
678. Neumann Richard, 20
679. Neumann Rudolf, 30
680. Neumann Dr. Hilda, 48
681. Neumann Dr. Paul, 65

682. Neumann Julius, 55
683. Neumann Katherine, 56
684. Neumann Gertrude, 57
685. Nowak Siegfried, 20
686. Ochshorn Gisa, 28
687. Orenstein Leopold, 19
688. Pachtmann Haja, 55
689. Pachtmann Marcel, 28
690. Pais Mosek, 55
691. Pais Erna, 18
692. Pais Itta, 45
693. Papo Danko, 30, dental technician from Šabac
694. Paschkes Rosita, 22
695. Paschkes Walter, 27
696. Paul Serel Basia, 52
697. Paul Isidor Jakob, 44
698. Penner Gittel, 49
699. Penner Simon, 51
700. Perlmann Moritz, 33
701. Petschenik Abraham Hirsh, 49
702. Pfeffe Heinrich, 33
703. Pfeffer Siegfried, 32, from Germany
704. Pfeffer Anna, 34
705. Picker Rachel, 28
706. Pinkascheviæ Theodor, 20
707. Pinkus Kurt, 29
708. Platschek Siegfried, 20
709. Plaut Herman, 32
710. Politscher Eugen, 20
711. Pollak Heinrich, 32
712. Pollak Aranka, 53
713. Pollak Julius, 59
714. Polonsky Susa, 31
715. Polonsky Gerhard, 36
716. Pomerant Eli, 48
717. Pomerant Max, 48
718. Pompan Jakob, 57
719. Pompan Regina, 50
720. Pragan Rudolf, 21
721. Preis Gisela, 22
722. Preis Otto, 22
723. Preis Friedel, 18
724. Preis Walter, 21
725. Preminger Hudia, 35

726. Preminger Emil, 42
727. Preminger Mela, 51
728. Preminger Heinrich, 56
729. Prucker Friedal, 21
730. Pulgram Hermann, 33
731. Puretz Sarah, 48, Born Schönals Lea
732. Rat Elsa, 21
733. Rechnitzer Hedwig, 41
734. Rechnitzer Jakob, 33
735. Rehberger Richard, 33
736. Reinhold Hermina, 21
737. Reiniger Martha, 13
738. Reis Lilli, 26
739. Reis Friedrich, 27
740. Reis Simche, 32
741. Reiser Molo, 45
742. Reiser Lemel, 49
743. Reismann Elsa, 27
744. Reismann Julian, 32
745. Renhold Adolf, 25
746. Repstein Nita, 26
747. Rewelsky Hermann, 31
748. Richter Hans, 21
749. Riegler Elsa, 41
750. Riegler Leopold, 46
751. Riegler Julia, 56
752. Riegler Julius, 61
753. Riese Karl, 19
754. Rosenbaum Kurt, 19
755. Rosenbaum Ludwig, 31
756. Rosenberg Paula, 33
757. Rosenberg Rudolf (Rudolf-Viktor), 20
758. Rosenberg Herbert, 19
759. Rosenberg Irma, 31
760. Rosenberg Karl, 43
761. Rosenblum Moritz, 21
762. Rosenblum Traute, 25
763. Rosenblum Wolf, 23
764. Rosenstrauch Adelheid, 36
765. Rosenstrauch J. Abraham, 49
766. Rotenstreich Rachela, 41
767. Rotenstreich Karl, 48
768. Rosenstingl Gyula, 21, from Germany
769. Rosenthal Leitzer, 35, from Poland
770. Rosenthal Günther, 21

771. Rosenthal Karl, 28, from Germany
772. Rossmann Rosa, 46
773. Rossmann Josef, 52
774. Rosner Edita, 32
775. Rosner Cäcilie, 32
776. Rosner Friedrich, 71, Vienna
777. Rosner Else, 9
778. Rosner Walter, 29
779. Rotberg Eva, 20
780. Roth Giser Elisa, 20
781. Roth Giser Lothar, 29
782. Roth Margit (Margarete), 32
783. Roth Aleksander, 37
784. Rothstein Feiga, 30
785. Rothstein Asig, 28
786. Rotter Ernestine, 39
787. Rottmann Sara, 43
788. Rottmann Jakob, 43
789. Ruchhalter Amelie, 19
790. Rubensohn Werner, 20
791. Rübner Alfred, 35, from Germany
792. Ruff Artur, 35
793. Russa Avram, 17, student from Šabac
794. Russa David, 25, clerk from Šabac
795. Russo Jeanne, 53, housewife from Šabac
796. Russo Dr. Haim, 65, doctor from Šabac
797. Sachs Adam-Adolf, 20
798. Salomon Ella, 20
799. Salomon Hermann, 53
800. Salomon Laura, 44
801. Salomon Judith, 19
802. Salter Sofia-Gisela, 44
803. Salter Erwin, 49
804. Samori Eduard, 48
805. Samueli Nacman, 49
806. Samueli Regine, 48
807. Saphier Erwin-Robert, 20
808. Saphierstein Arthur, 20
809. Säufer Amjaram-Naftali, 49
810. Säufer Hanna, 49
811. Sechter Emil, 38
812. Seefeld Irma, 27
813. Seelinger Siegbert, 27
814. Seelinger Lotte, 27
815. Seidler Lewek, 53

816. Seidler Sabine, 43
817. Seidner Hermine, 49
818. Seidner Stella, 19
819. Seif Abraham, 44
820. Seif Frieda, 44
821. Seinblüth Josef-Mosko, 59
822. Seinblüth Feiga, 54
823. Seinmann Josef, 32
824. Seinmann Xenia, 29
825. Seisse Wolf, 37
826. Seiwach Regine, 20
827. Siegel Berish, 32
828. Silber Haja, 44
829. Silbermann Emil, 32
830. Silbermann Josefine, 29
831. Simonović Rakila, widow from Šabac
832. Singer Abraham-Haim, 59
833. Singer Salim, 50
834. Singer Karl, 24
835. Sklarek Georg, 51
836. Sklarek Else, 49
837. Smejansky Ester, 56
838. Sonntag Hertha, 19
839. Spiegel Johann, 20
840. Spiegel Max, 23
841. Spiegel Ernest, 33
842. Spiegel Elsa, 19
843. Spiegler Erich, 30
844. Spiegler Alice, 39
845. Spielberger Albert, 25
846. Spielberger Paul, 21
847. Spitz Käthe, 21
848. Spitz Kurt, 26
849. Spitz Elisabet, 39
850. Spitz Emanuel, 47
851. Spitzer Alice, 31
852. Spitzer Ernest, 44
853. Spitzer Jana, 26
854. Spitzer Otto, 35
855. Spira Moses, 28, from Poland
856. Springer Käthe, 23
857. Sprung Gusta, 48
858. Sulfer Rudolf, 35
859. Sulke Max-Herman, 20
860. Süssmann Karl, 50

861. Süssmann Therese, 50
862. Süssmann Max, 20
863. Sprung Mandel, 48
864. Swintalsky Haim, 42
865. Szabo Viktor, 47
866. Schächter Rifka, 63
867. Schächter Josef, 33
868. Schächter Anna, 32
869. Schaner Franzuska, 39
870. Schapira Ignatz, 39
871. Schapira Minna, 47
872. Schatzker Jetta, 41
873. Schein Isak Levi, 50
874. Schein Herner Rifka, 48
875. Schenk Dr. Nathan-Aron, 28
876. Schenk Anna, 29
877. Scherf Salomon, 43
878. Scherf Gusta, 43
879. Schimper Scharl Stella, 31
880. Schindler Walter, 30
881. Schleifer Erwin, 30
882. Schlesinger Elka, 30
883. Schlimper Robert, 25
884. Schmetterling Karl, 43
885. Schmetterling Malka (?)
886. Schmittmayer Kela, 20
887. Schmitz Ernst, 22
888. Schneider Robert, 23
889. Schneider Albert, 27
890. Schneider Haim Pinkas, 37
891. Schober Ernst, 27
892. Schober Gisela, 27
893. Schober Josef, 29
894. Schönfeld Stella, 44
895. Schaner Theodor, 44
896. Schram Simon, 44
897. Schram Josefine, 41
898. Schreiber Leib, 50
899. Schreiber Max, 19
900. Schröter Anna, 39
901. Schröter Leo, 33
902. Schulemann Walter, 32
903. Schwachter Ignatz, 34
904. Schwadron Moses, 53
905. Schwadron Oskar, 24

906. Schwalbe Inge, 22
907. Schwamm Otto, 33
908. Schwamm Klara, 30
909. Schwarzblattel Otto, 36
910. Schwarzblattel Jannet (Jenny), née Dickmann, 27
911. Schwarz Egon-Eugen, 47
912. Schwarz Paula, 44
913. Schwarz Gustarv, 32
914. Schwarz Marcel, 20
915. Schwarz Stefanie, 54
916. Schwatzer Kurt, 54
917. Schweber Sara, 56
918. Schweber Markus, 55
919. Schwerger Malvine, 19
920. Stegl Fritz, 36
921. Stereifler Jonas-Jakob, 53
922. Stein Leo, 47
923. Stein Alice, 43, Zasavica
924. Stein Berich Leo, 28
925. Stein Moritz-Martin, 34
926. Stein Kurt, 22
927. Steinberg Leo, 23
928. Steiner Paul, 20
929. Steiner Edith, 49
930. Steiner Otto, 32
931. Steiner Franz, 44
932. Steiner Artur, 37
933. Steiner Hermann, 21
934. Steiner Julia, 20
935. Steiner Hans, 21
936. Stelper Kurt, 28
937. Stern Josef, 48
938. Stern Emil, 38
939. Stern Else, 42
940. Stern Mathias, 26
941. Stern Rudolf, 33
942. Stern Aladar, 35
943. Sternberg Bassia, 52
944. Sternberg Fabian, 52
945. Stolz Haim, 41
946. Strauber Dr. Solomon, 29
947. Strauber Franziska, 27
948. Strassmann Wolf-Leib, 43
949. Strassmann Isak, 33
950. Streifler Lotta, 33
951. Strübel Herbert, 20
952. Talert Egon, 31
953. Tannenbaum Herman, 19
954. Tannenbaum Ernnst, 22
955. Tannenbaum Robert, 32
956. Tauber Salomon, 30
957. Tauber Josef, 28
958. Taubenschlag Werner, 20
959. Trebitsch Herta, 20
960. Tuchfeld Herbert, 18
961. Tutter Heinrich, 21
962. Tutter Jetti, 21
963. Ullmann Kurt, 20
964. Urban Eduard, 29
965. Urban Ella, 29
966. Versändig Moses, 40
967. Verständig Malka, 37
968. Waldmann Malvina, 40
969. Waldmann Ernst, 63
970. Waltuch Fritz, 24
971. Wassermann Rifka, 44
972. Wassermann Simche, 44
973. Wassermann Friedel, 40
974. Weigel Walter, 34
975. Weinberger Emanuel, 61
976. Weniberger Martha, 45
977. Weitraub Sara, 32
978. Weitraub Moses, 42
979. Weinstein Sabina, 47
980. Weinstein Sandor, 20
981. Weingarten Betty, 20
982. Weinstock Haja Ides, 46
983. Weiss Eva, 16
984. Weiss Ruth, 17
985. Weiss Lisabeth, 19
986. Weiss Alexander, 20
987. Weiss Franz, 21
988. Weiss Fritz, 25
989. Weiss Gerold, 26
990. Weiss Karoline, 31
991. Weiss Adelberg, 39
992. Weiss Ester, 32
993. Weiss Frieda, 27
994. Weiss Rudolf, 40

995. Weiser Helene, 34
996. Weiser Georg, 39
997. Weissberg Mordoko, 43
998. Weissberg Bulin, 36
999. Weissberg Siegfried, 20
1000. Weitz Angela, 58
1001. Weitz Dr. Ignatz, 52
1002. Wellwahr Elwire, 27
1003. Wellwahr Emil, 26
1004. Wellisch Melanie, 34
1005. Wellisch Ernst, 33
1006. Wenig Hansi, 41
1007. Wettendorfer Bernat, 70, pensioner
   from Šabac
1008. Wettendorfer Alexander, 35, from
   Šabac
1009. Wettendorfer Franz, 32, from Šabac
1010. Werthim Alfred, 21
1011. Werdiheim Karl, 20
1012. Wesel Feiga, 23
1013. Wesel Paul, 29
1014. Wickelholz Ella, 25
1015. Widder Eugen, 30, from Slovakia
1016. Wieselberg Minna, 21
1017. Wieselberg Artur, 25
1018. Wieselmann Max, 19
1019. Wiesner Amelie, 49
1020. Wiesner Daniel, 60, engineer
1021. Wisternitz Hans, 20
1022. Widowsky Mordoko, 23
1023. Willner Wilhelmine, 42
1024. Wimmer Gottlieb, 45
1025. Wimmer Rachel, 41
1026. Wimmer Haim, 31
1027. Winkler Alexander, 23
1028. Witsches Sofie, 52
1029. Witsches Salomon, 46
1030. Wiesinger Ernst, 14
1031. Wohl Karl-Heinz, 19
1032. Wolfsohn Ester-Emma, 61
1033. Wollisch Dr. Friedrich, 38
1034. Wollmann Juliette, 46
1035. Wünschbancher Erich, 19
1036. Zámory Manfred, 17
1037. Zimmermann Lydia, 53

1038. Zimmermann Samuel, 60
1039. Zewitzger Robert
1040. Zuckerberg Zittel, 61
1041. Zuckerberg Anna, 33
1042. Zwicker Berta, 44, from Zasavica
1043. Zwicker Josefina, 48
1044. Zwicker Suzanne, 16
1045. Zwicker Siegfried, 56
1046. Zwicker Robert, 32
1047. Zwicker Ilona, 32
1048. Zwicker Julius, 43, from Vienna
1049. Zwicker Franz, 22
1050. Zwiebel Sofie, 40
1051. Zwiebel Süsskind, 41
1052. Zwirn Egon, 22
1053. Zeigfinger Benjamin, 41
1054. Zenner Rossa, 51, from Vienna
1055. Zenner Haim, 54, from Vienna

Today there are no Jews in Šabac.

Today Zasavica is a nature park, a special reserve.

Today in Zasavica one finds a picturesque woods, boggy meadows, wide banks and waterways, a wealth of plant and animal species, especially old, endemic and rare ones, and their communities, and a historical heritage that stretches back to distant times. Today in Zasavica visitors are offered tourist experiences: rest, recreation, boating and enjoyment of nature.

In May 2011 in the Zasavica special reserve there were recorded three new species of butterfly: the Brown Hairstreak (*Thecla betulae*), the Mourning Cloak (*Nymphalis antiopa*) and the Green Hairstreak (*Callophrys rubi*). The butterflies in Zasavica are protected, they fly.

Today Zasavica is lovely. And full of life. Several indigenous animal species wander freely through the reserve. There are Podolski cattle, and Pulin sheepdogs, five families of beavers and more than six hundred Mangalica pigs, so-called woolly pigs—*Wollschweine*—adorned with black eyelashes. Mangalica pigs are robust, resistant to disease, stress and all climates. The woolly pigs love to roam, they have a great need of movement, walking, of coming and going. The great freedom of movement is made possible by their powerful legs, strengthened by sturdy trotters. Unlike so-called thoroughbred strains, Mangalica pigs have no deformations in their locomotive apparatus, and are equally at home on plains,

mountains and hilly meadows from the Alps and Pannonia to the Carpathians in the east and the Balkan mountain range in southeast Europe. Mangalicas love mud.

Oh, and most important: in the Zasavica Special Nature Reserve a farm has been established with one hundred members of a species known as the Balkan donkey, for the time being the only donkey farm in this part of Europe. Donkey milk and meat are used to make unique and expensive cosmetics and dried meat products. Donkey milk is high-quality milk, it has a low percentage of fat and a high percentage of protein. So, in the Zasavica Nature Reserve donkey milk is used for making face creams and body creams, and it is possible to buy enough of that milk (at least seventy liters) at forty euros per liter for a bath à la Cleopatra, for maintaining the softness of the skin. Yes, donkey milk is exceptionally expensive milk because donkey mares do not give much milk, at most 150 to two hundred milliliters in four milkings a day, so in two years one mare will only give twenty or so liters. But this milk does not contain bacteria, so it does not need to be pasteurized, it has sixty times more vitamin C and additional medicinal qualities. It is preserved by freezing.

Donkey milk cream—25 euros
Donkey milk soap—5 euros
Donkey milk liqueur, 1 dl.—10 euros
Donkey meat sausage, 1 kg.—15 euros
Donkey meat salami, 1 kg.—20 euros
There. That would be the Zasavica Nature Park today.

My father was a religious fanatic, Rudolf Sass finally confesses to himself and to the psychiatrist Kaplan. *A literate religious fanatic and a successful merchant. My sister died before the war, in unexplained circumstances. She was fifteen. I wanted to cast light on those circumstances, at some stage. No one ever talked about my sister's death in our house. No one talked about anything in our house. An uncomfortable hardness ruled*, says Rudolf Sass.

After graduating from high school, Rudolf Sass leaves the small town, not far from Šabac, where the Sass family had settled at the end of the war. *I didn't miss anyone*, says Rudolf Sass. *My mother— under the absolute dominance of my father, frightened and weak; my brothers, they got by somehow. I only regretted leaving my grandfather, with whom I had long, quiet conversations, I told him about my Jewish friends, who gave me money, just a few coins so that I could go to the cinema or buy sweets. Nevertheless, I decided that when I got stronger I would go home, I decided I would go and say to my father, You were a cruel and bad parent.*

So:

It is 1946. Rudolf Sass secretly takes three one-hundred-dollar bills out of his father's safe. He needs them to cover his living costs until he finds work. Rudolf Sass changes one bill on the black market and puts the money into his pocket. He hides the other two bills in his shoes. He walks twenty kilometers to the railroad station.

In the noisy smoke-filled station restaurant, Rudolf Sass orders tea and takes off his shoes, which are rubbing. His feet are swollen and bloody. The banknotes are crumpled, torn and smudged. Unusable. Rudolf Sass trembles, he is beside himself. He climbs onto the train. Limping. In the distance he hears a terrible voice, a deep, furious voice yelling, *Stop, Rudolf, stop!* His father is running along the platform, red in the face and waving a clenched fist. The doors close. The train leaves.

Rudolf Sass finds a place in a run-down student dorm, a room shared with two others, he does newspaper and milk rounds, plays basketball, gets a scholarship, he fits in, it is all meager but secure. He studies. He passes his exams. Now and again he goes to the theater, tickets are cheap, he has friends, he has a girlfriend, then he doesn't, then he does again, life works, it goes on. He has no contact with his family. No one calls, no one visits. From time to time he exchanges letters with his grandfather. His childhood gradually disappears in the trash heap of his confined past, in the storehouse of days buried under his new life.

Some ten years later Rudolf Sass's arms and legs occasionally swell again, and the tendons in his thumb and forefinger stiffen. These are irregularities that do not disrupt the rhythm of his life. The problem is diagnosed as an angioneurotic edema, that is, a psychosomatic illness, that includes allergies.

It'll pass, say the doctors.

It'll pass, Rudolf Sass repeats.

Poor Rudolf Sass. He cannot free himself from the problems of his body.

It is 1984. Rudolf Sass (57) has been living in Switzerland for a long time now, eighteen years. He is a specialist, an anesthesiologist, at a private clinic in Lausanne. When he's not working, when he rests, he looks out at Lake Geneva and the mountain range in the distance. He is married to Laura, a nurse who works in the same clinic. At home they speak French. They have a daughter, Tina (16). When he is agitated, Rudolf Sass notices his heart occasionally skips a beat, his pulse becomes irregular. *What now? These extrasystoles do not bode well*, he says, and goes for a checkup. The tests reveal no anomalies. However, Rudolf Sass is convinced that this inner fluttering is connected to the discussions he has been having for some time with his wife Laura about his visit home. *I'm going with you*, Laura insists. *No, I'm going alone*. Rudolf Sass is determined. And so, Rudolf Sass goes to his homeland to carry out his mission, to bury his years-old nightmare, to cast the rotten, irritating burden out of his good, stable Swiss mountain-lakeside life, to tell and show his father what he thought and what he still thinks about him. But his father is no more, his grandfather has also died, in the family house only his mother is left. After his return to Lausanne, the extrasystoles retreat. But it is another event that contributes to the fact that Rudolf's heart starts to beat properly again, quietly and regularly. He breaks off a love affair that has long been bringing chaos and disquiet into his spick-and-span Swiss life. And so, for a few years Rudolf Sass feels well, apart from the occasional recurrence of his allergy symptoms, redness of the face and swelling of his hands and feet.

Time rolls. Rudolf Sass ages. The clinic where he works is in financial difficulties, a crisis, savings have to be made at home and at work, the future is uncertain, old age too. Tina marries, not a doctor as Rudolf Sass had hoped for, but a stockbroker whom Rudolf does not like. At his son-in-law's insistence, Rudolf Sass invests his life savings in some shares and loses all his money. Soon after that his itching starts again, his *pruritus ani. Still I keep functioning. At work, at home, at table and in bed. No signs of depression*, Rudolf Sass assures himself.

But troubles keep coming.

Rudolf Sass's son-in-law falls ill with tuberculosis of the lungs.

His condition worsens and he is moved to the Vaudois University Hospital in Lausanne. Rudolf Sass is upset. In addition to his wife and himself, he must now provide for his daughter Tina's family. In 1988 she gives birth to Emma. His son-in-law is increasingly ill, spitting blood. The doctors invite their colleague Rudolf Sass for consultations. One evening, as he is walking in the hospital grounds with his arm around Tina's shoulder, a chance passerby calls out, *Now what, you're seducing your own daughter!* Rudolf Sass feels his cheeks burning, his heart starts beating rapidly and his head begins to pound. That night Rudolf Sass cannot sleep. *I'm going to be ill,* he keeps saying, *I'm going to be ill.* His anal itch gets worse—Rudolf Sass is saddled with a deep depression. Rudolf Sass avoids seeing patients, fearful that he might attack or injure them. He is afraid to be with his wife, with Tina and little Emma. Terrified and confused, Rudolf Sass does not understand what is happening, despite his hope that, as soon as his pruritus is cleared up, he will emerge from the dark. *That mental blindness in Rudolf Sass is astonishing, the blindness provoked by the chance remark about him and his daughter,* says Andreas's friend the psychiatrist Adam Kaplan. *The apparently harmless remark of a passerby reactivated in him a suppressed sense of guilt in connection with his wish for the death of his son-in-law, and his guilt about his fantasies of renewed control over the lives of his daughter Tina and his granddaughter Emma, Rudolf Sass reacts vehemently, maintaining that he is doing all in his power for his son-in-law's recovery.*

Fantasies about death and lust are completely alien to my nature, maintains Rudolf Sass; *I am convinced that my depression is a result of the physical state I am in.*

It was only when I told him that his pruritus could perhaps be a sadomasochistic expression of suppressed hatred for his son-in-law, and possibly for his wife, that Rudolf Sass began to listen to his body and his emotions. You see, said Adam Kaplan to his friend Andreas Ban, *the first outbreak of pruritus in Rudolf Sass coincided with investing in those shares at the insistence of his son-in-law, a classic identification of money with the anus—we learned that at grammar school. The uncontrolled scratching with which Rudolf Sass attempted to relieve his anal itch points to the sadomasochistic nature of his conflict. One should also remember that he stole his father's money for his escape to university, and particularly the episodes from Rudolf Sass's early childhood when he tries unsuccessfully to help his friend Kari Kriss. All these episodes involve money.*

Rudolf Sass brings his first dream to a session with Adam Kaplan. *The dream is about fingernails, about the bloody, bitten nails with which Rudolf Sass tries to climb a tall tree,* Adam Kaplan says to his friend Andreas Ban. *Running away from his wife, Rudolf Sass finds himself surrounded by believers deep in prayer. According to the Talmud, believers are obliged to burn the cuttings from their fingernails, and to examine their nails carefully during prayer. The nail is dead matter,* says Adam Kaplan, *the nail is a symbol of death, it must be destroyed because it threatens the body and the soul. The bloody bitten nails in Rudolf Sass's dream symbolize the suppressed aggression he feels toward his wife whom he considers responsible for the loss of their property. The believers symbolize the castration which threatens Rudolf Sass's superego. And here, finally, the return to his father,* concludes Adam Kaplan.

Yes, that return to our fathers about whom volumes have been written and are still being written and will always be written. Fathers who like evil spirits inhabit our bodies even after they are dead, who never really die, who burn with us in the flames of the crematorium, holding us protectively to their chests or sending us dire, threatening looks, sometimes shaking a belt or stick at us. Even when we become fathers, we do not succeed in killing our own. Overcome with a desire for revenge, we kill our fathers in dreams and poems, in plays and stories, in films, to assuage our guilt, we send them prayers for forgiveness. So Rudolf's father's fanatical Catholic beliefs pursue Rudolf Sass all his life, they catch him, disappear, then grab him by the throat again. Like a branded beast Rudolf Sass bears the stamp of his family, torn between abandoning himself to his masochistic being and the need to be free from his suppressed anal-sadistic impulses. Rudolf Sass, in life and death united with his mild permissive grandfather and his sadistic father.

But there is another story, unfinished, a hazy story, that undermines Rudolf Sass's life, the story of his father's role in the massacre of Šabac, even if that role amounts to the unwillingness to help, the simple refusal to see and silence. Rudolf Sass will never discover whether or how much his father, on the other side of the River Drina, served the Ustasha regime of the Independent State of Croatia, because he never asked anyone or researched anything, because he never had time, is that it? Life pulled its strings which Rudolf Sass obediently accepted, in the end, by anesthetizing his Swiss patients, himself becoming numb, quiet, reconciled to his polished inner being in which he stored his family filth.

Andreas Ban would have called Adam Kaplan, even traveled to Belgrade, to ask him, *Adam, what's happening to me, I've lost the key*, because Andreas Ban trusts his friend from his secondary school days. But Adam Kaplan is no more. In 1998 Adam killed himself with his father's pistol.

What now? Should he, Andreas Ban, write something about his own father? Or—about himself as a father? Vain delusions. He had put the puzzle together up to a point, solved the little rebus, and after too many years its images had arranged themselves into a panorama he no longer needed, which he was pushing away and burying. But.

In 2006 or 2007, he no longer remembers when, at the funeral of his cousin Clara who dies of glioblastoma, while the priest is performing his one-act play over the open grave which, with sagging faces, the congregation accompanies like the chorus in classical tragedy, with the singsong refrain of *our sins, our sins*, Andreas Ban is approached by an elderly woman who in a whisper says, *In 1942 my brother, a Zagreb student linked to the National Liberation Movement, served time with your mother in an Ustasha prison, while your uncle, also Clara's uncle, Dr. Bruno belonged to the university Ustasha command and came to lectures in his uniform.* At funerals one learns all kinds of things. One skeleton is laid into the ground, another rises up. Andreas Ban leaves Clara's burial broken and beside himself. His family too drags with it slimy trails of evil, he too can play this game, before his eyes a cracked family photograph now flickers, a distorted mirror, its silver peeling away. How is it that for sixty years not one of his relatives has ever mentioned the wartime and postwar past of his uncle Bruno, later a scientist of world renown, an expert in the biological protection of agricultural and forest cultures, one of the founders of the postwar Agricultural and Forestry School in Sarajevo, member of the Academy of Sciences of Bosnia and Herzegovina, that uncle Bruno who succeeds in curing his carcinoma of the testes, while metastases slink through his sister, Andreas's mother Marisa, gripping her and devouring her until they snuff her out. How come, Andreas Ban wonders, but too late, too late, how was it that uncle Bruno ended up in Sarajevo in 1946, when his family, Andreas's, on both his mother's and his father's side, had no connection with Bosnia and Herzegovina? Does the new government send him as punishment, just as many collaborators of the NDH are after the war scattered all over Yugoslavia to bring progress to the remote, devastated or backward regions, the way Lovro Matačić is sent to Skopje in 1948 to develop the musical life there, the Lovro Matačić who in 1941 leaps out of his tailcoat into the uniform of a home-guard lieutenant colonel, and by decree of Slavko Kvaternik is appointed supervisor of home-guard music overseeing all NDH military orchestras and nurturing close friendships with prominent political and military figures in Germany and the NDH.

Throughout the war, noble Mata-čić, in addition to performing in Croatia, travels through Austria, Germany, Italy and Romania, through countries in which at that time *sangre puro** was a sanctity, and at the invitation of another, more significant and greater musical personage of the twentieth century, the famous Wilhelm Furtwängler, stands in front of the Berlin Philharmonic Orchestra  while all over Europe potential geniuses vanish in scorched flakes through chimneys, are shoved into collective pits, rot in forests

* On April 30, 1941 Pavelić brought in the Decree on Race, that is "on the protection of the Aryan blood and honor of the Croatian nation," which was repealed on May 3, 1945.

or hang from town lampposts, while the sensitive urban population, shortsighted and tongue-tied, those who enjoy the power of music to ennoble the soul, clap and chant "encore!" Matačić served his time in Stara Gradiška, and after a five-year enforced stay in Macedonia, continues to rise in his own and others' eyes until he sails into legend. While Furtwängler is to this day the subject of plays, biographies, historical studies and films, with the aim of disentangling the wartime and postwar entanglements of that egocentric, but indisputably talented and highly educated musical figure, known to some as Monopoleon, whereas in Croatia all that remains of Lovro Matačić is a minor touched-up myth and the Lili and Lovro Matačić Foundation that gives grants to talented young musicians. When Andreas Ban mentions Matačić to acquaintances, they say, *No need to poke around there any more, all there is to know about Matačić is known already.* Who knows? What do they know?

In December 2004, Andreas Ban is living in Skopje when the Macedonian National Theater puts on an exhibition of photographs, documents, posters and texts on "the life and creative opus of the great Croatian musical maestro Lovro Matačić." There are gaps in this exhibition, the years 1941–45 are missing, the years when the noble conductor goes to Stockerau in Austria, as depicted in the film "Fighters for Croatia" (1943), and says, *You know what, I'm just visiting our soldiers to brighten up their lives with music.* From what he remembers of that Macedonian exhibition, Andreas Ban cannot be sure that he saw photos of the "supreme military bandmaster" (Matačić), assigned to the Office for the Spiritual Care of Members of the Armed Forces of the NDH, conducting in Vienna a German-Croatian military concert with music ensembles from the German Wehrmacht. Andreas Ban does not remember that exhibition at the Macedonian National Theatre in Skopje in 2004, organized by the Zagreb Lili and

Lovro Matačić Foundation and the Croatian Embassy in Skopje, supported by the Macedonian Ministry of Culture, nor does he remember whether he had seen the Easter edition of the paper *The Croatian Nation* printed in honor of the founding of the Independent State of Croatia, which included a text by Jerko Skračić (*Poglavnik, Leader, longing of all Croats, / May the power of Providence forever protect you / Let your firm hand rule over us / Let your firm hand be our Leader!*) and musical notation composed by Lovro Matačić for the march "The Song of Croatian Freedom."

Whom should Andreas Ban ask about his uncle Bruno? Perhaps his family, his Partisan, antifascist family had included other protectors of their own little lives, other adherents, followers—Ustashas. Whom to ask? Almost all of them are dead, including those who are still alive.

Did Bruno collaborate with the Ustashas? Andreas asks his ninety-two-year-old father, now when it is too late. His father says nothing. Andreas Ban asks again. His father says, *Many people collaborated.*

Why was he sent to Sarajevo? asks Andreas Ban.

I don't remember, his father says.

Andreas Ban had read somewhere that wars are orgies of forgetfulness. The twentieth century has archived vast catacombs, tunnels of information in which researchers get lost and in the end abandon their research, catacombs that ever fewer people enter. Stored away—forgotten. The twentieth century, a century of great tidying that ends in cleansing; the twentieth century, a century of cleansing, a century of erasure. Language perhaps remains, but it too is crumbling. A great burden falls on twentieth-century man and he drags himself out from under it, damaged. Did Pliny write somewhere that nothing in us is as fragile as memory, that dubious ability which builds and rebuilds a person. Whom should he now ask? How can he sort out that family defeat? Family secrets surface unexpectedly and too late. Whenever a person wishes to remember, up comes oblivion (or death), ready to pounce.

Whom should he now ask?

In 1941 Bruno has a fiancée, Judita, this Andreas Ban knows. Judita is a philosophy student and a Jew. Through his connections, Andreas Ban presumes his Ustasha connections, Bruno sends Judita secretly to Trieste, where for Andreas Ban the story breaks off.

What happened to Bruno's fiancée Judita? Andreas Ban asks his ninety-two-year-old father now that it's too late.

Which Judita? his father says.

Perhaps that small, brave, loving gesture goes some way to redeeming Bruno after the war. But as luck would have it, in 1949 Bruno marries Klotilda, an ethnic German about whose past Andreas Ban knows nothing, except that she was blonde, and lucid, methodical, rigid and tidy. Andreas Ban could have called his ninety-year-old uncle Bruno and clarified all those questions, but since after Klotilda's death her family used lies and trickery to appropriate the burial plot of Andreas's grandmother, Bruno and Marisa's mother, so that now he, Andreas Ban, does not know where someone will lay his cremated remains, he no longer communicates with Bruno. When Bruno comes from Sarajevo for the funeral of his sister, Andreas's mother Marisa, without even once in the preceding two years of her illness visiting her, and people are mourning, many from all over Yugoslavia, friends and Marisa's former patients, Klotilda does not attend the service but fries veal cutlets, dozens of veal cutlets, calmly and with dedication so as to feed all who later come to the apartment. Andreas Ban does not ask anything then, it is not the right time. Now, when he is fighting a duel with his own body, a duel from which, ah, he knows, he will not emerge the victor, all that remains is for him to pick through other people's lives to get some distance from his own. Otherwise, Andreas Ban, already lethargic, is waiting for the approaching waters of Lethe to wash over him. Granted with occasional feeble twinges. But, Andreas, *you can demolish a city, burn a card, scratch a marble, but you cannot remove a word from a brain, understand?*

Klotilda and her family, did they collaborate with the Nazis? Andreas asks his ninety-two-year-old father.

Leave me alone, his father says.

Andreas's father is now a semi-invalid. He has bedsores. He acquires the bedsores after an operation for a broken hip. When bedsores appear, they are often followed by sepsis from which older patients quickly die. But Andreas's father holds on, he does not let go. He says, *These bedsores aren't healing, I'll have them my entire life.* How extensive is a whole, an entity? Andreas's father lives in a state-run old people's home in Zagreb because he does not have an apartment of his own. Andreas's father's second wife and her son assure Andreas and his sister Ada that their father is on his way out, that is why he has to go into a home. He is not on his way out. He cannot get to the toilet so he shits in diapers. That's all. Andreas's father calls Andreas and tells him about his fucked-up dignity. About how tired he is. Andreas's father is completely lucid. His French is still good. And his English is good. When they talk, Andreas Ban and his father occasionally throw Italian words and phrases into their conversation as well. But nevertheless his second wife and her son still put Andreas's father into that home. Because he can no longer walk, because he is infirm. Now when Andreas goes to visit his father in that home, he meets the sons and daughters of other old and infirm residents, some of whom do not know who they are nor where they are, they just lie like corpses and their mouths gape mechanically as the staff shovel spoonfuls of thin gruel into them.

In the bed next to Andreas's father lies a former Ustasha whose surname is Boban. He is ninety-seven, after the war he fled to

France and has now returned to die in the bosom of his mother-land. He is the cousin of Rafael Boban, the half-literate boor and cutthroat, commander of the Black Legion, who used to tour markets before the war selling spangles and tobacco. The Boban in the bed beside Andreas's father steals other people's belongings, sweets, sugar, teabags, paper handkerchiefs, sometimes even cash. With tiny, tiny steps he creeps into neighboring rooms and thinks that no one can hear him because he is completely deaf. When the nurses catch him, they just say *tuttuttut* and shake their heads while he acts dumb. So, willy-nilly, the Partisan and the Ustasha reach a "reconciliation." In an old people's home. In silence. In infirmity.

There is also an old woman who often comes into Andreas's father's room and wails, *Take me home, please take me home.* There's another, she is stylish, but her eyes are empty. She just comes in, stands there and says nothing. Andreas asks her, *Is there something you need?* and after a pause she says, *Closeness.* As though she were a Beckett character. Andreas asks her, *How old are you?* but again she says nothing, says nothing then whispers, *Very old*, because she does not know, because she does not remember. That woman looks well groomed and her hair is expertly cut.

There is a stench of urine in Andreas's father's room.

In that home Andreas listens as the sons and daughters of those lying there desperately call the staff, *Please come, Dad has shat himself, Mother has soiled herself.* Andreas's father says, *I didn't pass a stool for three days, then I had a good shit over Christmas.* And he says, *I go down to the ground floor by myself, in the elevator, in my wheelchair, and play chess in the living room.* And he says, *We used to play Preferans until our third player died.**

* Preferans. An Eastern European ten-card plain-trick game with bidding, played by three or four players with a thirty-two-card piquet deck. A sophisticated variant of the Austrian game Préférence, which in turn descends from Spanish Ombre and French Boston.

When Andreas comes to visit his father, he brings the strongest combinations of vitamins and minerals to help him hang on to life a bit longer, he gives him pocket money because Andreas's father says, *I've never been so poor.* Andreas takes his father out of the home in his wheelchair, he takes him out to lunch, they drink good wine, eat scampi cocktail and laugh. He pushes him through the streets to breathe in the air. They go from bar to bar and smoke. They both have cold hands. Sometimes they reach for each other's hands and talk, linked together. About the past, about the future, about the music that will be played at Andreas's father's funeral: *"Lovely land, Istria dear,"* play that for me, says Andreas's father.

Andreas's father sells the apartment which he worked for together with Andreas's mother, then gives half the money to his other wife. Then he moves into his stepson's apartment. His stepson has several apartments and he thrusts under Andreas's father's nose a declaration (certified by a lawyer) according to which Andreas Ban's father agrees to be moved out by the stepson into a home when he becomes infirm or begins to lose his marbles. Andreas's father signs the declaration. Andreas's father did not lose his marbles, but he made a fool of himself. Andreas's father spent his half of the money, the money from the sale of his apartment, on renovating the apartment which he moved into with his second wife, the apartment belonging to his stepson who stipulated how that apartment should look. So Andreas's father is left without additional funds, with a small pension that barely covers his stay in the state-run old people's home. Andreas's father had been a tall, very tall, handsome man. He had a degree in electrical engineering. He was friends with painters and writers. He owned their paintings and books. All that disappeared, the pictures disappeared and

---

* "Krasna zemljo, Istro mila," the Istrian anthem.

the books were thrown out or given away. Especially the books with dedications. Andreas's father had traveled all over the world, he was well known. He had associated with many political figures, with Tito and Nehru, with Kerensky, with Louis Alojz Adamič, with Nasser, with Nimeiry, with Olof Palme and Urho Kekkonen. Urho Kekkonen gave Andreas's father a very large transistor, long ago, when transistors had just become fashionable. Ranković* had it in for him. And some other Croatian politicians had it in for him. It does not matter who, they are dead now. Photographs bear witness to Andreas's father's life, Andreas keeps them. The oil paintings are not at Andreas's place or at his sister Ada's. Andreas's father has now shrunk. He has no clothes either. He has no shoes or winter coat or cap or gloves or scarf, so Andreas brings him his own for their "walks." Because they think, that woman and her son, that Andreas's father will never go out again. Out of the home, out of his bed, out of that waiting room. So they keep bringing him pajamas and tracksuits. He is very thin and fragile, Andreas's father. Andreas would like to move his father closer to him, but his father says no. He wants to stew in his own stupidity. He has sobered up and puts up with it. That woman now visits him in the home once a week, as though he had gone on some kind of cure, to a spa. She brings him apple pie. She is bored now, that woman, because she no longer has someone to quarrel with, no one to shout at. She is quarrelsome, pathologically jealous. Andreas and his sister annoy her, she insults

* Aleksandar Ranković was a Yugoslav communist of Serb origin, considered to be the third most powerful man in Yugoslavia after Josip Broz Tito and Edvard Kardelj. Ranković was a proponent of a centralized Yugoslavia and opposed efforts that promoted decentralization, which he deemed to be against the interests of Serb unity; he ran Kosovo as a police state and made Serbs dominant in the Socialist Autonomous Province of Kosovo's nomenklatura. Ranković supported a hard-line approach against Albanians in Kosovo, who were commonly suspected of pursuing seditious activities.

them, Andreas's father's previous life annoys her. She has hysterical attacks and dreams up vile stories. She is old too, and totally uninteresting. She is not nice to look at, she was never good-looking, and Andreas likes beauty. That woman has a lot of poison inside her. Politically, she is quite fanatical, right-wing. Andreas does not like to be in her company, she makes him tense. In the home, they like Andreas's father. Andreas's father is cheerful. Andreas's father is outgoing, he talks to people, listens to their stories, when he plays chess he wins. Very few manage to work out what goes on inside, in Andreas's father's chest, perhaps only Andreas Ban and Ada. What is now going on in Andreas's father's chest is pain. And pressure. It seems that Andreas's father is carrying a pneumatic chamber. He has had enough, Andreas's father. He says, *Leave me alone.*

Words, and with them images, hook themselves onto the brain like anchors and wound it.

Anchor.

Kindzal.

Many people still wriggle out with the defensive platitude *We didn't know. We didn't know about the persecutions, the camps, the slaughter then, we don't know about the disappearances, the torchings, the new camps and killings today.* That is what Wilhelm Furtwängler says too, justifying himself by saying he saved—he no longer remembers how many—Jews, especially musicians in "his" Berlin orchestra. Then an American researcher asks him, *Why was it necessary to save Jews if people didn't know?* Then Furtwängler falls silent.

Oh, there were other Matačićs and Furtwänglers in the course of the Second World War, there were plenty both before and after it, they exist today and they always will. Prominent and important musicians, conductors and composers who believed and still believe that, not art, but their art is more significant for humanity than a person. Herbert von Karajan, with his Nazi party card from 1933, membership number 3,430,914, and Victor de Sabata, Mussolini's close friend … Andreas Ban does not even wish to think about writers. About painters and actors, about singers and filmmakers who "stay and serve." But Otto Klemperer leaves, Bruno Walter leaves, Fritz Busch, Arnold Schoenberg and Alexander von Zemlinsky leave. Toscanini refuses to conduct in Nazi Germany, Oskar Danon leaves (to join the Partisans), and when he mentions this to those acquaintances of his, they say, *They were Jews or Serbs, they were saving their skins,* as though those who stayed and served were not. Why does Furtwängler play for Hitler's birthday? Why does he play at Nazi rallies? Why does he shake Goebbels's hand after one of his concerts? Why is his recording of Bruckner's Seventh Symphony broadcast immediately after Hitler's death? Had the Nazis by any chance won the war, would Furtwängler have taken shelter in a more secure place? Would he have withdrawn his anti-Semitic pronouncements? It is a dubious, rickety justification that would suggest anyone is indebted to these artistic giants who are also human monsters, dwarfs. The world would have survived without their music, without the Papadopouloses and Baranovićs, without various Leni Riefenstahls, because new ones would have come, as they have, maybe even better ones. Andreas Ban sees the whole hodgepodge of defensive statements dragging themselves through history like slime as an apologia *pro vita sua,* by means of which not only individuals but also governments endeavor to justify their service of the ideologies of Fascism, Nazism, Ustashism and, in the last analysis, of pathological patriotism.

In the afterword to his novel *The Guiltless* (*Die Schuldlosen,* 1950), Hermann Broch states that political indifference is closely linked to ethical depravity, that is, that politically innocent people are to a considerable degree ethically suspect, that they bear ethical blame, and stresses that the German populace did not feel responsible for Hitler's coming to power because they considered themselves "apolitical," in no way connected with what was happening around them. And what about the "apolitical" Croatian populace, which is selectively apolitical? How does it cope with what was happening and is still happening around it? It doesn't. It enjoys the music and applauds. And writes rigged history.

The Pope visits Croatia again. The new one. Once again people fall into a trance, they shout, *We love you, Pope.* When the previous pope was exhibited to the people, when they drove him all over Croatia, the people chanted, *We are the Pope's, the Pope is ours*, and asked him to stay, *Stay with us, Pope, stay with us*, they begged him frantically, as though they were dying.

At the end of the eighteenth century, the nobleman Jean-Louis Alibert (1768–1837) is preparing for the priesthood but recognizes in time the limitations of the strictly controlled masked ball, the costume theater of illusion, of blindfolded, repetitive, even threatening imagination, so he decides to study medicine and becomes a renowned dermatologist and later personal physician to the French king, Charles X. In his book *Physiologie des passions, ou Nouvelle doctrine des sentiments moraux* (1826), Alibert studies the way in which passion and emotion affect morality. Alibert writes about courage and human weakness, about integrity and finally about melancholy and depression, in other words, about phenomena long ago identified in a world which never was and never will be equally good for everyone. So why is Andreas Ban upset, why does he stay clenched in the embrace of a gigantic octopus whose tentacles crush his lungs, his heart and his brain, whose black ink clouds his vision?

Alibert tells two little stories about the two faces of melancholy, about melancholy as a creative force which enriches and inspires the fragile human species, and about melancholy as a negative force which drags people into depression and despair. So, as he examines an old copperplate engraving on which the founder of Stoic philosophy Zeno of Citium (fourth century B.C.) sits with slumped shoulders and a mournful face in the shade, with some kind of parchment on his knees, Alibert extols him as an example of humility and courage, as a heroic figure with enormous influence over the life of Athenians because of his encouragement of their patience, virtue, freedom and honesty. Andreas Ban would like to embark on a polemic, a quarrel, with Zeno of Citium, but also with Alibert, because when it is applied in practice, all that talk turns out to be senseless. Zeno is not prominent in public life, he sees government and laws as fate, he believes that a Stoic, virtuous man does not have the strength to oppose the powerful, so all that remains for him is to withdraw into solitude, into his small restricted privacy. How much has man changed since the fourth century B.C.? Why is Andreas upset? In *The Eighteenth Brumaire of Louis Bonaparte*, Marx says clearly, *Men make their own history, but they do not make it as they please; they do not make it under self-selected circumstances, but under existing circumstances, given and transmitted from the past. The tradition of all dead generations weighs like a nightmare on the brains of the living.*

Alibert also writes about Anselm, an intrusive patient in the Bicêtre hospital known as Diogenes who, because of his inflated ego, his unfounded ambitions and imagined philosophizing, maddened by the idea of saving the world, in the end, isolated, goes mad.

So, Andreas Ban knows what is happening to him, once he even goes to his doctor and tells her: *I'm depressed*, although he is not quite certain about the level of melancholy and depression running through him. *I'm depressed*, he tells his doctor, who does not ask questions, does not rummage through Andreas Ban's innards, she just says, *All right*, and prescribes some pills.

The tablets (antidepressants) do not help. They damage Andreas Ban's intestinal flora, so instead of eliminating through his pores vapors of "black bile," he runs to the toilet five times a day, forevermore, endlessly, because new shit is constantly amassing. Once he even shat himself as he was hurrying up the hill toward the drugstore, his sphincter slackened and out of him poured accumulations of muddy waters, surprisingly odorless, silted up for decades in his insides where his organs float. He kept tightening his buttocks and walked more and more quickly, while down his legs ran the substance of himself disappearing. *I'm no longer fit for this world*, he mumbled, breathless and feeling through his pockets for his little pump, which was not there. The antidepressants cast Andreas Ban into a still deeper depression, so he gives up the tablets.

Gastroscopy, orders the specialist six months later, *tomorrow morning, on an empty stomach, no liquids, no solids.*

Andreas Ban comes for his gastroscopy appointment at noon. He is thirsty and irritable. The nurse says, *Take out your dentures*, Andreas Ban says, *Take out your own*. The nurse asks, *Do you have asthma?* Andreas Ban says, *Yes. Then we'll do it without anesthetic*, says the nurse. They push a rubber tube down to the bottom of his stomach and delve and push while he grunts like a pig for the slaughter there in the half dark of the underground clinic. They hand him a little picture of his stomach in shades of red, black and brown. *This is your stomach*, says the doctor, *it's full of craters, completely corroded.* Who is eating and straining whom, Andreas Ban his innards, or they him? *What now?* he asks. *Make peace with yourself*, says the doctor and prescribes him new medication. *Checkup in six months*, he says. Six months later other issues present themselves, so Andreas Ban's corroded stomach has to wait.

What was it Freud said? Melancholy is a pathological form of mourning, the melancholic does not succeed in fully grieving for the loss of an object (Elvira? Marisa?), a place (Belgrade?), an ideal (ah, from time immemorial the world has been going through periods of madness to take a small step toward reason, says Broch), and so the melancholic omits, rejects the final process of grieving, he refuses to grieve, even masochistically enjoys that refusal of confronting his sorrow. In this matter, the melancholic is so militant, says Freud, that in the end he swallows the lost object, incorporates it into his being, transforms it into the storehouse of his ego and keeps it like a ghostly double. Since the melancholic refuses to part from the lost object, with time that lost object pursues him, so the melancholic gradually abandons the outside world and languishes in the underground of his psyche. In other words, melancholy would be a pathological form of mourning, a sick flight from reality, a flight from the outside world into a refuge, into the inner world of the psyche. What if reality is sick, what then? What if the inner world is destroyed, in ruins and robbed, where to then? So, in grief, the world becomes poor and empty, while in melancholy the ego is like some kind of abandoned archaeological discovery that has been dug up. Yes, the melancholic is a radical atheist who in his hollow discourse worships a dead god.

Andreas Ban knows all this. Nevertheless, despite the insidious, elusive pain that bores through him, all is well, inside it is finally quiet. Quiet and dead. *Tot. Mort.* Lifeless.

As when snow falls on the coast and a silent film is played. People are perplexed, they cannot cope, they buzz mindlessly, they leave work early, cars crawl, buses are late, trains stand still, while the snow, really light and insignificant, does fall, and the little town is transformed into a huge soundproof chamber in which one cannot hear one's own breathing. Andreas loves it. He breathes deeply (the snow conceals his asthma), he walks (as briskly as he can), if he falls, it will be soft, *This snow is a gift*, he says, because the snow is a complete image with fifty-year-old layers of his life under different skies, under vaults that are far from the lid here, what is snow doing in Rijeka?

Then it rains and his faint hope melts, the broad canvas of Andreas's life vanishes, the small town becomes even smaller, once again it emits a din, a senseless street din, heavy as a wet army blanket. Faces emerge on the sidelines and conversations echo on the sidelines and once again he, Andreas Ban, emerges, he who for twenty years has been on the sidelines.

Then, since the years pass and no more snow falls, as a product of a false longing, in the small coastal town a skating rink is opened and named "The Sea Snowflake."

His body is heavy, lazy and immobile, he does not know how to get rid of it, it drags after him like cargo, he drags it around on his back, bent over, he moves it within himself trying to steal from it little shallow breaths. This struggle with his body devours his thoughts whose landscape flattens, brown and deformed. His tongue grows into a huge rough beast frantically thrashing inside his mouth, trying to get out. Andreas Ban moves away, looks at himself and sees an exhibit in the bizarre collection of stuffed animals of the Victorian taxidermist Walter Potter, imprisoned in a small glass cage (so as not to get damaged). He is kept company (in neighboring glass containers) by squirrels drinking tea, festively dressed kittens at some kind of a wedding, a freak cat with two tails and three legs on its back, a dozen albino rats getting drunk in an empty inn, cicadas playing cricket. Here are gentlemen lobsters (lobsters do not grow old), scientist-lobsters in suits with spectacles on their noses, a heap of anthropomorphic scenes in which Andreas Ban too features as a monstrous creation, half-human, half-bestial.

*

While Andreas Ban is talking about Zemun with three unknown men on a bus, a skilled pickpocket takes his bag with his documents. His identity card is gone, his bank cards gone, his passport gone. After twenty years Andreas Ban returns to his Belgrade apartment, opens the mailbox and out of it fall letters, flyers and a multitude of pills.

That is when he receives the invitation to Amsterdam.

Andreas does not have a respectable suitcase. All his cases are worn because they were cheap and they have traveled back and forth. Some do not have handles, some have lost wheels, the Chinese one has broken in two.

Buy this Samsonite one, the shop assistant tells Andreas, *only three hundred euros. That's class.*

I am class, says Andreas. *That's why I can't buy the Samsonite.*

So he borrows a suitcase.

Andreas Ban had also advised some of his patients, *Go away somewhere*. Travel, that "little death of departure," as Virilio puts it, reduces the tension of impasse and brings (temporary) oblivion. So Andreas Ban, wrapped in his extended "aesthetic of disappearance," lands on a little island of time in which tomorrow does not exist, in which yesterday is buried. On a quiet, free-flowing illusion.

George Hendrik Breitner, *Oudezijds Achterburgwal, Amsterdam (Het Kolkje)*

The flight from Belgrade to New York has a stopover in Amsterdam, where Andreas Ban leaves the airport and stays for three days. It is the mid-1970s. Andreas Ban is twenty-something, he has energy and a soaring step. In his pockets he carries his university degree, a few love affairs, after the tumultuous and disappointing year of 1968, an unsuccessful battle with bureaucratic Communist Party officials and the frightened employees at the psychological support center of a Belgrade municipality, after which he was dismissed, then a two-year stint as a psychology lecturer on an evening course at an open university and—a Fulbright scholarship to study for a master's degree in the United States. Andreas Ban does not remember where he stays in Amsterdam, he does not remember what he does with his vast amount of heavy luggage, or where and what he eats. Bertolucci's *Last Tango in Paris* has just been released, provoking conflict between the protectors of morality across the western hemisphere and the aesthetes, the rebels, for the most part left-wing. Andreas Ban does not remember in which Amsterdam cinema Marlon Brando and Maria Schneider unfurl their life stories, but to the present day he retains their bottled-up sadness which has for almost forty years been overflowing from a, let us say, fictional reality into one that time is wearing out and breaking into pieces. Andreas Ban does not know exactly when *Last Tango* danced in Yugoslavia, with a "delay" of several years certainly, anyway now it makes no difference, neither Marlon Brando nor Maria Schneider is alive. In Yugoslavia *Last Tango* was first banned for minors, and screenings, of an abridged version, began at eleven p.m. or later. It was not shown on television until 1981.

In a small Amsterdam theater, then, in the 1970s, Andreas Ban sees a production of Beckett's one-act monodrama *Not I* (premiered on the small stage of New York's Lincoln Center in October 1972), and walks through the Red Light District. At that time, Andreas Ban knows nothing about Holland, nothing about Amsterdam, a peripheral stopping place on the way to a different world (and life), but it seems that the images and aromas of their mutual three-day seduction settled in one of those mysterious little chambers of the mind that we believe have disintegrated, crushed by the years, and turned into grains, into insignificant markers of our past, only to open up again unexpectedly, even several decades later, uninvited, swollen with vitality, introducing slight disorder into our reality. Now Andreas Ban sees that the twentieth century has been rattling off the same old story, but he had to grow old to grasp it. *Not I* is set in a dark space in which just one ray of light illuminates a woman's mouth placed up high, three or four meters above the stage, and, at lightning speed, logorrheic, breathless, that mouth tells its story, our story; in the darkness lit by one penetrating beam. The creature, reduced to a mouth, is hearing a tale buried in profound silence which the audience does not grasp, but it catches it, almost in flight, remnants of the life of the unnamed woman who after many years of silence has been converted into her own (or someone else's?) mouth. The audience members catch scorched flakes, particles that fall, billowing, onto their shoulders and chests, so that the small stage appears to be turning into a repository, a storehouse of carbonized corpses. What can be made out is a disjointed narrative about a life without love, about desertion, violence, deaths and disappearances, about aimless wanderings through devastated landscapes. Round and round in a circle. There is no new beginning, there is no beginning because there is no end. Both *Last Tango in Paris* and *Not I*, combined with the Red Light District where young and old, fat and thin half-dressed women sit in windows behind which can be glimpsed cheap narrow beds with crumpled sheets, are nothing but a soundless cry (or plea?), unavoidable and showing no way out. A search for a new voice that ends in defeat. In the 1970s, *Last Tango in Paris* and *Not I* and the Red Light District destroy the norms of craft and profession, and introduce confusion into tidily arranged lives. Later, at the end of the twentieth century, art had largely relaxed (imploded?), people were inured to prostitution, time had stopped undulating, it had begun to stoop and to age unattractively, with a stench.

It is with these thoughts, almost forty years later, in February 2010, that Andreas Ban lands once again on Dutch soil.

In Amsterdam it is raining, it is cold and windy, Andreas Ban cannot get his umbrella out because his hands are occupied, for a long time he has wished for a third hand, like some kind of third eye, one that would protrude at his waist in the shape of a hook, on which he would be able to hang various objects, nutritional and professional. As soon as he gets home he will buy one of those shopping carts that all better-off old ladies drag back from the market, even if he has nothing to put in it. His hair is as wet as if he had surfaced from water, which he has, he has surfaced from dreariness *croatica* and come up into—he has yet to see what. Andreas Ban takes a taxi to Spuistraat, pronounced Spaustraat, he is met—with a bottle of chilled wine and white roses on the windowsill—by lovely Fleur van Koppen (herself like a flower) with abundant red hair, bright-red-painted lips, all transparent and smiling, a more beautiful version of Hanna Schygulla as he remembers her from "The Marriage of Maria Braun."

Perhaps he should describe the apartment. Previous residents on the Writer-in-Residence Program of the Dutch Foundation for Literature do that pedantically, enchanted. The apartment is beautiful, in the very center of the city, spacious and light, on two levels, fashionably and minimally furnished. It is warm inside, Andreas Ban goes barefoot, singing (?!) as he walks up and down the polished white wooden stairs that lead to the gallery where the bedroom is, while outside it snows. The apartment is on the third floor, high up, on one side Andreas Ban has a view over the whole of Spui Square, where there are bookshops and a great deal of activity, in fact it is a square of books (on the ground floor is the famous Athenaeum bookshop), on the other side he looks out at "his" broad, noisy Spuistraat, studded with little cafés and restaurants, a street that cuts across the medieval cobbled lanes, dark and mysterious, in which footfalls roll along quietly until they step onto the bridges and canals, where they become silent. But the windows, the windows in the apartment and windows in Amsterdam entirely satisfy Andreas Ban's fetishism, his enchantment with glass. In the apartment, windows fill the entire length and almost the height of the two long living-room walls; it is as though Andreas Ban is in a glass box out of which he can fly whenever he wishes.

Andreas Ban did not write in Amsterdam. It would be a shame to write in Amsterdam, a waste of time, fiddling about with the unimportant when one was caught like this in a three-week-long embrace with an unknown host. In Amsterdam Andreas Ban tries to forget, to erase old images, what was left of them, with new ones. Amsterdam—an opportunity for approaching extinction.

Andreas Ban does not have time to research the whole city, its peripheral areas, open spaces and parks. He circles around the center, revolves around its core. Like a spider's web, the eight-hundred-year-old trajectories linked by bridges and canals catch the walker in their labyrinths, sometimes constricting the lungs so that Andreas becomes breathless. That shortness of breath, that rhythm of short breaths, that breath of short breaths, that breath shortness, that short breath of breaths, that short inhalation, exhalation, will like a tedious cat slink behind Andreas Ban throughout his stay in Amsterdam.

In the center of the city one enters into amazing, concealed past times, familiar or dreamed, painless, into slow-moving time that flows over reality and at night moves behind the looking glass. Unlike Camus's hero Clamence who follows the concentric circles of Amsterdam down to his (own) ninth circle, below sea level,

Andreas's twenty-six-day surf through Amsterdam is neither deep nor probing, but horizontal and random, more like a curveball. It narrows and stretches, entirely in keeping with the new century, disoriented but monotonous and flat, leading nowhere. (That other journey, Clamence's and Camus's, into the center of the absurd, is long since over for Andreas Ban.)

The stairways are narrow, their ceilings low. The stairway in Andreas's building is also spiral, large suitcases barely make it. Furniture is taken into buildings with cranes and winches—through the windows. The inner spaciousness is at odds with the narrow, constricted outer space.

In an irritatingly fast and noisy age in which it seems that only pedestrians roll along lazily, in a time of hysterical convulsions, Andreas Ban sinks, like an untreated and incurable epileptic, into a miraculously dense timelessness, into a misty past, there on the third floor of the building at 303 Spuistraat, surrounded by glass.

And after a long time, almost twenty years, Andreas Ban seems to have arrived. Home. And after a long time (almost twenty years), he buys flowers for his refuge. Andreas Ban surrounds himself with roses. A bier or feast day?

The television channels keep showing the same advertisement for *pommes frites*. In this persistent advertisement members of a family aggressively and euphorically produce loud crunching noises as they munch little potato sticks. Andreas Ban turns off the set. He finds a radio channel with music, a good background for that month-long production, that February show, that little winter dream. (There is no sun, heavy sky, trees with bare branches, snow and sleet, wind, deserted neighborhoods and parks, canals filled with brackish water, bridges covered with moss, days of sticky dampness.) The Middle Ages, semidarkness and mystery, surface out of everyday life. Closed circular orbits destroy the illusion of continuity, around them gapes the surreal emptiness of abandoned reality. Time disappears, erasing history.

Andreas Ban hears the clatter of clogs on cobbled streets, the swift steps of fair-skinned women moving in their long, wide skirts, heads lowered, through the radial, dark alleys he hears the hoofbeats of draft horses distributing barrels of beer, the flutter of the wings of white Dutch caps.

It was on Spui Square, beneath the windows of the building in which he is staying, from 1965 to 1966, that the Provo movement, said by some to be the precursor of the student protests of 1968, seethed, gathering around the statue of the Amsterdam orphan, *Het Lieverdje*, nowadays visited by tourists who first stare at it, then at their maps, for the most part either blessedly ignorant of the recent past, or not interested.

The not exactly monumental little statue of the cheerful orphan caught executing a dance step, the work of the sculptor Carel Kneulman (1915–2008), was in fact the stimulus for the ludic and seemingly apolitical Provo movement, that began as an antismoking campaign after a tobacco company had donated *Het Lieverdje* to the city. Today, when the desires and dreams of the young are turned toward a somewhat less extravagant but more existential consumerist reality, passion, perceptiveness and originality seem to have sunk into the porous, sandy Dutch soil, into the polluted waters in which the planet Earth floats. As well as initiating provocative happenings that mocked authority, the monarchy and the obedient masses, the Provo movement began as a nonviolent organization that demanded what were not even especially radical social changes: the white chicken plan called for the Amsterdam police (known as blue chickens) to become social workers; the white bicycle plan asked for white-painted bicycles to be left unlocked for public use; the white homes plan pushed for the legal occupation of abandoned living spaces, including the empty royal palace on Dam Square, to house young people and solve the problem of squatters. As an anarchist movement of the young inspired by Marcuse, Provo set Holland alight by demanding a higher level of tolerance toward minorities, national and sexual, and other marginalized social groups, becoming the first European postmodernist antiauthoritarian movement to promote the freedom of the individual. Then, in May 1966, after increasingly frequent police arrests, beatings and threats, Provo sank into compromise. Artists and philosophers staged their happenings at midnight, usually on Saturdays, gathered around *Het Lieverdje* on Spui Square under Andreas's very window, where now at midnight it is quiet and deserted. But around the corner outside Café Hoppe, into the small hours and regardless of weather conditions, there gather dreamers, former anarchists, now aging, gray-haired and paunchy, nonviolent but noisy, who sing, sometimes even dance, and exchange worn-out dreams that disintegrate into shreds. Café Hoppe, founded in 1670, is exactly opposite the building in which Andreas Ban lives, not twenty steps from one entrance to the other. Café Hoppe is well known in that it was regularly frequented by the beer magnate Freddy Heineken, until in 1983 he was kidnapped with his chauffeur and released for a ransom of some sixteen million euros in today's money. At that point, he stopped going there, then, in 2002, he died. Freddy's empire, worth around three billion euros, is now run by his daughter Charlene de Carvalho-Heineken, reputed to be the richest woman in Holland. She does not go to Café Hoppe. Café Hoppe is one of the innumerable noisy, crowded *bruine cafés* scattered through Amsterdam, so called because of the layers of cigarette smoke that seeped from the walls. In the next-door café, smoking is permitted from 6 p.m. until closing time, and Andreas Ban would go there with Ljerka or Leo (who came for a week's stay) for a glass of wine, sometimes he would go alone and stand at the bar or sit beside a low window that looks onto Hei Steeg, an alleyway redolent of the aroma of freshly baked cakes, espresso and marijuana. There was magic in the possibility of taking a leap from one world into another. While in Rijeka, the postmidnight unarticulated weekend yelling of our young people engenders an arrhythmic beating of his heart and a rhythmic clenching of his jaw, the Amsterdam celebration makes Andreas Ban smile and prompts a strange, displaced yearning.

Marcuse died more than thirty years ago. Andreas Ban has two copies of his *One-Dimensional Man*, one from 1968, the other from 1970 with Andreas's mother's signature, which Andreas finds in 1978 when the family clears out Marisa's belongings, a store of treasures from her life to them unknown. Both copies of *One-Dimensional Man* are scribbled over with notes, comments, exclamation marks, question marks and underlined passages. Today Andreas Ban sees that his mother Marisa, a doctor, a neuropsychiatrist, led a double life, one part remains to him forever closed. Marcuse too got lost somehow, he has settled in one of those remote little chambers of Andreas's brain, on the tiny doors of which is written "picnics in the desert" and which open almost conspiratorially quietly, unexpectedly. Thus, when on Spui Square, in the Academic Cultural Center, the historian and culturologist Professor Frank van Vree, Professor Guido Snel and Andreas Ban had spoken before some hundred people about history and about his book, a small room in which for thirty years now Marcuse, Marisa and some others had been hanging around, voices, soft or agitated, opened up and Andreas Ban heard, he saw, emerging from that room, first on tiptoe, then with ever surer steps, in almost military formation and lining up in front of them, figurines, statues, torsos, heads, smiles, which then took over the stage. Instead of the story of his book, a different story occupied the podium. The story of a technologically advanced, so-called free democratic society in which institutions exist to limit freedom, suppress individuality and creativity, blur exploitation and prevent, even punish, the acquisition of new experiences, identities. They talked about the way society is in fact controlled through the imposition of false needs, and how criticism of society is effectively and systematically suppressed by being infiltrated into institutions. They spoke of a closed technological society which creates a new totalitarianism, and in it there is no place for those outside the process of production. About the fact that the only way out of the comfortable, rationalized, undemocratic freedom offered by developed industrial civilization is through rebellion. About the fact that revolution is possible only through awareness, but that awareness in itself demands revolution. Then Eric Visser, director of De Geus publishing house from Breda, invited a dozen of those present for beer and snacks and the whole din quietened down, the spirits returned to their cells, snow fell.

In Holland, the word for cinema is *bioskoop* and people kiss three times.*

Garbage is put out on Tuesdays and Thursdays—Andreas is told—in front of one's building, and left on the sidewalk. It looks horrendous. Paper and glass go in special containers on Koningsplein (a six-minute walk away). So Andreas Ban fills a big black bag with vast quantities of discarded paper and drags it to Koningsplein, in the rain. There he finds a square metal box about a meter high (smaller than the dimensions of Andreas's black plastic bag), with a slit like those on mailboxes. Andreas cannot believe

---

* The Serbian word for cinema is *bioskop*, and the Serbs kiss three times, as opposed to the "Croatian" word for cinema, *kino*, which is in fact German, the Croatians kiss twice on the cheek. This refers to the Croatian nationalistic attitude toward the Serbs during and after the dissolution of Yugoslavia.

what he is supposed to do. He leaves the bag to soak in the rain and after that he no longer separates anything. Yet another absurd case of wasting time on the unimportant. Gathering grains of sand in the desert. But people are obedient, they like to separate their trash, to recycle the debris of their own and other people's lives. Following a diktat, they fly to embrace goodness, which they shift around in their pockets the way men scratch their balls, then they sleep soundly.

Fleur invites Guido, De Geus editor Ilonka Reintjens, who arrives from Breda by train, and Damir Šodan, who comes by train from The Hague where he has spent more than ten years at the ICTY* translating those endless, tedious documents, what a shame. Throughout Holland people mill and buzz around, slithering as though they had a grasp on time, not the other way around. They go to Brasserie Harkema, which prides itself on its domestic system for purifying and bottling drinking water in their own Harkema bottles, and the menu includes a description of the process of its filtration, the addition of mineral components and treatment with ultraviolet rays. *That is why*, they stress at Harkema, *the water at Harkema is not water from a tap, but mineral water, of markedly better taste. But, if you wish*, they recommend at Harkema, *you may always order a glass of ordinary water, which is free of charge.* After dinner Andreas Ban takes Damir Šodan to his local bar, where they smoke and drink cognac, then around midnight Damir jumps onto a tram, from the tram onto a train to The Hague, while Andreas totters up the spiral staircase to his garret. Good, simple activities, stress is presumably lurking elsewhere. Damir did not talk about his poems, Damir Šodan is an excellent poet, so he does not need to talk about his poems, but Andreas,

* International Criminal Tribunal for the former Yugoslavia.

standing with him at the bar, in the smoke and din, in Amsterdam, in Spuistraat, listened to Damir's lines, voices, whispers steal out of a book on the shelf of his Rijeka room, slip out of Damir's letters to wild wanderers, nomads, once to a migratory nightingale that "drives away more powerful and important birds ... although in essence there is nothing to see," he listened to words knocking against buildings (Spinoza's and others') in the black nights, followed them from Bombay to Brioni, from Lisbon to the forests of Norway, from Nečujam on the island of Šolta to Saint Petersburg, he watched them travel along "black meridians," sail in old boats, and he felt fine, even if he does not remember whether he and Damir talked at all or simply smoked and drank. Like Šodan's Bakunin, that night Andreas dreamed about "little weasels in the snow" under which he crawled wondering whether the time had perhaps come to die.

The following day Andreas Ban discovers that hollandaise sauce has nothing to do with Holland, that it is a French dressing, and once again his days pass peacefully.

Cooking shows have long been universal hits. It might be worth asking why. Particularly since they are becoming increasingly tedious, unwatchable and indigestible. Since there is an ever-greater number of poor people, particularly those for whom TV shows are their only mental superstructure, these shows are also offensive. Lively performances by smiling chefs take place in elegant kitchens where high-quality pots and pans are used, the ingredients are expensive and often exotic. As Andreas fears that when he retires his nutrition will be reduced to chicken wings and innards and that he will, heaven forbid, go to the market just before it is blasted by water cannons to pick up a few rotten apples and discarded salad leaves, he finds this nutrition craze nauseating. There are even shows in which strangers pretend to be friends and dine at one another's homes evening after evening, stroll through rooms, rummage in cupboards and wardrobes, and taste food, then appraise it or comment on it unkindly. The ambience of the homes is often kitschy, the walls are decorated with framed needlework and puzzles. But alongside that particular trend there are also a number of cooking shows in which dishes are produced from wild herbs, except that those wild herbs do not grow everywhere. Such shows are cooked up, their presenters say, to arouse interest in "neglected" vegetables and cheap but healthy food.

On Dutch TV Andreas Ban follows the preparation of salads and stews made from common purslane (also known as verdolaga, pigweed, little hogweed, red root, pursley, and moss rose, *Portulaca oleracea*), which he had picked the previous summer with Liljana Dirjan on Rovinj's Punta Corrente. The Dutch chef sautés the fleshy leaves in butter, Andreas and Liljana had eaten it as a salad. Cookbooks say that purslane is a tasty wild plant that grows in spring and summer, of a mild salty-peppery flavor, which is not entirely true, it is a rather insipid little plant with a slightly bitter tang. To encourage consumers to make dishes from purslane, what is stressed without exception is that it contains Omega-3 fatty acids (currently "in"), then vitamins A, C and B, followed by minerals, numerous antioxidants such as magnesium, calcium, potassium and iron, and a whole lot more. How much purslane should be eaten for the human organism to get stronger, no one writes, no one says. Cookbooks and TV shows emphasize that it is good to combine purslane in salads with tomatoes, eggs, capers, olives, sheep's cheese and salted anchovies, which once again suggests original recipes devised for idle consumers with deep pockets and no imagination.

The Dutch supermarket chain Albert Heijn was founded in 1887 and, of course, took its name from its founder. Those AH supermarkets can be found throughout Amsterdam. There are big ones and small ones, some better than others. Near Andreas's building there is a small AH in which Andreas Ban finds shopping challenging. The tills are placed close together, so close that it is impossible for a cart to get through. In that small, constricted AH, there is always a crowd and everyone is in a hurry, people do not pack their goods tidily in bags, they just sling them in. Andreas finds it comforting that these markets are open every day, including Sundays, until 10 p.m., but even so they are always crowded. So Andreas goes in search of a larger Albert Heijn where he could, in a more leisurely way, discover Dutch and imported foodstuffs, and get lost. He got trapped in Amsterdam's web of bridges and canals, walking into the wind and the rain, with no hat or umbrella and without a map. Then, on the other side of the street he catches sight of Dubravka Ugrešić. Straightaway he asks her, *Dubravka, is there a larger AH in the neighborhood?* and she says, *I don't know.* They stand for a while, smoking, Dubravka Ugrešić and Andreas Ban, and they produce sentences resembling long strips of elastic that rhythmically stretch and loosen, there, in an empty Amsterdam street at five p.m., as it is getting dark. Then Andreas Ban goes on his way, although it would have been nice if he and Dubravka had ducked in somewhere for coffee or tea, but it is not the right moment. Staggering along, Andreas Ban sets off toward his house and on the way discovers on the corner of his Spuistraat and another street, it does not matter which, a vast AH, which as far as groceries go, fills the soul with calm. In that AH, Andreas Ban has time to communicate with the Dutch (who are very well-disposed to foreigners), listen to their advice in the matter of various Japanese, Chinese and Indian spices (which he does not use), no one pushes or pursues him, he is relaxed, he finds his soy milk, buys strawberries, a bottle of Chilean red wine and four kinds of cheese, some goat's, some cow's—Holland produces first-class cheeses in unimaginable combinations.

*

The Dutch like to eat. They nurture a culture of eating.

The winter of 1944–45 in occupied Holland was so harsh that it led to great hunger. Around thirty thousand people died. The Dutch remember that winter as the *Hongerwinter*, it is etched in their collective memory. That winter of 1944–45 brought back the misfortunes of all wartime winters, the distant ones and the more recent, such as the Sarajevo winters. Andreas learns that then, during that *Hongerwinter*, in the absence of any other sustenance, the Dutch ate tulip bulbs and sugar beets, making them into puree, porridge and sweets. In that winter of 1944–45, horses vanished because they were eaten. Trees vanished because they were cut down for fuel. Those who did not die became seriously anemic and clinically depressed, and the women infertile. Today there is a great deal of research into the consequences of that hunger on the human organism, as though hunger had disappeared. One such study concludes that Audrey Hepburn suffered all kinds of ailments because she went hungry in Amsterdam in 1944–45, that she acquired respiratory problems and edemas, and her blood count was low. Perhaps this is why the Dutch enjoy eating so much, talking about food and watching cooking shows, perhaps they are curing the trauma that is now etched into their genetic code and has become a tiny (Dutch) archetype.

So, as he strolls through Amsterdam's familiar floating Bloemenmarkt (a flower market opened as early as 1862), not ten minutes' walk from his apartment, and sees all kinds of gigantic bulbs, three times bigger than celeriac roots, before Andreas Ban's eyes pops up the image of that famine and the situation in which flowers were turned into porridge. Then he buys ten small wooden tulips of various colors to give to people when he gets home. There are all kinds of stories about the Dutch tulips that arrived in Holland in the middle of the sixteenth century from the Ottoman Empire, when it would seem mass hysteria reigned, known as "tulipomania." Tulipomania in Holland reached its height in February 1637, when it is said that one bulb was sold for four fat oxen, eight fat pigs or twelve fat sheep, for two tonnes of butter, five hundred kilograms of cheese, and so on to the point of complete madness. There was a similar floral hysteria in the Victorian age, the so-called "orchid delirium," when fanatical orchid collectors sent their researchers to all corners of the world in order to look for new species.

Sylvia Plath wrote about tulips:

> *The tulips are too excitable, it is winter here.*
> *Look how white everything is, how quiet, how snowed-in.*
> *I am learning peacefulness, lying by myself quietly*
> *As the light lies on these white walls, this bed, these hands...*
>
> *I have let things slip, a thirty-year-old cargo boat*
> *Stubbornly hanging on to my name and address...*

Then Andreas Ban remembers Operation Black Tulip and hurries to his apartment to watch the life of his neighbors across the street for a while, because he had promised himself that during his twenty-six-day stay in Amsterdam he will not research the obscenities of the Second World War. Rest from dragging all that worn-out baggage around, he said to himself, my own and other people's, find a more cheerful occupation here, in Amsterdam. Go shopping, he said to himself, there are great bargains, buy shoes. He made a start, but feebly. He kept pushing the past away, Go back to your catacombs, he told it, but, like a slimy rivulet it surfaced and trickled around him, under his feet.

Like this:

Operation Black Tulip was carried out from 1946 to 1948. Its aim was to drive out of Holland all Germans, most of whom had settled there long before the war. It was not logical that all Dutch-Germans collaborated with the occupier. When Andreas Ban mentioned the Dutch Resistance Movement in conversation, Amsterdamers would say *Bah* and wave their hands, *It was a lousy resistance movement*, they would say, *Holland had a lot of collaborators*. Such generalizations are rotten, but that's what it's like in war (and afterward). Individual destinies sink, small lives merge into one great false mass event that keeps repeating its statistical story. In the end, 15 percent of the German population was driven out of Holland, that is, 3,691 civilians, because Operation Black Tulip was abruptly halted. According to the assessments of historians, however, it is presumed that around 170,000 citizens of Holland (of whatever national allegiance) had cooperated with the Nazi regime at a time when the entire population of Dutch-Germans was around twenty-five thousand souls. So the Dutch-Germans were probably meant to serve as sacrificial lambs on the national altar of innocence. Of course, Operation Black Tulip was a joke compared to the ten million Germans during the war and afterward forcibly scattered all over Europe; ten million disoriented people (many guilty, many entirely innocent), dragging their miserable bundles, streaming west from Hungary, Czechoslovakia, Poland, Yugoslavia, Romania and the USSR, leaving behind the smudged traces of spent lives, which—like the crumbs of bread that Hansel and Gretel scatter behind them to retrace their steps home (but that's a fairy tale)—became sodden in the passing of time. That's how it is in wartime. Who cares about trifles? Names disappear, small lives bury themselves, forget themselves, or decay in old picture albums and slide off deathbeds.

Operation Black Tulip began on September 10, 1946 with arrests in Amsterdam, in the middle of the night. It was a Tuesday and it was raining. People had one hour to pack their belongings, fifty kilograms per person. The remainder of their property, including apartments and houses, firms and factories, was confiscated by the state. Then the human cargo was transferred to camps on the eastern border, most to Marienbosch, then to Germany, to the British occupied zone. In 2009 the Dutch census counts a population of 379,559 Germans living in Holland.

In 2010, Geert Mak, a popular left-oriented and politically committed Dutch writer and journalist, winner of multiple awards, and a lawyer, visits Croatia to promote his book *In Europe*. Andreas Ban asks him to speak about Operation Black Tulip. Geert Mak looks at Andreas Ban blankly, *I don't know what you're talking about, I know nothing of Dutch Operation Black Tulip.*

Zwarte tulp, says Andreas Ban, *doesn't it ring a bell?*

Nee, nee—no, no.

Yes, for big history, historical tributaries dry up at once. Vanish. In their bed not even silt remains, nothing in the memory from which it would be possible to read a name, an existence, a small story, long since extinguished.

Throughout Andreas Ban's stay in Amsterdam, the blinds on the windows of an apartment across the street had been down. The windows were right next to each other and, as in Andreas's place, they probably stretched along the whole wall of a room. A woman lived there whom Andreas Ban had never seen, but she regularly hung her clothes out to air, or to straighten out the creases. Andreas Ban observed the appearance and disappearance of combinations of skirts and tops, dresses and jackets, slacks and shirts. First a little black dress hung by the window, disappearing in the evening. In its place came a brown skirt and a yellow pullover, in the morning they too disappeared. And so it went from day to day. The woman was roughly five foot eight, she weighed approximately 125 pounds, she went to work around eight a.m., came back around six p.m. and put the lights on. And (not witnessed by Andreas) hung her outfit by the window for the following day.

Another tenant had the head of a huge stuffed stag on his wall, its antlers branching into gigantic fans. He had chairs on which no one sat.

A third tenant had furnished his living room in shades of black and white, but his lamps were yellow. The walls were covered with paintings and the shelves were full of books. Andreas watched him eat, talk on the telephone and laugh. In the bedroom the double bed with orange sheets was never made. Then he vanished, he was not there for four days, the bed gaped empty, and Andreas grew worried. Then the shutters came down, he was back.

Andreas Ban bought shoes. Three pairs. Given that he walks less and less, with more and more difficulty, the shoes would remain new. Andreas nurtures a special tenderness for shoes. And for glass jars.

He did not escape the Second World War.

Andreas Ban calls in at the Athenaeum Boekhandel on the ground floor. All those people, all that milling around, the leafing through pages, the buying, the cash registers dinging—a quiet festival. New editions in various languages, old editions in various languages, whatever he looks for, he finds. As soon as he got to Holland he noticed Hemon's *Best European Fiction* series published by Dalkey, with stories by Štiks and Ušumović, as though Igor and Neven and Saša were all there in Amsterdam, so Andreas sits with them in that little café on the corner, and tales of their lives start to flow, tales which, despite the war, had after all somehow turned out OK. When he came back to Croatia, Andreas went to see Marko in the Ribook Store to tell him how it had gone. They spent a whole hour sitting on the sofa, drinking coffee, and no one came in. Just one girl looking for decorative little address books, which the bookshop does not stock, so her appearance did not count. Then Marko said, *I sold one book today—about I.T.*

The Athenaeum Boekhandel is run by Herm Pol. Herm Pol is the striking, tall, gray-haired and well-read director of the Athenaeum Boekhandel, with whom one can talk about literature, he has a definite opinion about the books he orders. In Herm Pol's shop Andreas buys Harry Mulisch's *The Discovery of Heaven*. He does not have anyone in Amsterdam to discuss that book with, in Holland the book came out a long time ago. It is a thick book, 736 pages, that does not require a pencil for underlining. Mulisch, whose mother was Jewish, had a personal, probably unsolved problem with Nazism, a family trauma he wove into his writing. So, in the novel *De aanslag*, in English *The Assault*, made into a film (and awarded an Oscar many years ago for best foreign film), Mulisch settles scores with his father, a "soft" Nazi, thanks to whom he and his mother were not deported to Auschwitz. Many elements in *The Discovery of Heaven* are redundant, there is all kinds of content in the novel, from Greek and Jewish mythology, the student uprising of 1968, classical mysticism, the Holocaust, astrophysical theories, Renaissance and other philosophies, to incomprehensible constructs, endless "cruel twists of fate," incredible convolutions of plot, chance meetings and deaths, love trios and quartets, so much stuff stacked up that ideas and sentences barely breathe, crushed in an asthmatic clinch.

Andreas Ban also buys Jonathan Littell's *The Kindly Ones* (in its French original *Les bienveillantes,* awarded the Prix Goncourt in 2006), which is 903 pages long, because people are still writing and discussing it, and concludes that the man (Littell) is not normal. Littell, like Mulisch, hooks on to mythology, to the Erinyes who are meant to take revenge on his narrator, but who tenderly grant him amnesty (as he was granted amnesty or was rather bypassed by all the courts that tried Second World War criminals), and the narrator, that Nazi Dr. Max Aue, an engineer and music lover, a latent and potent married homosexual in an occasional incestuous relationship with his twin sister, this emotionally castrated executioner who kills his mother and stepfather now that he has dodged justice, lays out his life before the reader, describing it in senseless and tedious detail (the battle of Stalingrad—more than one hundred pages), and manages, oh lord, a lace factory, and this not remotely delicate soul runs through his fingers that most delicate of all fabrics, which then seems an additional desecration. Worst of all about Littell's book is that it is written in a language which is not, but aspires to be, literature. It is hard to find a justification for such a hideous confession in which at the very outset the narrator (Aue) states that he does not regret anything he has done, that what he did (and he committed diabolical crimes), he did with his eyes open, that he was only doing his job. Dr. Max Aue also affirms that he had realized that thinking is not always a good idea, so why then the need for fanatically obsessive descriptions of war and finally his diabolical address to the reader, *You might also have done what I did, because everyone, or almost everyone, in a given set of circumstances, does what he is told to do. I am a man like other men, I am a man like you. I tell you I am just like you!* Nowhere in 903 pages is there a single word about the possibility of choice (which Dr. Aue has), about the possibility of rebellion, about guilt. Ironically and superficially, the book is dedicated to the dead. All this might have been digestible had Littell's book had a sense for language. It is the tedious report of a deranged mind. And for an analysis of the development, survival and functioning of deranged minds, of perverted sadists, there is no need to use the backdrop of Nazism, the pathological ideology of the Third Reich, the setting of war.

On February 17, 2010, Andreas Ban reads a report from Ljubljana of an unheard-of scandal that has shaken Slovenia, news of the prominent doctor Saša Baričević who was maimed, torn apart and finally killed by his three bull mastiffs, because Dr. Saša Baričević was in fact a woman and, it is presumed, had used the dogs for sexual intercourse, which they could no longer tolerate. What about pedophile priests? And incestuous monsters who for decades rape their own children in bunkers? Those are Dr. Max Aue's kin.

Andreas Ban said to Herm Pol, *This is all too much, both Mulisch and Littell, give me a Cees Nooteboom to get over them.* Then Herm Pol said, *Come back on Wednesday, I'll introduce you to him.*

The third book that tried to drag Andreas Ban into the Second World War was right on target because it was not a book about the war at all, but about a complex journey in search of one's self, about poetry, it is poetry, about socialist poverty from which some fine souls are born, about love, about the quest for roots that leads nowhere because roots are an illusion, about legends, about a myriad of dreams that twinkle in constellations that people pointlessly drag through their lives. In his book *Everything is Illuminated* Jonathan Safran Foer entangles his reader in the hard knots of human destinies, but leaves space for laughter, allows him also to think. This is a book with images that fly after the reader like little swallows, they flutter, it is a fairy tale which frightens and heals.

Andreas Ban then talks with Herm Pol about the Dutch language which he finds more difficult to pronounce than to speak, because of the guttural sounds that demand practice to be correctly pronounced. Had he stayed longer in Amsterdam, Andreas Ban would have embarked on the adventure of learning Dutch, it would have been fun to do, although in Holland almost everyone speaks English.

These Dutch gutturals, says Andreas Ban to Herm Pol, *as if we were in Africa*, and Herm Pol says, *You know, during the Second World War the Germans learned our language and tried to pass themselves off as Dutch, but it was precisely those joined consonants that they could not produce, so we would immediately recognize them.*

The buildings on the canal along Herengracht are the most elegant. They are the palaces of wealthy merchants from the sixteenth and seventeenth centuries. Very nice to look at.

Fleur and Guido said to Andreas, *Go to the Tuschinski Cinema on Reguliersbreestraat, it's near your house.* Reguliersbreestraat is not a particularly wide street and armies of consumers march along it in both directions, the street is full of all kinds of shops, cramped fast-food snack bars with plastic chairs, tables and cutlery, in which the food is prepared by people from every continent, who do not raise their eyes to look at the architecture. So Andreas Ban passes along that street, Reguliersbreestraat, several times from top to bottom, finding not one exceptional building until he searches for numbers 26–28. Squeezed in the embrace of boring gray multistory blocks, the Tuschinski Cinema gleams oddly, almost comically transposed, adorned in the Art Deco style with elements of both the Amsterdam School and Jugendstil on its facade.

Then Andreas Ban begins superficially to research the story of Tuschinski, and once again comes across a small, forgotten trace of the past planted monumentally at 26–28 Reguliersbreestraat; the life of a dreamer buried in the foundations of a building of entertainment, a building on whose walls today, from celluloid tapes (or virtually from digital cameras) stream tales that both concern us and do not.

Abraham Icek Tuschinski (in Polish Tuszynski) was born near Łódź in 1886 and murdered in Auschwitz in 1942. He erected his building for the citizens of Amsterdam to discover a path to illusion, to cheerful, benign lies meant to brighten their existence, but in the end he himself was unable to escape the greatest horror of the twentieth century.

A tailor by profession, Tuszynski reaches Rotterdam from Poland in 1903, with the intention of emigrating to America. In circumstances that cannot now be explained, he does not board the intended ship and, instead of pattern-cutting and sewing, he throws himself into building vaudeville and cinema halls. As early as 1911 he opens in Rotterdam the Thalia, the Royal Cinema, the Scala and the Olympia and, in 1928, yet another luxurious hall, the finest Dutch cinema, the Tuschinski, built in 1921. After the outbreak of the Second World War, during the German bombing of Rotterdam in May 1940, Tuschinski is left without his box of dreams. The Amsterdam cinema changes its name to the Tivoli and becomes a Nazi deportation center. On July 1, 1942, Abraham Icek Tuschinski and his wife Mariem Ehrlich are taken off to the Dutch concentration camp of Westerbork, and then to Auschwitz, where soon afterward the two of them, holding hands, watched the last roll of their life's film as showers of gas clouded their memories.

There were several other occasions when Nazism ambushed Andreas's Amsterdam days, but mostly he kept it at bay.

Every Friday Spui Square is flooded with covered stalls, gazebos, displaying new and secondhand books. There are old editions, bibliophile exemplars, new editions, postcards, prints, records, children's books from the beginning of last century, history books, intermingling languages and publishers from all over the world. Coffee is brewed, beer poured, information exchanged, a great scholarly bookish family hums and buzzes from nine in the morning until six in the evening. From his bedroom window on the gallery, in the attic, Andreas Ban follows that piling up of ideas between covers, whether it is raining, snowing, blowing a gale, the stallholders do not give up. Andreas Ban goes down to the square, looks around, happens upon a stall with English books and to his horror reaches for a copy of Primo Levi's *If This Is A Man*. A little red light comes on in his head, he shudders, enough, Andreas, he tells himself and for thirteen euros buys a copy of *Lewis Carroll Victoriaans Fotograaf* (Amsterdam: Meulenhoff-Landshoff, 1979), as a memento and for pleasure.

At three points, marking the vertices of a huge imaginary triangle, Spui Square is framed by identical sculptures of the conceptual artist Lawrence Weiner who lives partly in New York, partly in Amsterdam. These sculptures do not remind one of Demnig's stumbling stones, but they are for stumbling on. They are steel structures resembling open books placed on the ground, roughly one meter by one and a half (Demnig's blocks are small, ten centimeters square, and they are shiny). On one page of Weiner's open book it says: *Een vertailing / van de ene taal in de andere*, and on the other: *A Translation / from one language to another*. People sit on these "books," children climb on them, and onto them one can put purchased books and other goods. It is clear that, as an artist, Weiner does not exactly nurture a love of the visual and the sensual, he seems to recoil from the image, relying above all on the power of the word.

Weiner probably does not write; if he did, he would have realized how impotent the word has now become, how anemic it is today, dry and useless. Nowadays, to bow down before words, when any fool scatters them around thoughtlessly as if brushing dandruff from his shoulders, is almost moronic. Besides, Weiner's rigid, dark-steel "books" are ugly, aggressive, and as cold as the blank gaze of a damaged mind.

The photographer Evert van Kujik tells of meeting and photographing the singer, accordion player and busker Nenad Banda. Evert van Kujik shows Andreas Ban two of his photographs of Nenad Banda on Spui Square some Friday long ago, weaving a glimmering stage full of flux for shoppers, a stage no doubt more exciting and potent than Weiner's rigid one. The photographer Evert van Kujik tells Andreas that until the outbreak of the war, Nenad Banda taught in a secondary school in Vinkovci, that he came to Amsterdam in 1993 and had a hard life. He says of Nenad Banda that he hovered between reality and longing, like an angel, only superficially immersed in mortality. Nenad Banda died in 2006 of lung cancer, at the age of forty-three. He left a wife and a five-year-old son and emptiness, a dull silence on the squares and market places of Amsterdam.

Photography and facial surgery are Andreas Ban's two unrealized dreams. Psychology and writing are for him no solace, they are but the debris of the transposed world that Andreas Ban wished to make, at least for his personal enjoyment. So, in the bathroom in Rijeka, in a now rusted transoceanic trunk which absorbs clouds of damp with every shower, for three decades an old Opemus enlarger, trays, tongs, timers and unopened packets of long since unusable photographic paper have been rotting, because even if there were the possibility of Andreas Ban ever returning to his dream, hours are tolling—*too late, old man.*

In Belgrade, Andreas Ban developed photographs in his kitchen, on nights when there was no moonlight, and dried them in the miniature bathroom with no window. He had saved up around two thousand dollars for an Olympus with the requisite lenses, and asked his father to help him with the customs and import. His father said, *Forget that idiocy, save your eyes.* That was in the mid-seventies. Today Andreas Ban's eyes are completely shot, myopic and glaucomic. Perhaps his father had been right, perhaps Andreas Ban should have simply looked at green, not at any kind of blackness, not at any kind of darkness. And ironed out the convolutions of his brain.

Into the gray mailbox Evert van Kujik drops for Andreas Ban a book of photographs by August Sanders (sixty portraits of Germans taken between 1913 and 1928), a gift, and two studies for him to look at, one with the powerful works of socially and politically committed (there, it's possible) Dolf Toussaint, and the other of the softer nostalgic George Breitner (1857–1923). Toussaint's book of photographs of Amsterdam's working-class district Jordaan, taken in the 1960s, sells for three hundred euros or more.

Alongside one of the central Amsterdam canals, an elegant hundred-year-old building in Keizersgracht houses the Foam photography museum. The display of photographs at that time by Alexander Rodchenko, still barely known to Western European

audiences, draws observers into a time that crackles with passion, political and social upheaval, cruel prejudices, merciless killings, into a time when the world is being broken and torn apart, when rebellious and provocative art springs from the magical debris of the past. Into a time forever lost. A time whose energy spilled into the twentieth century like Niagara Falls, with a terrifying crash, to leave, now in the twenty-first, a shallow stream, a trickle, a little stagnant water at the bottom of which roll the darkened and slimy pebbles of memory. Rodchenko's portraits of Lilya Brik, Mayakovsky and Osip Brik, his buildings and structures taken at sharp angles, often from below, arouse both unease and longing. Their large size and bizarre details suck observers in and, traveling through the dark tunnels of a time warp, they reach open landscapes, where even the air boils. Out spring Dziga Vertov, Lev Kuleshov and Sergei Eisenstein (invisible in the exhibition), Boris Pasternak recites poems, Andrei Voznesensky brings him his first verses, Kazimir Malevich waves a paintbrush, Maya Plisetskaya dances, Picasso smiles, the international avant-garde marches with a firm step, there, buried in the depths of the earth.

The first exhibition of photographs that Andreas Ban visits during his émigré escapade to Toronto is by Albert Eisenstaedt. At that time refugees from Yugoslavia, among them Leo and Andreas, spend their days in government offices that advise refugees in wealthy Canada on life in general—on nutrition, on personal hygiene, on learning the language, looking for employment (with higher or lower prequalifications), after which some travel into depression, others to "European Meats," where meat has passed its sell-by date and is sold off cheap, while yet others sip coffee and stretch out pastry sheets.

It is summer. In Yorkville (Toronto's "bohemian" quarter) everything pulsates, washed and stylish. Andreas Ban knows where to find the Mira Godard Gallery and in it Motherwell, Larry Rivers, Frank Stella, Lipchitz; nearby are also the Galerie Dresdnere, Evelyn Aimis Fine Art and the Nancy Poole Studio. They display Warhol, Rauschenberg, Safdie, de Kooning. Irena Klar is in the Hollander York Gallery, while John Walsh is in Kinsman Robinson. But he goes to a button seller.

At that time, in 1995, Eisenstaedt is ninety-seven. He does not come from New York to Toronto because it annoys him to maneuver up and down steps in his wheelchair. He prefers to look into the distance from the Time-Life skyscraper and, by then already only in his thoughts, take snaps. And remember.

As a button seller Eisenstaedt is useless. Instead of selling buttons, he fiddles with the lens of a camera he was given as a present, so his boss fires him. He feels better. He is free. He is a free Jew in Germany. A free marksman aiming at dancers, beggars, faces, streets. He becomes a well-known and sought-after photographer. In the early 1930s he begins voyaging through the world. He records for himself, not yet knowing that he is also recording for posterity. No more buttons in his life. Yet he nurtures a strange, suppressed tenderness to that clothing detail. That tenderness is there every day as an echo, reminding him of how it all began.

In 1930, in Berlin, he takes pictures of little girls in ballet schools, in Paris of a man with a doll in his hand near Rue St Denis, and a rehearsal of "Swan Lake" at the Opéra. In 1931, from Paris ("Destitute Men, Notre Dame Cathedral"), he goes to Volendam, Holland, where he spends time with art students (1932). He returns to Berlin to immortalize Jascha Heifetz conducting the

Berlin Philharmonic, then goes to St Moritz ("Skating Waiter"). In 1933, at a first night in Milan's La Scala he photographs ballerinas again, Milanese, coachmen and the poor, he photographs young nuns in Turin, in New York in 1934 poodles on Fifth Avenue, and in Venice, that same year, the first meeting of Hitler and Mussolini. Then, in Tannenburg, Germany, Hitler at the funeral of von Hindenburg. Associated Press sends him urgently to Geneva to catch Joseph Goebbels at the meeting of the Fifteenth League of Nations, extolling the wisdom and strength of his Führer. In the first row stand reporters, asking questions. Goebbels smiles for the cameras. Then everyone leaves. Eisenstaedt raises his camera, Goebbels fixes his gaze on him. In the focused eye of the camera and the sharp eye of Goebbels fateful decisions shimmer. In 1935, Albert Eisenstaedt abandons Germany forever. *I succeeded in taking everything with me. Three years later, I would have ended up in a gas oven*, he would say later.

Through Paris, Albert Eisenstaedt reaches New York at the right time. Modeled on popular German photo-magazines, Henry Luce is preparing to launch what has become the legendary *Life* magazine.

Eisenstaedt becomes one of the first four "house" photographers.

With more than 2,500 photo-essays and ninety-two covers of the leading American magazine in his portfolio, Eisenstaedt remains to this day the father of photojournalism.

The Circle Gallery is also in Yorkville. As its name suggests, it is a round gallery. In it, one looks around and circles. Spectators circle around the universe of Albert Eisenstaedt and no longer know whether the whole of the twentieth century is revolving around them or whether they are traveling along some imagined orbit through history captured at the moment of its creation by the click of the button of a gifted button seller.

Eisenstaedt has never visited Toronto. The Circle Gallery has no ramp for his wheelchair. So he misses the last exhibition of his life. He dies on August 24, 1995, a little more than a month after its closure.

In the same Amsterdam street, Keizersgracht, some two hundred numbers further down from the Foam museum, there is another small private photography museum, Huis Marseille. This Marseille House, built in 1665, belonged to a wealthy French merchant whose ships sailed from Marseille to Amsterdam and back. It is a cold, windy day, it is raining and getting dark. After Rodchenko, Leo and Andreas hurry down Keizergracht, while Canada runs after them. In the Huis Marseille on the three floors of that narrow building are displayed works by the Canadian photographer Edward Burtynsky. These are color photographs in which there is almost no color, no blue sky or lush vegetation, photographs of enormous dimensions, two meters square, maybe more, and on them Burtynsky "talks" about the phases of oil exploitation and about the impact of that exploitation on landscape and on people, although people seem to have been brushed out of his photographs. If they are in some, they are reduced to the point of invisibility, they have to be looked for. These reduced people, even when they exist in Burtynsky's photographs, are hardly noticeable because they are dark and greasy, completely merged into the devastated landscapes covered in smudges, streams and lakes of thick black gold. As a partially reassuring contrast to Burtynsky's photographs, on every floor of the Huis Marseille there is a view (beyond closed windows and balconies) onto an inner garden with a summer house and orderly horticultural fantasies, in spring and summer probably awash with lively colors and shades of green, but now, in February, only dead leaves dance on the central plateau and the shiny bare branches of tall trees knock against the windowpanes like silent goblins.

At the time of Andreas and Leo's Canadian emigration, Ken Saro Wiwa was hanged in Nigeria. Ken Saro Wiwa was a fighter for human rights, a candidate for the Nobel Prize, a poet. As a result of a trumped-up accusation by the then military regime with the ruthless General Sani Abacha at its head, he was tried at a military court. The international community protested, but Ken Saro Wiwa and eight of his fellow fighters were nevertheless hanged because the military regime in Nigeria did not care about protests from the international community, because the military regime in Nigeria needed dollars from oil exploitation, because the Shell Company (officially named Royal Dutch Shell, *originally a Dutch and British firm with its head office to this day in The Hague*) has its biggest wells in Nigeria and because Shell is today a multinational company in which the USA also has its fingers.

The land in the valley of the Niger River is devastated. This is the valley inhabited by the Ogoni people, from whom the family of Ken Saro Wiwa spring. In 1995, the land of the Niger River Valley was a military zone. Andreas Ban does not know whose zone it is today, but the land is polluted, nothing grows there any longer. On that land the children are hungry and the water is poisoned. There is nothing there for fishermen or farmers. The Ogoni people get no compensation for their lost lives, their lost land, their lost waters which once, long ago, served half the state of Nigeria. The military regime of General Abacha killed people in the Niger Delta. The Niger Delta is the most densely populated area of Africa, with almost six hundred inhabitants per square kilometer.

There are oil pipelines everywhere. Because of aging installations, in some places the oil leaks into the earth. Nothing will grow there for the next thousand years. The earth is hard, baked, dead; it is possible that there are still little islands of fertile soil five meters beneath the black petrified crust.

The military regime in Nigeria hangs Ken Saro Wiwa for accusing the Shell Company of genocide. The Shell Company does not wish to make a statement. The Shell Company has no intention of halting oil extraction in Nigeria. Particularly if Ken Saro Wiwa is out of the way.

Many people are killed. Many homes burned. They rebelled. They will not rebel any more. The military regime in Nigeria was quiet for a few more years. And Shell is still tranquil.

So, some threads delicately entwine over there in Holland, un-expectedly. The unruly Rodchenko and his powerful vivid formats vanish beneath the burned inhuman slabs of Burtynsky, as though they had been covered over by a vast cement block and sunk into non-existence. Then Canada, buzzing in Andreas's head, drawing him into a space and time from which he believed he was amnestied. And Shell there in The Hague, the site of the International Criminal Tribunal for war crimes committed on the territory of former Yugoslavia, where translators from the former shared territory do their work, translators whom Andreas Ban knows from a former life, some even come to the launch of the Dutch edition of his book in the splendid Selexyz bookshop in the famous Hague Passage. *Run, Andreas, run*, he told himself, in vain.

In Amsterdam, Andreas Ban watches gay men dancing in the street, holding hands, walking with their arms around each other, unafraid.

Andreas Ban drinks tea near the University in Café de Jaren, which is as big as a beer hall, with Frank van Vree, who will be moderating the launch of Andreas's book. Frank researches memory and remembering and is writing a book, *In de schaduw van Auschwitz* (*In the Shadow of Auschwitz*), and talks to his students about memory and remembering, about what fragile, unreliable and sometimes capricious phenomena they are; how they take on many different forms—tame and wild, truthful and deceitful—when they are chiseled into monuments, transposed into films, when they are photographed, when they make fiction and history, when they are sealed in documents. *As far as the Second World War is concerned, Auschwitz has become a point by which to calibrate behavior, the symbol of a tolerant society*, says Frank van Vree, *but alongside Auschwitz there are many stories, deliberately forgotten or tendentiously distorted.* Then Frank got onto his bicycle, rode to his car and drove off. *I live with my family in the country*, he said, *quiet and green there.*

Do you talk with your tutors about fascism? Andreas asks his fourth-year students, and they just look at him and say nothing. Then someone says, *No.* Then someone else adds brashly, *It's not in the curriculum, it's not online.* Immediately Andreas wants to start an argument, but instead he hands the students a short text by Umberto Eco, a little piece about ur-fascism, to warm them up, and they read it out loud in the class, and Andreas Ban asks them, *Are there any elements of fascism in Croatia?* after which silence bursts into the dark aura of fear. These students are registered for various subjects—history, literature, philosophy, languages—they weave, twist, wind, dabble, scratch around in facts, after which they turn deaf and set off into the world terrifyingly muted. The majority. So, when the past and present unexpectedly leap up in front of them in a feverish embrace, in an embrace of love and hate, blindness and passion, when they smirk at them in their dreams and waking hours, they swat them away as though they were horseflies, plug headsets into their ears and shake their heads. Like puppets on a string, they wait for someone to give them the gift of movement under the skies of the unmoving.

One night, into Andreas Ban's half-sleep strolls Leeuwenhoek, the guy born in Delft in the middle of the seventeenth century, and the whole business of how he develops the microscope and with it discovers bacteria, parasites, blood corpuscles and much more, and Andreas sees too his mother's old microscope from her student days, in a huge wooden box which magically disappears in the 1950s (sold for five kilos of oranges), and which Andreas Ban and his sister open piously and secretly, so as to observe through its lenses their first paramecia and amoebas, those *single-cell protozoa* inhabiting muddy marsh waters, which *change their shape as they walk on false legs*, which are in fact, simple as they are, very complex and greedy *protozoa* that resist any artificial, laboratory engineering of their own species.

The Prix Goncourt for 2009 is won by the French-Senegalese writer Marie NDiaye for her novel *Trois femmes puissantes* (*Three Strong Women*), and so there is a meeting held about the Goncourt prizes to which Andreas Ban does not go, because at the same time in the Academic Cultural Center across the road from his building there is a discussion about the thirty-one-year-old Afghan politician, activist and fighter for the rights of her nation and especially women, Malalai Joya. There is a lot of information about Malalai Joya online, about what she is fighting for and how, where she has given talks, on which continents, at which universities, in what forums, in which international papers she has written; which prominent names, from Chomsky to Naomi Klein to journalists, parliamentarians and politicians, have spoken about her anticorruption activities, offering her (moral) support. But something here does not add up. It is as though an absurd drama is being acted out behind the scenes of Western civilization, a burlesque to prick the conscience of the world, a conscience dulled by many of those who support Malalai Joya. The book that Malalai Joya writes with the Canadian journalist Derrick O'Keefe, published in the US as *Raising My Voice* and translated into many European languages (with titles such as *A Woman Among Warlords* or *Au nom de mon peuple*), is being launched that evening by De Geus in its Dutch edition. One can enter the hall only if registered in advance, at the door there are security personnel or plainclothes police, and there are more in the audience. As a member of parliament, in 2003 Malalai Joya took the microphone and, demonstratively removing her black scarf, used the three minutes she had at her disposal to let fly a volley at the so-called democratically elected Afghan government, in particular its wartime leaders, profiteers and criminals (who enjoy the support of the US and members of NATO). Then a campaign was launched against her. In 2007, Malalai Joya was deprived of all political rights and thrown out of parliament, after which she survived several assassination attempts and was quite ironically offered the protection of the United Nations Security Forces. Nowadays she travels incognito in a burka, is guarded by armed professionals and has no permanent address in Afghanistan. Andreas finds it touching and exciting to observe this young, fragile, beautiful woman completely spellbound by her mission. Using the language of agitprop, demonstrations, anger and accusation, a simple language without circularity, without nuances, a language that has the effect of a mantra, with one sharp thought at its core—the one about "the freedom of the people"—a language comprehensible to her half-educated and manipulated "brothers and sisters," a language carrying the burden of an almost fanatical belief in "a better tomorrow," the language of revolution and revolutionaries, which still rings in the ears of fifty-year-olds and those even older, and whose faded traces sink into the dug-out crevasses of history, a direct language, almost flaming, used by this decisive woman, the embodiment of all stereotypes of a woman revolutionary, to address her indifferent and spoiled audience which cannot think of a better plan for frittering away a rainy evening. Childishly utopian, spoken almost in a trance, her final call to her drowsy Dutch audience rings out (an entreaty Malalai Joya probably addresses to all the assemblies of Western civilization before which she stands): *Rise up against the intervention of your country in Afghanistan, let us fight for our freedom on our own; we have thrown off the Taliban, we will throw off Karzai. I want to live, but I am not afraid of death. I am afraid of silence. And to those who wish to remove me I say: You can pluck a flower, but you cannot prevent the coming of spring. If they kill me, they will not kill my voice, because it is the voice of all the women of Afghanistan. I am just a symbol of the struggle of my people and the servant of their ideals. If they kill me because of what I believe, then let my blood become the inspiration for emancipation and my words be a revolutionary paradigm for the generations to come.* This pathos-filled, somnambulist, archaic and cliché-ridden rhetoric uttered in the midst of a shallow, consumerist civilization, whose greatest concern is the ecological separation of waste, seems to be the only possible rhetoric for the disenfranchised and uneducated. That is why what Malalai Joya is doing in her country is more important than the way she presents it in the Western market, because those are goods the Western market does not buy: Malalai Joya's illegal schools for girls, schools in cellars and private houses during Taliban rule, her sharp public condemnation of religious fundamentalists, her childhood spent in Iranian and Pakistani refugee camps (after the Soviet invasion of Afghanistan), her struggle against the inclusion of former mujahideen in the current Afghan government, and, not at all unimportant, her awareness, her public admission of the importance of her own education which will procure her a rhetoric on a par with that of prominent Western politicians and thinkers who now bow paternalistically before her.

After that performance that will do absolutely nothing for Malalai Joya and her people, Andreas Ban goes for a drink with Rashid Novaire. Rashid Novaire is a Dutch writer with a fine oval face and skin the color of white coffee, born in 1979 to a Dutch mother and a Moroccan father. In 2005, Rashid Novaire appears in Zagreb and Zadar at the European Short Story Festival, and the literary journal *Zarez* publishes two of his poems ("India" and "Herons in Cairo"). Rashid Novaire writes novels and poetry. In the bar, Andreas and Rashid do not talk about literature, or perhaps a bit, obliquely. Rashid talks about a book that is lying in his belly, buried, and which, as time passes, is turning into a clump, heavy and painful. Rashid is beginning to break up that clump by collecting pellets of his family's past. In 2008, his novel *Roots* comes into being. Thus Andreas discovers:

Once upon a time there was a fair-skinned, blue-eyed Polish woman of German origin. From Danzig (?). At the beginning of the Second World War, after the German invasion of Poland, bewitched by the Führer's promises about the upright future of the upright Aryan race, this fair-skinned, blue-eyed Polish woman of German origin resolves to make her contribution to that future. She commits no crimes, she does not inform on any Jews (if she does, Rashid will never know), she just gives birth. So this Polish woman of German origin brings ten children into the world and for her effort receives Hitler's Cross of Honor of the German Mother, *das Ehrenkreuz der deutschen Mutter*, popularly known as *das Mutterkreuz*. Because, as the Nazis liked to say (and in a similar vein the Catholic Church claims), *Your body is not your property but the property of your family—your homeland*. After the war, this proud Polish woman is not driven out of Poland with all those Germans who stumble around

Europe looking for somewhere to settle down. But her children leave, one after another. The daughter of the by now elderly Polish woman of German origin starts a family in Amsterdam, where *her* daughter falls in love with a young Moroccan immigrant and they have a son. The son becomes a Dutch poet and prose writer, while the old Polish woman of German origin renounces her granddaughter because she marries a man of "impure" blood, color and race. However, the old Polish woman of German origin dies soon afterward—so no problem. *That granddaughter is my mother*, says Rashid. *You never know where you are with history, you never know where the truth lies. In what actually happened or in what we would like to have happened. History is a dangerous seductress.*

Andreas Ban casts a glance around the bar. He looks behind him. The bar is full of guests, and noisy. A small bar with the patina of a dangerous past. A frowning barman. At the counter stand big fair-haired men, muscle-bound men with tattoos, men of stiff military gestures. Andreas Ban sees how he and Rashid shrink, slip off their chairs. A strange wind blows through the *bruin café*, it gets dark and cold. From somewhere in the distance comes that famous maudlin "Horst-Wessel-Lied." *Imagination can play all sorts of tricks on us*, says Andreas Ban, *let's get out of here. But expand the story of your great-grandmother*, he says. *And visit Poland.*

Guido Snel takes Leo and Andreas to the Turkish restaurant Diwan, in the Jordaan district. They eat all kinds of snacks, they are brought ten dishes with food for picking at and dunking. Some of the foods are familiar, meatballs for instance, *tarator* salad, *ajvar*, but some are new to Leo and Andreas, and spicy. The pieces of baklava are unusual and slip down the throat. When Andreas Ban had strolled through Jordaan on his own (before Leo came), although all the tourist guides describe it as a lively and picturesque workers' district, there had not been any liveliness anywhere. It was windy, clouds hung like rags from the bare branches, the canals were murky. The shops were shut and little balls of gray winter silence rolled across the squares. As he walked, Andreas had stumbled across a relatively small statue of Theo Thijssen (1879–1943), the Netherlands' best-loved children's author. Theo Thijssen stood outside the Theo Thijssen Museum, in fact outside the house where Thijssen was born, which Andreas Ban does not enter. The statue of Anne Frank is small. Andreas does not visit the Anne Frank House either, because there are too many people lining up outside the museum and Anne Frank has been turned into a populist Dutch brand as though she belonged in Amsterdam's Madame Tussauds. A writer from Turkey who had lived in this literary Amsterdam apartment before Andreas had been to the wax museum and had his photograph taken in an embrace with Obama. The photograph of the Turkish writer had been fixed into a virulently red frame, but he had forgotten it on the fridge.

The night that Leo and Andreas walked to Jordaan with Guido, it sparkled everywhere, as though it was New Year.

In The Hague Andreas also visits a large historical photography exhibition and an exhibition of the Blue Rider,* then once again sinks into a deep blue depression because of the times he is living in. It is cold in The Hague too. Andreas Ban spends two days staying with his friend Zoran Mutić, otherwise from Sarajevo, plunged in Zoran's family war story which he already knows in detail, but still, he always wants to hear it again. Zoran is a first-rate translator of poetry and prose from modern Greek, yet in The Hague he now translates documents and indictments, all

---

* The Blue Rider (der Blaue Reiter). A group of Russian immigrant and German artists (including Vasily Kandinsky, Alexei von Jawlensky, August Macke, Franz Marc and Gabriele Münter) founded in Munich in 1911.

kinds of bureaucratic legalistic tangles; instead of dealing with lyrical souls he concerns himself with crooks and collects films that he will not get around to watching and books that he does not have time to read.

On the way to the Gemeente museum (while Zoran is at work), Andreas Ban catches sight of a telephone booth in which a smiling Stalin is waiting, illuminated by a table lamp with a pinkish-white shade. What if, instead of  Stalin with his twisted wing mustache, that syphilitic degenerate and pervert with his stubby sawn-off mustache had been crouching in the telephone booth, the guy who had caught venereal disease from a Jewish prostitute in Vienna in 1908, after which he imagined that God Himself had sent him to eliminate the "Jewish disease" that was raging throughout the world?

In The Hague Andreas Ban goes to lunch with Joško Paro, the Croatian Ambassador at the time. First Andreas Ban and Joško Paro talk about literature, then about agreeable activities such as learning Dutch and painting, then they move on to Tudjman and the 1990s, Andreas is initially tentative, then relaxes completely, because Joško Paro turns out to be a critically minded collocutor, so the salmon they are eating slips merrily down Andreas's throat. Afterward, when Andreas goes off to his launch, Joško Paro says, *Be careful, the Dutch are very direct people.* After the launch, Paro's warning is clarified: a middle-aged man approaches Andreas Ban and says, *I'm a psychologist, what you wrote is good, but your reading was terrible, promise that you'll never read like that again.* Better that than Croatian artificiality, constrained politeness.

After the launch, Mirjana Staničić from the Croatian Embassy invites Kirsten from De Geus, Zoran and Andreas to dinner in a businessmen's restaurant, where all the guests are men who speak softly, dressed in dark suits and expensive shoes. It looks conspiratorial.

In The Hague Andreas Ban does not manage to see the sea. Zoran says, *You can't swim in the sea at Scheveningen, it has currents that sweep people away, never to be seen again, so why would you look at it?* and Andreas trusts Zoran.

In The Hague Andreas Ban also visits an exhibition of Czech glass because it is on his way, and as he looks at those creations full of imagination and color, not exactly appealing heaped up like that, he recalls the 1960s when people used to travel from Yugoslavia to Czechoslovakia for ugly crystal glasses, jugs and cake sets, and then arrange them in glass-fronted cabinets, mostly for prestige and wonderment.

In The Hague it is below zero. Snowflakes sprinkle the days. Ellen Elias-Bursać, who also translates for the Tribunal and books as well, when she has time, takes Zoran and Andreas to De Boterwaag Café to get warm. As far back as 1682, butter was sold in De Boterwaag Café, so in the middle of the café that looks more like a beer hall with its old stone floor, stands an authentic weighing machine from that period, a huge decorative object, wrapped in nostalgia, around which the customers eat and drink tea.

Chinese New Year falls while Andreas Ban is in The Hague, festivities and din, crowds everywhere, especially in the Chinese quarter. The Chinese quarter sprang up on the terrain of the former Jewish shtetl of impoverished Ashkenazy immigrants. That is why Ellen Elias says, *I have my own Jewish story, you know.* That was something Andreas Ban did not expect. There in The Hague. Those stories running after him like little ducks sliding over the frozen lakes and canals, then stumbling on the hardened Hague soil. Ellen's family was originally from Krakow, and before the Second World War most of its members moved to America. Some did not manage to leave and they simply—vanished. As soon as he had returned to Amsterdam, Andreas received a photograph from Ellen Elias of her grandfather Nathaniel M. Elias, a New York chemical engineer who, as a witness for the prosecution and on behalf of several government agencies of the United States, testified in Nuremberg at the I. G. Farben trial. And there in The Hague, as they are wandering through the Chinese quarter, Ellen says, *Come, I want to show you something.*

They enter a small urban park with leafless trees and step onto the empty children's playground surrounded by new four-story apartment blocks with red and yellow facades. In the middle of the playground are six shiny climbing frames of various heights that resemble chairs (there had been seven, one was stolen). It is only when one gets very close, when the gaze focuses on each individual rung, that one notices, written in crooked children's handwriting, with letters of unequal size resisting order and severity, male and female names and beside each name in brackets a number indicating age. According to an explanation written on the ground nearby, Andreas Ban discovers that these are the names of some of the two thousand and sixty-one (2,061) Jewish children from The Hague consumed by the war, many of whom "played here and went to school across the road." Andreas Ban discovers that the Nazis had taken these children, two thousand and sixty-one (2,061), aged between six months and eighteen years, from their parents (the parents were rounded up a few streets away), and from the open space in front of the school, precisely on the site of this "playground," sent them in special wagons first to Westerbork concentration camp or to Vught transit camp, then to Auschwitz, Sobibor, Bergen-Belsen and Theresienstadt. The monument is the work of the artists Sara Benhamou and Eric de Vries and was erected in 2006. Later, Andreas Ban researches several families from The Hague to find out where and how the parents, brothers and sisters, the relatives of the children who had been taken away had ended up. In some cases deaths were shared, familial, sometimes the mothers died with their daughters and sons, sometimes the children died alone.

For instance Flora Bachrach (3), born in The Hague on November 16, 1939, at 13 Spaarnedwarsstraat, was deported in a children's convoy from Vught via Westerbork to Sobibor in June 1943 and killed on July 2 of that year. With her were her sister Klara (6), born on December 26, 1936, and her brother Sine (1), born on May 30, 1942. Seven days later, on July 9, 1943, their thirty-five-year-old mother Bertha Bachrach-Dessaur, born September 18, 1907, was killed in Sobibor. One can only imagine her heartrending pain as before her eyes dance the smiles of her children, one of whom was still toddling around in diapers and forming his first words.

The Weinreb family lived at 70 Hasseltsestraat, in Scheveningen. David Weinreb, born May 15, 1941, in The Hague, dies in Westerbork camp on April 27, 1943, and is cremated three days later. Two weeks later he would have been two years old. The urn containing his ashes is in the Jewish cemetery in Diemen in section U, row 5, grave number 6. There is no information about the other members of the Weinreb family. So, it is presumed that David's parents and their two remaining children survived the war. One could carry on like this for ever: follow the histories of once-living people and converse with their ghosts. But people do not have the time.

One other thing: the deportations of Jews from Holland began on June 15, 1942, and continued until September 13, 1943. Some 101,000 people were taken away (and killed). The Hague assembly center was first situated in Scheveningen prison, then in the "vacated" Jewish orphanage in Paviljoensgracht.

When the sun illuminates Rabbijn Maarsenplein, the six chair-ladders gleam. The shafts of silver arrows rebound from them in all directions, they fly in a circle, into the air, left to right, bury themselves in the ground. But down these chair-ladders long shadows also glide, pouring over the playground and spreading beyond its edges. Then darkness falls over the merry memorial to the murdered children.

In Holland, Andreas Ban did not look for Demnig's stumbling blocks. But still, standing rooted to the spot in the children's playground in The Hague, unable to summon the strength to climb even onto the lowest chair-ladder, he remembered how Demnig repeated ad nauseam: *People are forgotten only when we forget their names.*

Tenuhemo min hashamayin
May Heaven comfort you

Erna Aalsvel (15)	Isidor Abrahams (2)
David Abrahams (13)	Jacob Abrahams (10)
Elfrieda Abrahams (4)	Judith Abrahams (5)
Helene Abrahams (10)	Machiel Abrahams (7)
Helene Minna Abrahams (17)	Menno Samuel Abrahams (8)
Henri Abrahams (10)	Michel Abrahams (18)

Mirjam Minne Abrahams (9)
Raphael Abrahams (2)
Abram Abram (13)
Meyer Abram (16)
Mietje Abram (11)
Mozes Abram (8)
Regina Abram (4)
Willy Abram (4)
Abraham Abramowicz (17)
Heinrich Adler (10)
Hanna Agsterribbe (3)
Jozef Agsterribbe (4)
Rachel Agsterribbe (18 mths)
Rachel Hanna Agsterribbe (5)
Salomon Agsterribbe (3)
Hans Julius Ainstein (13)
Benjamin Aizenfeld (12)
Anton Alter (10)
Carla Alter (8)
Clara Alter (2)
David Alter (3)
Elisabeth Alter (14)
Eva Alter (12)
Frederik Alter (7)
Hartog Alter (9)
Hennie Alter (11)
Johanna Alter (9)
Julia Truida Alter (12)
Louis Alter (2)
Marcel Alter (5)
Meijer Alter (10)
Meijer Alter (10)
Mirjam Alter (5)
Philip Alter (4)
Rosette Alter (3)
Bryndil Lya Altman (8)
Channa Altman (9)
Berta Ament (12)
Dora Ament (18)
Klara Marie Ament (16)
Norbert Ament (15)
Betty van Amerongen (2)
Levie van Amerongen (10)
Annette Estella Ancona (2)
Dina Appelboom (12)

Jaantje den Arend (7)
Leendert den Arend (8)
Marcus den Arend (2)
Hartog van Arend (4)
Käthe van Arend (12)
Mozes van Arend (8)
Elga Sara Aronstein (15)
Salomon Asser (16)
David Bachrach (16)
Engel Bachrach (11)
Flora Bachrach (3)
Hijman Bachrach (7)
Klara Bachrach (17 mths)
Klara Bachrach (6)
Lina Bachrach (13)
Thea Henriette Bachrach (5)
Lena Baks (5)
Jacob Ksiel Balamut (4)
Peretz Chaim Balamut (8)
Pesel Balamut (7)
Fredy Barchasch (9)
Marcel Barchasch (11)
Ralph Barchasch (10)
Carla Betty van Baren (3)
Herman Jacob van Baren (12)
Alexander Barendse (5)
Annie Barendse (17)
Betje Barendse (4)
Elizabeth Barendse (4)
Estella Barendse (8)
Hijman Manasse Barendse (11)
Isaac Barendse (6)
Isaac Henry Barendse (3)
Isaac Jacob Barendse (17)
Jansje Barendse (18)
Wolf Barendse (8)
Wolf Alexander Barendse (7)
Louise Bertha Bargeboer (18)
Jacob Beck (13)
Sofie Jaantje Behr (8)
Juda Bekker (18)
Richard Herman Bekker (13)
Sophia Bloeme Bekker (14)
Lea Evalien Benedictus (2)
Anna van den Berg (15)

Louise van den Berg (12)
Max van den Berg (17)
Robert van den Berg (20)
Hermann van der Berg (16)
Mindel Berglas (4)
Perl Berglas (4)
Margherita Berkelij (6)
Marianne Beradine Berkelij (5)
Philip Herman Berkelij (8)
Benjamin Izak Berkovics (4)
Elvira Berkovics (6)
Samuel Berkovics (2)
Betta Berlijn (11)
Ester Besen (16)
Gusta Besen (10)
Adolf Herman Besthof (17)
Anna van Bever (16)
Emanuel van Bever (9)
Alexander van Biene (8)
Mozes van Biene (12)
Willem van Biene (12)
Leo Biermann (2)
Alexander Blanes (13)
Eliasar Blanes (16)
Lion Blanes (17)
Samuel Blau (8)
Barend Blik (5)
Gabriel Blik (2)
Leentje Blik (7)
Nathan Blik (3)
Joel Mozes Bloemendaal (6)
Mozes Isaak Bloemendaal (16)
Siegfried Salomon Bloemendaal (4)
Carolina Esther Bloemkoper (12)
Clara Suzanna Bloemkoper (7)
Jacob Bloemkoper (9)
Lea Bloemkoper (11)
Margarethe Meta Bloemkoper (4)
Marius Jo Bloemkoper (5)
Bertha Hanna Blok (5)
Cato Blok (14)
Esther Blok (13)
Harry (Tsewie) Blok (13)
Henri Willem Blok (13)
Henriette Lena Blok (7)

Jacob Blok (11)
Justine Blok (15)
Marcus Blok (11)
Mietje Blok (8 mths)
Ribca Blok (17)
Rosette Blok (18)
Sophia Blok (13)
Gerda Ella Blom (9)
Marina Blom (6)
Sientje Blom (8)
Alida Boas (3)
Benedictus Israel Boas (12)
Aaron Bobbe (15)
Anna Bobbe (4)
Anna Bobbe (16)
Barend Bobbe (15)
Benjamin Bobbe (4)
Clara Bobbe (16)
Debora Bobbe (9)
Hanna Sophia Bobbe (16 mths)
Herman Bobbe (2)
Jacob Levie Bobbe (12)
Jacob Louis Bobbe (7)
Jetje Bobbe (17)
Klaartje Bobbe (3)
Louis Bobbe (2)
Louis Bobbe (10)
Marieka Bobbe (14 mths)
Maurice Bobbe (17)
Rachel Bobbe (12)
Rebecca Bobbe (12)
Rika Bobbe (17)
Saartje Bobbe (5)
Samuel Joseph Bobbe (9)
Andries Boekbinder (17)
Anna Boekbinder (5)
David Boekbinder (17)
Kaatje Boekbinder (17)
Mozes Boekbinder (7)
Salomon Boekbinder (7)
Simon Boekbinder (13)
Jacques Herman Boeken (18)
Louis Carol Boeken (15)
Carla Jeanette Boeken (8)
Josua Boesenach (12)

Jacob Bornszteijn (7)
Simon Boutelje (6)
Abraham Bouwman (11)
Eduard Brandeis (14)
Elizabeth Brandeis (15)
Erica Charlotte Brandel (12)
Jacqueline Yvonne Brandel (7)
Ferdinand Brandel (7)
Louise Selma Brandel (6)
Maurice Ivan Brandel (7)
Mozes Brandel (18)
Simon de Brave (17)
Juliette Leni Bril (14)
Jacques Brilleslijper (9)
Simon Brilleslijper (7)
Mozes van Brink (12)
Rozetta van Brink (11)
Fanny Brodman (2)
René Brodmann (15 mths)
Carla Bromet (10)
Emanuel Bromet (6)
Henry Rudolf Bron (10)
Jacques Jan Bron (11)
Louise Bronkhorst (15)
Mozes Bronkhorst (12)
Sara Bronkhorst (17)
John Jacques Bueno de Mesquita (7)
Jacob Campignon (5)
Albert Louis Cohen (3)
Alica Cohen (17)
Alice Elisabeth Cohen (17)
Benjmin Cohen (9)
Cato Cohen (13)
David Cohen (18)
Frederika Cohen (3)
Gretha Cohen (11)
Hanny Cohen (14)
Hans Jozef Cohen (12)
Heintje Cohen (13)
Herman Davey Cohen (16)
Jacob Cohen (7)
Jacob Cohen (8)
Jacques Cohen (16)
Jeanette Helena Cohen (15)
Joan Cohen (14 mj.)

Jozef Cohen (18)
Louis Cohen (13)
Marcus Cohen (5)
Max Adolf Frits Cohen (11)
Louise Paula Cohen (17)
Mozes Cohen (18)
Nico Louis Cohen (10)
Paulina Kay Henriette Cohen (6)
Roosje Cohen (15)
Salomon Cohen (17)
Samuel Abraham Cohen (16)
Sara Cohen (15)
Sophia Martha Cohen (6)
Pincu Simon Cohn (11)
Helena van Collem (11)
Samuel van Collem (14)
Aaron Tobias Colthof (1)
Jacob Isidor Colthof (3)
Isaac Con (15)
Celina Rosa Cosman (18)
David Cosman (10)
Elisabeth Cosman (11)
Isaac Cosman (15)
Joseph Cosman (8)
Rosa Hermina Cosman (13)
Simonne Clara Cosman (16)
Emanuel Creveld (19)
Gretha van Creveld (17)
Hendrika van Creveld (15)
Hendrika Roosje van Creveld (12)
Henny van Creveld (8)
Hester Roosje van Creveld (6)
Jacob van Creveld (17)
Jetje van Creveld (4)
Louis van Creveld (16)
Carla Croiset (6)
Ernst Cukerman (6)
Sophia da Cunha (13)
Abraham Dagloonder (17)
Eduard Dagloonder (2)
Estelle Dagloonder (16)
Esther Dagloonder (7)
Fritsje Dagloonder (12)
Joseph Dagloonder (12)
Joseph Dagloonder (14)

Joseph Dagloonder (16)
Klara Dagloonder (8)
Leendert Dagloonder (15)
Marcus Dagloonder (17)
Simon Dagloonder (10)
Jack Joseph van Dal (14)
Alfred Dick van Dam (7)
Hartog van Dam (8)
Heiman van Dam (11)
Izaak Nathan van Dam (11)
Isidoor Bram van Dam (10)
Jacobus van Dam (11)
Sibilla van Dam (17)
Abraham Willem Danser (5)
Marianna Danser (16)
Markus Danser (4)
Meyer Danser (3)
Roza Danser (15)
Sophia Danser (6)
Sophia Danser (14)
Bloeme Davids (5)
Louis Davids (3)
Betty Davidson (11)
Isidoor Davidson (7)
Suzanna Davidson (8)
Aaron Dessaur (12)
Anna Dessaur (17)
Rachel Dessaur (14)
Simon Dessaur (13)
Sami Diamant (14)
Aron Djament (3)
Elka Djament (8)
Riwka Djament (6)
Eva Dormits (14)
Jozef Dormits (12)
Josina Marja Drukker (12)
Esther Druyf (3)
Henriette Druyf (6)
Henriette Rebecca Druyf (7)
Isaac Druyf (9)
Salomon Druyf (17)
Chana Dryter (3)
Herbert Leopold Eisenmann (9)
Jacob Eisenmann (16)
Relina Gudula Eisenmann (12)

Sally Eisenmann (13)
Jacob Elburg (9)
Johan Arie Elburg (1)
Henriette Rosetta Elion (14)
Daniel Markus van Engel (15 mths)
Robert van Engel (6 mths)
Milan Engelmann (5)
Olaf Engelmann (12)
Hartog Jacques Engelsman (11)
Rebecca Engelsman (6)
Sigmund Isaac Engelsman (3)
Arnold Engers (13)
Regina Rozetta Englander (17)
Philip Ensel (16)
Ella Epstein (16)
Albert van Eso (17)
Selma Fredy van Esso (13)
Henriette Martha Eyl (5)
Rika Jeanette Eijsmn (4)
Ilse Lea Ferber (16)
Jeanne Ferber (5)
Richard Ferber (7)
Sara Ferber (7)
Henriette Sophia Feitsma (10)
Jacob Jonas Feitsma (14)
Joseph Henri Feijten (17)
Ester Findling (15)
Hennie Findling (12)
Herman Findling (4)
Herbert Fink (15)
Renee Fink (14)
Debora Finsij (13)
Judith Eleonora Fischer (10)
Yvonne Fischer (7)
Maurice Isaac Fischzang (8)
Ber Flam (11)
Lea Flinker (14)
Mozes Wolf Flinker (18)
Karel Anton Fonteijn (17)
Betty Maria Frank (13)
Jacob Meyer Frank (16)
Martijn Salomon Frank (16)
Meyer Jacob Frank (15)
Philip Leonard Frank (14)
Salomon Frank (6)

Salomon Barend Frank (4)
Samuel Frank (4)
Aron van Frank (17)
Beletje Veronica van Frank (15)
Ezechiel van Frank (11)
Henri Sara van Frank (17)
Henriette van Frank (9)
Lea van Frank (4)
Paulina van Frank (13)
Veronica van Frank (15)
David Franken (11)
Heijman Karel Franken (10)
Klara Franken (4)
Lena Julia Jacoba Franken (6)
Ellen Margit Freimann (15)
Herman Emile Frenkel (15)
Aaron Fresco (13)
Aaron Heinz Fresco (17)
Abraham Fresco (7)
Adele Fresco (13)
Alexander Fresco (15)
Anna Fresco (8)
Anna Fresco (17)
Calman Fresco (13)
David Fresco (17)
Dora Fresco (2)
Elias Fresco (18 mths)
Elias Fresco (9)
Emanuel Fresco (15)
Esther Fresco (14)
Fanny Elise Fresco (2)
Helena Fresco (9)
Hester Fresco (17)
Isaac Fresco (14)
Jacob Simon Fresco (2)
Jacques Fresco (9)
Jonas Fresco (14)
Jozeph Fresco (16)
Klaartje Fresco (8)
Louis Aaron Fresco (12)
Louis Fresco (18 mths)
Maurits Fresco (6)
Margaretha Fresco (13)
Rachel Fresco (18 mths)
Raimond Fresco (2)

Sara Fresco (4)
Arnita Friedberg (14)
Emil Friedmann (12)
David de la Fuente (8)
Gompel de la Fuente (11)
Marianne de la Fuente (16 mths
Elisabeth Fuld (16)
Henriette Fuldauer (14)
Isidora Davida Fuldauer (13)
Selly Fuldauer (14)
Rosa Gabes (11)
Benjamin Gans (16)
Bloemina Gazan (17)
Eli Abraham Gazan (12)
Grete Gazan (5)
Jozef Gazan (14)
Juda Gazan (9)
Julie Gazan (3)
Marcus Meier Gazan (11)
Levie van Geens (13)
Sophia van Geens (17)
Alexander van Gelder (14)
Arthur Izak van Gelder (12)
Hartog van Gelder (17)
Jitschak Nechemjah van Gelder (4)
Ruben Chizkiah van Gelder (6)
Nico Meyer van Geldere (18 mths)
Salomon Nathan van Geldere (4)
Bertha Rosetta van Gelderen (11)
Johan Meyer van Gelderen (16)
Jozef van Gelderen (16)
Berta Gerstl (10)
Koenraad Huib Gezang (16 mths)
Anni Glattstein (9)
Heinz Gobas (16)
Joseph Tobias Gobets (15)
Esther de Goede (6)
Felix Gokkes (3)
Isaac Gokkes (8)
Isidore Gokkes (13)
Simon Gokkes (15)
Rigina Goldberg (7)
Asscher Selig Goldman (7)
Chaja Perl Goldman (6)
Chuma Goldman (2)

Hinda Ida Goldman (5)
Israel Goldman (13)
Sylvain Louis Goldstein (14)
Alexander Abraham Goldwasser (13)
Slata Charlotte Goldwasser (11)
Nico Gompers (15)
Barend Leon Gosler (6)
Henri Eduard Gosler (2)
Jacques Max Gosler (3)
Bernard David Gosschalk (16)
Johanette Gosschalk (8)
Ester Gottlob (14)
Schabse Gottlob (16)
Sientje Goudenburg (3)
Herman Goudsmid (9)
Maurits Goudsmid (11)
Michel Goudsmid (15)
Riwka Ethel Goudsmid (5)
Benjamin Henri Goudstikker (16)
Jacques Goudstikker (17)
Isaac le Grand (17)
Trude Pia Grätzer (15)
Marco Grimberg (15)
Abraham Grinbaum (4)
Jerach Grinbaum (2)
Joseph Grinbaum (6)
Isaac Grishaver (9)
Raphael Grishaver (7)
Betty Nanette Groen (11 mths)
Flora Groen (15)
Hendrik Groen (14)
Hanna Louise Groen (7)
Klara Groen (16)
Emanuel de Groen (5)
Aaron Jacob de Groot (9)
Anna Thea de Groot (5)
Fritz Louis Jozeph de Groot (11)
Arnold Salomon de Groot (5)
Hans Salomon de Groot (8)
Jacob Abraham de Groot (9 mths)
Jeanne de Groot (4)
Mourits de Groot (16)
Robert Isaac de Groot (6)
Salomon Jacob de Groot (5)
Sophie de Groot (8)

Theodora Anna de Groot (3)
Esther Grosswachs (11)
Malka Grosswachs (10)
Sarah Grosswachs (6)
Taube Grosswachs (4)
Paul Grosz (6)
Abraham Grün (11)
Gilda Grün (6)
Josef Grün (9)
Majer Herz Grün (2)
Siegfried Grün (10)
Maurits Grynbaum (8)
Betty Judith Haagens (18)
Aron Haagman (8)
Elisabeth Haagman (12)
Gabriel Haagman (2)
Hijman Manasse Haagman (4)
Roosje Haagman (10)
Emmy de Haan (16)
Fietje de Haan (18)
Kitty de Haan (15)
Ilse Sara Haas (8)
Alice Renate de Haas (17)
Edith de Haas (16)
Henderina van Hachgenberg (16)
Rebecca van Hachgenberg (6)
Salomon van Hachgenberg (16)
Sara van Hachgenberg (13)
Sophia Engeltje van Hachgenberg (2)
Alida Hakker (10)
Calman Hakker (16)
Debora Jeanne Hakker (7)
Frederika Hakker (13)
Heintje Hakker (13)
Isaac Hakker (4)
Jacob Hakker (16)
Jacques Hakker (8)
Joseph Hakker (5)
Lea Hakker (7)
Maurits Hakker (14)
Mina Hakker (14)
Rachel Hakker (3)
Rebecca Hakker (16)
Sara Hakker (5)
Simon Hakker (10)

Suze Hakker (13)
Anna Halper (16)
Frieda Halper (13)
Lothar Halpern (12)
Joseph van der Ham (16)
Abraham Hamburg (5)
Engelina Hamburg (3)
Esther Hamburg (6)
Joel Hamburg (8)
Joseph Hamburg (4)
Abraham Hamme (5)
Anna Hamme (14)
Harry Hamme (7)
Harry Hamme (9)
Hartog Hamme (10)
Joel Hamme (12)
Joel Hamme (13)
Louis Hamme (5)
Magdalena Hamme (4)
Magdalena Hamme (8)
Mala Hamme (2)
Margaretha Hamme (6)
Salomon Hamme (15)
Salomon Hamme (17)
Sara Hamme (4)
Salomon Happe (5)
Betty Alida Harschel (4)
Klara Harschel (12)
Salomon Harschel (4)
Max Paul den Hartogh (8)
Sonja Jacqueline den Hartogh (6)
Mathilda Etty Hartogs (11)
Marcel Haut (8)
Eduard Hendrix (9)
Dolly Hertz (17)
Emanuel Herman Hertz (8)
Josephine Hertz (14)
Helen Cheftsibah Hertzberger (8)
Jacques Maurice Hertzberger (10)
Rinah Henriette Hertzberger (6)
Abraham Hes (14)
Salomon Hes (17)
Paulina Heijligers (10)
Alex Mark Heijmans (11)
Henri Juda Heijmans (16)

Jeannette Anna Heijmans (13)
Max Leo Heijmans (13)
Hans George Hildebrand (19)
Ruth Hiller (15)
Jetty Bertha Hillesum (17)
Frank Gunther Hirsch (18)
Judith Cato van der Hoek (12)
Rudolf van der Hoek (17)
Godfrey Hoepelman (4)
Johnny Hofstede (5)
Elisabeth de Hoop (14)
Jacob Hornman (10)
Gustaaf Isaac van der Horst (2)
Louis Zadok van der Horst (3)
Aaltje Huisman (14)
Aron Huisman (13)
Cato Huisman (15)
David Huisman (13)
Ester Huisman (18 mths)
Faigla Huisman-Abramowicz (18)
Hendrik Huisman (13)
Hendrika Huisman (16)
Jacob Huisman (6)
Jacques David Huisman (4)
Lea Martha Huisman (10)
Mozes Isaac Huisman (15)
Louis Hijman (11)
Rachel Hijman (12)
Angele Hijmans (7)
Hartog Jacob Hijmans (10)
Jacques Hijmans (11 mths)
Sarah Hijmans (9)
André Ikkersheim (17)
Elisabeth Ikkersheim (7)
Izaak Heiman Ikkersheim (12)
Louis Ikkersheim (4)
Margaretha Ikkersheim (11)
Margaretha Elisabeth Ikkersheim (13)
Salomon Ikkersheim (14)
Willem Daniel Ikkerheim (16)
Renee Anna Isaac (15)
Sulamith Ismann (18)
Salomon Israel (9)
Alexander Jacobs (8)
Alida Femmina Jacobs (8)

Marie Jacobs (11)
Maurits Jacobs (3)
Rosine Jacobs (14)
Sonja Josephina Jacobs (11)
Suzanna Irene Jacobs (4)
Henriette Lilly Jacobson (5)
Nehemia Jacobson (4)
Sophia Annie Jacobson (16)
Bertha Jeger (15)
Frieda Jacobi (5)
Friedrich Jamenfeld (15)
Eduard Isaac Jas (18)
Hester Jas (5)
Abraham Jeret (16)
Dorota Jolles (14)
Nathan Jolles (12)
Alfred de Jong (17)
Alida de Jong (12)
Emanuel de Jong (6)
Emanuel Ernst de Jong (6)
Harry Jacques de Jong (7)
Heintje de Jong (8)
Hesseline de Jong (9)
Isaac de Jong (9)
Judith de Jong (17)
Leonardus de Jong (14)
Marianna de Jong (14)
Marie de Jong (10)
Menno de Jong (3)
Nanny de Jong (13)
Roosje de Jong (6)
Saartje de Jong (16)
Sarintje Edith de Jong (8)
Schoontje de Jong (16)
Willem de Jong (6)
Antoinette Clara de Jongh (12)
Clara Antoinette de Jongh (17)
Felicia de Jongh (9)
Jack Leon de Jongh (6)
Rudolf Leon de Jongh (3)
Samuel Maurits de Jongh (15)
Jack Kaas (16)
Johanna Jeanette Kaas (16 mths)
Jules Floris Kaas (16)
Max Kaas (14)

Jozef George de Kadt (2)
Flora Kallus (5)
Hermina Kallus (4)
Malka Kalter (11)
Henrietta Rebecca van Kam (15)
Louis Benjamin van Kam (16)
Bella Kamm (3)
Jeanette Kamm (9)
Cirl Lea (Cilla) Kaner (10)
Jacques Kanis (2)
Jacob Reginald Kat (13)
Leendert Kat (17)
Annette Katan (17)
Benjamin Katan (6)
Elie Katan (16)
Hendrik Jacob Katan (16)
Jacob Katan (18)
Maurits Jacob Katan (15)
Abraham Kattenburg (14)
Gretel Katz (13)
Louise Katz (6)
Myra Katz (6)
Willy Katz (3)
Bernhardine Josepha Kaufmann (16)
Hannah Ida Kaufmann (13)
Donald Frederik Keizer (18)
Friederique Anna Keizer (10)
Sophie Johanna Alice Keizer (13)
Berta Keller (12)
Frieda Malie Keller (3)
Judith Keller (14)
Isidoor Kets de Vries (11)
Sera Kitty Kets de Vries (9)
Bertha Kahn (4)
Elie Keijl (16)
Esther Kahn (8)
Henny Kahn (14)
Mina Erni Kahn (11)
Sara Kohnraad (9)
Hanny Kirchner (14)
David Kirghijn (7)
Regina Klausner (2)
Abraham Salomon Kleerekoper (10)
Mirjam Kleerekoper (6)
Abigael Chajah Klein (2)

Edith Klein (3)
Jeanette Rosa Klein (10)
Marcus Eljakoem Klein (4)
Sara Klein (6)
Ronja Kleinkramer (18 mths)
Manes Mozes Kleinman (13)
Abraham van der Kloot (4)
Betsie van der Kloot (13)
Ester Gajo van der Kloot (13)
Eduard van der Kloot (9)
Eva van der Kloot (17)
Eveline van der Kloot (9)
Frederika van der Kloot (9)
Frederika van der Kloot (5)
Isaac van der Kloot (18)
Juda van der Kloot (14)
Martha van der Kloot (14)
Max van der Kloot (9)
Mozes van der Kloot (13)
Salomon van der Kloot (11)
Samuel van der Kloot (16)
Sophie Alida van der Kloot (13)
Arthur Kloots (12)
Dora Kloots (8)
Heiman Kloots (7)
Louis Kloots (6)
Lyon Joseph Kloots (11)
Samuel Kloots (14)
Sientje Kloots (4)
Mandlem Klueger (14)
Debora Clara Knap (6)
Abraham Koekoek (12)
Alexandrine Koekoek (12)
Berenice Koekoek (10)
Henry Martin Koekoek (5)
Isaak Koekoek (6)
Lena Koekoek (9)
Levi Koekoek (8)
Mathilda Koekoek (15)
Roza Koekoek (13)
Salomon Koekoek (4)
Samuel Koekoek (6)
Sara Koekoek (13)
Malvine Kohn (13)
Sylvia Kohn (15)

Elizabeth van Kollem (16)
Rachel van Kollem (13)
Salomon Simon van Kollem (2)
Joseph de Koning (5)
Louis de Koning (15)
Willem de Koning (8)
Harry Koopman (8)
Isaac Koopman (15 mths)
Joseph Koopman (5)
Nico Koopman (14)
Rudolf Koopman (5)
Felix van Koppelen (19)
Sara van Koppelen (5)
Jettie Korach (12)
Sophia Louise Koren (3)
Cywie Korn (14)
Jeanette Kornalijnslijper (6)
Bernard Kosiner (10)
Gitly Kosiner (14)
Bernard Kosman (19)
Philippus Kosman (8)
Sara Kosman (15)
Doortje Hanna Koster (8)
Elisabeth Koster (17)
Elisabeth Bilha Koster (8)
Emanuel Koster (8)
Eva Koster (17)
Israel Koster (13)
Louis Victor Koster (16)
Malke Cyrel Kowal (12)
Herbert Krakauer (17)
Muriel Norma Krakauer (13)
Gerard Edward Krausz (6)
Sientje Kronenberg (9)
Ignatz Kroo (7)
Alida Kropveld (7)
Jacques Jozeph Kunstenaar (7)
Lion Kunstenaar (16)
Mary Kunstenaar (12) Bernard Kupfer-
    schmidt (6)
Ethel Kupferschmidt (5)
Eva Regina Kupferschmidt (3)
Rose Kupferschmidt (15)
Carolina Jeanette Kwetsie (4)
Emanuel Kwetsie (9)

Jaantje Kwetsie (11)
Louis Adriaan Kwetsie (18 mths)
Donald Lakmaker (14)
Gerald Lakmaker (17)
Sophia Elisabeth Lakmaker (2)
Judith Lamport (15)
Frits Robert Ralph Lange (6)
Henrietta Betje de Lange (8)
Hetty de Lange (8)
Mirjam de Lange (13)
Samuel de Lange (5)
Anna Mathilda Lansberg (14)
Antoine Cornelis Lansberg (8)
Martin Victor Lansberg (18)
Albert Lauer (11)
Alexander Lauer (13)
Joseph Lauer (6)
Olga Lauer (15)
Heinrich Maijer Laufer (14)
Ella Marianne Leefsma (12)
Margaretha Flora Leefsma (15)
Theodora Judith Leefsma (8)
Abraham de Leeuw (6)
Alexander de Leeuw (7)
Bernardus de Leeuw (14)
Gabriel de Leeuw (15)
Hanna Rozetta de Leeuw (9)
Herman Max de Leeuw (5)
Marianna de Leeuw (7)
Philip Isaac de Leeuw (13)
Richard Gerrit de Leeuw (5)
Sara de Leeuw (14)
Frederique Yvonne de Leeuwe (16)
Alexander Jacob van Leeuwen (12)
Alida van Leeuwen (5)
Anna van Leeuwen (7)
Barend van Leeuwen (3)
Betje van Leeuwen (2)
Calman van Leeuwen (3)
Cato van Leeuwen (17)
Clara Deborah van Leeuwen (4 mths)
Ester van Leeuwen (11)
Hadasse van Leeuwen (9)
Helena van Leeuwen (11 mths)
Isaac Elias van Leeuwen (11)

Izak van Leeuwen (2)
Johanna van Leeuwen (7)
Jacob van Leeuwen (3)
Jacques Jacob van Leeuwen (16)
Josephina van Leeuwen (12)
Lea van Leeuwen (6)
Levie Efraim van Leeuwen (13)
Levy van Leeuwen (8)
Levy Alexander van Leeuwen (9)
Marianna van Leeuwen (2)
Michiel van Leeuwen (4)
Mina van Leeuwen (17)
Mozes van Leeuwen (11)
Mozes Jacob van Leeuwen (7)
Nathan van Leeuwen (2)
Nathan van Leeuwen (9)
Rebecca van Leeuwen (7)
Roosje van Leeuwen (12)
Salomon van Leeuwen (13)
Samuel van Leeuwen (3)
Sara van Leeuwen (9)
Sara van Leeuwen (11)
Susanna van Leeuwen (6)
Wolf van Leeuwen (13)
Mina Lefkowicz (10)
Sarah Lefkowicz (9)
Zili Lefkowicz (12)
Debora Leibel (12)
Gitel Leibel (17)
Sara Leibel (15)
Simon Lelie (14)
Aaron Lelyveld (3)
Dora Lelyveld (14)
Hartog Lelyveld (8)
Herman Lelyveld (18)
Jacques Lelyveld (5)
Martha Lelyveld (6)
Mourits Lelyveld (7)
Rebecca Lelyveld (14)
Roosje Lelyveld (18 mths)
Samuel Lelyveld (14)
Sientje Lelyveld (12)
Aron Leman (12)
Aaron Lens (18)
Aaron Lens (13)

Anna Lens (14)
Anna Lens (15)
Betje Lens (14)
Betje Lens (10 mths)
Boas Lens (6)
David Lens (11)
Eliazer Lens (17)
Elkan Lens (14)
Esther Lens (16)
Flora Lens (15)
Helena Lens (11)
Henriette Lens (10)
Jaantje Lens (3)
Jaantje Lens (14)
Jacob Lens (9)
Jacob Lens (3)
Jeanne Lens (5)
Joseph Lens (15)
Max Lens (15 mths)
Mietje Lens (3)
Rebecca Lens (9)
Rosa Lens (4 mths)
Suze Lens (7)
Alexander Leons (12)
Anna Therese Leons (16)
Rosa Suze Leons (7)
Simon Leuiken (6)
Eduard Nico Leverpoll (14)
Anna Levie (13)
Eva Jenny Levie (9)
Rachel Levie (15)
Sonja Vrouwtje Levie (15)
Benjamin de Levie (11)
Frida de Levie (7)
Bernarda Antoinette Levin (9)
Bernardine Selma Clara Levin (11)
Louis Emanuel Levin (16)
Louis Michel Simon Levin (14)
Micheline Zerla Levin (9)
Sara Marianne Levin (5)
Marcus Levisson (5)
Menno Jacob Levisson (2)
Salomon Elias Levisson (17)
Selma Levy (18)
Alida Levij (1)

Marcus Levij (1)
Hans Lewenstern (15)
Paul Igor Francois Lewin (8)
Cili Liebfreund (15)
Gemmi Liebfreund (8)
Leizer Liebfreund (9)
Kitty Alida de Liema (12)
Rozette Esther van Lier (3)
Siegfried Lievendag (14)
Eva Lipfrajnd (16)
Daniel Jacob Lorsch (11)
Levie Isaac Lorsch (17)
Edith Lewi (10)
Jacob Löwi (5)
Hanny Lunski (12)
Leo Lunski (14)
Henriette Maarsen (17)
Suzanna Maarsen (15)
Elisabeth Manheim (11)
Emanuel Manheim (8)
Salomon Manheim (14)
Alexandra E. Manuskowski (9)
Leonard Manuskowski (2)
Louis Manuskowski (6)
Louis Manuskowski (4)
Rebecca Roosje Marcus (6)
Joel Maschke (10)
Jacques Mathijse (12)
Bijnja Matz (7)
Bijnja Matz (15)
Eduard Meinbach (9)
Harry Meinbach (16)
Leo Meinbach (10)
Maurits Meinbach (12)
Julia Margaretha Melkman (10)
Phyllis Mendel (17)
Sientje Francina Mendel (11)
Annie Mendels (7)
Hans David Mendels (4)
Jet Mendels (13)
Betty van Menk (10)
Jacqueline Elisabeth van Menk (8)
Jozeph van Ments (13)
Benedictus van Mentz (10)
Robert van Mentz (10)

Mieke Meuleman (3)
Jenny Meijer (17)
Nanny Meijer (8)
Ruben Meijer (2)
Rudolf Johan Meijer (2)
Bernard Meijers (4)
Estella Meijers (5)
Hubert Emanuel Meijers (17)
Salomon Meijers (6)
Herbert Michaelis (13)
Anita Eva Kathrin Milch (5)
Philip Aron Milikowski (18 mths)
Eva Minzer (7)
Liane Minzer (5)
Benzion Mitmann (13)
Simon Mitmann (3)
Abraham Mof (8)
Kitty Mogendorff (11)
Marcus Mogendorff (10)
Hadasse Mok (11)
Bernard Jacob Mol (18)
Margarethe Mol (14)
Isidor Monderer (10)
Jacob Monderer (2)
Marcus Monderer (7)
Regina Monderer (9)
Rosa Monderer (6 mths)
Salomon Monderer (4)
Louise Jeanne Montezinos (5)
Esther Morowicz (3)
Sara Rachela Morowicz (4)
Klaartje Morpurgo (13)
Herman Felix Moses (12)
Isidor Karel Moses (17)
Hadassa Mossel (12)
Mosche Mossel (13)
Sifra Mossel (10)
David Mozes (9)
Hein Mozes (10)
Serina Mozes (15)
Bernard Muhlrad (13)
Adele Nabarro (12)
David Nabarro (11)
Marcus Nathan (18 mths)
Betty Neuburger (10)

Konrad Neuburger (13)
Jacob Neuburger (10)
Bernard Neugreschl (2)
Herman Neugreschl (17)
Lazar Neugreschl (15)
Sara Neugreschl (4)
Tobias Neugreschl (13)
Joseph Neuwit (14)
Nico Niekerk (10)
Salomon Niekerk (12)
Wilhelmina Elisabeth Niekerk (17)
Henriette Sara Noach (4)
Josina Sara Noach (18 mths)
Emanuel Noort (8)
Nicolette Noort (10)
Betsy Norden (16)
Ruckla Nosek (15)
Salomon Notowicz (7)
Hartog Nussbaum (13)
Jozef Nussbaum (15)
Lea Nussbaum (11)
Sabina Nussbaum (14 mths)
Gerzon Oberstein (16)
Bert Oesterman (8)
Eliazer Oesterman (14)
Emanuel Oesterman (5)
Joel Oesterman (11)
Mozes Oesterman (16)
Sander Oesterman (8)
Sara Oesterman (12)
Maurice Opdenberg (18)
Rachel Opdenberg (15 mths)
Hans Oppenheim (16)
Gusta Orgel (10)
Israel Orgel (12)
Heiman Os (16)
Jetje Avro Os (16)
Mietje Os (14)
Rosa Nora van Os (17)
Anna Ossendrijver (17)
Leo Benjamin Aaron Ossendrijver (6)
Rozetta Soelamith Ossendrijver (2)
Henriette Louise Delphine van Oven (8)
Elisabeth Pais (6)
Simon Pais (17)

Mietje Papegaai (13)
Edith Paradies (5)
Peter Paradies (8)
Anna Parser (14)
Rosa Parser (14)
Sander Parijs (6)
Abraham van Pels (18 mths)
Jozef van Pels (12)
Rebecca Emma van Pels (2)
Roosje Peper (8)
Saartje Peper (11)
Rachel Pezaro (17)
Joseph Piller (17)
Aaron Polak (7)
Abraham Polak (16)
Alexander Polak (12)
Aron Polak (3)
Betty Polak (17)
Chaja Sara Polak (8)
Channa Polak (11)
Clara Polak (16)
Elisabeth Polak (8)
Flora Jacoba Polak (10)
Heintje Polak (11)
Hendrica Polak (15)
Hendrica Polak (13)
Isaac Polak (11)
Isaac Maurits Polak (4)
Johanna Polak (16)
Judith Hadassa Polak (9)
Louis Polak (14)
Max Polak (13)
Nathan Polak (14)
Philip Maurits Herman Polak (16)
Samuel Polak (8)
Shoelamiet Ruth Polak (8)
Vogeltje Polak (16)
Abelia Poons (15)
Abelia Poons (10)
Abelia Poons (7)
Betsie Poons (13)
Charlotte Poons (12)
David Poons (14)
Gerard Poons (17)
Gerard Poons (18)

Herman Poons (7)
Harry Poons (2)
Harry Alexander Poons (2)
Isidor Poons (16)
Izak Poons (10)
Jacob Poons (5)
Leon Mozes Poons (16)
Margretha Poons (14)
Philip Poons (12)
Rachel Poons (15)
Salomon Poons (11)
Sara Poons (13)
Simon Poons (9)
Susanna Poons (6)
Gerson Pots (9)
Sara Pots (10)
Louise Ada van Praag (17)
Maurits Asser van Praag (7)
Richard Alexander van Praag (5)
Rosine Geertruida van Praag (8)
Eva van Praagh (10)
Helene van Praagh (13)
Louis van Praagh (11)
Maurits van Praagh (9)
Mietje van Praagh (8)
Eliazar Meijer van Praagh (3)
Philip van Praag Sigaar (16)
Rachel van Praag Sigaar (10)
Anna Prins (16)
Elias Prins (11)
Elizabeth Prins (10)
Esther Prins (6)
Grietje Prins (4)
Hadasse Prins (2)
Max Prins (6)
Mathilda Prins (5)
Paulina Sara Prins (4)
Salomon Prins (8)
Samuel Frits Prins (14 mths)
Sara Prins (6)
Serafina Wilhelmina Prins (9 mths)
Sophie Prins (11)
Jacob Prusicki (8)
Sally Prusicki (11)
Meijer Pijpeman (10)

Selina Rebekka Pijpeman (3)
Bernard Antoon de Raay (4)
Julia Rachel de Raay (8)
Joseph Rapaport (17)
Ernestine Emma Helena Raphalowiz (14)
Marcel Philip Raphalowiz (17)
Duifje Ruth Tsippora Reens (6)
Louis Juda Reens (5)
Herman van der Reis (16 mths)
Moses Karl Reiter (16)
Judith Ricardo (10)
Willem Ricardo (12)
Ela Wolf Roenbergh (15)
Eduard Roet (14)
Jacob Roet (11)
Jeanette Roet (6)
Jozef Roet (16)
Marianna Rofessa (17)
Rachel Rofessa (5)
Rebecca Rofessa (2)
Hans Roodenburg (11)
Henny Roodenburg (9)
Simon Roodenburg (14)
Elisabeth Roodfeld (13)
Rebecca Roodfeld (17)
Isidoor Roos (15)
Dientje Jansje Roseboom (13)
Jeanette Roza Roseboom (9)
Adolph Rosenbaum (18)
Jack Rosenbaum (6)
Mimi Betsy Rosenbaum (13)
Nathan Rosenbaum (16)
Abraham Fritz Rosenberg (18 mths)
Isi Rosenberg (7)
Lina Bluma Rosenberg (4)
Herman Rosner (8)
Markus Rotter (15)
Szulim Rotter (17)
Jenni Sonja Rozdau (17)
Aron David Rozenblum (15)
Reina Rozevelt (17)
Abraham Rudolf (5)
Isidoor Max Rudolf (2)
Marjem Schewa Russ (15)
Schulem Russ (17)

Simon van Rijk (16)
Izaak Sachs (13)
Chaje Sara Sack (5)
Jacob Sack (5)
Mirel Henny Sack (3)
Oskar Sack (9)
Rebecca Sophia Salzedo (7 mths)
Kurt Sander (15)
Aaltje Sanders (2)
Anna Sanders (5)
Betje Meta Sanders (16)
David Sanders (8)
Elisabeth Sanders (8)
Helena Sanders (7)
Isaac Sanders (17)
Joseph Sanders (9)
Josua Leendert Sanders (9)
Leon Sanders (9)
Meta Sanders (13)
Rosette Sanders (11)
Rosette Josephina Sanders (7)
Salomon Sanders (9)
Aaltje Schaap (13)
Aaltje Schaap (10)
Abraham Schaap (5)
Aleida Schaap (8)
Barend Schaap (4)
Henriette Charlotte Schaap (2)
Manuel Schaap (10)
Chaim Alter Schachter (7)
Hella Sara Schachter (10)
Mina Schachter (17)
Salomon Siegbert Schachter (11)
Max Scharfstein (8)
Reni Henriette Scharfstein (11)
Jettie Elisabeth Scheffer (3)
Rachel Frederika Scheffer (2)
Salomon Asser Scheffer (11 mths)
Salomon Kosman Scheffer (2)
Henriette Schellevis (7)
Willy Schilo (18)
Antje Schnitzler (13)
Eva Helena Schnitzler (10)
Kaatje Schoonhoed (7)
Rachel Schoonhoed (8)

Ernst Walter Schott (12)
Hans Peter Schott (17)
Hendrika Juliana Schram (6)
Betje Schrijver (14)
Hermanus Schrijver (16)
Annie Schuier (13)
Hartog Schuier (18 mths)
Herman Schuier (14)
Branca Schupper (6 mths)
Hela Schupper (18 mths)
Judith Schupper (10)
Malke Schupper (18)
Tonia Rachel Schupper (4)
Carl Schurmann (8)
Werner Schurmann (17)
Esther Schuijer (18)
Rachel Schuijer (13)
Abraham Victor Sealtiel (17)
Benjamin Sealtiel (6)
Betje Sealtiel (14)
Betje Sealtiel (5)
Bilha Esther Sealtiel (11)
David Sealtiel (5)
Elisabeth Sealtiel (4)
Emanuel Sealtiel (13)
Jetje Sealtiel (14)
Simon Sealtiel (8)
Suze Sealtiel (13)
Zadok Sealtiel (14)
Gita Siebzehner (10)
Hinda Siebzehnner (16)
Hirsch Jacob Siebzehner (7)
Sara Kreindla Siebzehner (14)
Josef Zewi Sigmann (16)
Lieselotte Silberschutz (8)
Belia Sils (5)
Boas Silverenberg (2)
Carolina Silverenberg (2)
Robert Frans Simon (4)
Henri Jacob Simons (13)
Meijer Jacob Simons (18)
Leon Sips (3)
Betje Slier (6)
Dina Slier (4)
Isaac Slier (9)

Berta Slomovits (16)
Frederika Slomovits (14)
Levie Sloves (14)
Joseph van der Sluis (12)
Sara van der Sluis (2)
Simon van der Sluis (18 mths)
Christina van der Sluijs (7)
Judith van der Sluijs (8)
Benvonida Rachel Snoek (7)
Dora Snoek (8)
Esther Snoek (12)
Helena Snoek (10)
Isaac Snoek (11 mths)
Jacob Snoek (15)
Simon Alexander Snoek (6)
Abraham Soep (16)
Elia Regina van Son (8)
Max Henri van Son (4)
Siegfried Robert Spanjaard (4)
Claudette Jeanne Speelman (11)
Irma Andrie Speelman (12)
Jean Speelman (15)
Max Jacques Adolf Spetter (17)
Abraham Speijer (9)
Abraham Speijer (5)
Emanuel Speijer (7)
Engel Speijer (18 mths)
Joseph Speijer (4)
Judith Speijer (6)
Louis Speijer (5)
Mietje Speijer (3)
Mozes Speijer (16)
Mozes Speijer (12)
Robert Sem Speijer (7)
Sara Speijer (12)
Simon Speijer (10)
Simon Speijer (8)
Simon Speijer (16 mths)
Sophia Speijer (15)
Ernst Spicker (15)
Flora Sonja Spier (13)
Johan Benno Spier (11)
Amalia van Spier (18 mths)
Keetje van Spier (7)
Sabina Spindel (11)

Charles Splitter (7)
Harry Splitter (16)
Judikje Spreekmeester (16)
Salomon Spreekmeester (10)
Aaron Springer (16)
Henry Springer (13)
Marc Leo Springer (7)
Andries Jacob Stad (6)
Catharina Stad (11)
Esther Stad (5)
Hans Stad (7)
Hendrik Stad (12)
Joel Stad (9)
Maurits Stad (8)
Max Stad (14)
Rosina Stad (18 mths)
Sara Stad (3)
Bernard van der Stam (7)
Isaac Jacob van der Stam (11)
Joseph van der Stam (13)
Max van der Stam (12)
Edith Esther Staszewski (8)
Hanna Maria Steinbock (8)
Pinkas Steinmetz (5)
Rosa Steinmetz (11)
Salomon Steinmetz (9)
Susi Steinmetz (13)
Betje Stern (13)
Marja Stern (17)
Reina Stern (6)
Alfred Sternfeld (9)
Charles Sternfeld (18 mths)
Louis Sternfeld (7)
Rudolf Sternfeld (10)
Amalia Sophia Stimmer (5)
Brandel Stimmer (18 mths)
David Leib Stimmer (6 mths)
Chaim Stimmer (7)
Ita Stimmer (8)
Mirjam Stimmer (3)
Helena Betty Stodel (6)
Celine Stork (16)
Izaak Salomon Stork (13)
Jozef Stork (11)
Karel Stork (8)

Leo Izaak Stork (17)
Louis Stork (9)
Fanny van Straaten (16)
Jacob Hans van Straaten (19)
Jacqueline van Straaten (13)
Betty Stranders (3)
Hans Stranders (6)
Sara Hanna Stranders (2)
Clara van Straten (8)
Hijman van Straten (4)
Hendrika Martha van Stratum (7)
Levie Israel van Stratum (14)
Nico van Stratum (7)
Antonia Elisabeth Strauss (6)
Hilletje Johanna Strauss (3)
Levie Strauss (5)
Jacob Stretiner (8)
Eva Stub (11)
Karl Stub (9)
Herman Suntup (14)
Samuel Swaab (13)
Jacob Swaan (11)
Johan Swaan (18 mths)
Isidore Ezechiel Swart (12)
Abraham Edgar Swarts (10)
Herzs Bernard Szachter (18)
Moses Mordcha Szachter (15)
Samuel Eli Szachter (17)
Breindel Liebe Szrajbman (11)
Jacob Szrajbman (7)
Sara Szrajbman (8)
Schalom Szrajbman (10)
Rubel Sztycer (17 mths)
Sem Sztycer (4)
Sylvia Sztycer (3)
Abram Szymonowicz (7)
Izak Tarcica (13)
Jacob Tarcica (5)
Rachel Tarcica (16)
Levie Tas (15)
Heintje Theeboom (17)
Joseph Theeboom (15)
Sientje Theeboom (13)
Abraham Tokkie (16)
Bertha Tokkie (10)

Betty Tokkie (3)
Judith Tokkie (14)
Nathan Tokkie (5)
Sophia Tokkie (17)
Wolf Tokkie (15)
Dora Tonninge (17)
Helena Tonninge (17)
Aron Moses Trachtenberg (15)
Elias Trachtenberg (11)
Jette Anna van Trommel (10)
Joseph van Trommel (8)
Carolina Rebecca Trompetter (18 mths)
Joseph Bernard Trompetter (8)
Wolf Trompetter (6)
Arnold Troostwijk (11)
Georg Troostwijk (9)
Bertha Turfrijer (14)
Marcus Joseph Turfrijer (18 mths)
Arnold Turksma (5)
Betje Turksma (9)
Duifje Turksma (7)
Esther Rebecca Turksma (5)
Isidor Turksma (18 mths)
Isidor Turksma (9)
Marjan Turksma (2)
Mietje Turksma (13)
Paula Turksma (14 mths)
Salomon Turksma (17)
Sander Turksma (12)
Simon Turksma (8)
Theodora Turksma (4)
Theresia Theodora Turksma (18 mths)
Hartog van Tijn (4)
Jette van Tijn (11)
Lion van Tijn (10)
Marianna van Tijn (17)
Mozes van Tijn (8)
Nathan Abraham van Tijn (4)
Nathanie van Tijn (11)
Renee Ullmann (16)
Edgar van Veen (14)
Sandra Joyce van Veen (4)
David Veerejong (15)
Klara Vegt (13)
Isaac van der Velde (9)

Jacques van der Velde (9)
Louis van der Velde (5)
Eliazer Henri Velleman (14)
Ernest Salomon Velleman (12)
Esther Mary Velleman (11)
Greta Elisabeth Velleman (9)
Hans Samuel Velleman (14)
Herman Velleman (16)
Kitty Evaline Velleman (2)
Maurits Velleman (14 mths)
Pinas Velleman (17)
Wladimir Iljitsch Velleman (11)
Esther Verdoner (15)
Joel Verdoner (14)
Sara Verdoner (15)
Betty Kitty Verveer (12)
Eveline Rosa Verveer (13)
Henry Verveer (11)
Joel Verveer (4)
Malka Verveer (16)
Max Verveer (14)
Eliaser Vet (13)
Frouke Betsy Vet (11 mths)
Israel Vet (12)
Jetje Vet (11 mths)
Meijer Vet (9)
Siegfried Vet (9)
Abraham Veterman (12)
Jetje Veterman (10)
Sophia Rebecca Veterman (14 mths)
Jacques Vieijra (16)
Paul Alfred Vieijra (13)
Jacob Vischschraper (13)
Johanna Vischschraper (8)
Eddy Louis Viskoper (3)
Elias Jacob Viskoper (6)
Johnny van Voolen (8)
Abraham Eliazer Voorzanger (4)
Dora Voorzanger (2)
Elisabeth Voorzanger (18 mths)
Lijdia Regina Voorzanger (18)
Hanna Irma Vos (14)
Rudolf Vos (16)
Elisabeth Sara Vreedenburg (5)
Joseph Vreedenburg (9)

Alfred Saul Hartog de Vries (13)
Aron de Vries (9)
Arthur Max de Vries (12)
Barend de Vries (12)
Carolina Roza de Vries (18)
Esther de Vries (6)
Hartog Louis de Vries (9)
Jacob de Vries (2)
Kaatje de Vries (11)
Martha Anna de Vries (18 mths)
Oskar Joseph de Vries (14)
Selma de Vries (17)
Vogelina de Vries (8)
Jacobine van Vriesland (4)
Maurits Willem van Vriesland (17)
Alfred Leo Vrieslander (4)
Bernhard Vriesman (17)
Robert Vriesman (7)
Jeanette Bertha Wachs (13)
Laura Wachtel (14)
Abraham Wahrhaftig (11)
Chaim Wahrhaftig (9)
Edith Wahrhaftig (19)
Esther Wahrhaftig (6)
Gusta Wahrhaftig (2)
Samuel Waisvics (9)
Freddy Efraim Wajnberger (7)
Harry Michael Wajnberger (13)
Andries Jacques Walg (9)
Elisabeth Walg (12)
Frederik Jacob Walg (15)
Levie Abraham Wallach (2)
Jacques Kopel Wang (5)
Jesaja Wang (15)
Juda Wang (15)
Emmy van Weezel (3)
Harry Wegner (11)
Robert Moritz Israel Weil (15)
Aaron Weiman (18 mths)
Gerta Weiniger (15)
Helene Weiniger (11)
Meijer Weiniger (13)
David Weinreb (18 mths)
Siegmund Weis (2)
Suze Weis (10)

Willem Weis (5)
Roseliana Rochma Weiss (5)
Clara Dororha Weissbraun (9)
Isaac Weissbraun (7)
Siegfried Weissman (15)
Esther Weiszbard (17)
Feigel Weiszbard (13)
Pepi Weiszbard (10)
Esther Wertheim (15)
Michel Wertheim (6)
Freddy Wessely (17)
Betty Louise Weijl (11)
Elly Dorette Weijl (11)
Jacqueline Weijl (13)
John Bernard Weijl (8)
Lijda Betty Weijl (16)
Maria Eva Wiesel (8)
Bertha de Wilde (18)
Bettha de Wilde (6)
Siegfried Izak de Wilde (14)
Ariette Wilk (14)
Ise Wilk (8)
Daniel Wilkens (5)
Leonardus Wilkens (7)
Duifje de Wind (15)
Jacques Winkel (18 mths)
Joseph Winkel (17)
Joseph Samuel Winkel (3)
Mordechai Winkel (15)
Sara Winkel (16)
Israel de Winter (14)
Levi Israel de Winter (7)
Nico Louis de Winter (18)
Philippus de Winter (14)
Samuel de Winter (17)
Schoontje de Winter (12)
Joseph Ruben van Wittene (16)
Elisabeth Wolf (11)
Joseph Mozes Wolf (12)
Josephina Wolf (9)
Levy Wolf (12)
Schoontje Naatje Wolf (3)
Szalom Wolf (12)
Salomon de Wolf (10)
Anna Rachel Wolff (8)

Bertha Susanna Wolff (10)
Edith Gusta Wolff (6)
Elisabeth Wolff (11)
Esther Wolff (3)
Israel Barend Wolff (4)
Joseph Wolff (13)
Leentje Wolff (16)
Maurits Wolff (9)
Nannie Wolff (11 mths)
Frederik de Wolff (12)
Jacob de Wolff (17)
Leopold Israel Wolitzer (16)
Louis Worms (5)
Isaak Leon Wijnberg (12)
Jacob Wijnberg (2)
Selma Wijnberg (13)
Wilhelmina Wijnbergen (2)
Geziena Sophie Wijnman (16)
Louisa van Yssel (16)
Paul Zaitschek (16)
Jacques Zeldenrust (8)

Roland Hartog Zeldenrust (11)
Jacques Zeligman (16)
Sophia Zeligman (15)
Mirjam Lea Zell (12)
Oscar Zell (10)
Willy Zell (14)
Aron Simon Zilberstein (9)
Gretha Rebecca Zilberstein (6)
Maurits Zisner (17)
Geza Jozef Zoest (10)
Adolf Zucker (17)
Josuah Zuckerhandel (4)
Israel Zwaaf (10)
Jansje Zwaaf (5)
Izaak Zwarenstein (16)
Joseph Zwarenstein (17)
Marjo Zwarenstein (12)
Dora Zijtenfeld (18)
Henick Zijtenfeld (16)
Moniek Zijtenfeld (15)

Sometimes it is as if Andreas Ban sees Lethe rise from its bed and splash the porous ramparts of memory. Flooding fields, cities and people. And when it decides to withdraw, it drags after it carpets of the past and the shaky present and buries them in its dense silt. And he hears Hypnos and Thanatos shading the world with the fluttering of their wings. Then he ought perhaps to reach for poets. Even for someone playful such as the Dutch poet Toon Tellegen who, with his seemingly absurd images and unrestrained language returns people to reality and makes them hop. Who asks, *Shall I go, shall I conclude that life is insignificant, shrug my shoulders and go? Or shall I stay?*

In the course of that February 2010 in Amsterdam, Andreas Ban "feels his way" through his surroundings, tourist-like. Had he stayed longer, he would have begun to live an everyday life. He would have looked for work and he would have written. Leo and Andreas leave the apartment on a Sunday morning. Washed sheets and towels are drying in the guest room. There is food in the fridge, coffee, olive oil, rice, tea and pasta in the wall cabinet; white and yellow flowers in vases, books he has read, too heavy to take back to Croatia, on the shelves. They leave the keys with a neighbor who works at the Athenaeum bookshop, as though they are going away for a short time, as though they will be back soon. The taxi comes on time, it's sleeting, the street is familiar, the number 2 and 5 trams, which start from around the corner, are familiar, the owners of the café opposite unlock the door and switch on the lights, they are familiar too, the journalist in the building next to theirs is carrying a bag with the bread and milk he has just bought—they say good morning and goodbye.

At Schiphol Leo sets off for terminal 2, for Zurich, Andreas to terminal 3, for Zagreb. As though they would meet in a few hours' time "at home," for lunch.

The world had shrunk further.

Andreas Ban does not travel anymore.

After Amsterdam, invitations come, little excursions, Warsaw, Edinburgh, Paris, Ljubljana, Koper, Rotterdam, Piran, Lillehammer, London, Budapest; all two- or three-day meetings, pointless discussions, the usual parrotlike questions. Like a wound-up tin toy, Andreas Ban tottered off "into the wide world" with an empty head and came back tired, immobile, *wound down*, plunged once again into *stasis*.

In Croatia no one invites him anymore, no one offers him anything, no little job of any kind, no fee that would have enabled him to augment his budget, to round out his little existence, which now, soon, soon, would become a really small, very quiet, closed, stifling existence. One more month, one more paycheck ... Andreas Ban counts, counts off his tepid life.

Besides, why should anyone call on him, who is he to "them"? And why would *he* call on anyone, who are they to him? And why ask, now that twenty years have passed, do you have some little (intellectual) job for me? He will buy (he must do so now, before that pension arrives), yes, he will buy one of those small carts and set off, limping, to collect empty bottles.

But, no.

The three garbage bins under his window have a regular visitor. The visitor comes around midnight and systematically, tidily, with astonishing enthusiasm, classifies the contents. He swiftly separates the sorted garbage into little plastic bags and places the bags on the ledge behind the bins and on the outdoor tables of the nearby beer hall, closed at that time; running from left to right, in small skipping steps, he gets out of breath. The homeless man then places the sorted garbage in the entrance of Andreas's building, because the door of Andreas's building does not lock automatically. Sometimes the homeless man sleeps with his garbage in the hall of Andreas's building, sometimes he shits beside his garbage. In the past, Andreas Ban would see that bearded homeless man at small exhibitions, spreading his stench of trash, but he does not see him there anymore. When he meets him in the street, the homeless man greets Andreas with, *Hello, brother.*

It is midnight. The first night train passes with a fearful shriek. The homeless man takes garbage out of the bins with increasing speed, hysterically, in a panic. The garbage truck is approaching the bins. The workers are already at the bin, they want to wheel it over to the truck where it will be lifted pneumatically and emptied. The homeless man does not let them. He hugs his bin, there is a struggle, a battle for the bin, for the trash. A quiet battle, without words. Andreas closes his shutters. And his window.

The next morning Andreas Ban opens his wardrobe where his beautiful, expensive, perfectly kept tuxedo hangs. He takes off the plastic cover and lays it on the bed. The shirt is clean, ironed, perhaps discreetly yellowed at the edges from being untouched. Andreas Ban takes out the bow tie, the black silk socks, the patent-leather shoes. On the bed lies an elegantly dressed corpse without a head.

Andreas Ban puts on his formal clothes. He looks at his reflection in the crystal mirror (on his grandmother's chest of drawers) out of which surfaces his youth to meet him, now sorrowfully misshapen. Because his vertebrae have shrunk by five centimeters,

his trouser legs drag on the floor, he cannot walk because he trips on them, so he stands still. Because of his large belly he is not able to do up either his trousers or his jacket, he just blinks and squints, staring into the misted mirror waiting for that other Andreas to come out of it, young and slim and smiling. They look at each other. Neither Andreas Ban breathes. Neither Andreas Ban moves. The young and the old Andreas Ban take each other's measure while over them both fall tiny particles of white dust that glisten in the semidark room. They glisten, both Andreas Bans, the past one and the present one glisten. Then, through a crack in the closed wooden slats slips a dirty ray of sunlight and blinds them, wipes them out and they vanish. Through the room a fat black fly buzzes nervously.

Dressed like this, in his expensive, perfectly preserved but tight tuxedo, under the jacket of which flap the tails of his half-buttoned shirt, Andreas Ban sits on the floor, with his unlaced patent-leather shoes on his feet, and starts leafing through his piled up, sorted books, the ones he is finally prepared to part with, the collection which, he now sees, he has been pointlessly collecting and, like some kind of demented hamster, dragging back to his overflowing stores. He rearranges them, moves them from one pile to another, volumes once carefully (he is surprised with how much zeal) acquired, bought, exchanged, some even stolen, whose covers, authors, titles, contents he still remembers although they are increasingly shrouded in undulating whiteness, and a mournful dankness is creeping into them. The books are arranged for discarding, for libraries, for the secondhand shop, and Andreas Ban sorts them again, haphazardly, chaotically and crossly, *Oh, what a lot, there's something of everything*, he says, beginning to leaf through them, beginning to read even with a kind of mild gaiety running through his body.

Unnecessary ballast, seen from close up—trash. *Books, adornment of my solitude*, Andreas Ban says now, *to be estranged as soon as possible*. Suddenly he sees des Esseintes, the one who wears a white velvet suit and waistcoats threaded with gold, the one who instead of a tie puts a posy of dog violets in the open neck of his shirt, and Andreas Ban looks at the paintings and engravings with which he, that des Esseintes, adorned his solitude, which, indestructible as a dirty, perhaps even bloody stain, weighed down by this whole burden of beauty, nevertheless mercilessly broke into reality, flooding the floors, walls, the air in which the two of them now float half-dead. But Andreas Ban is not Jean des Esseintes. Jean des Esseintes had money, a lot of money with which he nourished (adorned) his solitude, cramming it frenziedly with beauty until it became so weighty (that solitude of his) that it had to say *I have grown too heavy, I am leaving you, adieu.* He, Andreas Ban, cannot return the way Jean des Esseintes returned, forcibly, to the tedious happiness meant for the poor, because for that, for the lethal and empty happiness meant for the poor, Andreas Ban does not have and never will have so much as a fillér* with which he could camouflage that tedious happiness.

* Fillér. The name of various small coins throughout Hungarian history. It was the one-hundreth subdivision of the Austro–Hungarian and the Hungarian korona, the pengő and the forint.

Listen, Andreas,
the whole secret is to know how to get started, to be
able to concentrate the mind on a single point, to at-
tain a sufficient degree of self-abstraction to produce
the necessary hallucination and so substitute the vi-
sion of the reality for the reality itself. I tried. In the
long run the experiment was unsuccessful, but it
brought peace.

> *Jean, I have already concentrated my mind on a single*
> *point to the degree that neither dreams nor hallucina-*
> *tions can reach me, nor can nature.*

All right, nature has had her day; the sickening mo-
notony of her landscapes and skyscapes have tried the
patience of refined temperaments. When all is said and
done, what a narrow, vulgar affair it all is, like a petty
shopkeeper selling one article of goods to the exclusion
of all others; what a tiresome store of green fields and
leafy trees, what a wearisome commonplace collection
of mountains and seas!
One should have a lot of paintings.

> *I sold my paintings. Now I wander through deserted*
> *landscapes getting lost.*

You see, I sensed such a degree of stupidity, such hatred
of all my own ideals, such contempt for literature and
art and everything I love, implanted and firmly fixed
in the mediocre brains of these tradesmen preoccupied
to the exclusion of all else with schemes of swindling,
that I would rush back home in a fury and lock myself
up with my books. Worst of all, I hated from the bottom
of my soul the new generation of self-made men, the
hideous boors who feel themselves bound to talk loudly

and laugh uproariously in restaurants and cafés, who
elbow you, without apology, on the sidewalks.

        Oh, yes, the new types, for most of them life is so simple
and shallow. I had students who had not heard of Sar-
tre, of Freud, of Darwin, one girl told me that the Sec-
ond World War had begun in 1945 and ended in 1950,
another that Camus had lived in the eighteenth cen-
tury. There are those who believe that The Bridge over
the Drina is a five-act play, that Hamlet is a novel. For
some the middle ages lasted until the nineteenth cen-
tury, which is, all right, a fact one might accept. Eighty
percent of my students had never been to the theater, 99
percent had never gone to a single art exhibition. What
have I wasted my life on?

I too suffocated from the torrent of unnecessary words
that kept on coming, constantly repeating themselves and
indicating nothing, showing nothing, from that impov-
erished lexicon of suppressed and monotonous colors, from
the dull gaze of dead eyes, that followed me like molting,
half-wild stray dogs, I found it all painful and nauseating
and in order to survive I made my life into a game.

        A game, what kind of game? A wild game, an unin-
hibited game or a game with rules you had to follow?
With strict or not so strict rules, with sensible or senseless
rules? With your rules or theirs? A game in solitude, a si-
lent game? Your games require money that I do not have.
Paul Virilio states: The future lies in unimaginable soli-
tude—one of the elements of which is play, which sounds
nice but is blasé and pretentious, because playing in pov-
erty does not bring any comfort—it brings destruction,
self-destruction, disappearance and extinction.

So Andreas Ban sits on the floor of his already half-empty living room, in his tuxedo, and for the umpteenth time leafs through his library, arranges and rearranges books, transferring them from one pile to another. He ought to have carried out this triage long ago, twenty years ago, when he sent that rickety six-ton truck loaded with his packed-up life to his sister's Croatian address so that he would not appear suspect to the authorities.

A hundred and eighty-two packages, large boxes, packing crates lined with straw—for oil paintings, engravings, rugs, ornaments and for a yellow Chinese porcelain dish, as fine as tissue paper, transparent—all that arrives preserved, pointlessly whole and displaced: *According to the Law on external commercial trading, article 118, Implementation of ruling on temporary control of import and export— paragraph F, According to the instruction to customs, posts 01/5 D-4803/1 of 11.05.1992,*

List of personal effects for export/removal
Ada Ban—from Serbia to Croatia:

box 1 books
box 2 books
box 3 books
box 4 books
box 5 books
box 6 books
box 7 sweaters
box 8 sweaters
box 9 curtains
box 10 books
box 11 books
box 12 books
box 13 books
box 14 books
box 15 books
box 16 shoes, winter boots
box 17 books (encyclopedias)
box 18 books (dictionaries)
box 19 records
box 20 records
box 21 books
box 22 books
box 23 books
box 24 books
box 25 books
box 26 books
box 27 glass, ornaments, Leo's
    books
box 28 kitchen appliances,
    electrical

box 29 records, cassettes
box 30 books
box 31 books
box 32 books
box 33 books
box 34 books—Leo
box 35 books—Leo
box 36 books
box 37 books
box 38 shoes
box 39 toys
box 40 quilts, pillows, bedding, tablecloths
box 41 books, manuscripts—America
box 42 books
box 43 ornaments
box 44 bedding
box 45 bedding
box 46 shelves
box 47 shelves, chandeliers, lamps
box 48 sound system, speakers
box 49 clothes
crate 50 engravings
box 51 Leo's record player, towels
box 52 chairs, quilts, blankets
box 53 various
box 54 books, Leo's
box 55 glass, writings, criticism
box 56 criticism, prose, documents
box 57 literary texts, essays, documents
box 58 items of furniture, dishes
trunk 59 furniture, glass, ornaments, glasses, towels

box 60 crockery
trunk 61 rugs—Bukhara, Tabriz, Shiraz
crate 62 mirror, crystal
trunk 63 ornaments, glass, lights, TV, framed, glazed posters
box 64 glass, tumblers
box 65 winter clothes
trunk 66 suitcases, clothes
box 67 clothes
box 68 cases, clothes
box 69 slides, books, theater
box 70 photographs, kitchen pots
box 71 gas bottles
crate 72 furniture
box 73 lamps—table and standard
trunk 74 rugs—white, Kashan silk
box 75 lampshades, cushions
box 76 small rugs 3
box 77 coats, jackets
78 washing machine
79 refrigerator
80 freezer
81–90 kitchen cabinets
91 sink
92–95 tables: desk, kitchen table, Biedermeier table, low cherry coffee table
96–102 chairs
103–105 shelves—antique, standing
106 skis 2 pairs
107 bicycles 2
108 antique bergère
crate 109 oil paintings 5
crate 110 oil paintings
trunk 111 engravings, glazed 10

and so on, beds, wardrobes, antique chest of drawers, stove, vacuum cleaner, heaters, space heaters, Opemus 4 enlarger, armchairs, settee, stools, Louis XV-style chairs, up to number 182.

Signature:

Ada Ban

Ranka Tajsića Street 40/IV

Belgrade, May 14, 1992

Passport no. C 513211 Belgrade

His professional books Andreas Ban puts aside (after all)—for the secondhand shop.

Mikloš Biro, *Suicide: Psychology and Psychopathology*

Mikloš Biro, *The Psychology of Post-Communism*

Hermann Broch, *Poetry and Cognition*

Pavel Medvedev, *The Formal Method in Literary Scholarship*

Oh, a series of books by the once-respected psychiatrist Vladeta Jerotić who in the 1990s goes completely insane and, along with his nation, sinks into the murky waters of mystical and religious madness:

here are Jerotić's

Psychoanalysis and Culture from 1974, then

Sickness and Creativity

Between Authority and Freedom

Neurotic Phenomena of our Times

Neurosis as a Challenge

Psychodynamics and the Psychotherapy of Neurosis

Man and his Identity, Andreas's last Jerotić, bought in 1989.

Then,

L. L. Thurstone on intelligence,

Alfred Kinsey (an old, first edition, Marisa's book),

Fritz Perls, founder of Gestalt therapy, who also researches the importance of dreams,

here is Abraham Maslow and his humanist psychology, *A Theory of Human Motivation*,

then Chomsky, several titles,

here is Rollo May, "the father of existential psychotherapy,"

and the renowned Leon Festinger (*A Theory of Cognitive Dissonance*), who researches the way in which disharmony between belief and behavior leads to psychological tension that makes people change their convictions to justify their present behavior, which many of Andreas's former colleagues acknowledge, while at the same time they succumb to farcical proselytism. Festinger also writes about how groups exert pressure on the individual with the intention of breaking him, of compelling him to succumb to their collective norms and aims, the "schooling" that Andreas Ban has been through several times, including now, at this university.

William McDougall on human behavior, then

Gordon Allport on personality psychology and on various aspects of opportunistic behavior.

Adler, a heap of Adlers on individual psychology,

Ellis, Albert Ellis—*The Practice of Rational Emotive Behavior Therapy* (REBT),

four books by Karen Horney, two in English, two in an appalling translation into "Montenegrin."

He could give someone this Milton Erickson on hypnotherapy,

the behaviorist Hans Eysenck had never interested him,

Harry F. Harlow studies the behavior of monkeys and children's psychology—for the trash,

the complete works of Freud, in the original and translations, also individual editions, too much Freud,

Rivers, *Instinct and the Unconscious*,

Kurt Koffka, *Perception: An Introduction to the Gestalt Theory*,
William James, *Principles of Psychology I & II*,
Jung, lots of Jung, scribbled on, with comments in the margins,
why was all that Jung necessary?

Bertrand Russell, *The Analysis of Mind*, and several other Russells not in this pile, where are they?

Oh, Gustav Le Bon, and his *déjeuners du mercredi* with Valéry, Bergson, Poincaré and others, *The Crowd: Study of the Popular Mind*,

then old Abraham Myerson—*The Foundations of Personality*,

here is the now blind Elliot Aronson with his famous books *The Social Animal* and *Social Psychology*,

Fromm, complete works, some in Serbian: *Psychology and Religion*, *The Art of Loving*, *Escape from Freedom*,

some in English: *Man for Himself: An Inquiry into the Psychology of Ethics*, *The Forgotten Language: An Introduction to the Understanding of Dreams, Fairy Tales and Myths*, *The Sane Society*, *Socialist Humanism*, *The Anatomy of Human Destructiveness*, and so on, bye-bye, dear Fromm,

and here is R. D. Laing,

stop, Andreas, enough.

It is getting dark, Andreas's back hurts, he stirs himself with difficulty, turns onto his knees and crawls on all fours to the pile of philosophical titles, here are Nietzsche, Machiavelli, Wittgenstein, A. J. Ayer (*Language, Truth and Logic*), here is Heidegger, *Being and Time*, Husserl is here, and David Hume, and Descartes, oh, Lord, *le temps perdu*, and Marcuse, and Merleau-Ponty, and Marx, and Kristeva, and Todorov, and Bauman, and Kołakowski, Kierkegaard and Jaspers, to whom Andreas Ban returned a few months ago, he kept going back to many of them until recently, until three or four years ago, so many people had sat on his shelves and called to him, talked to him, so many years, forty, spent pointlessly, in having frightened students gaze at him inanely, stare at him and mouth incoherent phrases they had learned by heart, students who had no clue what he was telling them (because that was not in the curriculum, in which most of the content had been absurdly curtailed, ground up, modified, disconnected, the whole world presented out of context, out of time, senselessly), and so Andreas Ban sees his petty teaching career as a thirteen-year act of self-defecation, *as the ultimate destruction of his physical, psychological and intellectual being.*

What Andreas Ban would most like now would be to burn all these books together with their authors, most of whom are in any case already dead. Today there is barely room for them in the world. Trash is squeezing out his fellow travelers, just as it is squeezing out him, Andreas Ban, too. In many homes there are ever fewer shelves, and if there are any they are used for displaying little gondolas, model churches, ashtrays, pebbles and miniature cacti. Booklets, hundreds of booklets are now loaded onto e-readers, which their owners peck at in airports, on beaches, in cafés, to pass the time.

Why bother with the secondhand shop. His books might be bought by some other lost souls, already damaged, half deranged, but most probably they would not be bought by anyone.

Andreas Ban opens the window of his room high up on the fourth floor (no elevator) and from the nearest pile of rejected books he takes one at a time and starts to tear out pages. Off goes Dostoevsky, off goes Bernhard, off goes Montaigne, so Andreas Ban dismembers his former companions, philosophers, psychologists, psychiatrists, poets, off goes Tsvetaeva, off goes Gombrowicz, off goes Kafka, like weightless black-and-white birds they all fly toward the polluted sky, then abruptly plunge onto the flat space in front of his building where the garbage bins stand. Andreas Ban could fly off after them, fly with them, but long ago, in the twenties of the last century, in the smoky Paris cabaret Au Lapin Agile, Pierre Mac Orlan whispers to the despairing Utrillo: *My dear Maurice, melancholics don't kill themselves,* so Andreas Ban declines.

He feels like playing, but he has nothing to play with. In the course of his life he collected no objects other than books. And glasses. He has a collection of old glasses from everywhere, bought at flea markets all over the world and in upscale antique shops. He sometimes washes them and admires their sheen. Through these glasses Andreas Ban looks at reality which curls and twists gaily, in which objects and phenomena of various colors dance, distorted as in some surreal dabbling. What a collection! Goblets, odd wine glasses, robust tumblers for water and chunky beer glasses, delicate little liqueur glasses, champagne flutes, all in different dimensions but all with fine, thin rims, there are Bristol blue glasses, a tall black and a tall white glass of *avventurina*, a *lattimo* glass water tumbler and one of Andreas's favorites: a pink glass made in 1896 for the Millennium Exhibition in Budapest, bought with Elvira, for Elvira, in a remote shop in Szentendre one autumn of love.

He shuts his cabinet.

He did not even collect stamps, or brochures, long ago he used to collect postcards with reproductions of the works of famous and not so famous painters, at the time when he still visited international museums and exhibitions, three large boxes lie in the storeroom, he dragged them too from Belgrade! Oh, Andreas.

Benjamin collected objects, Benjamin collected toys. They say (experts write) that this was Benjamin's creative project. Bullshit. They say Benjamin as a collector was filling some kind of void, what kind of void? In their repetitiveness, Benjamin's "voids" resist any collector's passion, ever present, no collection can be placed inside them other than the ruins which they had always been. The "wise heads" rattle on about "the life story" that pulsates in collected objects, about memory, about history. They say Benjamin wants to reify the past, Benjamin sees in the collector an obsessive compulsion toward the reification of the legacy of the past, transforming it into a vast wealth of valuable goods, goods that have no monetary worth but nonetheless represent invaluable treasure. Oh, Lord.

Benjamin is playing, Benjamin is evoking childhood, and in the objects he collects, shifting them in his hands like pieces of a broken puzzle, he tries to step out of the world of memory into the world of dreams, which turns out to be impossible. For two cold winter months, from December 1926 to February 1927, Benjamin walks around Moscow digging up his days in search of a sense of existence, to save himself, rescue himself, redeem humanity—and into his intimate collection, his jumbled collection, he inscribes both the past and the present and his doomed future:

When he is not resting in his Moscow room reading Proust and nibbling little marzipan sweets, Benjamin visits toy stores, besieges toy museums, searches the streets, finds, examines, buys and stores in his trunk (in his memory):

carousels with movable figures of horsemen,

a little girl on a swing,

a wet nurse with a baby in her arms,

dancers made of clay and wood,

musicians made of porcelain.

He buys a miniature wooden sewing machine whose needle is moved by a special handle,

a little lacquered box for various trinkets,

he buys a papier-mâché doll that sways on top of a music box

I saw a boy on the street carrying a board with stuffed birds

I saw a man who was selling small skates pour les poupées

I saw tapestries showing Adam and Christ in white against a green ground, naked, but bereft of genitals

I saw a "red" funeral procession: coffin, hearse, harness, all were red
in a glass case I saw a landscape hanging on the wall with a me-
chanical clock built into it; the mechanism was broken and the clock
whose strokes had once set into motion windmills, water wheels, win-
dow shutters and human figures no longer functioned.

I saw a man selling small cages made of glazed paper and contain-
ing tiny paper birds

I also saw a real parrot, a white macaw, sitting on a basket contain-
ing linen goods a woman was selling to passersby

in a trunk I put away all my lovely toys and manuscripts
doll's house furniture made by convicts in Siberia
three wooden whales with the Earth on their backs
a samovar Christmas-tree ornament
a box in the shape of a duck
I bought a kitsch postcard, a balalaika and a little paper house
I found a carved wooden axe—for children
a whole world, worlds

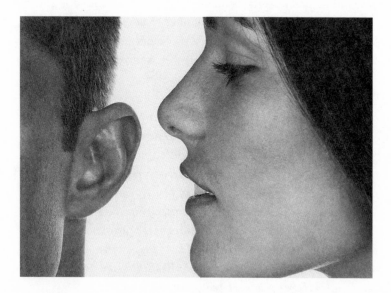

Melancholics do not kill themselves, with their solemn Masses they pollute the air; they are the lackeys of a dying society. Blessed and isolated in the rooms of their comfortable Grand Hotel Abgrund built on the *edge* of an abyss, on the *edge* of nothingness and the absurd, in the interval between extravagant dishes and so-called entertainment, they ponder over that chasm, groping in the dark, feeding on the cadavers of the new, "new age" madhouse so similar to the old one, the famous Salpêtrière, say, that town within a town with forty-five buildings, with streets and squares, with gardens and glades and a beautiful old church. At the end of the nineteenth century, 4,383 people live and work in the Salpêtrière hospital: 580 employees, 853 "alienated" people and 2,950 mentally or physically handicapped, including some children. Salpêtrière, originally a gunpowder factory, becomes the dumping ground for the Parisian poor, a prison for prostitutes, a refuge for the mentally disabled, for criminals, epileptics and the homeless. With time, the old mental hospital is modernized, like a faithful dog it runs after reality, so an increasing number of nonresidential patients go for "treatment" there. Otherwise, Salpêtrière was well known for its enormous population of rats. No, Andreas Ban is not a melancholic. His sickness has a different name.

Old age and memory weave themselves into time and come increasingly to resemble braids; time is in fact a whirlpool in which past and present events circle, prehistory and posthistory, in an eternal embrace. And as the future collapses, as there is in fact no future, the time that is coming is wrapped in the past like a scroll becoming the underground world of the future, a world obsessed with everything old. And so empires collapse, the leaders of gangs parade like statesmen, and under their equipment people become invisible. Therefore, no stories emerge from a disintegrated past, only lifeless images. There is no construction without stitches, everywhere there are fragments, because it is out of ruins, out of wrecks, out of discarded parts that the new comes into being.

Andreas Ban glances around the apartment. On the stove the crouching granite Eskimo woman is still waiting, her legs folded beneath her, her hands thrust into a stone wrap, looking like a little black ball so small that it fits into the palm. Legend has it that the Inuksuk protects and feeds those who give it a home. It brings them security and accompanies them on dangerous journeys. The Inuksuk is spirit and tenacity, tiny and quiet as it is. Andreas has kept his Inuksuk on the stove for years now, its face turned toward the door. She, that Eskimo woman, does not stir, just as Daruma does not stir for years in his cave, so his legs and arms atrophy, they shrivel so much that Daruma becomes round, like this Eskimo woman of Andreas's. Daruma's vigil lasted a long time, such a long time that every now and then he would be overcome by sleep, so as a punishment he cuts off his eyelids, believing that thus he will stay awake for ever. And today, as souvenirs, Darumas of various sizes carved out of jade, onyx, granite, ivory, marble, alabaster, with eyes wide open, are circulated in the markets without it being known whether they are still looking at the world around them or whether they are already completely blind. Andreas's little Eskimo woman smiles and blinks.

People write to him.

Strangers write to him about their darknesses. They do not demand anything, they present him with the pasts that chafe them, they try to shake off their personal and family nightmares by sending them to him. He no longer knows what to do with all those stories, with other people's lives, with spirits that swirl through the air in front of him. There are disintegrating people, there are terrible stories. When he reads those painful tales, Andreas Ban is overcome with shame at his twenty-year blindness in the course of which he observed only his own inner eye rooting through him, his own disintegration, his own breakdown, and he bows his head, leafs through those pages, carries them from room to room and in the end puts them away in a file labeled "Destinies." It is only now that Andreas sees how many superfluous people this small town amasses, keeps and stores in its jails, how many people float in timeless voids imprisoned in their own lives which become alien stories circulating through their bloodstreams. Why had he not gotten to know those people? Why did he not seek out those superfluous people, those prisoners, he ought to have found them and touched them. As it is, he, Andreas Ban, now has no one to write to.

There is one letter to which he never replied. The letter is undated and Andreas Ban cannot remember when it arrived, how many years ago he had put that letter aside intending to do something with it, perhaps write to the person who sent it. In some places the letter is smudged with the imprints of his coffee cup, and the pages are already brittle with age. In that letter L. says that he had heard a radio play written by Andreas Ban (Andreas Ban has no clue which play it is) and that it left him very upset and sad because he belongs to the generation that had lived through all of that. (*Which play is that?*) L. says that he is seventy-seven years old, that he is in the deep autumn of his life and is beginning to see the end which is coming frighteningly close, that is what he writes: *frighteningly close*. L. writes that he has always been a rebel, that he worked as a journalist, that he had fought against injustice, that then came surveillance, persecution and imprisonment, that he had gone to Czechoslovakia in 1968, where he was awoken on August 21 by Russian tanks, that in Prague he had joined the intellectuals—actors, producers, writers—who on those Russian tanks had drawn in chalk five-pointed stars with swastikas in their centers, he was arrested there, in Czechoslovakia, and taken handcuffed to the Austrian border, after which he, L., ended up in Germany and stayed in Germany for twenty-three years. In Germany, writes L., he meets all kinds of people very like those Andreas Ban describes in his play (*Which play is it?*), among them a certain translator named Pavel, who later confesses to him that he personally shot schoolchildren in Kragujevac,* that he had watched their school caps fly off their heads, that he had used a Maschinengewehr 42, a Šarac, L. writes, although that Maschinengewehr 42, that machine gun was produced in Nazi Germany and used by the Wehrmacht from 1942, while the Šarac was produced under the MG42 license in Yugoslavia much later as the MG53, by the firm Crvena Zastava.

L. says that as early as 1964 he writes about death camps, about Dachau, but also about the crimes committed by Israeli soldiers against the Palestinians, about which, he says, he has written a novel which speaks of two swallows drinking nectar from an agave flower, because the agave blooms only once in a hundred years. L. gives a detailed account of the plot of this novel and says that he will send Andreas Ban the manuscript so that he can see how it all works, how the events become entangled and disentangled. (The manuscript never arrived.)

Then, L. writes that new generations have no clue about much of what occurred in the Second World War, even young Germans who ought to know those facts very well do not know them well enough. In questionnaires, L. writes, to the question what does the word "Hitler" define, some reply that Hitler is a make of car. L. writes about his pain, about the large scars he bears on his soul because of past and present injustices, because of the vile world we live in. So he has written a play about all this, he says. But L. can no longer bear that burden, he needs distance, he says, and in the seventy-seventh year of his life he begins to write a novel about love.

* The Kragujevac massacre was the murder of Serb, Jewish and Roma men and boys in Kragujevac, Serbia, by German Wehrmacht soldiers on October 20 and 21, 1941. All males from the town between the ages of sixteen and sixty were assembled by German troops and members of the collaborationist Serbian Volunteer Command (SDK) and Serbian State Guard (SDS). An entire generation of secondary school children were taken directly from their classes.

Just before New Year (*which?*), L. concludes that there are no new years nor old years, that time neither comes nor goes, but we are the ones who go.

L. ends his letter with the statement that he is ending his letter because he does not want to write too much about himself and asks Andreas Ban not to reproach him for the typos because he, L., is in fact half-blind from diabetes and is typing from memory, and when he wants to read something he has to use a magnifying glass as big as the biggest apple. L. adds that he is not in fact from these parts, he was born in the Banat, on the three-way border of Hungary, Romania and us, that is what he wrote: *us,* and that he had *settled here, in these parts,* a long time ago but that he is now a widower. And, despite the fact that he is almost blind, L. writes that he does some painting, oil on canvas, and has taken part in several exhibitions.

Maybe today Andreas might even have replied to L., although he does not know what he would have said to him. The letter has been waiting too long. Maybe the diabetes means that by now he is completely blind, perhaps he has had his leg cut off, perhaps his arm, or both arms, have been amputated, so that he can no longer type, or perhaps L. is no longer even alive.

Andreas Ban does not pay attention to his swollen, painful knee. That right knee piped up suddenly, unannounced, but Andreas Ban does not wish to communicate with it. So his knee becomes insolent, increasingly insolent and high-handed, it asserts itself when Andreas goes down the stairs and when he climbs up to the fourth floor. That knee is capable of giving way, falling into its own hole, then Andreas collapses, and his knee is gleeful. At each step, his knee announces itself with an ill-mannered snigger and starts to drill, to aim its arrows into Andreas's hips and between his eyes.

His back makes itself known ever more often as well, *we're disintegrating,* Andreas's vertebrae howl, after which Andreas begins to sway down the hall to relieve them, those crushed vertebrae. Andreas goes to bed with increasing trepidation, because after just two or three hours a dreadful pain starts up around his pelvis, a fierce rending that sends surging waves through his entire body and he sinks, suffocating. Then he turns over and groans, tosses, gets up, sits down, throws himself onto the floor, gets up, walks (limps), makes himself coffee, and with yearning apprehension crawls on all fours back to bed hoping (by deceit) to snatch just a bit more sleep. Four years have passed since his doctor's advice to *mess around in the garden*, where Andreas Ban had, of course, not messed around, believing that he would work out a way to soothe the rattling of his demented vertebrae. Four years, just what the neurosurgeon gave him.

There are days when Andreas greets his pains with open arms. They fall into his embrace like rotten apples, drum on his chest and send their echo through his body. In his embrace, those pains slowly drain and like an infusion, drop by drop, flow toward his insides until they flood them with a thin layer of dark damp. Then time narrows to the present which is becoming short and shallow, and he no longer has anything to reflect upon, nowhere to wander off to, nothing to remember, he is jammed in the void of a miniature world. Andreas Ban no longer exists, there are only parts of his body—the left breast, the lumbar, sacral and cervical vertebrae, the right knee, the broken arm, the broken leg, the corroded stomach, sluggish intestines, the blocked bronchi, black lungs and half-blind eyes—parts of his body and organs which in the restricted present sometimes collide, sometimes pass each other by.

Waiting rooms, prescriptions, appointments, magnetic resonance imaging—then more waiting rooms, prescriptions, appointments, all that shifting from one hospital to another, from one doctor to another, all that jostling, all that senseless expense of time to finally, after a year or maybe two, go back under the knife, after which one could develop bedsores, after which his body would abandon him entirely and he would watch through a mirror as it flounders toward exitus. Andreas Ban will pop up in front of Andreas Ban, stand beside him and watch his crippled hobbling, his jerking movements and his grotesquely distorted face. There will be moments when the other Andreas Ban, dressed in an old, tight, black suit (a tuxedo?) will turn his back on Andreas Ban and, silent, motionless, simply wait for his double to blow him away. There will be days when the other Andreas Ban will appear like a transparent shadow, when he will lie down beside the first, throw his arm over his shoulder and whisper always the same little ditty:

> *Partout où j'ai voulu dormir,*
> *Partout où j'ai voulu mourir,*
> *Partout où j'ai touché la terre,*
> *Sur ma route est venu s'asseoir*
> *Un étranger vêtu de noir*
> *Qui me ressemblait comme un frère.*

When horses spend a long time in stables, isolated in their boxes, they become agitated and bite themselves. They bite their haunches, their bellies, their groins, neighing loudly and kicking furiously. As soon as the horses are harnessed to any task, they calm down. This applies to domesticated horses, wild horses don't do such terrible things to themselves. Domesticated horses can be soothed if they have company, not necessarily equine. It could even be hens that peck around among their legs.

The most effective method of counteracting equine self-harm is castration, it is applied just once and the effect is enduring.

Oscar Artiz was a relatively healthy man in late middle age. But, with time, his rheumatic problems became so serious that they prevented him from performing his regular job. Oscar Artiz worked on building sites, he was constantly on the move and carried heavy loads. After two years of illness, Oscar Artiz becomes, well, a bit depressed, his behavior is unusual, one might say strange. He keeps repeating: *I killed my sister*. One morning, he leaves his apartment, telling his landlady: *I won't be long, I'll be back for lunch*. But he does not come back. Two days later the police find Oscar Artiz, naked to the waist, lying in a field in the suburbs of the town where he lived. He is wearing only trousers, socks and boots and has numerous wounds to his head, neck and chest. Oscar Artiz, with almost no pulse but conscious, capable of following questions yet too weak to answer them, is taken by ambulance to the local hospital. A wound to his neck is festering and full of maggots, not bleeding. Eight hours later, Oscar Artiz dies. The autopsy finds no abnormalities in his internal organs or his brain. All his organs had an adequate supply of blood, so the doctors' commission concludes that death was not caused by bleeding. There were more than four hundred cuts and stab wounds on his body, mostly superficial, although the muscles on the back of his left hand, on his fingers and neck were damaged. The largest wound, the one on his neck, began at the lobe of his left ear and ended under the center of his lower jaw. So, Oscar Artiz has wounds all over his forehead (5 stab wounds), on his chin and neck, in his left armpit and on the left side of his rib cage (27 stab wounds), on his chest (72 stab wounds), on his abdomen (168 stab wounds), on his left arm: on the palm (24), on the fingers (15), on the wrist (4), on the forearm (6), on the dorsal side of his left arm: on the hand (2), on the fingers (3), on the wrist (2) and on the forearm (6), on the right arm: on the palm (26), on the wrist (12), on the dorsal side of the right arm: on the hand (2), on the wrist (10), on the fingers (21).

The wounds were made with a relatively blunt pocketknife which was found close to where the unfortunate Oscar Artiz was lying.

Conclusion: the number and nature of the wounds inflicted are typical of cases of self-harm and nervous breakdown. Medical history records an impressive number of similar cases, even more extreme than the case of Oscar Artiz.

They called him Laid, the little Arctic fox. He was born in a zoo. He was one of the eleven cubs in a litter produced by the "married couple" who had arrived in town the previous year. As a rule,

Arctic foxes are exceptionally resilient; they survive temperatures as low as -50°C, in treeless lands, frequently covered with snow. They have small ears and pads covered in fur so that their step is quiet and careful. A week after they come into the zoo-world, vets separate Laid, the smallest of the litter, and Zig, the largest, from their parents to be hand-reared. Laid and Zig seem to progress just as well as the cubs left with their parents. But, after forty-nine days of living apart, Laid wakes at two o'clock in the morning and starts biting his foreleg, yelping desperately. An examination of the little polar fox does not reveal any anomalies, but, to be on the safe side, the cub is put on a six-day course of sedatives (0.3 milliliters of pentobarbital). Laid self-harms several more times with varied intensity. Then he is fitted with an immobilizing collar, which he tolerates. He is given antibiotics to prevent infection of the wound on his foreleg. For three weeks Laid is calm, he does not harm himself. Then, suddenly, thirty-seven days after the first episode, he tries again. They send him to the veterinary clinic where they hope that specialists will discover the cause of his unusual behavior. After a detailed physical and neurological examination, the university veterinary clinic cannot identify any anomalies in the little Arctic fox. Soon afterward, Laid begins to self-harm again, so the vets again sedate him. Forty-eight hours after he is taken to hospital, Laid dies. A thorough autopsy is carried out and no lesions that could have caused Laid's strange behavior are found. There were no abnormalities in his brain. Laid was diagnosed as suffering from "idiopathic behavior disorder." Laid's brother Zig developed normally, as did the other cubs in the litter.

When he was taken in, Sol Basco had abundant black hair and a thick mustache. After several months of hospitalization, Sol Basco pulls the hair out of his head and face. Sol Basco pulls out his hairs with such dedication that he is soon left without hair, eyebrows and beard. He also pulls out the hairs from his armpits and his pubic hair. The doctors are unable to cure his mania. Sol Basco remains in the Psychiatric Department of the University Clinical Hospital in Belgrade.

Pepita Bobadilla. Andreas does not know whether she is still alive. *Call me Pepa, call me Pepa*, she kept saying, and they called her Pepa. She was treated by Andreas's mother Marisa, who said, *Such people need not be treated at all.* Marisa's patients used to visit the Ban family, and on feast days they also came to lunch, sometimes several of them at once. True, there were patients who never came. Some of Andreas's mother's patients were quiet, others were not. Marisa loved her patients.

Pepita cut her hair short and unevenly, with nail scissors. She liked to show off her underwear, *Look how clean it is*, she would say, *I'm a clean woman*. Pepita Bobadilla, Pepa, was fat, but firm, she talked rapidly and a lot and she smelled of baby cream and walnut oil. Later, she would often bring flowers to Marisa's grave, whether she still does Andreas Ban cannot say, everything is far away, including his mother's grave, and Pepita has probably died. Pepa used to light small yellow candles beside the flowers, the yellow candles went out right away because there's always a breeze over Marisa's grave, it's that pine tree. Andreas and his sister had transplanted the pine from a pot into the ground beside their mother's headstone nearly thirty-three years earlier. The pine was small then, now it is tall. How it managed to grow so bushy is a mystery; cemeteries are constricted and crammed, generally overcrowded. The pine waves, as though it is saying come—or, perhaps, flee!—and it makes the air sway, sprinkles it with the Mediterranean. That is unusual. Andreas's mother's graveyard is a continental graveyard where the painter Paško Vučetić lies, also Mediterranean, and his wife Marija, in polished, dark coffins.

Their remains, placed in those coffins long ago, have already rotted, nothing but brittle bones and gray dust, devoid of any trace of human form. The little transplanted New Year tree, bought in an earthenware pot at a Belgrade market, had also been displaced, dug in, interred somewhere it did not belong. So, Andreas is now beside the sea, Marisa is not, and here beside the sea he has not one important grave, not one to visit.

Pepita Bobadilla wore nylon petticoats edged with nylon lace, yellowish, because nylon turns yellow with age. Pepita—Pepa—adored everything nylon and plastic: plastic containers of all shapes, sizes and colors, nylon clothing and nylon curtains, she also had green plastic sunglasses. Pepa liked to bring small gifts, two oranges for instance, which reminded Andreas of the 1950s, of smiling poverty woven of difficult improvisations. The maroon wax tablecloth Pepa once gave him had until recently covered his kitchen table, a miraculous remnant of his past life. As the maroon plastic tablecloth was worn out, stiff as a cadaver from lying there and being wiped clean for twenty years, Andreas had recently thrown it out.

Junk, nothing but junk, he had said as he filled black trash bags.

Pepita Bobadilla, the Ban family's Pepa, who called Marisa her "doctor-sister," suffered from trichotillomania. Like Sol Basco. Only, Pepa was at liberty, Sol was not. Pepa never entered a hospital (thanks to Marisa), Sol never came out again. Of all her hairs, Pepa most liked to pull the private ones. *Look how smooth it is*, she showed us, *look—it's clean and soft*, she would show us from the doorway and then would give Andreas and his sisters two moist kisses because she always had a dewy upper lip, even in winter. *I want to see*, Andreas's sister once said, but Pepa replied, *No. I pull the hairs when I'm alone*, she said, *I pull them when I don't know what I'm doing*, she said, *when I don't know what to do, I won't let you look, no.*

Beside the folder marked "Destinies" there is another thick folder, a little suitcase made of transparent pinkish plastic, with the label "Tests and results." In that folder languishes Andreas Ban, disassembled. In that folder lies Andreas's blood with all its components, with the thrombocytes, leukocytes, erythrocytes, with glucose and cholesterol, with triglycerides, with keratin, here are AST, ALT, FFT, ALP, and those markers CA125, CEA and CA 15-3 which, for the time being, rise and fall within the limits of what is normal; in the folder is Andreas's urine in varying shades of yellow, with sediment and specific weight, with bacteria or without, with proteins or with none, depending, with traces of blood or with none; in the folder Andreas's fragmented body languishes, tidily classified into subfolders, by organs; the pink folder also contains Andreas's breast, viewed from different angles, from the biopsy, from the process of incision through radiation, here are quantities of ultrasound scans of his breast; here are his kidneys (with little accumulations of sand), his liver (with cysts), his whole abdomen. The pink folder also contains Andreas's vertebrae, Andreas's lungs, Andreas's knees, Andreas's broken arms and legs. The pink folder contains innumerable results from spirometer tests, there are recommendations for an array of asthma pumps, powders and tablets; here are Andreas's intestines (in color), here are the electric beats of his heart, more or less regular, and here are ten years of reports on measurements of Andreas's optic pressure, which from time to time goes berserk, sky-high. In it, in this pink case, as in a shrine, as in a temple, Andreas Ban's assets are stored. Thanks to that folder Andreas Ban is able to move away and hand over (bequeath) his body to others—oncologists, neurologists, surgeons, physicians, pulmonologists, ophthalmologists, laboratory technicians, physiotherapists, pharmacists—for short or long-term use. Sometimes Andreas Ban hugs the little pink case, presses it to his chest and walks with it through his darkened rooms, as if rocking a weak child. *How light I am*, he says. When he takes the pink folder to doctors, they rummage through it in silence, root around in it, dig about, muddle everything up, while Andreas sits to one side, watching. Then he says, *I'm off. You've got all of me there, on those bits of paper, in miniature.*

By now Andreas Ban has been thoroughly examined, although he is still under constant surveillance. Internal and external. Thanks to the pink case it is possible to follow the slightest of Andreas's deviations and departures from the normal. As time passes, the folder swells. He will have to get another one, a different color, so as to differentiate himself from before and after. That one will be made of transparent black plastic and in its bottom left-hand corner Andreas will stick a little zebra with a blue glint.

So, since he arrived, twenty years ago now, there had been and there still are people with whom he could have become friends, who could have become close to him, he sees now, now that they write to him. Oh, yes, he was invited to their homes, for spinach pie, for bean stew, for lamb soup, for *yaniya*, he had wheat berry with whipped cream and without, he had eaten chestnut puree, he had licked teaspoons of thick rose and watermelon syrups, he would arrive with some book or other, with flowers, with a bottle or two of good wine, he had talked, casually, almost gaily, about the past, he had talked with his accent (*Damn it, man, he has Belgrade fur*), there had been card games or chess, and then—he would return home heavy, lame and sad, *it was all an illusion, shreds, crumbs, a charade*, he would say and plunge once again into his impoverished, dried-out solitude. He could have had some people over, he could have, his dried-cod ragout and his *baccalà mantecato* are first-class, his crème caramel is unsurpassed, his black risotto, his *minestras*, his *pasta e fagioli* and his *pastitsada con gnocchi*, then, his *brodettos*, his fritters … he had full sets of various crystal glasses with gilt rims, glasses for every kind of drink, he had silver cutlery and a special set for fish, he had Toledo tablecloths for twelve people, a white one and a pink one, although none of that was needed, he could have invited people to goulash with polenta (he makes that well too), to sausages or chicken breasts, to tripe, and then what? Now it is over, now even if he wanted to, he could no longer gather those people together. What could he offer them? They would look at each other in silence, in the half-dark of his half-empty rooms, in winter dankly cold, as though they were in some home for the infirm and abandoned. Those others, those who had and still have a single-track past and a present without creases, arranged in drawers named "life," in which there are no wars, no displacements, in which weddings are all alike, just as funerals are, in which there is no life, those people he could not invite because they floated in their safe határs where the lawns are soft and one's steps springy, while he had fallen out of the frame, hanging and swaying from a rusty hook and creating disorder. What would they talk about? What would they touch upon?

That last letter had fucked him up. In the days when he was still traveling, he had been surprised at how unknown lives whispered their stories to him, the way they would spring up from nowhere, leap out at him and roll along after him, straddle him, dangle from him as in his youth he had dangled from moving trams, and they would not let go until he (the psychologist Andreas Ban), with a *hush, hush, dear friends,* would free them from their bad dreams and nightmares. And now, it turns out that he need not have gone away, need not have researched, leafed through, listened to, watched anything. Here, under his nose, in this small, forgotten, forgetful town, languish the same kinds of stories, scattered through cemeteries, stuck to names, pressed onto photographs, left to lie around like excess, like redundancy.

S. Trajković begins his letter by stating that he must finally tell his story because, having kept it locked up for fifty or sixty years, it is rotting, but to his astonishment it refuses to go away, it keeps recycling, that is what he said, it recycles, spreading its stench, it is eating into him and in this imprisonment he sees that he is disappearing. *I am the prisoner of an incidental historical tale, a secondary historical drama*, says S. Trajković, *and now my own life is eliminating me.*

After that S. Trajković relates to Andreas Ban the contents of a documentary about two subspecies of chimpanzee, one of which is strikingly aggressive. Periodically, without any provocation, these aggressive chimpanzees, particularly the males, S. Trajković stresses, organize themselves into military formations and attack, torture, dismember and in the end kill members of the other subspecies so similar to themselves. From the documentary, S. Trajković discovers that this is a unique phenomenon in the animal kingdom and experts find it incomprehensible. *Otherwise*, says S. Trajković, *when these chimpanzees are not attacking, mistreating and killing the others, they live peacefully alongside groups of all species and subspecies, and it is unclear what is going on in their heads to make them turn wild, that is to say, mad.*

S. Trajković then switches to his family story. He writes that his late mother, Suzana Atlas, daughter of Blanka Atlas, née Steiner, and Armin Atlas, came from Senta and that the Atlas family was one of the wealthier families in the Kingdom of Yugoslavia. Then S. Trajković writes that the outbreak of the war finds Suzana Atlas, later his mother, in Nice, in a private school *pour les jeunes filles de bonne famille*, and that despite her teachers' advice not to return to Senta, she does. Soon afterward, writes S. Trajković, Suzana Atlas, with her mother Blanka, is sent to Auschwitz. The deportation of Jews from the Banat region begins in August 1941, writes S. Trajković. His grandfather, Armin Atlas, is taken away in a special transport, while his uncle, Suzana's elder brother Gjuri, then studying medicine in Zagreb, evades arrest and joins the partisans. S. Trajković writes that the only one to return from the camps is his mother Suzana, while Blanka is killed soon after their arrival in Auschwitz. Armin Atlas apparently survived the camp, but on his way to Senta, independently and on foot—S. Trajković emphasizes—disappears. Uncle Gjuri died recently in Novi Sad.

On her return from the camp, Suzana Atlas finds the family house occupied by strangers, and for a time lives in a rented room, as a subtenant. She never sets foot in her house again. After the war, Suzana Atlas sees personal items, antique furniture, linen, coverlets, Persian rugs, Rosenthal dinner sets and much more in her neighbors' houses, writes S. Trajković. It is only in 2010 that S. Trajković goes for the first time to see the house, once the family home of the Atlas family. Today, the building accommodates a branch of Milošević's Socialist Party of Serbia, writes S. Trajković, and the house is in a state similar to Milošević's party.

S. Trajković writes that Suzana Atlas soon gets a job in a nationalized firm, since she speaks several foreign languages. She works as secretary to the director whose desk once belonged to her (late) father Armin Atlas. One of the numerous drawers of the desk cannot be opened, so Suzana contacts a workman who before the war—what a coincidence!—worked as head of a department in her father's firm. It turns out that the drawer was not locked, but jammed, with a golden Pelican pen and pencil in a snakeskin etui. That is one of the rare family objects that Suzana Atlas ever acquires, and *which*, writes S. Trajković, *I still possess and from time to time, as though it were some kind of unreal reliquary, I look at it and shift it between my fingers.*

Soon afterward, Suzana Atlas has a chance to leave Senta and after a number of trivial events, unimportant for this story, writes S. Trajković, she settles in Opatija, where she is given a job as librarian in the town library.

S. Trajković's late father, Veselin Trajkovski, was born in the village of Duf in Macedonia, into one of the poorest families in the region. Having graduated from the Academy of Commerce (doing physical work and making expert baklava by day and studying by night), by order of the Communist Party Committee of the Republic of Serbia, Veselin Trajkovski is transferred to Rijeka. Shortly before that, Mihajlo Trajkovski, father of Veselin Trajkovski and grandfather of the S. Trajković writing to Andreas Ban, is obliged, during the process of Serbianization of the Macedonian population and to keep his rented sweets and cake shop, to change his surname from Trajkovski to the Serbian variant—Trajković.

S. Trajković writes that as a child he remembers his parents arguing about their surname, his mother Suzana, née Atlas, insisting that it revert to Trajkovski, because, having learned from the dark game History had dragged her Stein-Atlas family into in 1941, she can still feel the breath of that capricious lady. So, Suzana Trajković, née Atlas, maintains that it will be *fatally dangerous*, writes S. Trajković, when one day their Croatian neighbors start believing that they, the Trajkovićes, are Serbs.

In the mid-1960s S. Trajković begins elementary school. To his mother's astonishment, he barely passes first grade, with a score of 2 out of 5. For "achievement" in the first half of his second year, S. Trajković gets a score of 1. Then S. Trajković tells his mother that in his classroom everybody sits with a partner and only he sits alone at a desk facing the class, not like the other desks, facing the teacher. S. Trajković tells his mother that his teacher has made him cardboard donkey's ears which she puts on his head like a hat, and she shouts at him not to use the Serbian words "hleb" and "mleko" for bread and milk but the Croatian ones, "kruh" and "mlijeko." S. Trajković tells his mother that he doesn't get a snack, so his friends share theirs with him. This was the 1960s, S. Trajković stresses in his letter, *I didn't know what the teacher was talking about.* Naturally, Suzana Trajković makes a fuss, the teacher disappears, S. Trajković gets his morning snack and good grades.

S. Trajković then writes about the multiple identities with which he lives in the wrong places, because *all identities are porous*, he writes, and all places inconstant. And, he writes, he is not the only person who lives such layered days. As a member of the Jewish community of this town, *if such a thing exists*, S. Trajković adds (making Andreas Ban wonder whether S. Trajković means the town does not exist or the Jewish community), S. Trajković gets two papers every month, *two journals*, he writes, *Ha-Kol* and the *New Omanut*. Although they are different, both journals deal with the Holocaust, printing personal and family stories from which he, S. Trajković, would most like to escape but cannot, so he locks himself *in the toilet, he hides*, he says, he *vanishes*, after which he returns again to a more or less normal life. So, writes S. Trajković, he lives a double life: the one in the toilet, where the bestialities of disturbed minds reside, and the one outside, in which he seeks glimmers of humanity. S. Trajković writes that then, in the 1990s, the stories from the toilet, with their fecal accompaniment, spill over *into our mild, half-Mediterranean climate*, and that under this sky, he, with his given name and surname, he, Slobodan Trajković, becomes superfluous and undesirable. Slobodan Trajković ends his letter with a Macedonian expression, *Od šta bega ne uteka!** and addresses Andreas Ban directly with the words: *You are not alone.* Then adds: *Thank you.*

---

* You can't evade what you're running from.

Then it was his eyes.

The story of eyes began before Andreas Ban enters the story. Martin had an eye issue, Gombrowicz loses his eyes on the deck of a large ship, outside the door to his apartment Andreas Ban finds a white kitten with one eye and no nose that dies the following day.

Martin was found to have a melanoma of his left eye. Overnight he went blind, bang, the tabular melanoma made its way to the surface and pierced his eye. They took the eye out. *That's the safest thing to do*, they said. Martin had big blue eyes, now he has a big blue eye. Andreas does not know what happened to the eye that was removed, he forgot to ask. If it was thrown into the trash, it could have been eaten by a cat. In the head, eyes are watery; when they are extracted they dry out and shrivel. Like raisins, like sultanas, like currants.

Andreas Ban used to call his son *Blue eye of mine* as an endearment. He will never say anything so lame to him again, he can't anyway, Leo's left. He won't mutter endearments to anyone anymore.

I have particularly sensitive eyes. The eye is the most sensitive organ. It is very easy to pluck out an eye.
        Who are you?
Gombrowicz. One day, strolling astern, on the boards of the deck I noticed a human eye. I asked the helmsman,

Whose eye is that? Did it fall out, or was it removed?
I didn't see, Sir, said the helmsman. It's been lying here
since morning. I'd have picked it up and put it in a box,
but I'm not allowed to leave the helm.

> *Martin has a little box for his eye too. Round and blue,*
> *because that's what his new eye is like, round and blue,*
> *like the old one.*

I continued my interrupted walk, debating whether to
tell the captain and Smith—the latter had appeared on
the steps of the forward hatch. There's a human eye on
the deck over there, I tell him, do you think that it fell
out, or that it was removed from someone?

> *Gombrowicz, an eye can't fall out just like that.*
Of course it can. In the waters of the southern Pacific,
while we were becalmed we lost three quarters of the
eyes of the entire crew. The eye is a flimsily attached
organ, a sphere inserted into a socket in a person, noth-
ing more.

Before he goes to bed, Martin places the eye in the little box, to rest, to close, then lowers his eyelid to cover the socket so that it does not gape wide, empty, so that during the night nothing accidentally falls into it, a fly, for instance. At the end of the day, the eye that was not removed is tired, and at night it too is left alone, lonely, it turns and rolls and cannot fall asleep. *I have problems with this new eye*, says Martin, *it will not obey. And it sees nothing*.

But Martin is alive. He has lost depth perception, the third dimension has gone and he walks on his toes, he has become agile and cautious, but he is alive. That man Granero died the instant the bull in the *corrida* pierced his eye and head with its horn, and people watched his right eye hanging and swinging like a puppet on a string as he was carried out of the arena.

Throughout history people have often gouged out each other's eyes, they still do, only in secret. Through history the plucking out of eyes moves from life into literature and painting, where it still lives. As with Dante's harpies, those winged monsters with the head and torso of a woman, and the tail and talons of a bird of prey, that feed on the leaves of oak trees where suicides crouch, where one such tree preserves the body of the jurist and diplomat Pietro della Vigno (1190–1249), who did kill himself by beating his head against the walls of his prison, but only after the Emperor Frederick II had ordered, *Gouge out his eyes.*

All right, an eye can fall out or someone can pluck it out, but there are cases of gouging out *one's own eye*, or eyes. This happens in delusional states, particularly religious. In 1876, Gastone Galetti works as a waiter in Vienna and Trieste, and, when he does not work, he visits churches to which he invites friends and acquaintances and interprets the Bible for them. In July of that same year, 1876, Gastone Galetti is on his way to Herzegovina to fight the Turks, but is arrested and interned. One morning the warden is startled by an unusually loud prayer coming from Gastone Galetti's room. On opening the door he sees the unfortunate man covered in blood, his right eye lying on the floor and the left one hanging down his cheek. Gastone Galetti is immediately taken to the Trieste mental hospital, where it appears he remained until his death many years later. This unfortunate episode took place on July 25, 1876. By the end of September, Gastone Galetti's eye sockets heal and Gastone assures the doctors that God had ordered him to do what he did and that he does not at all regret having obeyed God and that he hopes he will soon be able to see again.

Another known case is that of Albina Krota, who believed literally in the gospel according to Mark or Matthew, it does not matter which, because they both reel off the same horrors, *And if thine eye offend thee, pluck it out, and if thy hand offend thee, cut it off, and if thy foot offend thee, cut it off* (Mark 9: 43, 45, 47), *and if thine eye offend thee, pluck it out and cast it from thee* (Matthew 18: 9), so Albina Krota gouged out both her eyes. Albina Krota's wounds also heal quickly, but unlike Gastone Galetti, she is released from the madhouse as cured and as such, cured, she carries on roaming the world for a long time, interpreting the New Testament to people. It is interesting that both Gastone Galetti and Albina Krota, in a state of exaltation, often repeated, *Oh, nothing hurts, nothing hurts at all.*

For years Andreas Ban regularly assesses his eye pressure (the doctors warn him, *Take it seriously, you could go blind*), now there is also redness. *Your eyes are red, why are your eyes red? You've got very red eyes, do they sting? Do they itch?* people ask wherever he goes. Andreas Ban looks at himself, he looks at his eyes and concludes, *Yes, my eyes are red.*

I'm allergic to the antiglaucoma drops, Andreas maintains, but the doctors do not listen to what Andreas Ban is saying, they imagine the worst, they walk him from department to department, from allergists to epidemiologists, from one laboratory to the other, setting up additional examinations with additional waiting and hanging around in dark overcrowded clinics.

An eye swab is taken by scraping the lower eyelid on the inside.

Now, this is going to hurt, says the nurse and starts scraping both Andreas's eyes. Then she observes, *You aren't groaning,* then she asks, *Are you all right?*

Andreas says: *I've got a high pain threshold.*

Two weeks later Andreas Ban learns that his eyes are bacteria-free, although redder than ever.

The doctors order: *Allergy tests.*

At the allergy testing (12 subcutaneous pricks in each forearm) the allergist concludes, *You are allergic to fur and to animal hair in general, but that has no connection to the redness of your eyes. Do you smoke?*

What is this swelling under my eye, this little pillow? asks Andreas Ban.

Your face has drooped, says the specialist, *with age.*

All right, says Andreas Ban.

Do you smoke? My dad smokes and has pulmonary emphysema, says the specialist. *The problem with your eyes could come from contact lenses, stop wearing lenses. Go and see your ophthalmologist.*

Andreas Ban hurries off to his ophthalmologist (in a different building).

Could this redness come from contact lenses? Andreas Ban (after two or three hours of waiting) asks his ophthalmologist. *I've worn lenses for forty years,* he says, *should I switch to glasses?*

No, says the specialist. This young woman doctor is tall and good-looking, very good-looking. She moves swiftly, as though flying, and her hair billows. *You're better-looking without glasses,* she says.

And this swelling under my eye, is that from old age?

No, says the specialist, *it's from sleeping.*

Why are my eyes red?

You're allergic to the eye drops, concludes the specialist. That conclusion was reached six months after Andreas Ban had said: *I'm allergic to the eye drops.*

For a year after that Andreas Ban and the good-looking doctor try out antiglaucoma drops in many different combinations, and finally the specialist says, *The redness has gone. Your whites are clear.*

Your eyes are lovely. Open them wide.

I can't, says Andreas Ban. *My lids have drooped.*

Then, one night, Andreas Ban rushes into the emergency clinic, the emergency eye ward, and when (after three or four hours of waiting) he is in front of the doctor, he says:

I can't see out of my right eye. Everything's cloudy. And he asks, *Could it be a tumor?*

Andreas Ban knows that the games the eye plays are deceptive. There was another woman, Amalia Tanzabella, who had an operation on one eye and lay for a long time in hospital with a bandage over the treated eye. *This treated eye itches terribly*, Amalia Tanzabella tells the doctors, but the doctors, of course, pay no attention. Amalia complains so much, every day, ever more, not only of an itch but of unbearable pain, so the doctors finally decide to remove the bandage and examine her eye. When they uncovered that woman's eye, they saw that the eye had become a completely dead and unusable eye, because in it a colony of ants had made a large hole, and from that hole the colony was moving back and forth, swarming all over Amalia's face.

Another woman, Anita Frascati, complained for months of terrible headaches but the doctors could not find any irregularities in her health. Finally she has her eyes tested. The medical experts discover a twenty-centimeter-long worm that had wrapped itself around Anita Frascati's eye and was about to penetrate it. The doctors spend hours removing the worm from Anita's eye, cautiously, not to damage it, but the eye was already dead. Whether it was by chance that the victims of these attackers that do not ordinarily attack the eyes, but are benign, tame and quiet creatures, in tune with their natural surroundings, integrated into nature, close to the soil, whether it was by chance that the victims were women, Amalia and Anita, in other words female eyes, has not been investigated. Perhaps those horrors could have happened to two male eyes, yes, probably, but that was not the case.

While the woman doctor looks deep into Andreas's eyes, so close their noses almost touch, scenes from his life appear beneath their lids and flicker in many colors as if he were watching a film. Recently he had read that, before they disintegrate, some animals' eyes, say those of cattle, like photographic plates retain the images of the beings and objects that were in their line of sight at the moment they expired. Which images will dance in Andreas Ban's eyes if he goes blind?

It's not a tumor, says the specialist. *It's a cataract with pseudoexfoliation syndrome, you have glaucoma, don't you?*

Yes.

Andreas Ban then studies texts about possible complications from surgically removing the lens in the event of high eye pressure, which is when the inside of the eye flakes, or rather does not flake, but false scales build up, falling softly like dry snow by night, like powder snow. In the course of the operation the eye can burst—pow!—break and dissolve, leaving a hole in his head where there had once been his lively green eye, so that, like Martin, he would get a green glass eye which would look directly and sternly at nothing.

You have nice long eyelashes, says the specialist.

That's because of the glaucoma drops, says Andreas Ban. *My original eyelashes are short*, he says.

Andreas Ban's turn for the operation comes six months later, when he can no longer see anything out of that eye. As with his limping, it is only then that Andreas Ban discovers that many people cannot see out of one eye, or even out of either, that they stumble half-blind, sometimes totally blind, without complaint, just feeling the restricted world that surrounds them, treading carefully, with small steps, gently and anxiously. Anton, Nino, Fiona, Cecillia, Rikardo, Edita, they all say, *We won't have the operation, we're fine as we are.*

They almost did not accept him at the ward. He had not brought new, fresh results of numerous examinations, he had brought a pile of three-month-old results, and they want patients to go again and again for tests, they want to know their current situation. His ECG was no longer valid, the internist's findings were not valid, his blood count was not valid, the pulmonologist's findings were not valid. Nothing was valid. And this little eye procedure is conducted under local anesthetic which no longer consists even of an injection in the temple: the eye is wiped over with a deadening gel, so the patient hears everything and if he wishes he can even converse with the doctor carrying out the procedure, which Andreas Ban does. There was soft music playing, some light Mozart, and he asked, *Are you now sucking out my lens? Is my eye now empty?* and the doctor said: *Yes, I'm about to fit the new, clean lens, through which you will see clearly and sharply.*

OK, they had given him a tablet to bring his eye pressure down, to prevent his eye from exploding, but that was all. They took him in without fresh results, because the doctor is a clever and excellent doctor who, like Andreas, cannot bear filling in forms with little boxes, and what's more, she is good-looking and entirely normal, she does not always manage to put on her white coat because her patients keep flowing in so she examines them in her day clothes, and her day clothes are feminine, even provocative, and that small disobedience appeals to Andreas Ban, and he has an urge to embrace her.

In general, Andreas feels best around doctors. With them he has topics to discuss. He asks questions and gets answers, they try to solve his issues. They take care of him. They alone in this town.

Admission to the hospital takes much too long, first waiting one's turn, because some fifty frightened people wait outside, in the hall, then in the office within, where slow motion prevails, submerged in the irritation of the administrative women. At reception they still use inkjet printers, so it takes five minutes to print out a page, and admission documents consist of five pages or more. Besides, the scowling administrators ask a series of questions such as father's name?, mother's name?, which is completely absurd with older patients whose parents have probably been dead for a long, long time. When he told Victor about this, Victor said, *Your story is a joke compared to mine. Once they asked me: "Sex? Male or female?"* The administrator assigned to Andreas Ban also asked, *Do you have any disabilities?* At which he was faced with the dilemma of listing all of them, or picking out just one, so he said, *I've got no left tit,* at which the woman turned on him, *Mind your language!* she hissed, rolling her eyes.

Before the procedure, Andreas Ban dreams about gloves. *I've lost my gloves,* he says to the person in the bed next to him who lies back on his pillow, in his pajamas (his operation is scheduled for the following day, so why is he in pajamas?), with his arms crossed, looking straight ahead.

You've lost your gloves? I don't know anything about gloves, I'm a confectioner, says the one who is otherwise silent.

Someone said, we dream in order to forget, Andreas Ban tells the tongue-tied, half-blind confectioner.

I never dream, says the confectioner.

In Hans Christian Andersen there is a playful little dwarf by the name of Ole Lukøje who sends children to sleep and into cheerful dreams. Ole Lukøje approaches the little ones on tiptoe and scatters grains of fine sand into their eyes, which blinds them so they bow their heads and sink into slumber. Under each arm Ole Lukøje carries an umbrella, whose underside is splendidly illustrated, which he opens over the heads of the good children, so they enter into miraculous stories in which the world crackles with color, and another umbrella, black on the inside, with no illustrations, which Ole Lukøje uses to deprive naughty children of nocturnal excursions so they wake with difficulty, scared and empty. Ole Lukøje is an old dwarf, resembling a little Morpheus, perhaps even Morpheus himself, preparing for his final leap out of dreams into death. For Ole Lukøje has a brother also called Ole Lukøje and that brother visits people only once, closes their eyes, lifts them onto his horse and while telling them stories, carries them to the other side of reality. *My brother Ole Lukøje knows only two stories*, says Ole Lukøje on his seventh visit to a small boy called Hjalmar. *One of his stories is so magical that I can't describe it, while the other is so appalling that I have no words for it*. Then Ole Lukøje lifts Hjalmar up to the window and says, *Look, that's my brother Ole Lukøje on his horse. His other name is Death. You see, he doesn't look as terrible as he does in picture books, like a skeleton. Look, his coat is sewn with silver threads and he is dressed like a hussar, while behind him flutters a cape of black velvet that covers the back and the hooves of his horse. See them speed by!*

That is what Andreas Ban wanted to tell the confectioner who does not dream, but the confectioner was snoring and farting in his sleep.

That night, before his procedure, Andreas Ban listens to music on a little transistor he has brought with him. *If I go blind, this is what I'll do, I'll listen to music*, he says.

Then, in his hospital room lit by a forty-watt bulb (because why, in that hospital, in the eye department, would anyone want to read?), Andreas Ban, with his one eye, starts reading a letter from his friend the poet Ljiljana Dirjan, as he had not got around to it earlier.

Come to Skopje, Ljiljana writes, *I'll take you to the Matka Canyon, Matka is a tonic for the eyes. And I'll make you little Chinese nibbles.*

When he leaves the hospital (with a bandage over his eye), Andreas Ban is given a card for organ transplants, in case the new lens becomes detached. No matter where he is, with that card he can run into any clinic and there they will know at once how to repair it, what to put into that dead eye to bring it back to life.

The card, in the name of Andreas Ban, is called a *Patient Lens Identification Implant Card*, it contains: the name of the specialist, the date of the operation, all the dimensions of his right eye and all the dimensions and the make of the implanted lens. The card also contains the addresses and telephone numbers of the manufacturers of those lenses, in case, heaven forbid, of any blunder. So, as far as his eye is concerned, Andreas Ban is calm for a while. When he feels like excluding himself completely, blacking out his consciousness, obliterating it, turning his eyes into empty, blind eyes, into *white eyes* behind which there will not be any images or memories or vibrations, he will step into those белые ночи* (which are also called *black days*), he will step into the twilight, both the civic and the astronomical twilight when the Sun sinks.

There is another person who throws sand into eyes, an evil man who visits children who do not want to go to bed—Mr. Sandman. Children often do not want to go to bed, for children days are short, because they like to look, because they are discovering the world. But the Sandman says no. The Sandman determines how much of the world and what kind of world children may look at to remain obedient. So, when the Sandman throws a handful of sand into the eyes of disobedient children, their bloody eyes jump out of their heads and the Sandman collects them, tosses them into a sack and during the crescent moon feeds them to his young who sit in a nest and, like owls, have hooked beaks they peck with at the disobedient eyes of the disobedient children. And so, as time goes on, increasing numbers of tiny blind people of uncertain step roam the world, mysteriously quiet and like automata, like that beautiful Olympia, the great seductress, whose face had black hole instead of eyes.

For a month Andreas Ban is not allowed to lift heavy objects so

---

* White nights.

that his eye does not pop out, but he forgets his doctors' advice and lifts a lot of heavy objects and then through his socket streams a deep thick pain that beats against his brain like a boxer's knock-out blow. Then he hurries to lie down in the dark. Yes, light hurts Andreas Ban. Too much light is fatal for his repaired eye which now wants to look independently, without him, because it sees far and sharply. That is why, when he goes out, Andreas Ban wears very dark glasses, likewise on the advice of his doctors. Perhaps he should not have had the eye treated. Perhaps he ought to have detached himself from it, from that eye of his. What does Otto Rank say? Life is made up of separation. From one's mother, from oneself, from used-up times, all made up of bright or dark gradual separations, in stages. Until one's final disappearance.

He often has problems with his eyes. Andreas Ban. Once a splinter hit him in the left eye, piercing the white like an arrow and stopping him from closing the lid. Another time, as he was opening a bottle of champagne, the cork flew into his right eye, knocking it into his brain.

Perhaps he should be killed. Andreas Ban. Given a quick seni-cide, since he is already fading, evaporating, disappearing, van-ishing. Way back in Ancient Greece, the poet Hesiod, the histo-rian Herodotus and the geographer Strabo wrote about senicide, about the way the closest relations leave their old people (over sixty) in buildings without food or water until they expire. In the Balkans, killings of the old were lively and varied. Sometimes they not only killed the old people, but used their corpses for village feasts, for great celebrations. In some areas sons left their old peo-ple in remote places to die of hunger, or to be torn apart by wild animals, in some they suffocated them, and in others they buried them alive. Sometimes a whole village would be involved in the senicide. Then they would behead the old people or whack them on the nape of the neck with an axe or clobber them with poles, then drag them with wooden hooks to the graveyard. It is said that a man killed his father that way and on the road home threw away the hook. His little son, who had watched it all, picked up the hook and took it home. *Why did you do that?* asked his father. And the child said, *When you get old, I'll drag you with this hook.* To this day people still say: *He's ready for the pole.* In some places they were gentler; they just poisoned the old, so they died in installments.

Who should be the one to kill Andreas Ban? Leo?

Lobsters do not age.

Should he kill himself?

The French avant-garde killed themselves in a big way, theatrically and solemnly. Jacques Rigaut divulged his contempt for reality which was for him *le désespoir, l'indifférence, les trahisons, la fidélité, la solitude, la famille, la liberté, la pesanteur, l'argent, la pauvreté, l'amour, l'absence d'amour, le syphilis, la santé, le sommeil, l'insomnie, le désir, l'impuissance, la platitude, l'art* […] *il n'y a pas là de quoi fouetter un chat* […], affirming that suicide ought to become a vocation. Then in 1929 he really did shoot himself, having first marked out his ribcage with a ruler to be sure not to miss his heart. He was thirty years old. The writer and poet Julien Torma disappeared in the Tyrolean Alps in 1933. He was thirty as well. Jacques Vaché overdosed on opium at the age of twenty-four and expired with a monocle on his nose (1919). A. Alvarez who is, thank God, still alive (born in 1929) writes that Vaché was tall, elegant, refined and eccentric, he writes that when he met his best friends in the street, he would never recognize them, he never answered letters, never returned anyone's greetings. Then A. Alvarez quotes Breton quoting Bouvier who says that Vaché lived with a young woman whom he forced to sit immobile and silent in a corner of his room (as though she was that eyeless Olympia of Hoffmann's), while he entertained a friend. Vaché paraded through the streets dressed as a hussar, an aviator or a doctor, writes A. Alvarez. Andreas Ban reads A. Alvarez with pleasure, because Alvarez obliquely indicates a way for him, Andreas, to kill himself.

The boxer and poet Arthur Cravan, born in 1887 as Fabian Avenarius Lloyd, simply vanished in the Pacific Ocean near the Mexican coast in 1918. Perhaps Andreas Ban is behind schedule? Perhaps he should have killed himself sooner, then this situation would not have come to this. He would have avoided the current defiled reality, drowned in total silence, transcendental.

Be my guest, Andreas. Death is everywhere: heaven
has well provided for that. Anyone may deprive us of
life; no one can deprive us of death. To death there are
a thousand avenues.
      Seneca

> *Oh, yes, death is the infallible cure of all; 'tis a most*
> *assured port that is never to be feared, and very of-*
> *ten to be sought. It comes all to one, whether a man*
> *give himself his end, or stays to receive it by some other*
> *means; whether he pays before his day, or stays till his*
> *day of payment comes; from whencesoever it comes, it*
> *is still his; in what part soever the thread breaks, there's*
> *the end of the clue. The most voluntary death is the*
> *finest. Life depends upon the pleasure of others; death*
> *upon our own.*
>
>   *Montaigne*

Seneca killed himself out of vanity, not because he had nothing to live on. Montaigne did not kill himself. All that romantic talk about how life is a fiction and suicide a literary act is nothing but overwrought quasi-philosophical frivolity. Life in the dark, in the cold, is not a fiction. Illness that cannot be cured because the patient has no money for its treatment, is not a fiction. Hunger is not a fiction. Abandonment, shipwreck, heresy are not fictions. Suicide as rebellion, who needs that? Collective consciences have thick armor, like that of lobsters. Which do not age. Collective consciences, when some Primo Levi or Jan Palach or Tadeusz Borowski slightly instigates them, may stir for an instant, but then fall silent again.

He will not write anymore, he will not write anymore. Writing is worthless, useless, barren and utterly idiotic business.

> *You're right. Writing is an occupation in which you must prove your talent to those who have none.*

You are wrong, you Andreas Ban and you Julian Barnes. The whole age can be divided into those who write and those who do not write. Those who write represent despair, and those who read disapprove of it and believe that they have a superior wisdom—and yet, if they were able to write, they would write the same thing. Basically they are all equally despairing, but when one does not have the opportunity to become important with his despair, then it is hardly worth the trouble to despair and show it. Is this what it is to have conquered despair?

> *Yes, Kierkegaard. But we need books that affect us like a disaster, that grieve us deeply ... A book must be the axe for the frozen sea within us. Yours, Kafka.*

Andreas Ban shakes his head when such voices, such sophistry weigh on his brain. Dead voices, the voices of the dead.

Then it arrived.

The pension.

The pension of 1,327 kunas (177 euros).

The Croatian pension for fifteen years of work in democratic and socially sensitive Croatia. The Serbian part of his retirement riches will take who knows how long to come through, they tell him, maybe months. There, in Serbia, a further twenty-five years of past work lies in wait for Andreas Ban, for which, the very pleasant employees of the Pensions Office tell him, he will receive ten euros per year of employment, that is to say a further 1,875 kunas. What joy. Yet that humiliation could have been mitigated, deferred for two or three years, or even five, had the capering dean who raised his hand threateningly whenever anyone tried to interrupt his lengthy and repetitive tirades, had the dean mustered the nerve to speak out in his favor, in favor of Andreas Ban, instead of remaining undecided, and at the Senate meeting even against. Even the vice-chancellor of that university (ranked 1,338 on the list of world universities) could have mitigated that kick in Andreas Ban's ass, had he wished. But he did not.

But when the athletic Croatian Aryan bodies, wreathed in international gold and silver, those once combative, sculpted, muscular bodies, begin to fade and slacken forty years later, those bodies are branded with 1,100 euros a month by their sensitive homeland of Croatia, regardless of the income status of the owners of the bodies. To be fair, the thoughtful state of Croatia announces plans to reward the Paralympic bodies too, but with half that monthly allowance, because, after all, those bodies are somehow defective, invalid bodies, although still athletic. It figures. But it does not occur to the Croatian state to reward the mind, that elusive "excellence" (how grotesquely Croatia bandies about that hollow word) which hovers in bodies shriveled from sitting, writing and studying, in bodies that compose and paint and think while their muscles atrophy, their hemorrhoids swell, their vision weakens and their lungs collapse. To those miserable, nondescript physiques, often unpleasant to look at, the motherland allocates a monthly social assistance of 93.33 euros (for academicians), down to 66.66 euros (for those who have won major prizes) and forty euros (for those with lesser prizes), and that is after those bodies reach the age of sixty-five and prove their excellence with certificates and references. These thinking organisms also have to inform the local arbiters of "excellence" how many they share a household with, what their relationship to them is, what the names of all those members of the shared household are and when they were born, because should it be such a household, a warm family community, a *domus ruralis* with an open hearth around which its members gather and over which a pot of polenta hangs, then any kind of social support is entirely superfluous, because there is the family, that basic cell of society and life which in the twenty-first century has to take care of its waste. And, what is more, all these cripples, the creators rendered crippled, all this trash seeks crumbs of charity from the Croatian state, all are obliged to inform the Croatian state about their ownership of property, because heaven forbid that such properties should have several rooms, particularly in the event of family communities that have died out, or that there should hang on the walls of those properties oil paintings or engravings by famous artists, or that they should contain libraries, or, worse still, a concert piano. Because all that, that intellectual rabble, has to be annihilated.

I've been waiting a year for a reply from the Administrative Commission to allocate me regular financial assistance of forty euros, a colleague tells Andreas Ban.

Collect discarded bottles, says Andreas Ban, *you'll earn more.*

In the Department, they drop small contributions into a little bag for a farewell gift for Andreas Ban.

Andreas Ban puts a stop to that activity.

In the Department they plan a communal dinner at which they will present to Andreas Ban the gift that Andreas Ban does not want. *Are you fucking with me?* Andreas Ban says to them. *Forget it, forget me.*

The woman in the Department says, *So what, you'll live on royalties!* The woman who says *So what!* to Andreas Ban shouts, she always shouts when she talks. But when she says *What's up?* her lips pucker together like an asshole and emit a squeaky, conciliatory and slimy little question. When she says *What's up?* it is impossible to shout, the lips close and the breath has no way out.

Now, when he talks and when he writes (which he does only if he has to), Andreas Ban mixes languages as they float in his head. Like that Bertha Pappenheim (1859–1936), whom Freud, ostensibly out of discretion, calls Anna O., whom he never meets and about whom he knows very little. Breuer also rummages through Bertha's crisis, baffled by the mysteries of it, until she, Bertha Pappenheim, with her imaginative cathartic dramas, interprets what is going on with her. During that crisis, Bertha Pappenheim, whom Freud deprives of her name, transforming her into Fraulein Anna O. whom he deprives of personality, whose identity he crushes, imposing on her his image of her, as Bertha Pappenheim is crushed, pummeled and molded by the dull-witted overbearing puritans around her, her father, for one, and then that whole corseted end-of-the-century society, which does not permit her to finish school, let alone study at the University of Vienna, because the University does not allow women into its elite, even if some of them are more enlightened than the men whom the University of Vienna proudly takes under its wing, including Bertha's younger brother Wilhelm, who is clearly less intelligent than Bertha Pappenheim, who during her existential crisis, instead of studying, traveling and having a good time, is told to sit at home, make lace and tapestries, prepare kosher food and take care of her dying father, during that existential crisis Bertha Pappenheim forgets her mother tongue. Bertha Pappenheim understands nothing in her mother tongue, nor can she express herself in it, but instead she speaks fluently a refined English, French and Italian, which seems "strange" to Freud, and "bizarre" to Breuer. Although he is no expert, Andreas Ban believes that all of them, the prominent psychiatrists of the day, along with the Orthodox Jews who monitored her every step, and her family and friends were elegantly led up the garden path by Bertha Pappenheim who was telling them she no longer wished to communicate with them, their language was not hers. Bertha Pappenheim had to overcome the pain and fear through which she discovered that what awaited her was a life that did not belong to her but to a stranger.

Because, when they finally give up on Bertha Pappenheim, when they stop dragging her from one psychiatric institution to another and stuffing her with morphine, Bertha Pappenheim leaps into life. She sets up numerous institutions, kindergartens, orphanages, safe houses, educational centers, homes for fallen girls; she travels, gives lectures, translates important works of feminist literature, writes and publishes stories, plays, poems, both for children and adults, anonymously to start with, then under the pseudonym Paul Berthold and finally as Bertha Pappenheim; she meets people, she spends time with Martin Buber (philosophy of dialogue—you and I) and Henrietta Szold, then she dies of cancer, avoiding a second attack on her great work, on the Neu-Isenberg school and its branches, the total annihilation not only of her vision but also of the people whom her vision brought back to reality. The day after Kristallnacht, on November 10, 1938, the Gestapo orders the burning of Bertha's Neu-Isenberg schools throughout the Reich, and in 1942 deports its pupils and staff to the concentration camp Theresienstadt, where most of them die.

In 1954, Germany bequeaths Bertha Pappenheim a postage stamp.

CHONKIN: First-rate stuff! Takes your breath away. You make it from grain or from beetroot?

GLADISHEV: From shit, Vanya.

CHONKIN: What do you mean?

GLADISHEV: Simple recipe, Vanya. You take a kilo of sugar to a kilo of shit.... We react squeamishly to shit, don't we? But if you look into the matter you'll see that it's the most valuable substance on earth, all life comes from shit and returns to shit.

And so, Andreas Ban, transformed into a hybrid postmodern body, does not know how to get out of that body, how to abandon it, the way he (temporarily) abandons his semiurban refuge. But neither can he lend his body to others, because without him his body is an elusive object. His body is his otherness, which is after all not exactly alien to him. He no longer has a cat, his transitional object. She ran away and is likely dead, because she was a tame cat, unused to the outside world that to her meant nothing.

He is still disturbed (why?) when he forgets to take the medicine that blocks his hormone receptors, the medicine that ostensibly protects his nonexistent breast from being invaded by another tumor, that Armidex which he has to take for five years, four have passed, then what?

In Skopje, where in 2004 Andreas Ban muses about moving, he watches stray dogs marked with a yellow chip on the left ear roaming around the restaurants, and he feeds them secretly. *Stray cats are not marked*, Bogomil Gjuzel tells him.

It is the beginning of November 2011.

The days are still warm and sunny.

One Sunday morning Andreas Ban goes to Rovinj.

On the way to the bus station, Andreas Ban passes through the short main artery of the small town where a collective intimacy filled with loneliness circulates. He looks at women carrying bags, mostly with their right hands, with only four fingers. The women's fifth, little finger is free from the handle, while the others grip it. The women's pinkies bend like worms and shrivel in flight.

Women with straight hips pass by. Women with straight hips often acquire bellies, while those with full hips develop bigger behinds.

An ugly woman passes in black sateen slacks, with fungus on her skin.

Two street musicians, a guitarist with an evergreen repertoire and an accordion player who croons patriotic turbo-folk songs at the top of his voice. They both have upholstered chairs which they move to busy points of the pedestrian walkway where people promenade aimlessly in all directions, the walkway looks like a chaotic room, a walking room, a room to arrive in only to leave, like a vast room for collective dying. So, as he walks, Andreas Ban observes as the movement of the town collides with the breath and steps of its people.

In Rovinj, Andreas Ban sits in the square on the terrace of the café La Viecia Batana, drinks coffee and waits for Victor to bring him the packet he has ordered. It was in this café long ago that, during empty late afternoons, the philosopher and painter Carlo Michelstaedter from Gorizia, who shot himself in 1920, wrote his poems. Andreas Ban does not write poems and he will not shoot himself. The Sunday silence is suddenly broken by a brass band, Banda d'ottoni Rovigno, with which, as early as 1765, the *sapaduri*, *pescaduri*, *marineri* and *cavaduri* have brightened the days of laborers, fishermen, sailors and farmers. Otherwise, throughout its history, Rovinj sings. And weeps.

The terrace is half empty. Next to Andreas Ban, at a round table, sit seven middle-aged women, all seven in black, all seven with sunglasses on their noses and all seven with an intensely red drink in their right hand, which all seven middle-aged women raise simultaneously to their mouths. It is not clear whether the women are sorrowful or celebrating something while the brass band plays "Blue Night" and "Pretty Woman."

Where is that lovely hair? Andreas then hears a woman at the next table ask the woman to his left.

Something had to be sold, the woman replies.

The Gift of the Magi. It was probably the 1917 version, because when he saw the film in Manhattan he was not even six years old, and he cried. He had been taken to an evening of short films based on O. Henry's stories, in his memory the film is the one about the last leaf and the dying woman painter and the two create epiphanies in his head and body. The cinema was small, the seats wooden, the floor black, and the cinema smell of the early 1950s now blends with the smell of the sea in the Rovinj square where Andreas Ban waits for Victor in La Viecia Batana café, uncannily similar to the famous Pete's Tavern in Manhattan where O. Henry used to write his stories.

Then Jan, a painter born in Bradford to an English mother and a Polish father, educated in Cardiff, hurtles by on her bicycle. She has a gallery, Sotto Muro, in the old part of town, and she waves to him, *Hi, Andreas! Back again?* Andreas Ban met Jan Ejsymontt at radiation therapy, and after they had been bombarded with invisible Mevatron and Oncor rays, they would go for a white wine and talk about trains and cats. Later, that late summer of 2008, in the early morning hours, Andreas Ban and Jan Eysymontt would meet on the empty beach under the lighthouse and fling their scarred, radiated torsos into the sea to cool them. That year Jan made a picture in which a red ray cuts through the breast that had been operated on and visitors asked *What's that?*

A year later, Jan opened an exhibition entitled *That Day*, which was also called *One of 9*, an exhibition with new paintings and nine plaster torsos of mutilated women who had been operated on for carcinoma of the breast. The exhibition also contained fishermen's nets, stones from the sea, pebbles rimmed with tar, driftwood, there were music and flowers, red wine and Parmesan cheese, there were those who had been slashed and irradiated and those who had yet to be.

Andreas Ban often says, *When I die, play "Let the Sunshine In," sing as you carry me to the water and make sure it is a bright day. I want my funeral to be like Mrs. Batalita's.*

Mrs. Batalita ran a shop selling provisions in the old part of

Rovinj, in ulica Trevisol. She died in 1906, at the age of eighty. In her will she stipulated that on the day of her burial she wanted ulica Trevisol to be a cheerful street with music, and sweets to be handed out to the children. So the day of Mrs. Batalita's funeral was transformed into a festival about which people talk to this day. That is what he wants, a cheerful farewell.

Then someone on the terrace of La Viecia Batana says, *I have to climb up to the fifth floor*, and someone else says, *They gets* (I gets, you gets, he gets) *a heart attack from her voice*, and a third says, *Then night falled*, once again Andreas Ban is upset by the linguistic monstrosities of Croatian speakers. Then a woman says, *You didn't ask him nothing "by the way"?* at which Andreas is overcome by intolerance, so he turns and says, *Oh, you speak English,"by the way"?*

And that heavily made-up la-di-da says, *Cut the crap, old man.*

And he remembers the numerous diminutives that some people scatter all over the place, that drive Andreas Ban to distraction, and he becomes even more irritated, so when Victor finally arrives Andreas asks him, *What kind of country is this, a sycophantic Croatia, who are these Croatlets* (a diminutive they do not use), *when to them everything is so tiny and feeble, colorful and sugary?*

The latest is Serbling, says Victor. *I've brought you belladonna.*

Belladonna, also known as deadly nightshade, devil's berries, death cherries, beautiful death, devil's herb, which sound terrifying and threatening. Belladonna also carries a tamer name, *dog's cherry*, and an almost magical one, *fairy plant*.

Belladonna is a bushy plant that grows up to two meters high and contains atropine, still used today to dilate the pupils, while in the Renaissance women would drop the atropine into their eyes to make them shine. And so those idle Renaissance ladies, squeezed into their corsets, in their silk, brocade, velvet and cotton dresses walk around with dilated pupils, disoriented, half-blind, winking without knowing at whom and smiling foolishly into space. Their

eyes appear dark and deep, but are in fact *empty* and *colorless*. They were beautiful women, *le belle donne*, blinded fools.

Up until the First World War, in Europe most belladonna was cultivated in Croatia, in Slavonia and southern Hungary. Annual production was between sixty and one hundred tonnes of dried leaves and 150 to two hundred tonnes of dried roots.

Belladonna conceals its poison in beautiful mauve-black berries, and in its leaves and roots. The berries are full of dark inky juice, bittersweet, the size of cherries, and are as refreshing as a vitamin drink, so they tempt passersby: *pick me, pick me and fly away to the land of dreams.* Those poisonous berries nestle comfortably in little green, five-pointed cups and sway there quietly in the summer and autumn breeze. If consumed, just a few berries can kill a child, while an adult requires twenty to slip away, to set out for fantastical landscapes, because belladonna has a powerful hallucinogenic effect. In Istria, belladonna grows on shady slopes where the soil is moist. The plants bloom from June to August, while their fruits ripen from July to September.

Here you are, says Victor to Andreas Ban on the terrace of La Viecia Batana, without asking questions. *Here are the leaves and the roots and about a hundred fresh berries.*

It is cold. The apartment smells of darkness and damp. Andreas Ban switches on all the heaters and all the lamps. He climbs up to look at the electricity meter, it is spinning vertiginously. Andreas Ban smiles. He pours himself a grappa with rue and sets off limping down the hallway, swinging Victor's plastic bag. He waits for the warmth to pour over the parquet and lick at the walls. An hour passes. Andreas Ban settles into his gray armchair, takes the dried belladonna leaves out of Victor's bag, crumbles them and fills his pipe. The pipe was handmade by the renowned Emil Chonowitsch in the 1970s, it has the trademark chonowitsch–denmark, handskaaren. Andreas Ban was given the pipe in 1975 by the psychiatrist Erick Aho of Geneva, when Andreas Ban was there on a one-year training course in clinical depression, anxiety and phobia. Andreas Ban does not normally smoke a pipe. Back then, Erick Aho was packing up his life. His wife had walked out, taking their two daughters with her and selling their furniture. Erick Aho was left in an empty house with five or six camping chairs, a low plastic folding table and four blow-up mattresses. It was at that table that the psychiatrist Erick Aho sketched out his battered past for the psychologist Andreas Ban. Their backs were guarded by tall white bookshelves with no books. In a corner lay children's toys, some blocks, dolls and soft toy animals with no limbs. Through the dirty windows a garden with a swing could be seen. The lake was not visible. *I have a great collection of pipes that I no longer need,* said the psychiatrist Aho. *Here's one for you, it's elegant and sits nicely in the hand.* That is how Andreas Ban came by a pipe. Now he puffs at it.

Mild dizziness.

Tachycardia.

His pulse quickens.

His face burns.

Andreas Ban goes to the kitchen, his gait—stable.

Andreas Ban shakes half of Victor's belladonna berries, some fifty of them, into a yellow porcelain Chinese dish as fine as tissue paper, almost transparent. *Big blueberries,* he says. He sprinkles sugar over the berries and goes back to his armchair.

Belladonna soothes asthma attacks.

Belladonna is dangerous for people with glaucoma.

Belladonna is a trap for Andreas Ban.

Andreas Ban eats the sweetened belladonna berries. Slowly, one by one, six of them.

His lips become dry.

His vision clouds.

The pain in his back eases.

One berry.

In the distance someone whispers. Who is whispering? The voice is familiar but distorted. Andreas Ban never mistakes voices, Andreas Ban recognizes voices perfectly, he does not need faces. The voice comes closer, slips under the door and rises, stands upright and sways. Why is it swinging? It is a voice in lines, a voice resembling a prisoner, except that its stripes are red-black with little green dots in between. *I am a musical voice,* says the voice. Andreas Ban recognizes the voice of Strauss.

His mouth is full of saliva.

Perspiration.

Vertigo.

Andreas Ban rocks backward and forward in his armchair.

Two berries.

Pain in his eyes. Pulsing in his eye sockets. His eyes sting. The light sends arrows like the prickles of little albino hedgehogs into their whites. His lids flutter. They will not close.

Someone switches on the radio. Stalin is speaking. Stalin's face grows in Andreas Ban's room, swells like a balloon, hovers. Through the closed windows enter gigantic crabs. *We're Stalin's crabs*, they say, *we're the Red Army of Stalin's crabs, red royal crabs. We come from Norway*, they say, *and we are going to Gibraltar. There are ten million of us, we are indestructible.* The crabs cover the room, crawling, each weighs at least five pounds, the span of their pincers is more than three feet. One clambers onto Andreas Ban's chest. Andreas Ban gets up with difficulty. *I'll nip off your nose*, says the crab on his chest, *I'll gouge out your eyes, I'll break your hips.* The other crabs are devouring the room. What was left of the room. They devour the empty shelves, the chest of drawers, the crystal mirror in its gilt frame, they devour Andreas's rocking chair, the one made of black bamboo.

Five berries.

Piercing pain in his ears. His parotid glands pulsate, swell. An unbearable din in his head.

The tip of his nose tickles. His nose is red and swollen, blood drips from it.

The smell of a forest, the smell of rotten fruit, the smell of a corpse, the smell of freshly baked bread.

Andreas Ban would like to say something, words will not come out. They come in waves, from his stomach, a whole ball of hairy words rolls in Andreas Ban's mouth as though he is about to vomit but they just fall onto his tongue and sink.

Four berries.

The radio comes on suddenly. Out of it leaps a Chinese circus with two monkeys and a little curly-haired dog. The Chinese have pigtails and they sing women's opera arias. Andreas Ban cannot decipher them, a great din.

Pain in his teeth. His gums itch, bleed. His teeth chatter.

His stomach clenches. Nausea.

Small tortoises clamber up toward Andreas Ban's knees, then the twenty small tortoises line up along Andreas Ban's thighs and settle there. The twenty small bald tortoises raise their heads at the same time and stare at Andreas Ban. All the small tortoises' faces are Elvira's face, twenty little Elviras smile at Andreas Ban.

Leo hangs from the ceiling. *I dreamed of an army and acrobats*, says Leo. Andreas Ban stretches his arms out to him, tries to touch him, but Leo is transparent. *I am air*, says Leo. *I perform virtuoso saltos. Here's a bit of Kafka*, he says and from the ceiling starts hitting Andreas Ban with fat black worms. *That's not Kafka*, Andreas Ban wants to say, but he cannot.

His tongue is growing. It is like a gigantic strawberry.

Pain in his spine.

Pain in his stomach. He cannot cough.

Pain in his rectum.

Six berries.

A window pane shatters, a miniature bronze Glenn Gould falls at Andreas Ban's feet from the sky, he takes a white piano and his piano stool out of his back pocket, and starts playing Brahms in yellow gloves. *You've warmed the room up brilliantly*, he says, *I like it like this.* That lasts a while.

Then a flood. Andreas's living room is transformed into a lake. The lake fills, grows, on the surface of the lake float heads from

Andreas's albums. They bob around. Some heads have open eyes and they blink, others just look, some have no eyes at all. No one smiles. There are young faces and some very old faces.

Three berries.

Andreas Ban has shat himself. A thin green stool spreads over his behind, slips down to his knees. Andreas wets his pants. Worms wriggle in his penis.

On the floor lies an enormous treble clef, splattered with muddy earth. The tremble clef stands up and twists, in spasms. It dances. *My name is Tranquility*, it says. *I was exhumed in Transylvania. Three times.*

A shaggy white dog lifts its leg and pees against the wall of Andreas's room. The wall cracks, opens, and out of the wall come Andreas's father and Andreas's mother. *Put on a waltz*, they say. No music. Andreas's parents spin in silence, then they stop on a chocolate cake, he is wearing a white tuxedo and she a crimson evening gown. The white dog is sleeping on the rug that Glenn Gould has neglected to take away. *Shall I make you a kilt?* Andreas's mother asks him, *Scottish*, she says. Andreas falls onto his knees and eats the dog's food out of the silver dog bowl.

Four berries.

His testicles are hard. Swollen.

His breathing is uneven, spasmodic, rapid. A rasping cough causes pain in his left hip. Andreas Ban spits out a blood clot.

Palpitations. His heart drums in his head. His heart swells uncontrollably.

A hearse carries a coffin to an open grave. The road is rutted and the coffin jolts at an indecorously crooked angle. A yellow brocade cover with gold tassels pokes out of the coffin. The cemetery has hillocks overgrown with mauve grass. Through the cemetery float boats full of shoes. A blackbird lands on Andreas's shoulder. *Those are the shoes of the citizens of Sarajevo*, the blackbird whispers. Out of the shoes sprout sunflowers.

Three berries.

His knuckles are shiny, streaked with red lines, they rise like dough.

Jerking of his arms and legs.

His neck stiffens.

One berry.

Waterfalls gush down the windows. Out of the floor rises snow, it winds like a stalk and moves toward Andreas. It wraps around him, he is tied in snow chains, he cannot breathe.

His body temperature rises. Thirty-nine degrees.

I am an immortal unicorn, I am looking for my lost brothers who are lying at the bottom of the sea, says a blue animal speckled with little gold stars. Andreas Ban removes the gold stars, one by one, from the blue unicorn, and sticks them over himself. He is all golden and starlike.

Three berries.

His fingers are stiff. They tremble.

Shaking. Convulsions. His carotid glands pulsate. Madness in his eyes. His eyes are sightless.

Andreas Ban sways backward and forward like a paranoid schizophrenic. He waves, catches a ball, swivels his fingers, picks through wheat.

One more berry.

A young magician swings on a trapeze. Out of his hat fall ostrich eggs out of which leap: a football team of naked dwarf Hitlers, all the players lack their left testicle. Tiny black angels land on them singing:

> *Hitler had but one left ball,*
> *Mussolini had none at all,*

Stalin was three-ballin',
That's the dictators' rise and fall!

The door opens, Arnold Schoenberg comes in. He is singing too:

Behind Schoenberg comes Steve Reich on tiptoe, *Listen to my trains*, he says. The trains sing, they thunder and sing, they tell stories, the space fills with journeys, tracks spread out and join, they have nowhere to disappear to, in them lies history. Bosch arrives with a basketful of Lilliputians under his arm. Bosch scatters the Lilliputians through the room as though they were marbles, the Lilliputians roll around making faces, they jump all over Andreas Ban, slip into his trousers, into his pockets, his socks, under his eyelids, they slide down his back and snatch his berries. The music stops. The trains stop. Andreas Ban defends himself from the Lilliputians' attack, he yells, he screams, but produces no sound. A threatening dark silence reigns.

Then he loses consciousness.

Around Andreas Ban dance Parca moths. Andreas Ban lies on the floor, soiled, wet and blind. The room is in darkness.

Three days have passed. Clotho and Lachesis wave their wings and say, *Our work is done, bye-bye.* Atropos lands on Andreas Ban's heart, out of his bosom he takes a pair of scissors, hugs them, raises them up high and says, *This should be the end.*

Andreas Ban stirs. He slithers on his belly to the toilet. He pushes his finger into his mouth. He vomits. He drags himself to the kitchen, half fills a glass with dishwashing soap, dilutes it with water and drinks it. He vomits. He drinks a glass of diluted vinegar, vomits. He crawls to his medicine cabinet, dragging after him trails of vomit and green shit, he is wet and blind. Among his medicine he feels for his *carbo medicinalis* tablets, crushes ten of them with his teeth and swallows them. His throat is full of dust and tight.

Then he calls an ambulance.

For a week I've been trying to reach Andreas. He doesn't answer.

I send him text messages. Nothing.

He's not on Skype.

I telephone Andreas's sister, our Bubi, in Rovinj, she says, *We met about ten days ago. He came for lunch and he hugged me. That was unusual*, says Bubi.

I telephone his neighbor on the first floor, the neighbor has no idea.

I check the hospitals. Nothing.

I come.

The apartment is empty. There's some furniture, but there are no books, no ornaments, where the pictures used to hang, just yellow-brown tobacco-colored outlines of the frames. No clothes in the closets.

The kitchen is intact. As though someone was living there. There is food, there is wine. The fruit is rotten, flies dance around it.

Andreas's bed is covered with a red Bukhara rug, no bedding.

The blinds are down.

In the bathroom everything is as it was before, towels, soap, toothbrushes.

My room is untouched as well.

In Andreas's study there is no laptop. On the desk is a black folder with a label inscribed belladonna. In the bottom right-hand corner of the folder shimmers a little blue-and-silver zebra facing outward, about to step over the edge.

I have not corrected Andreas's manuscript. Many events and facts are missing from it. The manuscript has gaps. In the manuscript Andreas Ban skirts around facts and events which to him may no longer mean anything. The story of Andreas's father is incomplete, it's a long, dense story, a complex story from a painful time. The story of my mother Elvira is unfinished. The story of Ada has no past. My story is a stump.

All those stories trouble Andreas Ban, he does not succeed in guiding them to a happy ending, as though some game of destiny had bequeathed him the task—of unraveling other people's lives. Then he must have given up on them. On the stories that suffocate him. He lets them go.

This manuscript of Andreas's surprised me.

Up until I was twenty-something, Andreas and I were a little family in which life breathed in an orderly fashion. We went to films and to the theater, we visited exhibitions, we read, we ate modest meals, we sometimes traveled, together or separately, we talked a lot, few people came to visit, sometimes friends of Andreas's from his former life, then a celebration, activity, cooking, conversations, all the beds filled. Only Ada—Bubi—came regularly. We didn't have a ladder. The ceilings are very high. We had a cat. And a lot of noise outside the windows. On the whole, we didn't have any secrets. Maybe some small, intimate secrets. There were no big secrets. Or lies. I acquired more and more friends, Andreas fewer and fewer. I left. Andreas said: *Go. It's claustrophobic here.*

The end of summer 2009. Andreas and I go from Rovinj by boat to the Venice Biennale. In the Giardini, Andreas scampers into the exhibition pavilions and looks at the exhibits superficially, without interest, then he rushes out of the pavilions and lights a cigarette. *On the whole, crap*, he says, *art has gone flat*, he says. As we leave the Giardini, Andreas catches sight of the Hungarian pavilion and stops dead. *We have to see this*, he says, *this Péter Forgács. Péter Forgács talks about parallel lives, as does Péter Nádas, as does history in general, which is all parallel but tangled in knots.*

At the time, I didn't understand what Andreas was talking about.

The exhibition was called *Col Tempo*. Now, leafing through the catalogue of that exhibition and recalling Andreas's stories from another of Forgács's installations, which he visited in 2007 in Berlin's Jewish Museum, I succeed to a certain extent in understanding the story of Rudolf Sass, working out why it is important for Andreas (and for me).

The *Col Tempo* exhibition is made up of parallel events which connect the painful course of history into a quite logical image, reminding me of Andreas's episode with Carlo Ketz, the former husband of his deceased sister, the madman who steals other people's lives. The exhibition-installation *Col Tempo* offers a glimpse of the Other, as the curator explained to visitors.

That's Levinas, Andreas said, *when I see the other, I understand myself. To understand myself, to respect myself, I have to respect the other, because I am the other. And responsibility for the other is a fundamental human value. Without it, we become monsters. Besides*, said Andreas, *in every dialogue, even a latent one, between one artist and another, between the artist and the audience, between the artist and his work, whether it is a painting, music or language, is also hidden the self-portrait of the artist himself.*

I didn't understand what Andreas was saying. I didn't understand Péter Forgács's installation. I intended to read the catalogue when we returned home, but I didn't. It was a little volume of essays dedicated to the works, films and other visual creations of Péter Forgács.

We ate pizza and drank beer on the terrace of a trattoria near the terminal where the catamaran would leave for Rovinj. We had two hours and Andreas talked at length.

You see, he said, *in November 1939 individual groups of Jews were fleeing from Nazism and trying to get to Palestine in boats. Groups set out from Vienna, Berlin, Gdansk and Bratislava. But the winter of 1939 was so cold that the Danube froze and travel by ship was impossible. After all kinds of setbacks, instead of reaching Palestine, those Jewish refugees ended up in a small Serbian town, Šabac. And then, after the Axis forces occupied Serbia on April 6, 1941, all those people, more than a thousand of them, were shot or killed with exhaust fumes. You see,* said Andreas Ban, *it was only when I saw Forgács's installation in Berlin, that I discovered that almost simultaneously, but in more favorable climatic conditions, in the early autumn of 1939, some six hundred Jews from Bratislava did reach Palestine, did manage to survive. The Danube was still navigable then and from it came the beat of waltzes, which were quickly replaced by funeral marches. Those six hundred Bratislava Jews embarked on the riverboat Erzsebet Kiralyne, that is the Queen Elizabeth, mastered by the famous captain and amateur filmmaker Dr. Nándor Andrásovits who carried them across the Black Sea to freedom. Less than a year later, in the autumn of 1940, that same Queen Elizabeth, mastered by the same Nándor Andrásovits, sailed the Danube in the opposite direction, upstream, transporting the minority German population settled in Bessarabia, in the territory between the former Moldavia and Ukraine. These Germans were to be resettled within the borders of the German Reich. In his installation, Forgács uses amateur footage taken by Nándor Andrásovits on both journeys to tell two diametrically opposed émigré stories that do nevertheless touch, connected by the waters of the Danube. That Danube exodus, that Rippling Flow of the powerful European river, as Péter Forgács also calls his work, shows the world through a totality of facts. Because the world is determined by facts, and since facts are everything, everyone may or may not become a "case." With his eight-millimeter camera Captain Andrásovits records life on the boat. He records the faces of his passengers. He records expectations and hope. Love, even a wedding. Conversations, dancing and songs. The story is personal, not historical. There are no uniforms or weapons, no insignia. It is only through Forgács's intervention and through music that one discerns the muffled rumbling from the Danube foreshadowing a general catastrophe.*

Who were those Volksdeutscher?

At the beginning of the nineteenth century, the Russian Emperor Alexander I permits Germans from the German lands to settle in Bessarabia, on territory deserted in the wake of the Napoleonic wars. A hundred or so years later, the signing of the Ribbentrop–Molotov Pact between Hitler and Stalin led in 1940 to the repatriation of those ninety-three thousand Bessarabian Volksdeutscher to the Third Reich. The SS organized the deportations. Ships, among them the Queen Elizabeth, waited in ports, and from those ships, after sailing along the lovely blue Danube, the displaced farmers ended up first in German transit camps, then on the estates and in the houses of displaced Polish families in the western areas of occupied Poland. Then the men were mobilized and most of them never returned home.

A long time ago, said Andreas Ban, *through my friend the psychiatrist Adam Kaplan, I learned of the destiny of a certain Rudolf Sass. Like millions of other destinies, the destiny of Rudolf Sass moved along a trajectory which is parallel to some life's path of mine, and therefore also yours. It turned out that the destiny of a man I did not know, sent out ripples which affected my life. Facts and states of being that I recognize as my own. Little fears and painful doubts. That is why we delude ourselves if we think that other people's parallel stories will never rub up against ours. They will. In one form or another. In an expression, in some incidental, casually uttered statement, in some apparently insignificant encounter, also parallel, even if they never reach us directly.*

Endless parallelism confirms the connectedness of facts and lives. The gulf between the mind and the body.

If you look, you will see, said Andreas Ban, *Rudolf Sass, and not only he, could be recognized in us or we in him, in others. Somehow.*

The story of Rudolf Sass unsettled me. That was the first and last time, as we waited in Venice for the ferry to Rovinj, that Andreas mentioned Rudolf Sass. He said nothing about his destiny, about his life. I knew nothing about Rudolf Sass.

I am a doctor. I am currently in Zurich training in cardiology, on a modest grant. Andreas Ban has a good heart, healthy, he does not need my knowledge. I am thirty. At the university I occasionally run tutorials with the students, I assist my mentor. I have a student whose name is Emma Sass.

What do I do now? People disappear. Adults disappear. And children disappear. Many simply evaporate. As though they had never been. Andreas Ban must appear somewhere, he cannot leave me with such a burden. This burden oppresses me now, Andreas knows that, he will come back because of me, to make it easier for me. It is hard to completely erase history and memory, history and memory like to come back. They get under people's skin and penetrate their bloodstream. There, I have learned: people are invisibly connected without knowing it, they touch one another through lives that to them remain forever foreign, they step into times which they think are not theirs, they walk through landscapes which are new only to them but which have existed for centuries. That Rudolf Sass is proof. So, he will appear, Andreas Ban will come.

In the catalogue of that Venetian installation of Forgács's, *Col Tempo*, László Földényi asks:

Is it possible to carve a slice out of space?

And he says: *Yes, and then again, no.*

And he asks: *Can life be chopped up into pieces?*

And he says: *No. But then again, what makes it whole is the fact that it is made up of pieces; parts that can never be fitted together seamlessly. Life is full of cuts, says* Földényi, *even though we devote a large part of our energies to making the cuts invisible. We would like to believe that our life was coherent, seamless, with the stitching not showing and everything appearing to be smooth and logically constructed. Stitches, however, are even more conspicuous than cuts. Worse, they keep coming apart, again and again. These are what one might call the heavy moments in life; these are the times when one catches a glimpse of the divergent structure of life behind the stitches and cuts, when instead of what we are used to, we see something that is unprocessable, on which nothing lasting can be built.*

For those who have stepped through the looking glass, who have gone behind the screen, external time no longer exists. Death, when it comes, risks not finding anyone there.

LEO BAN, ZURICH

2012

ACKNOWLEDGMENTS

In *Belladonna* Daša Drndić has incorporated or quoted the words of a number of writers. If there is any writer whose work has not been acknowledged here, we will make due reference in any future edition.

Lines adapted from Édouard Estaunié's *Solitudes*, a collection of three novels published in 1922.

Excerpt from Joseph Conrad's *Under Western Eyes*, first published in 1911.

"Troy" ("And the wind brought people …") from Bogomil Gjuzel's *A Well in Time*, first published in English by Arc Publications in *Six Macedonian Poets*, edited and translated by Igor Isakovski (2011). Reproduced by permission of Arc Publications.

Lines adapted from Diana Budisavljević's *Dnevnik* (Diary) 1941–1945, Croatian State Archives, Zagreb, 2003. https://theremustbejustice.wordpress.com/2013/04/12/bravery-of-diana-budisavljevic-is-stronger-than-oblivion/

"The Scholars" by William Butler Yeats, written between 1914 and April 1915, and first published in the collection *The Wild Swans at Coole* in November 1917 by Cuala Press.

Lines taken from Emma Goldman's report "The Relation of Anarchism to Organization" submitted in 1907 together with Max Baginski to the International Anarchist Congress, first published in *Mother Earth*, 1907, then in *Anarchism and other Essays*, first published in 1910.

Karl Jaspers, *The Question of German Guilt*, Fordham University Press; 2 Rev Ed edition (October 31, 2000). Translated by E. B. Ashton. With a new introduction by Joseph W. Koterski.

Radomir Konstantinovic, Filosofija Palanke ("The Philosophy of the Province"), published by Nolit, Belgrade, in 1969.

Lines from Witold Gombrowicz's "The Events on the Banbury," in the short story collection *Bacacay*, translated from the Polish by Bill Johnston. Published by Archipelago Books, New York, 2004. Courtesy of Archipelago Books, New York.

Jacques Rigaut, lines from "Je serai sérieux comme le Plaisir", first published in Revue *Littérature N°17*, in December 1920.

Seneca, lines from the *Thebaid*, Book I. i.

Michel de Montaigne, from his *Essays* vol. 4, an excerpt from "A Custom of the Isle of Cea" ("Oh, yes, death is the infallible cure of all ..."), translated by Charles Cotton, published by Edwin C. Hill, New York, 1910.

Excerpt from Søren Kierkegaard, *Journals and Papers*, Indiana University Press (Bloomington, Indiana, 1967; London: 1968), edited and translated by Howard V. Hong and Edna H. Hong.

Lines adapted from Vladimir Voinovich's *The Life and Extraordinary Adventures of Private Ivan Chonkin*, Translated from the Russian by Richard Lourie. Published by Northwestern Uni Press; Reprint edition (March 29, 1995) by arrangement with FSG. Translation copyright © 1977 by Farrar, Straus and Giroux, Inc.

We also thank the following for the use of illustrations:

health-science-spirit.com, Walter Last (p. 7); Bundesarchiv, Bild 101I-191-1656-14 / Walter Henisch (p. 51); Jutarnji list archive (p. 72); Warner Chappell Music GmbH & Co. KG Germany (p. 120); United States Holocaust Memorial Museum, with the permission of Yehuda Koren and Eilat Negev (p. 164); Eva Kris (p. 195); Croatian State Archives, HR HDA 1561/00078 (p. 219); © 2006 Vladimir Faibyshev (p. 257); Alexander Lavrentiev (p. 262); AKG-images (p. 272); Sara Benhamou and Eric de Vries (p. 277); Bigstockphoto (p. 302); iStockphoto (p. 315); Jan Ejsymontt (p. 358); Rudi Valtiner (p. 360); AKG-images / Gilles Mermet (p. 368).

The list of names of 2,061 children deported from the Netherlands to concentration camps from 1938 to 1945 was compiled in 1985 by Kitty Coster and has been added to over the years by the Israeli Embassy in the Netherlands. The list of šabac Jews and Jewish refugees who were killed in Zasavica in October 1941, compiled in Belgrade on December 24, 1945, is kept in the Jewish Historical Museum in Belgrade.